ECHOES OF
WAR

ECHOES OF WAR

**BOOK ONE
IN THE ECHOES TRILOGY**

CHERYL CAMPBELL

SparkPress, a BookSparks imprint
A Division of SparkPoint Studio, LLC

Published by SparkPress, a BookSparks imprint,
A division of SparkPoint Studio, LLC
Phoenix, Arizona, USA, 85007
www.gosparkpress.com

Published 2019
Printed in the United States of America

ISBN: 978-1-68463-006-6 (pbk)
ISBN: 978-1-68463-007-3 (e-bk)
Library of Congress Control Number: 2019937838

Formatting by Katherine Lloyd, The Desk

For

Rich,

Kris,

Chris,

Allison,

and

Donna

CHAPTER

1

Dani spent her morning the same as she'd done countless other mornings. She was a survivor, and she planned her day with the intent to live to see the next one. She didn't know that she would die in a few hours, or that her next life's path would put her on a course to save the lives of countless others.

A tendril of smoke wafted up from the melting rubber as Dani held the candle's flame near the end of it. When the dull, black fragment of the tire's inner tube began to crack and smolder, she removed it from the heat. The thin piece of rubber would erupt into flames itself if she wasn't careful, and she'd have to start over.

She applied the softened edge of the inner tube to a crack in the aged insulation covering a copper wire lying on the top of the table. She poured off the liquid candle wax into a container for reuse later before moving the candle aside. Then she picked up the length of the wiring with both hands and worked the softened rubber over the crack in the wire's insulation until it filled the gap. The reinforced seal wouldn't last long, but it was the best solution she had for reusing the wires until she could scavenge something better.

Dani repeated this process for several minutes, until she had all the breaks in the insulation repaired. She tapped the rubber with her fingertip, and when she was satisfied that it had cooled enough, she slid the completed portion to the left to inspect the next foot of wire for more cracks. She resumed her melting-patching technique, working left to right, until the entire length of wire was repaired. Once finished, she carefully rolled the wire and placed it in a box with others like it.

The stench of burned rubber hung in the room. She lifted her knife and sharpening stone from the table. Miles stirred in her bed as she slid the blade along the stone, but Dani didn't try to silence the noise. He needed to get up anyway. She glanced at the dog bed made of blanket scraps on the floor next to the table where she worked. It was empty, and her chest ached. *I need to move that stuff out of sight so I stop looking at it*, she thought.

Her eyes stung with the thought of her dead dog; she placed the knife and stone back on the table, rubbed the hint of tears from her eyes, and passed her hands through her short, unruly hair. She sniffled as she pushed her chair back to stand. Her shadow danced on the wall in the candlelight while she adjusted her tattered wool trousers. She'd stolen the pants off a dead, human MP. For a small man, the dead policeman's pants were big—too big for her. His boots, however, were perfect.

Dani tucked her threadbare T-shirt into her waistband then reached for her belt, which—along with other articles of clothing—had been tossed aside when she and Miles tumbled into her bed last night. The thin, lumpy mattress on the floor wasn't much to sleep on, but she and Miles hadn't done much sleeping. She eyed his duty belt with his plasma pistol still holstered in it. A weapon like that would be much better protection for her when she was out scavenging than the knife and pistol she currently used.

She left Miles's gun and belt where they lay and instead lifted her jacket, the dead MP's jacket, from the floor and placed it on the back of her chair.

Miles groaned and rolled to his back. "You've been melting rubber again." He opened his eyes and blinked in the darkness. "Why aren't you using the lamp?"

"MPs were poking around the block yesterday, but they didn't find my lines tapping into their power. If I don't consistently pull from their grid, they can't catch me," Dani said. She tightened her belt around her waist and slipped the knife into the sheath on her belt. She sat in her chair again, unrolled another length of old wire, and began inspecting the insulation for gaps.

"How long have you been up?" he asked.

Dani shrugged without taking her eyes from her work. "A while."

"Jace steals wiring for you to steal power from the Commonwealth. Shit, Dani, you get caught and you're in a labor camp for a minimum of five years."

"How many years will you get as an MP sleeping with a Brigand and not arresting her for stealing from the Commonwealth?"

Miles groaned and rolled out of the bed in search of his clothes.

She hid her grin and pulled the candle close to begin the mundane task of melting the rubber. Miles's movements in the background quieted as he shifted closer to stand behind her. His hand touched her left shoulder.

"Not now, Miles."

She remained hunched over the table, focused first on heating the rubber and then on placing the melted edge in the right spot on the wire.

His warm breath blew across her neck just before his lips arrived.

"You're going to make me burn myself," she said, but she didn't tell him to stop.

His mouth moved up her neck, and his tongue touched her skin. She wanted to resist his advance, but the sensation made her close her eyes. A tingle and mild shiver coursed through her body from her neck to her groin. Her hands wavered, and the strip of rubber ignited in a flash of heat. The flaming piece of rubber landed on the back of the hand she was holding the candle with, and she bolted away from the table and Miles, dropping everything as she stood. The chair and candle toppled with her movement.

Dani dragged the back of her hand across the coarse fabric of her trousers, wincing from the pain of the burn.

Miles slapped the piece of burning rubber to the floor and grabbed his boot to put the fire out. With the room now completely dark, he fumbled with objects on the table to find a match to relight the candle. After a few seconds, he growled with frustration and abandoned the task. He tripped over the chair with a curse and turned on the lamp between the bed and table. He stared up at her while still kneeling on the floor and clinging to the lamp's pole. "I'm sorry."

"Fuck off." Dani sat on the bed and examined the burn on her hand. The melted rubber had stuck to her skin. In her haste to stop her flesh from burning, she'd tried to wipe it off. Instead, she'd torn her damaged skin and the melted rubber had smeared across more of her hand, taking more freshly burned skin off in the process. She picked up the canteen of water she kept next to her bed. Miles reached to help her, but she pushed him away.

Once she had the cap unscrewed, she poured water over her burn. The searing pain eased some, but not enough. As soon as the water trickled off her hand, air reached the exposed wound, making her hand feel like it was on fire again.

"You need to clean the burn to keep it from getting infected," Miles said.

"I do *not* need your help with this."

He continued to kneel on the floor, and his attention turned to the lamp. His eyes followed the cord down to where the bare ends of its wires wrapped around the posts of a car battery.

"Christ, Dani, you stole a battery out of one of the MP trucks?"

She placed the canteen on the floor and went to a stack of totes in the corner of her room.

"Forget what I said about the labor camp. They'll just execute you if they ever find out about half the shit you've taken from their supplies."

Dani shrugged. "I needed the battery so I could come off their grid to repair my wires. I used the candle today to save the battery you're now draining for me."

She lifted the first two totes off the stack and opened the third while Miles finished dressing in silence. She pulled a small metal box from the tote and brought it to the table. She righted her chair and sat with a heavy sigh to inspect her wound. Black remnants of rubber remained stuck to her skin at the edges of the burn. She'd have to leave them for now; the injury was too raw for her to properly clean it without taking something for the pain.

Miles pulled on his boots and paused. "You waxed my boots."

"Yeah."

"Thanks! Nothing is worse than wet socks." He finished lacing his boots and stood to button his shirt. Dani glared at him. She was still angry about the mishap, but she also loathed his uniform. The Commonwealth of North America's logo resided on the left side of his shirt; his last name, Jackman, was lettered on the right. "MP" was plastered in large letters to the outside of both his shoulders, and his second lieutenant insignia decorated his shirt collar. She'd always believed the CNA was stupid to advertise their military police members with the shoulder badges. It made them easier targets for Wardens. Still, she cared for Miles.

"Dani, I really am sorry. I didn't mean for you to burn yourself."

She squeezed a line of ointment over the burn and wound a roll of gauze around her hand to cover it. She wrapped a length of tape around the gauze and tore it off with her teeth. With the burn protected from the air, the worst of the pain eased.

"The MPs are raiding C Block today to clear it of Brigands," Miles said.

"Clear it? You mean 'kidnap civilians to be troops for the CNA.' Call it what it is, Miles. Don't hide what you do by giving it some name that helps you sleep better at night."

"I know you hate what we do, but it's the only way we can keep our numbers up against the Wardens."

"There are plenty of other ways to fight this war with the Wardens." She tossed the tape and tube of ointment back into the medical kit.

"Don't scavenge today, Dani."

She laughed and shook her head. "It's how Brigands survive, Miles. If I don't scavenge, I don't eat."

"I'll bring you food tonight."

"I'm going out today."

Miles sighed and snatched his jacket off the floor. "Avoid C Block. You don't have Brody to watch your back anymore."

Dani tightened her jaw.

"I'm sorry to bring him up. I know you miss him, but—"

Dani slammed the lid on the small medical kit closed, ending the conversation.

"Be careful today, please. Stay away from the Echoes."

She left the table and lifted her jacket from where it had fallen on the floor when the chair toppled. "Brigand Echoes are just like Brigand humans. We're focused on staying alive and free while you and the Wardens kill each other."

Miles put his jacket on and yanked the zipper up, covering his uniform top. "Fine! Go play with your Brigand friends today. But stay the fuck out of C Block!" He stomped out of her room and slammed the door behind him.

Dani slipped into her jacket, leaving the front of it open. She lived among the war's civilians, scavenging and stealing from the Commonwealth and Wardens alike. She didn't need to hide her identity. She turned the lamp off and walked out the door.

Brigands only had one goal: survive. They left the fighting to the idiots who wanted to kill each other.

CHAPTER

2

An upper corner of the tattered map sagged where it had torn free from the tape still stuck to the wall. Dani took another bite of her wafer and pushed the edge of the map up with the palm of her hand. She chewed while she studied the thicker lines marked over the city. Portland, Maine, was divided into six blocks. C Block was in the southwestern part of the city's remnants, which was also the location of the MP Stroudwater Barracks. The MP camp was near where the airport used to be, before the Wardens turned it into rubble.

Dani and her uncle lived in B Block in the center of the city, which was poor even by Brigand standards. B Block's population remained under a hundred, so an attack from either MPs or Wardens was unlikely. C Block offered the best opportunities to raid MP stores; in fact, it was the block where Dani had scavenged the wafer she was now eating. But given Miles's warning regarding C Block, she decided to tackle E Block, also known as the Old Port, instead today. With its old fishing wharves and numerous warehouses, E Block always had food and supplies waiting to be stolen. Poaching fish was one of the many crimes Dani had committed in that block before, and she planned to do it again today. Miles could have his raid and she could do her scavenging, and she'd still be far from the MPs' crosshairs.

"You need to stay in today," Jace said.

Dani glanced over her shoulder at the older man. He still moved without a sound—impressive for someone in his sixties. "I know about the raid, Jace."

He pushed the menagerie of tools in front of him on the workbench aside and placed his gnarled leather messenger bag on it. "Raid or not, you're staying in."

Dani sighed and continued examining the map.

"Dani."

"What, Uncle?" she asked, her tone sharp. When he didn't speak, she released the map and turned to face him. Without her hand to keep it up, the map's upper corner rolled back down the wall.

"What happened to your hand?"

"I was careless when I was repairing wire casings this morning. It's fine," she said. The ache turned to a throb when she held her hand by her side.

"I'll hunt today. Stay here to work on the wiring and take care of your hand."

She opened her filth-covered pack on the bench. "Don't bring back any more old wiring. I have plenty. I'll search the warehouses in the Old Port today for newer strips. The older wires work, but a nice length of something less ancient would provide more consistent power for us."

She spread out an oil-stained cloth and rolled two sets of wire cutters in the fabric to keep them from clanking together inside her pack when she walked. The most successful Brigands survived by not making noise, and Jace had trained her well.

"Keep an eye out for anything solar. Any size will do, but bigger is better. I'm close to having everything I need to make a solar panel so we don't need the Commonwealth's grid at all," she said as she continued to put more tools into her pack.

Jace didn't respond, so Dani looked up. "What?"

"You're not going out."

"We had this conversation yesterday. We're not doing it again today, Jace."

He reached for her pack; she moved it out of his reach.

"First Miles and now you are dictating how I will spend my day? Good luck with that."

"Please, don't leave B Block today. Will you stay if I ask nicely?"

Dani laughed at her uncle's attempt to be polite. "What's gotten into you?"

Jace's wrinkled hands found a screwdriver with a broken handle on the bench. He fiddled with it but didn't answer her question. His knuckles, bulbous from arthritis, bobbed as he turned the tool in his hands.

"Jace!"

His head came up.

"Why are you being weird? You've been acting strange for two weeks."

"No guns."

Dani groaned and removed the pistol from her belt.

Jace's sudden changes in behavior over the last two weeks had caused frequent arguments, mostly over Dani taking the pistol with her while scavenging. Each day he begged her to leave it behind, though she was safer with the weapon. Sometimes it was easier to just give in to his badgering. Today, she didn't bother pleading her case.

"Miles thinks *I'm* a pain in his ass. He should spend some time with you," Dani said as she placed the gun and holster on the bench between her and Jace.

"You should stop seeing him. He's an MP. He could turn

on us at any moment," Jace said, his eyes still on the tool in his hand.

"He won't."

Jace glanced up at her. "Why not?"

Dani shrugged. "I think he loves me."

The old man shook his head and groaned. "The CNA can't be trusted. Does he still hate Echoes?"

"Echoes announced their presence on Earth by blowing it to shit forty years ago, Jace. Plus, if you kill the bastards, their bodies renew, and they come back again for another round. Humans have a good reason to hate Echoes."

"Do you hate them?"

"No, but I'm fine avoiding Echoes and other humans to stay alive."

"Except you don't avoid Miles."

"He's not your concern. You and I survive just fine."

"I don't know how much longer we can."

Dani tilted her head. "How much longer we can what? Survive?"

He tossed the screwdriver back on the bench and passed his callused palm over his face. "It all starts with the dog."

Dani blinked and shook her head. "Huh?"

"Everything goes downhill once the dog dies."

A familiar twinge in her chest returned with the mention of a dead dog. "What dog?"

"*Your* dog. The one you always get that always dies, and then the shit goes sideways."

"*What* are you talking about?"

"I can't keep doing this. I keep getting it wrong."

"What's with the damn riddles? Start making some sense or I'm leaving."

He shook his head, his face pinched like he was in pain. "I don't know how."

"If I'm going to make E Block for supplies and return before dark, I need to go. Tell me what's going on."

"Stay."

"Why, Jace? You have to give me a reason for you acting like a freak about this. I don't understand what you're even talking about with dead dogs. Do you mean Brody? What does he have to do with whatever you're trying to say? Tell me. Please."

"I can't."

She rubbed the back of her neck and sighed with frustration. "I'm done with this guessing game." She grabbed her pack. "Figure out how to explain whatever the hell this madness is you're babbling about by the time I get back."

"Wait."

Dani finished securing the rusted buckles on her pack before slinging one strap over her shoulder. When Jace didn't offer any additional answers, she slipped her other arm through the second shoulder strap and tied the pack close to her body. Then she headed out the door to start her day, ducking to clear the metal piping running through the interior of the abandoned building they lived beneath as she went—a habit at this point.

As she neared the exterior walls of the building, she noticed that the sun was out. As much as she wanted to walk in the sunlight and enjoy the warmth, she forced herself to adhere to Jace's rules. She moved along the walls just inside the structure. Rats squeaked and scampered out of her path. In the winter, when scavenging undetected was more difficult due to the cold and snow, she and Jace dined on rats to stay alive. Tonight, she planned to eat fish. She hoped her deranged uncle's wits had returned by then.

She slowed as she reached the collapsed corner of the building—a casualty of one of the many Warden bombs used to capture New England decades earlier. The Echoes had attacked and captured every major city in the world, killing billions of humans in the process. They'd then declared themselves wardens over Earth. Fortunately, the Wardens occupying Boston hadn't bothered much with the smaller cities of Portsmouth, New Hampshire, or Portland, Maine, after the initial attacks.

The human and Echo Brigands sometimes formed alliances, but Jace had always insisted that he and Dani operate solo, just the two of them, as a team. The things he'd said—questioning their ability to continue to survive—worried her. She didn't want him to give up.

Food, she thought. *I'll get us some fish tonight. Real food. That should help ease his concerns.*

Four miles of avoiding MPs and other Brigands lay between her and the wharves. She left the shadows at the corner of the building, jogged across the deserted street, and slowed slightly to enjoy the sun. A dog barked in the distance, and Dani spotted another Brigand moving around another building. She increased her pace and moved back into the shadows.

CHAPTER

3

The MP patrols were predictable, as usual, so Dani avoided them with ease. She nodded to a group of three Brigands as she passed them. She'd seen the trio, two men and a woman, many times before in her movements between blocks, but she never stopped to chat.

The woman smiled in response to her nod, and Dani continued on her way. She had another mile before reaching the center of the Old Port in E Block. With the police occupied with the C Block raid, things were dead; Dani moved through the city without seeing a single MP.

After going another eighth of a mile, she stopped in the shadow of a building and checked her surroundings. No people moved about, and the only sound was the wind stirring leaves and debris through the streets. She took a step toward the sunlight—and someone grabbed her upper arm. Startled, she spun to strike the person, but another hand caught her wrist before her fist made contact. She blinked several times, and as her eyes focused, Jace's face sharpened into view.

"Stay in the shadows," he said.

Dani jerked her arm and wrist free from his grasp. Her heartbeat thundered in her chest, and she tried to calm the effects of the adrenaline surge. She slowed her breaths and regained some control. "You're a fucking ninja. Why the hell are you sneaking up on me, anyway?"

"I need to talk to you."

"*Now? Now* you want to talk? I so want to kill you."

"Not as much as you'll want to when I'm done."

Dani's brow creased with confusion. Her uncle stood before her, wringing his hands. He paused just long enough to gesture for her to follow him before resuming his nervous hand movements.

Dani followed Jace without speaking until he stopped near one of the many columns of a long-deserted parking garage housing rusted heaps of abandoned vehicles. The cars and trucks were barely recognizable after decades of Brigands scavenging metal, tires, wiring, parts, and anything else that could be utilized in some way.

"You may want to sit," Jace said.

Dani folded her arms across her chest—bumping her burn in the process. She flinched and shifted her posture. She had a hard time being defiant when the tiniest insult to her wounded hand sent shock waves of pain up her arm.

"Don't sit." Jace took in a deep breath that made his chest rise with the effort. He expelled the breath in a controlled manner before meeting her eyes. "You're not human. Neither of us is. And . . . I'm not your uncle."

Dani stared at him for a moment. Then a burst of laughter escaped her.

Jace scowled. "I'm not joking."

"Of course you are," Dani said, still laughing.

Jace shook his head.

Her smile faded and turned to a frown.

"It's the truth, Dani."

"I don't believe you."

"You think you're twenty-five years old, but you were originally born in 2058. Linearly speaking, you're closer to fifty-five. You've had a couple of resets."

Several seconds ticked by while Dani searched for her voice. When she spoke, her voice cracked. "I'm an Echo?"

Jace nodded.

"Not a human?"

"No."

"Couple of resets? You mean I've died twice?" Dani paced as she talked.

"Yes."

"So I'm fifty-five, and you're not my uncle? What are you?"

"Your brother. Half-brother. Same father but different mothers."

A nervous laugh escaped Dani's mouth, and she ran her hand through her already tousled hair. Her pacing stopped. "Bullshit. Echoes remember their past lives. I don't remember anything but growing up with you as my uncle. I have only lived as a Brigand, so I could not have been born before the war started."

Jace resumed wringing his hands. "Yeah. That's why this is so complicated. You're the only Echo I've known to forget their past when they reset. You . . . you forget all of it. You're an anomaly. You seem to displace everything except your survival skills each time. I think it's a subconscious thing."

Dani laughed again. "You're killing me with this."

"Please, just listen. You were eleven when the Wardens attacked and orphaned a few days later. Your mother and our father were Echoes, but the Wardens killed them again while they were regenerating. Their deaths became permanent. I was seventeen and took care of you, but you were killed when you were twenty-five. As long as Echoes don't suffer a catastrophic injury, like a beheading, or get killed mid-regen, they heal their damaged bodies and return to a younger point in life—usually somewhere in their late teens or in early adulthood. But you returned as a ten-year-old. I cared for you in your second life, but you died at twenty-five again. You're caught in a cycle and I don't know how to break it and keep you alive. What I do know is that you always get a dog, the dog dies, and you die a few weeks later."

She remembered his words from earlier that morning: "It all starts with the dog."

He shifted his messenger bag from his back to his side, pulled the flap up, and removed a tattered book from inside. "Here," he said, handing it to her. "I started writing everything down, trying to figure out how to break your loop. I'm old, Dani. I haven't died yet, so I don't know what age I will return to, or even if I will. I'm only half Echo. How do I take care of you again as an old man?"

Dani opened the book and flipped through several pages of notes. They blurred before her eyes. She turned to the beginning of the book and found a photograph of a family standing together: a man, woman, teenage boy, young girl, and dog in front of a tall, stone wall.

"I was the result from a relationship our father had with a human woman before he married your Echo mother," Jace said.

"Her?" Dani asked with a nod at the photo in her hand. "This is my mother?"

"Yes. Flip it over; read the back. Dad always liked having photos in his hand. He hated the digital shit."

"Jason, Dani, and Br—" Dani's hand shook, and she closed her eyes.

"Brody. You adopt a dog, and name him Brody. The one you lost two weeks ago, he's your third."

"Jason," Dani muttered. "Jace."

"Yes. See the year?"

Dani forced her eyes open. Her voice shook when she spoke. "2068." The child in the photo could easily be her. She placed the picture back in the book and turned more pages, glancing over the years and notes. She pulled out another photo of a young woman with a dog. The woman was her, no question; the dog wasn't her Brody, but it was similar-looking to him.

"I don't have any other pictures of you. Photographs and printing are luxuries we'll never have again."

She replaced the photo inside the book and closed it before passing the journal back to Jace. "Why didn't you tell me any of this before?"

"You're safer on this planet as a human, believing you're human. I'm telling you now because I am desperate to keep you from dying again. I'm old, older than I should be. Hardly anyone survives past fifty now with this war, and I'm well past that age. An elderly man can't care for a child."

"So this is about what you need?"

"Don't be stupid. I thought this life, your life, would be different, but I see the same events happening again."

Dani's anger flared, and she tightened her hands into fists, ignoring the throb it produced in her right hand. "You should have told me sooner."

"I'm sorry. I should have, but I didn't know how without making you panic."

"I'm not panicking! I'm fucking livid," she growled.

"I am sorry. Please, let's just go back home."

"I need time to think through this, and I don't want to be around you."

"I must stay close in case something happens to you, Dani."

"What will happen is I'll strangle you. Leave me alone, Jace. Give me time."

"I'll give you space. Go home, I'll scavenge our food today, and we can talk more when you're ready."

Her mind was too distracted for scavenging. Stealing from MPs required her full attention. "Fine. I'll head back to our block. But don't expect me to be home."

"If you die alone, you will be vulnerable until you recover from regenerating. If you're killed during that time, it's permanent. You don't get another chance."

"I've seen Echoes die; I know how it works."

"When you recover, you'll still be a child, without any memories other than your name. You'll be an incapacitated ten-year-old girl."

"I get it," she said, though she didn't truly comprehend anything he'd told her.

"I don't want you to be alone."

"Do I die the same way each time?"

Jace nodded. "Friendly fire."

"Oh, that's perfect."

"You die with a gun in your hand."

"This is why you've been so uptight and making me leave mine behind lately?"

Jace nodded again.

"I promise I won't get in any gunfights today," Dani said. She turned to leave the garage.

"Dani."

"Leave me alone."

When she didn't hear him follow after her, she glanced back. He remained where she'd left him.

Dani kept walking. Her thoughts were a jumbled mess, and she was desperate to find a place to sit and think. Everything she'd ever believed had just been upended. Jace was right. Shit had just gone sideways.

CHAPTER

4

Dani's mind wandered, shuffling the various pieces of information Jace had just given her. She had more questions for him, but she also didn't want to speak to him again for a while.

Maybe he's just fucking with me. Some sick joke. She shook her head.

The family photograph was old; that could have been any girl in the picture. There were plenty of reasons to doubt its authenticity. But the second picture she couldn't deny. That was her in that photo.

She stopped walking and closed her eyes, trying to remember the images better. Surely there was something in the second photo to prove Jace wrong.

The dog in both photos looked so much like the dog she'd recently lost. Brody, *her* Brody, had been a thick-built ninety pounds of muscle. Like the dogs in the pictures, he'd been dark-colored with a splash of white on his chest. When scavenging at night with him, Dani had smeared grease on his chest to cover the white fur. She absentmindedly rubbed her fingertips against her thumb, remembering the feel of his soft coat.

According to Jace, Dani made the same mistakes before

dying. But Brody hadn't been a mistake; she'd adored that damn dog. *I miss you, B.*

Her thoughts shifted again. *Do Echoes have Echo dogs that can return from the dead too?*

She didn't have the answer. She hadn't heard of this before with animals, but maybe that explained why she'd ended up with the same, or almost the same, dog in her last two lives plus this one.

Jace must be fucking with me. I can't be an Echo. This is madness.

"Sssss."

Dani's eyes flew open, and she turned her head toward the source of the noise.

The woman she'd seen earlier in the day slipped her head out beyond the shadow of a building. "Do you *want* to get caught?" the woman asked.

Dani blinked in response and used her hand to shield her eyes from the bright sun. She realized she was standing in an uncovered parking area overgrown with grass and weeds, completely in the open. "Shit."

"Yeah," the woman said.

Lost in her meandering thoughts, she hadn't paid enough attention to her surroundings. Dani sprinted to the nearest shadows, which happened to be where the woman was hiding.

The stranger stepped back, a wary look on her face, as Dani approached.

Dani held her hands up to show they were empty. "I'm not here to cause trouble. You've seen me around before."

"Why are you standing out in the open?"

"I, uh, got distracted. Wasn't paying attention to where I was going."

"That'll get you killed, y'know."

"I know." Dani moved to leave, then realized she had no

idea which direction to go in. "I'm a bit turned around. I'm in C Block, but where?"

The woman pointed. "Fore River is that way."

Dani winced. She'd been so deep in her mental fog that she'd missed her turn to go back to B Block. She didn't remember crossing the bridge, but she was now deep inside C Block. "MPs are doing a raid here today."

The woman's face paled with the news. "Today? My brothers are scavenging inside the block. Help me find them, please."

Dani's middle rumbled with hunger. C Block had the best food with the fewest guards. Her plethora of questions for Jace still clouded her thoughts, and she physically shook her head to rid herself of them.

The woman tilted her head and stared at her.

"Sorry. A little dizzy," Dani said with a shrug.

The woman didn't seem to notice the lie, and if she did, she didn't care enough to make a comment.

"I need to get my bearings before I go anywhere," Dani said. She stepped out of the shadows with her eyes cast upward and turned in a circle. She found a building she liked and nodded before moving back into the darkness. "Come with me or stay here, but I'm going to the top of that building. If the MPs haven't moved in yet, I'll help you."

"Your sightseeing will take too long. I'll go without you."

Dani nodded. "Thank you for catching my attention to bring me out of the sun. I hope you find your brothers."

The woman gave her a quick nod and was gone. Dani wished she'd thought to ask her name, but Brigands tended to have short life spans and even shorter friendships with others. Even Brody had outlived many Brigands she'd met—until one killed him. Her chest tightened and she focused her attention on the task ahead. She refused to rehash the details of the night her dog died.

Remembering Jace's warning, Dani decided to pass on stealing MP food today and just leave C Block. She jogged through the streets, hugging the seams where buildings met the ground, until she reached the tallest building in the immediate area. She climbed into the lower level of the structure through a broken window and waited for her eyes to adjust to the dark. Only fragments of wooden furniture remained; the rest had clearly been dismantled for firewood or crude weapons long ago. Walls had been ripped out at some point, too, and several studs were splintered or missing. She didn't loiter in the lower level long enough to figure out what kind of place the building might have been before the war. It didn't matter.

After finding a set of stairs, she crept her way up them one step at a time, pausing when the structure groaned under her movement. Not all Brigands were friendly. Squatters guarded their homes, even if they were nothing more than a closet. She stepped over piles of debris, noting as she did that the trash was a mix of old and more recent refuse. A decomposing rat lay among one of the piles she passed.

Part of the stairs were missing, so she couldn't go any higher. She slipped through an open door and tiptoed across the torn carpet and broken planks to reach a window. She used the sleeve of her jacket to wipe at the haze covering the glass and looked out over the block. She'd never know how she'd managed to wander so deeply into C Block. At least now she knew exactly where she was and how to go home.

The floor creaked, and Dani froze. She kept staring at the window before her but switched focus from the view outside to her reflection and the room behind her. Someone moved, and Dani turned.

The man facing her snarled, holding up a former table leg like a club. Dani reached for her gun and touched only her belt. She tightened her jaw and cursed Jace. She shifted her hand to her knife and paused. The man's sleeves slid down his arms, revealing emaciated, sore-covered limbs. His strength wavered under the weight of his weapon. He'd been starving for some time and wouldn't survive the winter.

She left her knife on her belt. "I just came up for a look out the window. I'm leaving."

He stalked closer. "Give me your pack."

Before she could answer, a series of shouts rose from elsewhere in the block. The man lunged toward her. Dani stepped aside, swinging her upper body away from the incoming club even as she extended her foot and tripped the man. He fell with a curse, and Dani darted to a window on the other side of the room. She swiped her hand across the film on the glass and peeked out. The raid had started.

MPs poured into the derelict buildings; Brigands scattered like ants.

The man lumbered toward Dani again. She lifted her heels from the floor, but otherwise forced her feet to remain still. She waited until he brought the club down at her again, then sprang to the side, grabbed his threadbare shirt, and shoved him away from her. His head collided with the wall; he groaned as he slid to the floor. She kicked the table leg away from his hands and left him behind.

She was moving past the first window on her way to the stairs when an unfamiliar, thumping noise emanating from the other side of the river stopped her in her tracks. She took a few steps backward to look out the window again.

Three helicopters were landing on the border of B and C Blocks. Black-uniformed Wardens spilled out of the helos and formed lines. A thirty-man Warden platoon had more advanced weapons than the Commonwealth. Warden rifles were of the same tech as the bombs they'd used to cripple the cities across the globe forty-four years earlier. One Warden platoon could engage a hundred CNA troops and likely win.

The C Block raid wouldn't be using that many MPs, so Miles and the other members trying to capture Brigands would be caught unaware by these Wardens and slaughtered. She'd never find Miles in time to warn him, but she couldn't escape C Block either. The Wardens were covering the border to B and the only decent bridge across the river. Fore River was too wide and too cold for her to swim across to E Block.

Her only choice was to move deeper into C Block and hide. She abandoned the room, skipped down the steps, and crawled back out the window she'd used to enter the building. She needed a good place to wait out the fighting—preferably something underground, in case the Wardens opted to use more firepower than their quake rifles.

CHAPTER

After completing his weapon checks, Miles lifted his duty belt from the table and placed it around his waist. Other officers moved through the armory, gathering and checking gear in preparation for the raid.

He'd just completed buckling his belt when the female ranking officer entered. He and all the other MPs came to attention.

"At ease," Major Houston said.

Miles and his fellow officers shifted their stance, but their backs remained straight.

"We have a change in orders."

Miles flicked his eyes toward the major, then ahead again. He'd been dreading this raid. He hoped it had been canceled.

"The Commonwealth of North America's military experts are changing tactics. We will no longer hold Portland but will instead evacuate and regroup," Major Houston said, moving between the two lines of MPs.

Miles glanced at the woman again without moving his head. Her uniform was cleaner and crisper than his had been in years. He assumed it was the better accommodations that came with rank—then remembered that he spent more nights with his

Brigand lover than he did with the other MPs in the Stroudwater Barracks. No wonder his clothes were in such bad shape.

The major's voice brought his thoughts back to the present. "We've received word that the Wardens are extending out from Boston. That includes north of the city. Their own raids have brought more Echoes to their ranks, and, of course, though they still have fewer numbers than our CNA field support divisions, they have the better tech. Our troops started evac-ing last night and left us as the only CNA forces in the region. Today's raid was to be the first of several before we left, but those orders have changed too."

If Miles had slept in the barracks the previous night, he would have noticed the ground troops moving out. Instead, this news surprised him.

"We will complete the C Block raid as planned in order to acquire as many human and Echo Brigands as we can to add to our ground troops," the major continued. "Any Brigands with decent skill sets or Echoes with any knowledge of their alien tech will become part of the CNA weapons development division. Use every resource to capture as many Brigands, especially Echoes, as possible. If we can't upgrade our weapons to match the Wardens, we'll never win this war. Questions?"

"The Brigands that don't come willingly?" an MP asked.

"Subdue them as needed with tranqs. I don't want our captures spending their first few weeks as CNA recruits recovering in the infirmary. Understand?"

"Yes, Major," Miles and the other MPs responded as a group.

"Complete the raid, return to the barracks, and pack your shit. We abandon Portland by sunset," Major Houston said and left.

Miles's mouth had gone dry; he couldn't swallow. The other MPs resumed their activities, and he turned back to the table. He pressed his palms against the top and leaned against them. He needed to warn Dani that the Wardens were moving north, but he would be neck deep in the raid for the next several hours. There wasn't enough time for him to go to her in B Block before he had to leave.

No one had asked where they were going once leaving the city, though there were only two choices when it came to escaping Portland. South landed them in a hornet's nest of Wardens. East was the Atlantic. They could only evacuate to the west or north.

He righted himself and took a deep breath. Dani was an expert at surviving, and he couldn't worry about her today. He holstered his weapon, an older-model plasma pistol he'd taken from a dead Warden. The newer models the Wardens had invented had twice as much power and held a charge three times longer than the one Miles had. Still, his weapon was more advanced than the ones most of the MPs carried; some of them used ancient revolvers like the one Dani carried. *Shit.* He couldn't stop thinking about her.

The routine of finishing his gear prep and joining the platoon he led helped settle his thoughts. He was responsible for two squads, twelve MPs in each. His platoon of twenty-five, including himself, plus two other platoons, had raid detail today. They didn't have far to march, since Brigands and MPs shared C Block.

He led his platoon to their designated location and waited while the others reached their positions. He stared at his watch, and at six minutes past the hour, he ordered his officers forward.

They caught two Brigands with ease—they were drunk—but the rest of their captures they earned. The scavengers scattered, spreading the word of the raid as they tried to escape. Miles barked a quick series of orders before firing his tranquilizer gun three times, hitting a fleeing man and boy in their backs but missing the woman he targeted. The man and boy stumbled for a few steps before falling. Louder concussion blasts sounded through other nearby buildings, and Miles recognized them as the sound of cannon nets being deployed. They used those to capture people grouped closer together. He despised these raids, but they were part of his duties as an MP.

Several Brigands poured out of a stairwell in front of Miles. One collided with him, taking them both to the ground. The young man reached for Miles's weapon, and Miles drove his knee into the man's gut. While the young man coughed, Miles rolled him to his side and placed a silver, one-inch-long rod on the Brigand's waist. The immobilization cuff, I-cuff, activated, forming a belt around the Brigand. The device generated an electrical pulse that prevented the wearer from moving voluntary muscles.

Miles left the young man on the ground and stood. Blood trickled from a wound somewhere on his scalp while he tried to determine the locations of his troops.

A cannon net boomed from an upper level of the building. He hadn't ordered his MPs to start sweeps up through the structure yet. He and several of his MPs finished applying I-cuffs to the Brigands they'd caught coming out of the stairwell before he did a head count.

"Corporal, divide your squad," Miles said. "Use half to secure the lower level and the other half to move these Brigands to the trucks to haul them out. Everyone else is with me." He didn't wait for the corporal to acknowledge his orders before leaving. He was eager to find out why some of his platoon were on the next floor up when they weren't supposed to be there yet.

He rushed into the stairwell and took the steps two at a time until he reached the door leading into the second floor. He led his troops through the shambles of rooms toward the noise of weapon fire, passing dead, gunned down Brigands. He holstered his tranq gun and drew his plasma pistol. His missing MPs were using live rounds.

He stepped into the room, and to his horror, three MPs stood over the bodies of slaughtered Brigands. One of the scavengers took his final breath as blood poured from the open wound across his throat.

Miles pointed his gun at the MP still holding the dripping blade. "Drop the knife, Anderson."

Anderson smiled. "He resisted."

"Drop the knife."

Anderson examined the blood on the blade instead. "Major Houston wants Echoes. The best way to tell the assholes apart from humans is to kill them, see if they come back to life. Those two were human," he said, tilting the knife at the two dead women tangled in a net with holes through their backs.

Miles kept his pistol pointed at Anderson but addressed his accomplices. "Surrender your weapons. You're relieved of duty."

The MPs shared a glance but didn't move.

A subtle, bluish color began to glow under the dead man's skin.

"Look!" Anderson said with a sneer. "We have an Echo! Major Houston will be so happy."

The blue color traveled beneath the Echo's skin, moving through his veins. His body slowly writhed as the man's body converted back to that of an older teenager. The wound across his neck filled with the blue liquid, replacing some of the red blood and healing the fatal injury. The Echo's body heaved as he drew in a noisy breath.

Anderson grinned. "Now is the best time to permanently kill them."

Miles kept his pistol aimed at his MP. "We need their memories to create better tech. We have our orders, Anderson."

The MP shook his head. "Nah. These fuckers invaded our planet three hundred years ago, hid among us, and attacked without cause. Billions of humans have died because of them. They need to die."

Anderson flipped the knife in his hand and raised his arm to plunge it into the helpless Echo's chest. Miles fired. The plasma pistol's blast tore a hole through Anderson's heart, launching him backward. He was a corpse before his body struck the floor.

Anderson's accomplices surrendered their weapons when Miles turned his pistol toward them.

"Sergeant Coulson, place these men under arrest," Miles said.

"Yes, sir," Coulson said and approached the rogue MPs.

Miles kept his weapon on them until Coulson activated the I-cuffs. She tapped a series of lights on the cuff belts that allowed the two men to move only their legs.

With the rest of their voluntary muscles immobile, Miles lowered his weapon. "Sergeant, stay with them until we return to the barracks to put them in a holding cell. James, Aeryn, carry the Echo to the trucks. Mitchell, gather up the net and reload the cannon. Take all the gear off Anderson for yourself; ditch that useless revolver."

"What about Anderson?" Mitchell asked.

"Leave him." Miles had six MPs left with him. His heart was not in this raid, much less in murdering Brigands. "Everyone else, we'll split up into two groups of two and one group of three to finish clearing the building. Anyone who decides to start murdering people for sport, I'll kill you myself. Let's go."

CHAPTER

6

Dani used less caution than before when moving through the city. She bolted across sunlit streets to move deeper into C Block. She stumbled for no obvious reason and crashed to the asphalt. While sprawled on her belly, the ground trembled, making bits of dirt and broken asphalt dance between her fingers. The Wardens were announcing their presence with earthquake grenades. She scrambled back to her feet, wobbling, the earth still shifting beneath her boots.

The building where she'd looked out the windows and left the starving man crumbled into a plume of dust. Her body trembled—not from the weapon's earthquake but from fear. She flinched when images of structures collapsing, including the children's hospital in Boston, flashed through her mind. Jace said she lost her memories when she reset back to ten years old, but apparently she'd retained pieces of her past, even if they were as small as the pebbles vibrating around her boots.

The tremor subsided and the shooting started. Dani couldn't see the Wardens yet, but she heard the unmistakable whine as their quake rifles powered up for a second before blasting their targets. An earthquake rifle's violent blast would stop a human's or Echo's heart even if he or she was shot in a limb. The Echoes would heal, and the Wardens took them. Several shots from a quake rifle could crumble a wooden house, and Warden quake grenades took down entire buildings made of concrete and steel.

Dani forced her feet in the direction of the raid. She had a better chance of escaping MPs than she did the Wardens. Brigands continued to scatter as she moved toward the raid's chaos. They shouted at her to turn around, but she ignored their warnings. A few laughed at her when she told them of the Wardens' arrival. A Warden attack on the remnants of Portland sounded absurd, even as her own words reached her ears, but she'd seen their helos landing by the river with her own eyes.

She skidded to a stop upon reaching an abandoned house—small in comparison to the others she'd passed, and farther away from the bulk of the other structures in the city. She hoped the Wardens wouldn't bother with such a small building.

She moved along the side of the building to the rear. The back door was open, and she paused to listen for any movement inside. She moved up the steps into the three-story home, creeping and praying the boards wouldn't groan or break beneath her boots.

She wanted to reach the top floor, get the best view of the area. She crept through the house to the second level and stopped when she caught a slight movement in the hall in front of her. She pulled her knife from her belt, her heart racing.

A man with a knife sprang from behind a closet door in the hallway, and Dani backed up, playing it safe but ready to engage the Brigand.

A woman's voice halted the man's attack. "Stop! She's a Brigand."

Dani peeked beyond the man's form. The woman who had called her out of the sun earlier was crouched on the floor behind the closet door. Dani took a deep breath to ease the side effects of the adrenaline coursing through her body. She sheathed her knife and waited for the man to lower his. "Found your brothers?"

"The MPs caught my other one," the woman said.

"I'm sorry." Dani hoped Miles wasn't the one who had broken up this woman's family. "Wardens landed north of the river and are moving through C Block."

"Wardens?" the man asked. "You led them here?"

"They didn't see me, or I'd already be caught."

"Caught?" the woman said. "Wardens only capture Echoes. Are you one of them?"

Dani tightened her jaw, annoyed by the slip. "Dead. Captured. Does it matter? I'm going up to have a look at the area. Find a better place to hide than a closet." She walked away without waiting for a response.

She arrived at the top floor and found a window overlooking the front of the house. Though she recognized the street by the other rows of rotting homes, her mind refused to focus. She'd practically confessed that she was an Echo. At least she hadn't told them she shared her bed with an MP who was part of the raid that had taken their brother.

She passed her hand through her hair and pinched her eyes closed. "Pull it together, girl," she said with a whisper. She took another deep breath and opened her eyes in time to see a Warden, plasma pistol drawn, approaching the front door. *Shit*.

She didn't have many options for hiding inside the house, and she'd make too much noise trying to find loose floorboards to crawl beneath. The stairs down to reach the back door would take her through the front of the house. Dani moved through the rooms and found the window she needed. She eased the window up, wincing when it creaked with the movement. A tree next to the house waited for her. She slid one leg through the window and almost had her second leg through when the

Warden fired his plasma pistol inside the house. Brigand men shouted as they charged the enemy, but their attack ended the instant the Warden fired more rounds.

Glass shattered as a Brigand dove out a window on the first floor and tumbled to the ground. Before the young woman could stand, the Warden shot her from inside the house. Dani flinched at the sight and almost lost her grip; she scrambled to cling to the window frame. If she fell, assuming she survived the fall, the Warden would shoot her.

She needed a better plan. Her mind shuffled through scenarios, and her thoughts stopped when the woman from the closet screamed. Dani heard her voice float up from the lower floor.

"We're Echoes," she said. "I swear."

"Let's see if you're telling the truth," the Warden said. His weapon fired, and the woman cried out.

Dani assumed the Warden had shot the brother, since the woman continued to sob. She glanced back at the tree, still waiting for her attempted leap. With a curse, she pulled her body back into the house. She soundlessly moved through the third level of the house and tiptoed down the stairs. She planned to continue down and slip out while the Warden was busy with the other woman.

Sneaking past the Warden wasn't going to be possible. He stood between Dani and her exit, but at least his back was turned toward her. A bluish light glowed from the body of the man on the floor in the hall. His sister knelt beside him. Dani picked up a length of wood from the broken stair railing, considering her options.

"He's an Echo, and a young regen at that. He'll make a fine reconditioning candidate. What about you?" The Warden aimed his weapon at the woman.

She glanced past him to Dani, who was now approaching him from behind, and the Warden turned.

Dani swung the piece of half-rotted wood, splintering it across the side of the Warden's head. He stumbled back, and she smashed what was left of the rail across his wrist, dislodging the plasma pistol. She hit him in the head again on the upswing. The Warden crumpled to the floor.

Dani groaned and cradled her burned, throbbing hand as she released the piece of wood.

"Thank you! Thank you," the woman said, sobbing with relief. She remained kneeling by her unconscious brother, now a boy no older than fifteen in oversized clothing.

Dani tried to ignore the pain in her hand. She reached for the Warden's plasma pistol and left her hand suspended an inch above it. Jace's words about her dying with a pistol in her hand made her stop. She pushed the weapon along the floor to the woman. "Take that," she said, already pawing through the Warden's gear. She noticed the name on his uniform.

Blood matted his dark hair from her first strike and swelling formed on his cheek from her second swing. Dani stole his knife, food, and water before taking the communication device from his jacket. She considered killing him. She and every other Brigand would be safer with one less Warden. But she wasn't a murderer.

The woman picked up the weapon and stared at it. "I don't know how to use this thing."

"It's not for you to shoot. Use it to trade with an MP in exchange for safe passage through their lines. Here." Dani shoved the food and water into the woman's pockets.

The boy's body shivered, a common result after an Echo reset to a younger age. Dani removed her jacket and wrapped him in it. She pulled his upper body upright, and his eyes fluttered open.

"Take him and go. Your other brother is likely still alive if he's with the MPs. It's the best you're going to get out of this shitty day."

The woman nodded.

Dani shifted to leave, and the woman grabbed her arm. "What's your name?"

"Dani."

"Thank you, Dani. I'm Rebecca. We won't forget this."

If I die, I will, Dani thought, but all she said was, "Good luck." She stood and, raising her voice, said, "Any other Brigands in this house, leave now while the Warden is out. When he wakes up, he's gonna be pissed."

She was amazed by the volume of scuffling sounds. Three Brigands scurried down the stairs from the third level and two more crawled from beneath floorboards on the second level to leave the house. The woman lifted her young brother to his feet, and Dani led the way out. Once outside, they parted ways. The woman's chances of getting her barely walking brother out of C Block safely were slim, but with that plasma gun, they at least had a chance.

Before leaving the house, Dani threw the Warden's comm into the tree she'd almost jumped into just a few minutes earlier. It bounced among the branches a few times before becoming lodged in a thick batch of leaves high in the tree. As she was fastening the Warden's knife to her belt, a quake grenade exploded, leveling half of the larger, abandoned houses up the street. Dani sprinted away from the destruction and toward the raid.

CHAPTER

7

Ps emerged from the ground level of a building to join other officers in the street. A few MPs herded their captured Brigands away while the rest gathered to talk. Dani crouched behind a dilapidated, rusted car frame on its side in the street. She was out of breath and wished she'd taken a drink of the Warden's water before giving it to Rebecca. She peeked around the edge of the car, and her chest tightened when she recognized Miles.

He spoke briefly with two other officers, gesturing sharply; then, with a quick nod, he broke away from the officers and began barking orders to the MPs who had just returned from loading their prisoners into transport trucks. The MPs started dragging objects from around the block to form makeshift barriers.

Dani groaned with frustration. Instead of fleeing C Block, the MPs were going to fight the Wardens, despite not even knowing how many they had to battle. They would die trying to hold the block.

Miles and his officers headed back into the building. Fighting from inside a building when the Wardens carried quake grenades was suicide.

Idiots!

Her head turned at the sound of a quake rifle's high-pitched whine. As she lunged for the other side of the car, the blast struck the car. She scrambled to escape the wreck as it tipped over, threatening to crush her. She got her body clear of the wreckage, but a piece of the car's frame snagged her pack on the way down, jerking her to the ground with it. Pain shot through her shoulder when she fell, but she was still alive.

She maneuvered her way out of the pack and knelt beside the car, simultaneously working to free the pack and looking for a place to run to. She quickly realized, however, that the sprint to reach any cover better than the car was too far and too open. She was fast, but she couldn't outrun a quake rifle. The Warden who had just shot the car would shoot her in the back as she fled.

She considered running to the MPs—a few of whom had just materialized back outside the building at the sound of the gunfire—and hope they'd protect her and that she could also later escape them.

That was a lot of hoping.

"Shit." Dani was right between the MPs and the Warden. At least the MPs were too busy worrying about the Warden to have even noticed her yet.

They opened fire on the Warden, who shot back at them. Dani left the car and her pack. The quake rifle obliterated one of the makeshift barriers the MPs had set up with one blast, sending debris into the air. Dani used her arms to shield her head as the debris scattered, but she didn't slow. Her arm and cheek stung as pieces of shrapnel bit into her skin. She ignored the pain and turned her body to lead with her shoulder. She leapt and crashed through a partially broken window on the ground floor of the same building she'd seen Miles disappear into.

Dani rolled and pressed her back against a wall. Her chest

heaved as she pulled in deep gasps of air. She'd thought Miles was stupid for entering the building, and now she was inside it too. But given the circumstances, this was her best choice. Any sane MP would ignore her presence right now, since she wasn't a threat. A much bigger threat was busy blowing holes in the MPs who were making their stand in the street.

Plasma pistols fired from a few floors above Dani. She crawled back to the window and poked her head up. Just as she located the Warden on the street, MPs fired down on him from somewhere above, killing him.

Dani eased her head out the window, looking up now, and recognized Miles leaning out from the third story. *Smart man to take the high ground, but don't stay there.*

The remaining officers in the street cheered the small victory, but Miles ended their celebration with more orders. "Strip him and reinforce your bunkers," he shouted down. "More Wardens are coming."

The street MPs left their positions, and five of them rushed to the car that had almost crushed Dani. They lifted the rusted frame and carried it back to use as cover. Another pair of MPs took the gear from the Warden, marveling at the quake rifle and body armor.

Look who's scavenging now. Fucking hypocrites.

The Warden's body turned blue, and one of the MPs shot him in the head with his own plasma pistol, ending his life forever. They left an almost-naked Warden lying in the street after stripping the corpse of the rest of his gear.

A movement across the street caught Dani's eye. It took her a moment to identify it. A Warden moved along the roof of a church, carrying what looked like a thick pipe.

Dani's eyes widened. "Miles!"

He didn't hear her, and he was still barking orders. The street MPs turned at her shout, but she was more concerned for

Miles. He was right in line with the Warden who was preparing to launch a quake grenade.

She prepared to shout for him again, but a strong forearm slipped around her neck from behind, cutting off her air. The MP dragged her away from the window and threw her to the ground.

She landed hard, but she immediately rolled to a crouched position and put up a hand.

"Stop! There's a Warden on the roof of the church across the street with quake grenades."

"Liar," the MP said. He reached for I-cuff on his duty belt.

Dani read the name on his shirt. "Mitchell, I'm not lying. Miles and the others will take a direct hit if they're not warned."

Mitchell stared at her. "How do you know Miles?"

"Uh." She couldn't truthfully answer the question without jeopardizing Miles. "He's almost caught me before." His last name was on his uniform, not his first name. Any moron would spot her lie, and Mitchell was at least at moron level.

"Brigand vermin," he said as he approached with the I-cuff.

She rushed him, driving her knee into his groin. He collapsed with pain, and Dani returned to the window. Several hands grabbed her and dragged her out through the window and into the street.

"Miles!"

Finally, his head turned at the sound of her voice. He stared down at her. "Shit."

Dani pointed. "Church. Incoming!"

Miles's gaze turned to the church. "Take cover!"

He and his troops fled the corner of the level they occupied. The quake grenade struck the side of the building seconds later, tearing a massive hole in the structure and raining chunks of concrete, glass, and beams down into the street. The MPs dropped Dani and fled. She scrambled to her feet and dove back through the window.

As soon as she landed, she curled into a ball and covered her head with her hands. Deadly debris crashed to the street, and the building shuddered with the impact of the grenade. A choking dust billowed from the street in through the window, forcing her to flee the area.

She crawled until she reached a place where she could breathe better. Coughing against the dust, she tried to wipe it from her face and eyes.

The ringing in her ears obscured Mitchell's return. He grabbed her arm, and she twisted it free of his grasp. He sank to his knees. Blood poured down the side of his face. More blood spilled from his abdomen, where a piece of metal had impaled him.

"Help me," he said weakly, gasping for air.

She wanted to spit a retort back at him for asking Brigand vermin for aid, but instead, she knelt beside him. "Sit still," she said calmly. "Rest."

He kept his eyes fixed on her and nodded. His breathing grew more ragged until his breaths stopped altogether. Even after he was gone, his dead eyes stared her.

She'd seen men die before. The war had killed this man, and it would kill her too. She found his flask and drank the last of the water in it. He had a newer-model plasma pistol in his holster. She eyed the weapon for a moment before taking it and his tranq pistol. She intended to tranquilize any MPs or Wardens that got too close. She didn't know what to do with the plasma pistol yet.

The Warden named Rowan had mentioned reconditioning the Brigand Echo. She didn't know what that meant but was certain she wanted nothing to do with it. The plasma pistol was a last resort, possibly to use on herself if cornered. Maybe that's what Jace meant by her dying of friendly fire. Jace's old revolver, if she had it, would only put a hole through her skull. She could heal and be a ten-year-old kid again. A plasma pistol would take her head clean off, and an Echo couldn't come back from that.

Deciding that she would worry later about what to do if she were cornered, she resumed moving through the ground level of the structure. Shots were fired from an upper level somewhere, and no additional quake grenades hit the building. The MPs must have killed the Warden on the church roof. *Only twenty-eight more to go.*

Dani found an actual hole in the wall and crawled into it to hide, rest, and think. She heard Miles's voice and wanted to go to him, but she forced herself to remain hidden. From her location, she could tranquilize anyone who ventured too close to her position. She peered through a tiny crack in the wall and waited. As soon as she had a clear path, she planned to make a dash to leave the structure, avoiding the part of the street from which the sounds of MP weapons were now erupting again.

CHAPTER

T he fighting moved from the streets into the building, and Dani remained undiscovered inside the wall. A pair of MPs cowered near her location.

"Where's our backup?" the male MP asked.

"Rani's platoon is pinned and can't get to us," the female MP said. "Half of Kipp's crew was flattened in the street. We're on our own."

"Jesus."

"Pray if you want. I'm fighting until I can't."

Several blasts from a quake rifle shook parts of the building from the interior as the battle intensified. For now, Dani was hidden and away from the worst of the battle. She planned to remain where she was until it was safe to leave—except Miles was somewhere out there, still fighting . . . and losing. Could she really leave him to die?

The woman grunted as she stood. "We need to get closer, see if we can flank the Wardens inside the ground floor."

Miles's voice came over their comm, and Dani was startled to hear his voice so close by.

"This is Jackman. We're pinned by at least three Wardens, one is acting as a sniper. Four of us left, one is wounded."

While he spoke, multiple shots from plasma pistols and

quake rifles sounded over the comm, making it difficult to hear him. Dani shifted and pressed her head closer to the wall separating her from the MPs.

The woman spoke. "Location, sir?"

"Coulson! Northwest quadrant. Part of the upper floor is collapsed. We have cover, but it won't last once the sniper finishes blasting everything apart with the quake rifle."

"We're on our way," Coulson said.

"How many with you?" Miles asked.

"One. I'm with James."

"Aeryn?"

"Killed by the quake grenade from the church."

"Mitchell?"

"Missing, sir."

"Hurry, Coulson."

"We're on our way, sir," she said.

Dani listened until the sound of their boots diminished to faint thuds, then unfolded her legs and emerged from her hole. She spotted the two MPs climbing over rubble as they moved toward the fiercest fighting. Dani followed at a distance, constantly turning and scanning behind her to confirm she wasn't being followed. The increasing noise of weapon fire as they neared the fighting hid any sound Dani might be making.

As she picked her way through the debris, there was a break in the cacophony of shots fired for a few seconds. The noise of something behind her collapsing halted her steps. The fighting resumed, and she scurried into an opening between chunks of concrete and metal. A few minutes passed. She held her breath as a pair of Wardens marched past.

Coulson and James would be dead before they saw their attackers. Worst of all, two more Wardens would join the fight against Miles, assuming he was still alive. Three uninjured but pinned MPs couldn't survive long against five Wardens.

Dani slid out from between the concrete blocks. She crept around the larger piles of rubble to move parallel to where she suspected the Wardens were walking. The firefight continued to hide any noise she made, and she was careful to avoid venturing into their peripheral vision and being discovered.

As she passed another pile of rubble, she spotted the Wardens—still stalking Coulson and James. She pulled the tranq pistol from her belt. The weapon's hiss as it fired wouldn't give her position away like the plasma pistol would.

She changed her path to circle around to her right, making frequent glances down to make sure she didn't trip on anything. After stepping over a dead Brigand, she decided to stop and take aim. The Wardens raised their weapons to fire on Coulson and James, but Dani squeezed her trigger first.

The first Warden gave a shout of surprise before collapsing. The remaining Warden fired his rifle nowhere near Dani's location. The two MPs fired on the Warden, but one shot from his quake rifle sent them scrambling away from the falling debris he created. Dani's tranq pistol hissed again, and the bolt struck the Warden in the thigh. He spotted her, but his steps faltered as he tried to shoot at her. His body struck the floor, unconscious from the sedative.

The MPs glanced around for their ally but didn't find Dani; she'd already ducked back into the shadows. They left their cover to kill the Wardens and steal their gear while Dani observed them from between cracks in the debris. As soon as the Wardens' bodies began to glow, James stabbed them in the neck, dispatching them permanently.

This was Dani's best chance to escape the fighting and the building, but she remained. Miles was still in danger. Of course, her own peril grew each second she lingered around the battle, too. Jace's words of warning repeatedly echoed in her mind, but her legs refused to carry her away from Miles. She wasn't sure if she loved him, but she knew she didn't want him dead. The MPs left with their new gear, and with a curse at her foolishness, Dani followed again. *If I don't die today, Jace will kill me anyway. Death by half-sibling must qualify as friendly fire, right?*

The noise of the firefight grew yet louder. Dani couldn't see Miles, but she noticed two Wardens focusing their attack on a single area. They fired from the ground while a third Warden fired from his position on top of a concrete slab that had partially fallen from the level above, blowing pieces of the building apart with his quake rifle. Miles had to be on the receiving end of the assault.

Coulson gave orders to James that Dani couldn't hear, but she watched their exchange and the woman's gestures. The MPs split up. James fired at one of the Wardens on the ground and missed. The Warden turned to shoot him, but Coulson fired first. Dani grinned; Coulson was smart. The female MP's kill was answered with return fire that sent her scampering for better cover. James moved over debris to reach her and exposed his location. One shot from the Warden on the slab blasted James off his feet. He was dead before his body landed on the floor.

Dani didn't have a good shot with her tranq pistol on either Warden. Coulson had stopped shooting back, and now Dani couldn't see her.

The sniper resumed firing on his original target while the remaining Warden stalked closer to where Coulson had disappeared. Dani was closer to the woman's last location, so she rushed to reach her first. The Warden fired at Dani as she moved but missed her by a wide margin. She found the MP lying on her side, covered in dust except for areas on her face where blood flowed. Dani checked her pulse on her neck, and the MP moved in a flash. Pain seized Dani's arm when Coulson grabbed and twisted her wrist.

"Aah! Stop! I'm on your side," Dani said. She realized how

silly her words sounded. A Brigand on the same side as an MP was ludicrous.

Coulson held Dani's arm in the painful joint lock so she couldn't move the limb.

"Here," Dani said. She moved her free hand slowly to her plasma pistol. She pulled it from her belt and turned the grip toward the woman. "Take it. That Warden on the ground is coming for you."

The MP held her arm another moment. Dani sighed when Coulson released the pressure on her arm to take the pistol.

Dani rubbed her sore shoulder and elbow. "Can you keep the one coming busy?"

"Yeah. Where are you going?"

"After the sniper."

"How? You gave me your pistol."

Dani pulled her tranq gun. "I have this."

Coulson's brow creased. "That was *you* who immobilized the two Wardens?"

"Lucky shots. Handle the Warden headed this way. I'll deal with the one up top. It's the only way to free Miles."

"You know Miles?"

Shit! "I heard him say his name over your radio. He said he was pinned with a few other folks, right?" Dani had screwed up again. Miles had only identified himself by his last name when he called for backup.

Coulson didn't seem to notice the lie. "If I can find James—"

"He's dead." Dani peeked around the corner of a piece of twisted metal. "Your Warden is twenty-five yards away. Ten o'clock."

Dani left Coulson to move along the perimeter. She glanced up often to keep watch on the sniper while looking to find a way to climb up without being seen. Shots erupted near where she'd left Coulson, and Dani silently wished the woman well.

She had no love for the MPs, but they were better than the murderous Wardens.

Her search along the ground revealed only two ways for her to reach the upper floor. One way would provide the sniper with an easy opportunity to blow her away. The second option was a difficult climb through a mostly broken set of stairs in a somewhat exposed stairwell. Once high enough, she could tranq the sniper with an unobstructed shot through a hole in the stairwell's wall.

She secured the tranq pistol in her belt and headed for the stairs.

CHAPTER

9

The first few steps in the stairwell were intact. Every step after was either waiting to collapse beneath Dani's weight or missing altogether. She climbed and crawled more than she walked. Halfway up, several steps were gone. She stopped to locate the sniper, hoping she could get a clear shot from her current position and wouldn't have to continue beyond the gap in the stairs—but a fallen beam from the upper level obstructed her view of the Warden, who, judging from the thunderous blasts that kept sounding, was still mercilessly firing on Miles and the other trapped MPs. Dani couldn't see Coulson, but the continued noise of plasma pistol shots told her that the MP and the Warden on the ground were still trading shots.

Dani adjusted her feet, crouched, and sprang upward. Her leap was a little short. Her arms reached the next step beyond the gap, but her chest collided with the edge, and now her swinging lower body threatened to drag her off the step entirely. She glanced down at the pile of twisted metal below, waiting to impale her. She struggled to pull herself up but didn't have the arm strength to do so. She swung one leg up and, body contorted, managed to hook her boot around a piece of the handrail still attached to the wall. Her grunts grew louder as she clawed her way out of her predicament.

Once she was out of danger from falling, Dani clung to the handrail and drew in deep, raspy breaths.

Whose brilliant idea was this?

She wanted to stay curled and clinging to the handrail a bit longer, at least until her pounding heart slowed, but Miles didn't have time for her to rest. She forced herself to continue up the stairwell. Debris fell as she moved, but the sniper was too deafened by his rifle's whine and the blasts that followed each pull of his trigger to hear the racket she made.

Three-quarters of the way up the stairs, she found the massive hole in the wall she'd spotted from below. She stopped on the crumbling steps and looked through. She had an unobstructed view of the sniper now—still lying prone on the slab and shooting down at the MPs.

She drew her tranq pistol and aimed it at the Warden. Body armor covered his chest and back, but his arms and legs were vulnerable to a tranquilizer dart. She lined up her weapon's sights with the back of his left thigh and steadied the weapon with both hands. She took a breath, released it slowly, and started to squeeze the trigger—and her boot broke through the step she was balanced on. Her body dropped; her arms struck the edge of the hole in the wall, sending the tranq pistol bouncing out of her hands. She scrambled to the next step, but it too began to crumble beneath her. She scampered up the remaining steps as the stairwell progressively collapsed behind her.

She reached the next level in the building and dove away from the stairs, hoping the floor was more stable. She flattened her body against an intact portion of the floor where it met a wall far from the collapsed stairs. She hoped the sniper couldn't see her. He had to have heard the crashing stairs, even with the constant noise of his quake rifle.

All shots from both the rifle and plasma pistols paused. *Yep, definitely heard it.* Though she desperately wanted to see where the Wardens were now and which MPs were still alive, Dani didn't dare move. If Coulson had been anywhere near the now-collapsed stairwell when it gave out, she was probably dead.

The pause was brief; the weapon fire quickly resumed, including that of the quake rifle, and as it did, Dani realized how odd it felt to be relieved that the fighting had resumed. Shots weren't being fired in her direction, so she had remained undetected.

The sound the quake rifle made before it was fired irritated her. Her shot at the sniper with the tranq pistol had obviously missed. She had two knives left for weapons. She could protect herself with a knife to some extent, but she was no expert at fighting with one.

Once again, she had the option of hiding where no one knew where she was and leaving the MPs to whatever fate awaited them, or trying to help Miles and hoping they both survived. With a curse, she moved from her position on the floor to a crouch. She returned to the edge of the floor where the stairs had collapsed. The angled slab of concrete where the sniper was lay almost below her. Any closer, and the falling concrete would have taken him out. *No such luck.*

She surveyed her surroundings. *Twelve-foot ceilings. Seven-foot drop to the slab, almost straight down. If you run, jump, and make it closer to the top of the slab, the seven-foot drop becomes four. You can almost land on the sniper to take him out. Have the knife out when you jump. No. My luck, I'd just stab myself with it. Tackle the sniper, then pull the knife. At least I won't have a gun in my hand to be killed by friendly fire if I die like Jace says I do, right?*

Dani passed both hands through her hair and shook her head. *God, this sucks.*

She moved away from the edge of the gaping hole in the floor back to the wall and took a deep breath.

Horrible fucking plan.

She pushed off the wall and sprinted over the twenty feet of intact flooring. She leapt across the gap, and her boots landed hard against the angled slab while her palms slammed against its surface. Pain shot through her burned hand, but there was no time to worry about that. She dashed toward the sniper.

He'd heard her landing. He rolled and swung his rifle upward. Dani lunged for him and slammed her shoulder into his chest. The rifle fell from his hands, and they skidded a few feet in a tangle of limbs. Dani escaped his grasp and drew her knife. He reached for his knife, but it wasn't in its sheath.

He had been injured at some point; there was dried blood on the side of his face. Dani's mind worked to find a way to defeat him, but her brain's gears halted when she noticed the name on his uniform.

"Rowan." Dani shook her head. "You're a tenacious bastard."

Rowan grinned. "I could say the same of you. Attacking me with my own knife, now that takes some nerve." He shifted his feet to move higher up the slab.

Dani moved parallel to him, refusing to let him have the higher area; she didn't want him to be able to rush down on her quicker than she could sprint up to meet him. Either way, she couldn't outfight him. She wished one of the MPs would shoot him before she had to do anything, but no one fired up at the slab. Her only option was to surprise him. He was a trained killer; she was a trained scavenger.

Rowan's boot skidded on loose debris on the slab, and Dani charged without hesitation. He then grinned, and she realized she'd fallen for a feigned slip. She was committed to her attack now, though, so she swung her blade at him. He slammed both of his hands into her wrist, one on each side, and the blade flew out of her grip. Before she could recover, he made a fist and swung it back toward her, striking her in the jaw just below the ear. Dani stumbled from the blow and fell on her back.

She blinked to clear her vision while she clumsily scrambled backward down the slab, keeping her eyes on the blurred shape still moving toward her.

"I really hope you're an Echo. I will kill you several times for this," Rowan said. He picked up his knife and lunged at her, poised to thrust his blade into her chest.

Dani rolled, pulling her second knife as she went. As he came down at her, she drove it into the side of his body, below his armor. The knife's hilt prevented the blade from going deeper than she wanted. His warm blood flowed over her hand. She twisted the knife, and Rowan cried out. She jerked her knife free from his body and scrambled away from his attempt to stab her again.

Blood poured from the Warden's wound, running in thin streams down the concrete. The hand he held over the wound turned red. He crawled up the slab, still holding his knife. Dani neared the top edge of the slab as he approached. Her vision remained blurred from his earlier punch, and she had nowhere else to go if he reached her.

Rowan slowed as loss of blood weakened his body. Before he could reach Dani, he collapsed.

Dani stared at the fallen Warden, waiting to see if he'd move again. The ringing in her ears lessened, and she heard the continued fighting on the ground.

"Goddammit, Coulson, kill that fucker already!"

Dani wasn't sure how much time passed before Rowan's body began its bluish glow. She scooted on her rump closer to him and rolled him to his back. His body writhed as he returned to a younger Rowan—in his early twenties. She pressed the tip of her knife to his throat, realizing as she did that her hand

and forearm were red with his blood. Her blade trembled; she shuddered and dropped the knife. "The MPs can kill him if they want him dead."

She crawled on her hands and knees to the quake rifle. Still dizzied by the blow she'd taken to her jaw, she picked up the rifle and stood. Pain exploded through her body when something struck her chest. The force blasted her off the slab, launching her into a ten-foot freefall to the floor below.

CHAPTER

10

Miles and his MPs cowered as more bits of debris fell on them. The sniper couldn't hit them with a direct shot, so he was focusing on blasting the building over them with his quake rifle, sending bits of debris showering down on them. The Warden would drop the building on them before he let them escape.

Miles wiped dust from his eyes. He had new blood on his hand, but he didn't know which latest part of his body was injured. He was covered in scrapes and cuts; another one didn't matter. This Brigand raid had turned into a slaughter of the Commonwealth's MPs.

He looked at his remaining three officers. Most of his team was dead now. Only a miracle could save the rest of them.

Where is Dani?

He hadn't seen Dani since her warning about the Warden on the church roof. He prayed she wasn't lying under a chunk of concrete.

Petersen had been injured in the last exchange they'd had with Wardens, before retreating to their current position. Garcia and Elmore had still been uninjured and fighting then, but severely outgunned. That was even more true now that Garcia was gone. A shot from a Warden had slipped through the rubble, killing her, five minutes after their retreat.

Together, the three surviving MPs crouched on the first floor of the building behind an entire section of the second floor that had fallen. The cinder-block wall protected them to a degree, and they returned fire when they could, but the Wardens' more advanced weaponry was keeping them pinned behind their wall—especially the quake rifle one of their attackers was firing at them from up on some debris across the way.

Coulson had answered his call for backup, but Miles didn't believe she and James would arrive in time to help. Now, after the latest collapse of debris on them, Miles wondered how much longer they would survive. Petersen was bleeding profusely from the wound to his thigh. Elmore had tied his belt around his leg, but that wasn't doing much to slow the bleeding.

The barrage of shots fired on their location lessened, and Miles assumed Coulson had arrived. She and James had either killed a Warden, or they were drawing the Wardens' attack to them. The sniper's attack didn't waver, though.

"What do we do?" Elmore asked.

Miles checked Petersen's pulse; the man was dead. He took the dead MP's pistol and passed it to Elmore. Miles retrieved Garcia's weapon and kept it. He leaned against the wall and rested on one knee.

"As soon as there is the slightest pause from the sniper, we bolt. This is our only way out," Miles said, waving one of his pistols to his left. "We can't stay here."

Elmore nodded.

"Then we find Coulson and James. If they're still alive, we help them kill the rest of these bastards. If they're dead, we leave. The Wardens won't show mercy to any human."

"Yes, sir."

The sniper's rifle fell silent, and Miles and Elmore scrambled to leave. The loud crash of another part of the ceiling collapsing surprised Miles, however, and he paused a moment too long. As Elmore escaped, a block of falling concrete clipped Miles's leg, tearing a long gash through his trousers and calf.

Miles crawled back to Petersen's body and removed the belt from the dead man's thigh. By the time he finished tying the tourniquet around his leg, the sniper had resumed firing on his position. He'd missed his chance.

More parts of the wall broke apart with the continued blasts from the quake rifle, and Miles decided he wouldn't wait for the sniper to finish bringing the wall and building down on top of him. He pushed himself to his feet, and pain shot up his leg. He took a few tiny steps, limping with each one. Miles readied both guns in his hands and prepared to leave the protective wall.

The sniper's rifle was quiet again, and Miles limped away from the cinder-block wall. He held both plasma pistols upward, but he didn't have a target. He couldn't see anyone on top of the angled slab of concrete above him. His eyes scanned what was left of the second level, but nothing moved. He moved away from the slab to search for the sniper's new location. With each slow, hobbling step, he left a single, bloody boot print.

Miles spotted the other Warden and glimpsed Coulson returning fire at her enemy. He didn't see James or Elmore anywhere. He wanted the sniper dead. Coulson's continued firefight with the other Warden created enough noise to obscure his grunts and curses as he limped around piles of concrete and twisted metal instead of climbing over them and exposing his position. The last thing he wanted to do was make himself a better target for the sniper.

He noticed movement in his peripheral vision. The sniper was standing at the edge of the slab, the rifle in his hand.

Miles fired.

In the brief second the sniper's body twisted with the impact, Miles realized his target's clothes were wrong for a Warden. He'd shot a woman in a T-shirt. His gut tightened when he noticed her short hair and the bandage on her right hand. Dani's body fell over the other side of the slab.

Tears burned his eyes, and without regard for the remaining Warden, Miles rushed to find her. "Please, no," he said repeatedly as he moved toward the slab, ignoring the dangers around him.

He reached Dani. He dropped both pistols as he sank to the floor beside her. She was lying face down, and pools of blood had already formed beneath her upper body and head. With trembling hands he rolled her to her back and groaned. "Dani. No, no, no. Why were you here? This wasn't supposed to happen."

Tears fell from his cheeks to her face as he leaned over her corpse. The hole in her chest was from his weapon. He groaned and placed his hand over the wound. It wasn't bleeding any-more. He lifted Dani and pulled her close.

"You weren't supposed to be here," he moaned. "I'm sorry, Dani. I'm so sorry."

He lowered his head and wept, still clinging on to her. Then a sudden pain tore through his back, and he rocked for-ward, stunned into releasing Dani from his arms. As he turned, another strike caught him in the head. He collapsed across Dani's body, unconscious.

"Killed by her lover this time, eh, Miles? Thanks for that," Jace said. He grabbed the back of Miles's collar to pull him off Dani. After lowering the MP to the ground, Jace reached into his bag.

A blue glow started at the core of Dani's body and grew brighter. Jace threw a tattered blanket over her to hide the light. The broken bones in her arm and skull shifted beneath the skin. The color spread to her face and limbs. Jace placed the two pistols Miles had dropped in his bag, then slung the pack over his head again, adjusting the strap so it fell across his chest. His arms free, he leaned over Dani's shrinking form and wrapped her tightly with the blanket, leaving enough fabric to drape across her blood-smeared face.

Dani's body continued to heal as she changed from a twenty-five-year-old woman to a ten-year-old girl. Jace pulled her now-oversize boots off and threw them several feet away, into the plethora of litter around them. He'd get her out of the adult clothes later.

All sounds of plasma pistols stopped, and Jace hoped the MPs had defeated the last Warden. He slipped the quake rifle's strap over his shoulder and scooped Dani into his arms. Her body moved inside the blanket as she drew in her first breath in her healed form.

Jace took a final look at the MP who had accidentally shot her. "I knew you were trouble," he said with a frown.

Miles stirred but didn't wake. Dani wouldn't remember him anyway.

As he'd done twice before, Jace carried his regenerated sister's body away from where she'd been killed.

CHAPTER
11

Jace moved silently through the rubble, Dani gripped tightly in his arms. He stopped every few steps to listen. The two remaining MPs, excluding Miles, were making enough noise between them to hide any moan Dani might make as she continued to recover. He passed by the base of the angled concrete slab and paused. The unconscious Warden Dani had defeated remained where she'd left him. She'd saved Miles's life long enough so he could shoot her by mistake.

His warning to her this morning had not changed her fate. She'd still died by friendly fire, with a gun in her hand.

A new noise began in the distance. The rhythmic thumping grew louder, and Jace started moving again, this time with less heed for a quiet escape. His progress halted when he rounded a turn and found plasma pistols pointed at his head. He froze before the MPs.

"Don't move," the man said.

Jace's eyes flicked between the MPs and his surroundings. He read the names on their uniforms. Coulson and Elmore.

Jace held Dani closer to his chest. "Please. My granddaughter was injured. I need to get her away from this building before more parts collapse."

"How did you end up with a quake rifle?" Coulson asked.

"I picked it up off the ground," Jace said.

"Where's the Brigand woman?" Coulson asked.

Jace shrugged. "Dead, I guess. She was shot, and I saw her fall."

"Give us the rifle," Elmore said.

"I need it to trade for medical care for my granddaughter. Let us pass, and I'll tell you where to find your injured MP. His uniform says Jackman on it."

The female MP stepped closer to Jace, weapon still raised. "How do we know he's still alive?"

"Because I didn't kill him when I had the chance. He is injured, though, and will need your help to stay alive. Those were more Warden helos passing overhead a moment ago. Shoot us if you want, but I'm not staying here any longer to wait for their reinforcements to march through," Jace said.

Coulson lowered her pistol, and Elmore did the same.

"Where's Jackman?" Coulson asked.

Jace turned and nodded his head. "He's lying on the other side of that slab. I suggest you find your man and leave while you can."

"Come with us, and we'll get your granddaughter the care she needs," Coulson said.

"And be forced into the CNA army after? No thanks." Jace walked forward and stepped between the officers. They didn't try to stop him as he left. He glanced back and saw them jogging in Miles's direction.

Daylight was waning and more Wardens were arriving as Jace made his way through the city. His body ached, and he was out of breath from carrying his sister for the last few hours. He had been in his mid-forties the last time he'd had to carry her. Now in his early sixties, his strength began to fail, exactly as he'd feared. He didn't want her near anyone else while she recovered, but if he was to keep her alive, he needed help.

Going against his desire to remain hidden from all others, including Brigands, Jace carried his sister to an abandoned home west of Portland known for sheltering Brigands.

He traded the rifle for a private room for one night, five days of food and water, and two sets of child-size clothing. The quake rifle was worth more than any other weapon currency. He followed the woman managing the house to the rear of the structure. Brigands lined the stairs going to the upper level, and he stepped around and over people staying the night on the floor. Whatever they had traded in exchange for accommodations didn't compare to a quake rifle.

Jace carried Dani to their room and placed her on the rumpled mattress on the floor as their host placed a sack on the floor containing the agreed-upon food, water, and clothes. "It's not much space," she said, "but it's private. This used to be a walk-in closet off the master bedroom. Can you believe people once owned enough clothes they needed a closet to walk through to get to them all?"

"No. It seems impossible that life was ever like that." Jace's face flushed at this unexpected small talk with a stranger.

The woman smiled. "Don't worry. We're Echo-friendly here. Who is she? And don't give me that granddaughter crap."

"My sister."

The woman nodded. "Need a hand getting her cleaned up and changed?"

"Yes!" Jace said, almost pleading. He reached for his bag. "I can pay you—"

"No need," she said.

He helped her unwind the blanket from around Dani's body. The woman left for a few minutes, and Jace removed

Dani's socks, now four sizes too big. He found a mostly clean rag in his bag and wiped at the smears of dried blood on her face. The woman returned with ragged cloths and a bowl full of water. Jace busied himself with the sack, moving the food and water to his own bag while the woman washed Dani. She hummed a song as she worked, and he groaned when he removed the impossibly small clothing from the sack.

"She's lucky to have you," the woman said as she took the clothes from Jace's hands. She dressed Dani in a faded blue T-shirt and tattered jeans that were still too big for her ten-year-old frame.

Jace placed the extra set of clothes in his bag and pawed through the bloodstained adult clothing the woman had tossed to the floor after removing it from Dani's tiny frame. He found a half-eaten food wafer in her pocket. He removed the empty knife sheath and water pouch from her belt. After stowing the water in his bag, he pulled her belt from her trousers. He rolled her pants, socks, and belt before putting them in his stuffed bag. He left the blood-soaked tee with a hole through the front. If she grew as quickly as she had in her former pre-teen years, she'd be back in the trousers and socks by the time she reached fifteen. Clothes were often harder to find than food these days.

The woman finished dressing Dani and gathered the T-shirt, rags, and bowl, now full of red-tinged water. "Where will you go?"

"I don't know," Jace said.

The woman nodded and left the room. Jace pulled his blanket over Dani's small form and stared at her for a moment. He stepped out of the room and leaned his back against the door. Most of the Brigands staying in the house slept, but a group of three men and a woman huddled in a corner of the former master bedroom that had been turned into a communal floor space for sleeping. Jace listened as they talked.

"We're going west," one man said with a nod at the woman next to him.

"You can't survive in the mountains long. You have no gear and the snow starts flying next month," another man wearing a dark jacket said. "We're going north, to Bangor."

"Yep, north," the third man said. "It's too rural for the Wardens to care about. There are less than a hundred Commonwealth ground troops there. Some MPs in the mix, but the Brigands control much of the area."

The woman frowned. "Until the Wardens arrive with their tech and blast everything to dust."

"Nah. There isn't anything of value in the north that the Commonwealth or Wardens want," her companion said.

"You're saying we should go to Bangor too?" the woman asked.

"It's not the worst idea we've ever had." He turned to the other man. "How are you getting there?"

"I have a man that can transport us as far north as Waterville. Three- to four-hour ride on back roads. It's all walking after that."

"How much is the transport?" Jace asked.

The Brigands turned to him at his question. "For you and the dead kid you carried through here?"

"She's not dead, just injured during the fighting today. She only needs a little time to rest, and she'll be fine," Jace said. "How much?"

The man in the dark coat eyed him for a moment. "Got another quake rifle?"

"No, but I have another weapon I can trade." He had two older plasma pistols stolen from Miles, a knife, and Dani's revolver, but he was careful to only indicate that he had a single weapon. He had enough problems caring for a child; he didn't need to set himself up to be robbed.

"Like what?" the man asked.

Jace grinned. "Nice try. In case you can't tell by my gray hair, I wasn't born yesterday."

"We're leaving mid-morning to meet my contact. Show me what you have then, and I'll decide if you and the kid can come."

Jace shrugged. "Fair enough." He turned to go back into the room but paused when the woman who had helped him returned.

She handed him another small sack. "Socks, a fleece, and a jacket. The boots will be too big for her, hence two pairs of socks."

Jace stared at the bag. He needed the clothes for Dani, but he also needed to trade for their transportation north.

"Don't worry about paying for these," she said. "I was about her age when my older sister was taken by the Wardens. I like to think my sister is still alive, but I can't imagine the horror of surviving as an Echo under Warden rule. Can you?"

Jace shook his head. "Thank you, for everything."

She nodded and left. Jace entered the room and barricaded the door with a chair. He placed the newest sack beside the mattress before sitting next to Dani. His shoulders sagged, and he stared at the floor. He perked up when a small hand emerged from the blanket, reaching for him.

Jace took Dani's hand, and she gave him a sleepy smile.

"Don't worry, Jason," she said.

He gasped; she had never remembered him before following a regen.

CHAPTER

12

Rowan moaned and opened his eyes. Still lying on his back on the concrete slab, he lifted his hand, which was covered in half-dried blood. He flexed his fingers, and the stiffer, dried blood cracked with the movement. He rolled over with a curse and clumsily pushed himself to his feet. He'd died with his knife still in his other hand, so he resheathed it. He picked up the Brigand woman's blade, the one she'd used to kill him. He considered discarding the inferior knife, but he decided to keep it. If she was still alive, he wanted to use it on her. His brow creased as he stared at the knife.

He should be dead, permanently. He wondered what had stopped her from finishing the job. He scanned the area, pieced together the events that had preceded her attack. He'd had four MPs pinned behind a cinderblock wall. During the fighting, the woman leapt to the slab from the second floor. Now she was gone, and so was his quake rifle.

Bitch.

He stumbled down the slab to reach the ground floor.

This was his sixth time dying. At least his recovery time was fast. He checked the bodies of dead Wardens and MPs in the area and found an older plasma pistol. The Wardens' throats were cut, and their weapons and armor taken. Rowan was lucky the MPs hadn't found him at the top of the slab, or he wouldn't be walking around now.

He searched the area but didn't find the woman. If she lived, she'd escaped.

Several rifle shots from outside the structure gained his attention, and he left the building. He smiled to see eight Wardens marching twenty-five captured Brigands and MPs at gunpoint through the street—but his initial jog to catch up ended after the first two steps. His side still ached from being stabbed. Pain following a traumatic death tended to take a few more hours to leave the body after regeneration.

The other Wardens recognized him, and Rowan raised his pistol skyward in greeting. After catching up to the group of captives, Rowan strolled past them, inspecting each face carefully.

"Sir?"

Rowan turned to the Warden who spoke.

The other man stared at Rowan's side, and Rowan looked down, noting his blood-soaked clothing from his flank to his knee.

"I'm fine," he said. "I'm looking for a Brigand woman. Small frame. Short hair."

"We don't have anyone fitting that description, sir. The people here are the only ones we've found thus far that are still alive."

Rowan frowned and returned his attention to the prisoners. "Brigand. Mid twenties. Short, dark hair and wearing a short-sleeved T-shirt and MP uniform pants. MP-issue boots. She had a bandage on her right hand. Anyone who can tell me where she is, dead or alive," he said louder, looking at the Brigands, "I'll let you go free as soon as I find her."

"We caught a woman who looked like that, but she got away when a Warden hit the building with a quake grenade," one of the MPs said.

"Nice try, but tough luck"—Rowan paused to read the name on the man's uniform—"Kipp. I saw her after the quake grenade. Anyone else? How about a name?" He paced in front of the Brigands. "Surely one of you knows her."

"Will I go free if I tell you her name?" a young Brigand male asked.

Rowan walked along the line of prisoners to face the man that spoke. "Give me her name, and I'll give you a head start. If you can avoid capture a second time, you're free."

The muscles in the man's jaw tightened and relaxed as he considered his chances of escape. Rowan tried to smile reassuringly at him, but it turned into a sneer.

"Dani. She lives in B Block, but I don't know where."

"Excellent! Last name?" Rowan asked.

"I don't know."

Rowan waved his hand, gesturing for the man to leave the line. The Brigand took a few cautious steps away from the others before bolting.

"Anyone else know her last name?" Rowan checked the plasma pistol in his hand. Despite having been used in a long battle against the Wardens, the formerly MP-owned weapon retained half a charge and roughly thirty plasma rounds.

The group remained silent, and Rowan turned away from them. He aimed his pistol at the fleeing Brigand and fired one shot. The young man tumbled forward and sprawled face down in the street. He didn't move again.

Rowan approached the Wardens still guarding the remaining captives. "Guess he couldn't avoid getting caught again," he said with a shrug, and the Wardens chuckled.

Another Warden approached, and Rowan smiled "Curtis! You're late to the party, as usual."

"I am," Curtis said. "Bad day? You're looking a bit younger than when I saw you yesterday."

Rowan rolled his eyes. "Yes."

Curtis snorted a laugh. "What is that? Five?"

"Six."

Curtis laughed louder.

"Shut up. You have a harder time staying alive than I do. We'll have a party if you ever reach thirty before another regen."

"Fair enough. This looks like it could be interesting," Curtis said with a nod of his head at the prisoners. "What do you plan to do with the humans? We could use them for labor."

"Yeah, but they'll just die and then we have to deal with bodies. Non-compliant Echoes are better at labor. They just keep coming back to work some more."

Rowan and Curtis shared a laugh while the prisoners shifted uncomfortably. Rowan enjoyed watching them suffer. The humans in the group would die in the next few minutes. But the Echoes would have an even worse fate.

Rowan addressed the guards. "Kill them all. Once you ID the Echoes, take them to the barracks to begin conditioning. Compliant Echoes will enter combat training. Non-compliant ones become laborers."

Pleas and promises to work faithfully for the Wardens erupted from some of the prisoners, but Rowan ignored them.

"Burn the human bodies," Curtis said to the guards.

"No." Rowan shook his head. "Leave them in the street. As soon as the Echoes are moved, we raid B Block. I have someone I hope to find there." With that, he raised his pistol and began firing into the group of prisoners. They tried to scatter, but the other Wardens also opened fire and cut them down.

In less than a minute, the captives lay in growing pools of blood.

"Who are you looking for?" Curtis asked as he holstered his pistol.

"A woman." Rowan pointed at his side.

"And your head?"

"Same woman."

"Ah. A fighter, and a good one. You're the most decorated mid-level Warden in the northeast. You don't go down easily for a reason."

"First time, she ambushed me. Second time, I had her until she pulled a knife from out of nowhere."

"Impressive. Sounds like she fights like you. Echo?"

"I don't know. Need to find her first. I hope she's an Echo, so I can kill her a few times as payback."

Curtis frowned. "Rowan, you have to start thinking of the longer game. We've been in this war too long without a decisive victory. We keep chipping away at the Commonwealths on each continent, but if we're going to win anytime soon, we need to do it with combat specialists. If she is conditioned to be a Warden, she'll excel in battle. If her mind doesn't accept reconditioning, we could use her to reproduce, gain more full-blooded Echoes in our ranks."

A few of the bodies glowed blue. Rowan walked over to one; he had regenerated as a child, no more than eight years old. He shook his head. "The younger the age they return to, the easier it is to condition them, but they take days to recover post-regen."

Curtis shrugged. "They'll become part of our ranks one way or another, regardless of age."

The Warden guards moved in to drag the healing Echoes away from the human corpses.

"Hmm, only four out of that group," Rowan said. "I want more."

Within three days, Rowan helped lead the Wardens in securing the city, clearing it of any CNA presence, and capturing hundreds of Brigands who didn't flee in time. They identified a quarter of those captured as Echoes and brought them into service.

A week after the initial attack, Rowan stood with three other Wardens before his superiors to receive commendations for the successes in taking Portland. He stood before those gathered and waited while those of a higher rank babbled about the Wardens' might. Everyone present had a physical outward appearance of fortyish years or younger. The original Echoes who came to Earth had perfected the genetic mimicry of humans, including the unwanted side effect of aging. Unable to remove that portion of the genetic code, the Wardens had instituted mandatory regens to keep their troops in prime condition. The maximum physical age for a Warden was forty-five. Even the highest-ranking Wardens, the regent and vice regents included, barely had a wisp of gray hair before they regenned to a younger age—keeping their titles when they did, of course.

Rowan knew he could do more for the Wardens if he obtained a higher rank. The commendation was well and good, but it wasn't the promotion he needed. After the brief ceremony, he left the gathering. Once alone in a corridor, he removed the medal from his uniform. He passed his thumb over the decorative ribbon and the glittering medallion below it. He wanted a different kind of award.

Dani's body never turned up in the searches; somehow, she'd escaped. Rowan tossed the medal aside, promising himself he'd find her. The woman that had bested him twice in one day wouldn't beat him in the next fight.

CHAPTER

13

Dani opened her eyes when large hands pulled her from the warm blanket she had pulled over her head. When her vision cleared, she made out a strange man moving about the small, dark room. She wanted to run, but her legs didn't work, and she sank to the floor. She crawled to a corner in the room and wedged her body into it.

The man approached. "Dani, I know you're scared, but I need you to put these on." He placed a pair of boots next to her feet and pressed two pairs of socks into her hand.

She didn't know where she was or why she was tucked into a narrow room. Her body ached, and her limbs didn't want to move the way she wanted them to. The man seemed somehow familiar to her, though.

"You remembered my name last night, Dani. Do you remember me still?"

Dani didn't remember anything from yesterday, or the day before that. She frowned and tried to remember *something*. Only a vague image of written words came to her mind. *Boston. Momma, Daddy, Jason, and Brody.* "Daddy?"

He shook his head.

"Jason?"

"Yes. I'm Jason, but you call me Jace."

"Jace," Dani said, though she didn't remember who he was. She leaned forward to view his face better but recoiled with a gasp when someone pounded on the room's door.

"We're leaving *now*," a voice on the other side of the door said.

"We're coming," Jace said.

Dani clutched her socks as Jace rushed to shove things back into his bag. He threw her boots in last and slipped the bag's strap over his head. She flinched as he hurried to her with a small jacket in his hands. He fed her hand, still holding the socks, through one of the sleeves, and placed her other hand through the remaining empty sleeve. He didn't bother with the zipper before scooping her off the floor. He put one arm under her rump and held her close to his body, his wide palm against her back. With no other choice than to go with him, Dani hooked her legs around his waist and wrapped her arms around the back of his neck.

Jace carried her out of the room. Dani turned her head to see where they were going, and she bounced against his body as he trotted to catch up with two men who were already striding out of the house. One man wore a dark coat, and the other wore a lighter-colored, longer coat. Jace followed them outside, and Dani drew in a sharp breath when the cold night air met her bare feet, hands, and face.

"Please give me another minute to finish dressing her," Jace said.

The two men stopped and glared at Dani as Jace lowered her to the ground.

"This will be the only time we wait for you, old man," the man in the dark coat said.

Jace took the socks from Dani's hands and unrolled them. "We won't slow you down once I have her dressed for the cold."

His hands moved in a blur of motion, putting the socks on her feet, grabbing the boots from his bag and slipping them on her feet, lacing them up tight. Jace shoved the remaining socks over her hands as substitute gloves, then zipped up her jacket.

"Can you stand?" Jace pulled her to her feet.

Dani wobbled.

Jace caught her and picked her up again.

"We'll leave you both behind if you slow us down," the man in the light coat said.

"She has a concussion," Jace said. "She'll be fine once she's had proper rest."

Another man and woman sprinted from the house and joined them.

"We changed our minds," the newly arrived man said.

"Thought you might after the Wardens sacked B Block overnight," the dark coat said.

Dani didn't know what a "bee block" was, but she remained silent.

"The Wardens will sweep the remaining blocks by the end of today," the light coat said. "Portland's lost."

Dani's curiosity won. "What are Wardens?" she asked Jace.

"Is she serious?" the woman asked.

"She hit her head yesterday," Jace said.

Dani opted to not ask her remaining questions. She assumed if Portland was lost that they were helping find him or her again.

The man in the dark coat grunted and led the group away from the house. Jace kept up with them, Dani in his arms. He wasn't wearing a coat, and his skin glistened with sweat despite the chilly night air. Sleepiness settled over Dani as she bounced along in his arms, and she leaned her head against his shoulder. She tried to remember more about the words she'd seen in her mind earlier, but they blurred. She closed her eyes, and one arm slid from Jace's neck.

She was jarred awake by a sharp jolt. She opened her eyes. She was in the back of a truck. The vehicle's engine raced and lurched forward then back again. Dani crashed into the other people in the truck. As soon as the truck stopped shaking, she reached for the side, panicked, ready to jump out. A hand snagged the back of her jacket.

"Dani!" a man's voice said. "Dani, you're okay."

She tried to twist free of his grip, but he continued to hold her. She stopped fighting him for a moment to stare at his eyes. She'd seen him before but couldn't remember when or where. And she didn't remember getting in the truck at all. Her chest heaved with a sob as tears filled her eyes, and the man released her jacket.

"I know you're scared and are having a hard time remembering things," he said with a soft voice.

The other people crawled out the back of the truck, and the men started yelling at the driver.

Dani wiped at her tears and shivered, though she wasn't cold. She stared at the socks on her hands. The daytime temperatures had risen, and the sun peeked between thick, fluffy clouds. Her clothes and boots were too big, and she remembered a narrow room.

This man had helped dress her—last night or this morning. She wasn't sure which. "Jace."

He nodded.

"I keep forgetting things," she said.

"It'll get better. I promise."

"Are we still looking for Portland?"

Jace's brow creased, and he shook his head. "What?"

"Old man, get out," a man in a dark coat said. "We have to push the truck out of the hole our blind driver couldn't manage to avoid."

Dark Coat, Dani thought. She remembered him a little. *Not a nice man.*

Jace helped Dani from the truck bed and carried her to the side of the rural road, shot through with cracked paving and potholes from years of frost heave and lack of maintenance. He lowered her, and she found she could stand on her own. He placed his bag at her feet. "If you're warm enough, take the socks off your hands and put them on your feet so your boots will fit better," he said.

Dani nodded and pulled the socks from her hands. Jace returned to the others. They discussed the best way to dislodge the tire while she removed her boots. Two of the men argued while Jace talked with three other men and a woman.

After getting the second pair of socks on her feet, Dani pulled her boots back on. She laced them tightly, and her feet didn't slide inside them so much. She stood and inspected her jacket. She considered taking it off, but another idea struck her. She could run away. The adults were busy talking, and none of them noticed her. Jace might not be a friend. He still hadn't told her anything—not anything she could remember, anyway—about who he was or why he was with her. He'd told the others she'd hit her head.

She stuck her hands in her jacket pockets and found a watch with a yellow band and a cartoon black-and-white dog on the face. The watch still ticked, but the time could be inaccurate. She turned her body to line the hour hand up with the sun and visualized an imaginary line between the hour hand and the twelve on the face of the watch. If the time was right, she now knew which way was south.

When did I learn how to do that? I don't know where I am, so I don't know which way to go.

She knelt and dug through the man's bag. She shoved some of the food in her mouth and chewed while she pulled a canister out. After taking a gulp of water to wash her food down, she replaced the canister. There were other items in the bag beneath a rolled blanket, but she didn't paw through them. She had food and water. The road was lined with numerous trees, she could disappear into them in an instant—but she didn't.

The truck lunged forward out of the hole after much grunting and swearing from those working to push it free. Jace was out of breath when he returned to her. "You okay?" he asked.

Dani nodded. "I had some of the food and water in here." She handed him his bag.

"That's fine."

"Where are we and where are we going?"

"We're in Maine, north of Portland. We're riding to Waterville using back roads, so it's taking us a long time to get there. After the ride, we'll rest and hike north to Bangor. Life should be easier there. Plenty of lumber, and I'm told we could even build our own little house."

"Why are we going there?"

"I'll explain everything once we start the hike. It'll be easier for us to talk then."

"Old man, let's go!" Dark Coat said.

Jace sighed and ushered Dani back to the truck. She grasped the top of the tailgate and stepped on the rear bumper to climb in. Jace followed and sat next to her. His gray hair and wrinkles made him look old and tired. He also looked sad. Each time she caught him staring at her, his eyes got shiny, like he might cry, despite the smiles he kept giving her. She didn't like him being sad; she decided to stay with him for the trip.

CHAPTER

14

Jace slowed his pace, and Dani did the same to remain next to him.

"Are you tired?" she asked.

"No, just letting us have a little more space between us and them so we can talk," Jace said.

Dark Coat, Light Coat, and the others hiked ahead of them. Dani didn't mind walking at the rear. Dark Coat was an annoying man that often barked orders at Jace and called him an old man. Last night she'd tried to put a spider in his blanket while he slept, but Jace had made her stop.

This morning was more of the same, but Jace never got angry at Dark Coat. Dani didn't understand why he didn't just punch him in the mouth to shut him up.

"Dani, do you know what year it is?"

"2068."

"No, it's not," Jace said before explaining the history of Echoes arriving on Earth and how they could heal their bodies after death to live as immortals, provided they weren't killed during their recovery period or separated from their heads. "They've been here since the 1700s, but the humans didn't know that for a long time."

"Weird. Why did they come to Earth?"

"An old war tore their home planet, Ekkoh, apart. That's 'Ekkoh' spelled e-k-k-o-h. The Ekkohrians lived on Earth, hidden and reclusive, for centuries. As their numbers grew, though, they dispersed and began living as humans—which created problems with concealing the fact that non-humans were on the planet. Rumors sprang up everywhere that aliens were on Earth. Still, they somehow remained mostly hidden until the war began. As soon as the attacks started in 2069, with technology the humans had never seen before, the militant factions revealed themselves as an alien race from Ekkoh. The humans called them Echoes, and the new name stuck."

Dani remained silent, absorbing this information that was new and yet felt somehow familiar to her.

"These factions wanted to take Earth from the humans, turn it into another Ekkoh," Jace continued. "They call themselves the Wardens of the planet. Most of the Echoes not involved in the attack joined forces with local governments to help them against the Wardens when the war began. The Wardens killed billions of people, humans and Echoes, bombing countless cities across the globe. The humans couldn't compete with the advanced alien tech, and they were forced to abandon the larger cities like Boston, where we used to live. We fled Portland last night because the Wardens moved north to take the city from the CNA."

"CNA?"

"Commonwealth of North America. After the war started, every nation was impacted by the attacks. Most of the leaders of the nations were killed or imprisoned. The United Nations reorganized. Each continent set up their own Commonwealth as an interim government. The temporary solution became more long term as the war continued. The Commonwealths still communicate with each other, but mostly everyone looks out for themselves."

Dani frowned. To her, this seemed like a bad way to run a government, but she didn't understand why she felt that way. Again, she got the sense that she knew all this somehow.

Jace continued. "You and I are Brigands. We're part of a mixed group of humans and Echoes, the civilians—or refugees, however you want to look at it. We're poor, and we scavenge for food and supplies. Successful Brigands are the ones that survive. Dani, the year is 2113."

"I hit my head *so* hard that I don't know what year it is or any of that history?"

Jace chuckled; it was the first time Dani had heard that sound from him.

"You don't have a concussion. I have always waited until you were older to tell you that you're an Echo, but since that has never worked out well, I figure it won't hurt to tell you now. It's safer to live as a human since so many humans hate, or at least distrust, Echoes. Even though you and I didn't start the war, some will still hate us."

Dani's feet stopped moving.

Jace turned to face her and knelt. "This is a lot of information to throw at you at once. Take some time to adjust to it."

"Who are you?"

"Your half-brother. We have, had, the same father."

"My parents are dead?"

"Yeah," Jace said.

"You're my brother?"

Jace nodded.

"You're ancient, and I'm a kid. Did I die?"

"Yes. Loosely translated, *Ekkoh* means *remember*. Each life you live is called an *Echo*. Most Echoes remember their past lives when they heal and come back. You don't. I think you displace your memories, stick them somewhere in your subconscious."

"I don't understand."

"Dani, you forget everything about your past each time you die—you lose everything except your survival skills."

She pulled the watch from her pocket. "That's why I knew how to find which way was south using this."

"When did you discover that?"

"While the truck was stuck. I used the watch and the sun to figure out the direction for south. I thought about running away."

Jace smiled. "I'm glad you stayed. You also return to a much younger age than most Echoes, so it takes you longer to recover physically."

"That's why I couldn't walk at first?"

Jace nodded.

"How did I die?"

He sighed and stood. "Let's talk while we walk so the others don't leave us."

She slipped her hand inside his—something that seemed to surprise him, judging by how his eyebrows disappeared into his hair.

After a moment of walking in silence, he told her about the day she died—how he'd followed her, but she was always too far away for him to help. "You went after a Warden sniper alone. He had you beat. You managed to kill him, but you couldn't finish him. You've never been a killer, Dani, and that's a good thing."

"You said I died. He didn't kill me?"

"When you stood to leave, one of the MPs you saved mistook you for the sniper, and he shot you. I finally reached you and took you away before the MPs or Wardens found us. I got us to that safe house for the night, and then I needed to get you out of Portland—and that's how we ended up with this crew." He waved his hand toward the small group hiking seventy-five yards in front of them.

She glanced up at him. "What's in Bangor?"

"More Brigands, fewer MPs, and no Wardens, so I'm told. Normally you and I avoid others. I train you on being a scavenger, how to survive, and how to hide in the shadows. You learn fast and are great at what you do, but—"

"But what?"

"You still die when you are in your mid-twenties, every time."

"That's a long way off."

A shadow crossed Jace's face. "Not as far as you think."

"Have you died before?"

"No. I'm half Echo, so I'm not sure what will happen to me if I die; I may not come back."

"Oh." Dani frowned.

They walked in silence for several minutes before she spoke again.

"Jace, do you teach me how to fight too?"

"I teach you some basics, but that's all. I don't want you getting dragged into this war."

"But we're already in it."

"Brigands are neutral. We don't fight for the Commonwealth *or* for Wardens, Dani."

"Maybe we shouldn't stay neutral. I helped the MPs before, right?"

Jace stopped and turned to face her. "Yes, and you died for it too."

"That was an accident. You said the Warden had me beat. Why was he going to win?"

"He was a better fighter than you."

"Since teaching me how to sneak around and scavenge hasn't kept me from dying, what if you teach me to fight too?" Dani asked.

He stared at her without answering.

"Jace?"

"Uh, yeah, I mean. . . ." He knelt again and took her hand. "I'm sorry. This part is new to me. This is different. You've never asked me to teach you to do anything other than scavenge before. Learning to fight will be new for you, since you haven't done it before. It'll be hard and won't come to you as easily as scavenging. Are you sure you want this?"

Dani nodded.

"Okay. I'll teach you the basics; you will likely remember most of it once we start. But we'll need to find someone to teach you the more advanced stuff."

Dani grinned. "When do we start?"

"I'll show you a few things tonight when we stop to camp. Now, we need to catch up to the others before we lose them."

She nodded and continued to smile. She took his hand again when they resumed walking, and Jace didn't appear so surprised this time.

When they stopped for the night, after they started a fire and ate, Dani sat in front of her brother. He showed her how to apply joint locks to wrists and elbows.

"Why are you bothering to teach a child that stuff?" Dark Coat said. "She's no match for a Warden and you know it, old man."

Jace ignored the question, but Dani hopped up and approached him.

"His name is Jace, not old man," she said. "You *will* address him by his name."

The man laughed. "Or what?"

"You flinch when you see a spider," Dani said. "I'll put one in your blanket tonight while you're sleeping. Eight hairy legs crawling on your neck. I tried to do it last night, but Jace wouldn't let me. You should thank him. He's nicer than me."

The man chuckled nervously as his eyes flicked to Jace.

"She's telling the truth," Jace said. "I may not wake up in time to stop her tonight."

The man's face hardened, and he pointed his finger at Dani. "No spiders!"

"Stop calling him an old man," Dani said.

"Fine," he said to her before addressing Jace. "This one's trouble."

"You have no idea," Jace said.

Dani returned to her brother to resume her lessons. Dark Coat was politer to Jace and avoided Dani the rest of the trip; she was fine with that arrangement.

CHAPTER
15

Jace kept his promise to teach Dani how to fight. For the next fifteen years, twice a day, she trained with those he hired to teach her. She only used her skills in real life a few times; twice to break up scuffles among Brigands, and once to end an attack from a Brigand who decided to try to take her pack. She broke his wrist, and he changed his mind.

As Dani grew up in their new location, Jace often told Dani how much easier their lives were in Bangor than they had been in Portland. Since Dani couldn't remember anything about Portland, or her prior lives, she had to accept his words as truth. He also always grinned when he said, "Other than you stealing every other day from the MPs, this is different!" She didn't understand that statement either, except for the stealing part. She was guilty as charged on theft.

Her brother's happy demeanor took an abrupt turn into anger when she returned from scavenging one day with a dog in tow. She arrived at their small, two-room house—constructed by Jace out of rough-cut lumber—and placed her pack on the floor. "Jace! I made a great find in Orono today."

Jace remained seated at the table, his back to her, cleaning his weapons. He didn't bother turning around when he spoke.

"What the hell were you doing there? Swiping books from the ghost town university instead of robbing the MPs blind of anything they don't nail down?"

"Well, yeah, I did take *one* book I found. Look," she said.

He turned his attention from cleaning his weapons to her. "Goddammit. No, no, no, *no*! Dani, no dog!"

Despite the yelling, the dog remained seated by Dani's foot, tail swishing back and forth on the floor. His tongue lolled from his mouth as he looked up at her and back to Jace. Dani couldn't help but smile at the dog. He was a bit thin from scavenging on his own, but at full weight, she guessed he would be around ninety pounds. He had a muscular build and was a mix of dark brown and black striping with a broad splash of white on his chest. She knelt and rubbed the top of his wide head, and he wiggled in response.

"Are you listening to me?"

She chuckled. "Not really. I'm keeping him."

"No!"

"Jace, relax. It's just a dog."

"God, Dani, no. It's not just a dog. This time was supposed to be different!"

Her temper flared, and she stood. "What the hell does that even mean?"

"Remember the part where you keep dying in your mid-twenties? The other part of that is you get a dog, the dog dies, and a few weeks later, you die too. Up until now you haven't repeated anything from that old cycle. No dog!"

Dani rolled her eyes. "You're overreacting."

"I'm the one that takes care of your ass every time you die. I'm an old man now. I can't do this again. It's a miracle I'm still alive. The human, even half-human, life expectancy has plummeted since the war began."

"And I'm grateful you've been there to care for me after

< 87 >

each regen, but I'm keeping the dog. I've already named him." Dani smiled.

Jace groaned and reached for his messenger bag. "Another Brody."

Dani's smile faded.

"Am I right?" Jace asked with a glance over his shoulder at her as he opened his bag. "Yeah, I'm right. Fucking dog. Here," he said and turned.

She took the photos from his hand, one of a family and a dark-colored dog with a white chest and the other of a young woman with a dog next to her. The dog was dark with white on its chest, and the young woman was her. Dani tried to swallow the sudden lump in her throat, but her mouth was dry.

"Turn the family picture over. Read the writing on the back of it," Jace said. He folded his arms across his chest and waited.

She did as instructed and after a moment, she found her voice. "I don't understand."

Jace took the photos back and tucked them inside his notebook before stuffing the book into his bag. "The family photo is pre-war. Our father, your mother, you, me, and a damn dog named Brody. That was before you died the first time. Second picture—clearly you recognize yourself in that one, right?— that's you and another mutt named Brody, about a month before he died and two months before you died, the second time. I never got a picture of you with the third Brody, and I sure as hell won't get one of you with the fourth. No dog, Dani."

"Why have I never seen those photos before? Why now?" Dani asked.

"Because *this* time things have been different. Well, up until now," he said with a wave of his hand toward the dog.

"You told me I die from friendly fire. How did the other dogs die?"

Jace tightened his jaw.

"Answer me!"

"They died protecting you."

"That's just fucking great, Jace. Your arthritis is killing you, and you can't scavenge like before. I need a new partner when I am out. I'm keeping him."

Jace snarled at the animal still sitting next to Dani, and Brody wagged his tail.

"So you just whip out these photos now, when it suits your argument? You've had them all along? What else haven't you told me, dearest *brother?*"

He returned her glare but didn't speak.

Dani stomped back out of the house with Brody. She completed her evening training and stayed the night with a few Brigand friends near the old library in Bangor. Brody remained with her through it all.

She woke the next day and set off for her morning training, Brody walking next to her.

She walked along the Kenduskeag Stream for three-quarters of a mile, crossed the bridge over the stream, and took a left to cut across the steeper hills to reach the old water tower another four hundred yards away. She took a drink of water before dropping her pack on the ground. She knelt and gave Brody some of the water, too, and most of her food, though she knew she'd be starving by midday.

She'd always liked the hill near the Standpipe, a water tower that had been converted into an architectural piece of artwork instead of a standard, round reservoir mounted on metal posts. It was surrounded by bricks that made it look more like a giant turret that belonged on a castle. It had been equipped with spiral stairs with windows leading to the top to a 360-degree viewing platform. The roof had long ago collapsed, and most of the windows were broken. The interior of the Standpipe was a hazard after years of neglect and abuse following the start of the war.

Gavin emerged from the tree line twenty-five yards away, and Brody barked, but with a wagging tail. Dani stood and smiled as Gavin approached.

"Still smiling to see me even though I kick your ass twice a day," Gavin said with a grin.

"Smiling for now. Though I will probably hate you like I always do in a couple of hours."

"I see you brought your vicious Brody back." Gavin patted the dog's shoulder. Brody's tail somehow managed to wag faster.

"Yeah." Dani wondered if she should change his name.

"How's Jace?"

Dani shrugged. "I didn't go home last night."

"Doesn't sound good."

"He's pissed about the dog. No point going home to have a fight."

Gavin laughed and gave Brody another pat. "Let's get started."

Two hours later, Dani lay in the grass on her back with a horrible throb in her right thigh, left ribs, and left flank. Her shirt was soaked with sweat, and she was out of water.

"I hate you," she said, marveling at how a man almost twice her age could still have so much stamina.

"Right. See you this evening." He wiped sweat from his face with one hand and headed for the forest. "The good news is you're actually getting better, Dani."

"I still hate you."

Gavin's laughter carried him into the trees, and he disappeared.

Dani managed to roll to her side and then to her rump on

her second attempt. She rubbed her sore ribs and lower back. Gavin had a nasty right hand that showed little mercy when she left her side unprotected.

When she was younger, Dani had progressed quickly with her combat trainers, always moving beyond what they could teach her—and then Jace found Gavin. He was a marine veteran, and other than that, Dani knew little else but his political opinions. Gavin had never agreed with CNA policies and their Military Police tactics, so he lived among the Brigands. She always wanted to follow him to see where he lived, but after their sessions, she was too tired and battered to bother. He'd been her instructor for the last seven years, and she doubted she would ever progress beyond his training. He was the toughest man she'd ever seen, with Jace in a close second place.

A rank odor reached her nose, and Dani picked at her shirt and sniffed. She winced at the smell and forced herself to her feet. "Can't meet Xan smelling like this."

Brody stared at her pack.

"The food in there is mine. Okay? Hope you like mushrooms or know how to catch your own fish."

She lifted her pack from the ground and shuffled back down the hill toward the stream with Brody at her side. She needed water and a quick bath. Her shirt should have enough time to dry during the walk back up the hill to the overgrown baseball field. Once she crossed Union Street to the west, the line almost splitting Bangor in half, she would be in MP territory. If caught she'd be forced into CNA ranks, but she didn't mind taking the risk to see Xan.

CHAPTER

16

Dani stripped for a quick swim and washed her shirt in the stream. Brody splashed through the water and leapt into the deeper pool to join her. She wanted to swim longer, but she was hungry and thirsty. She left the stream still tired but less sore from Gavin's punishment-disguised-as-training. Tonight's session was ground fighting, and tomorrow was to be a mix of aerobic and anaerobic conditioning. He only gave her a day off when he decided she'd earned it. She was ready for a break, though if what Jace said was true about her dying not long after getting a dog, she didn't want any time off—she wanted to be as prepared as possible for whatever was coming.

She dressed while Brody rolled his wet body in the grass, his tongue hanging out like he was smiling. She was already attached to the dog; she didn't want him to get hurt for her sake.

She rummaged through her pack, which gained Brody's attention, and he was back on his feet and beside her in an instant. She chuckled as she pushed his snout out of her bag.

She started a small fire and used her dented metal cup to start boiling water to refill her canteen. She foraged in the trees along the stream, picking a few plants to eat as she went along and collected mushrooms. She spotted a decent-sized fish, around ten inches long, in a shallow pool.

"Sit," she said to Brody, and he complied. Dani hadn't expected him to actually know what the word meant. "Wow. The person that had you before must be missing you, if they're still alive."

She snapped a thin limb from a tree and picked the twigs and leaves from it. She sharpened one end with her knife and moved along the rocks to the pool. The fish was still there. She waited, poised with her new weapon. With a quick thrust, she pierced the fish with the spear. She plunged her other hand into the water to grab the writhing creature. She looked over her shoulder at Brody. "Hope you like fish."

She returned to the fire, poured the boiling water into her canteen, and put another cup of water on to boil. She cleaned the fish and cut fillets. After threading the slices of meat over thinner strips of wood she made from the spear, she cooked them over the fire. By the time she put the fire out, she had a full canteen again, and she and Brody had eaten.

Her shirt was almost dry as she headed back up the hill. On the trail through the trees, she noticed three Brigand men sitting together. They spotted her and Brody, and she altered her course to move off the trail to go around them. One of the men shifted his seat to watch her pass, and Brody growled in response. The men didn't stand, and Dani glanced back a few times to make sure they weren't trying to follow her.

She patted Brody. Again, he'd surprised her. She had feared his friendly nature might make him want to greet strangers, as he'd done with Jace, Gavin, and her friends yesterday, but he understood the difference between friends and strange Brigand men. Good. A starving Brigand wouldn't hesitate to put a dog on the menu, and Brody was big enough that he could feed a few people.

Dani finished her hike back toward the water tower. She heard the voices before she saw the people, and she slipped through the trees to move closer to the field. Two women and four children walked in an open area. Three of the children were younger, around five or six years old. The fourth appeared older given his height. Their non-tattered clothing and groomed appearance concerned Dani the most. The women and children were Commonwealth families, and they were in Brigand territory.

Bangor's MPs and Brigands didn't tend to bother each other, except for Dani's routine theft of their food rations. The CNA had little interest in Bangor, so their troop numbers continued to dwindle while the MPs remained at the base. She guessed the women and children were likely MP families instead of CNA ground troop families. It didn't matter either way, but Dani found their presence unsettling. They were on the wrong side of the CNA–Brigand border. According to Jace, the Portland MPs often raided Brigand camps to capture CNA recruits, and Brigands returned the favor by stealing anything and everything they could from the MPs. Dani glanced down at Brody. He, too, watched the family, and his tail wagged as he did.

Dani made a hissing noise to get his attention. When he looked up, she shook her head and mouthed "No." Brody stayed with her. The families were alone in the field and seemed to be enjoying themselves—except for the older boy. He appeared disinterested in the others, and stayed a few paces away from them.

No one emerged from the trees to bother the women and children, so Dani moved on, hoping they wouldn't stay much longer.

When she and Brody arrived at Union Street, Dani paused. She crouched behind a tree and patted the ground with her palm. Brody lay next to her feet, and she put her hand on his side. An armored MP vehicle rumbled by without stopping. She waited until the sound of the vehicle's engine disappeared before moving again. She crept forward toward the street and watched for any movement. No MPs patrolled the area—thankfully, since Brody's bark rang out, startling Dani. She'd left him at the tree. He wagged his tail despite her glare at him.

"C'mon," she hissed, and the dog bounded from the trees to join her. "We have to work on your stealth," she said with a whisper.

The pair continued to the former baseball field, and Dani remained in the trees as she rounded the outfield.

She spotted Xan waiting near the half-collapsed dugout long before he saw her. "Hey," she said, and he turned. Brody growled, and she shushed him.

Xan smiled, but his eyes were on the dog. "Hey. Who's this?"

"A stray I found yesterday. How are you?" Dani asked before kissing him.

"Much better now." He kept his arms around her waist. He leaned in to kiss her again, but Brody pushed his body between them. "What the hell?"

Dani tried to push Brody aside with one hand. He didn't budge. "Move."

Xan scowled, released Dani, and took a step back. He shifted his posture as if preparing to kick Brody.

"Kick him and I'll break your leg," Dani said.

Xan froze and stared at her. "He's in the way."

"So?"

"I'll make him move if you won't."

Dani tightened her jaw, and Xan backed off. He stood balanced, no longer poised to deliver a kick. Instead, he folded his arms across his chest with a frown.

She snorted a laugh. "You're pouting now? I had no idea you could be so petulant."

"Petulant? Big word for a Brigand."

"Fuck you." She turned to leave.

"Dani, wait," Xan said, and she stopped. He tried to approach her again, and Brody growled. "Damn dog."

She couldn't conceal her grin. Brody might be a bit bony, but his size still intimidated Xan. Plus, Brody didn't care for Xan's company. Dani went through the list of people Brody liked and didn't like. Three skulking Brigands in the forest and Xan were on the shit list.

What kind of person wants to kick a dog? "Huh," she said, looking at Brody.

"What?" Xan asked.

Dani turned her attention to Xan. "Oh, just realizing how smart he is."

"You need to get rid of him. He's a bag of bones, anyway. You need to find your own food, you don't need to be bothering trying to feed him too."

"Don't worry about what I have for responsibilities. Is that also a big word for a Brigand?"

"I didn't mean—"

"Yeah, you did."

"The dog needs to go. He won't let me near you," Xan said with a wave of his hand at the animal.

Brody remained between Dani and Xan, and she appreciated the dog's presence. She liked Xan, but there was something about the man that Brody disliked in the same way he'd disliked the Brigand men earlier. Xan was attractive and smart, but she had just witnessed a jerk side of him she hadn't seen before. *Noted.*

"Me or the dog, Dani."

"Really?" Dani laughed. "You're such an ass."

"We've been seeing each other every couple of days for a few weeks. You've had the dog for one day!"

"I'm keeping him."

"Is she at least fucking you?" Xan sneered at the dog. "Because I'm not getting any."

Dani drove her fist into Xan's mouth. His head snapped back with the blow, and he covered his mouth with one hand after regaining his balance. Blood flowed from his lip, and he examined the blood on his fingers for a moment before glaring at her. "Bitch."

Brody's growl turned in to a snarl as he stalked toward the man.

Xan backed up a few steps, and Dani turned to leave.

"C'mon, B," she said. She smiled; she liked the sound of her dog's new nickname.

Brody joined her, and they headed back for the tree line, leaving Xan alone with his bloody lip.

CHAPTER 17

Once deep in the trees and back in Brigand territory, Dani stopped and rubbed her face with her hands. She took a deep breath and allowed the remainder of her anger at Xan to pass. She grinned. Punching him for his insult had felt great. She knelt and scratched Brody's ears and neck. He twitched his skin and used his rear leg to scratch harder at a place on his neck.

"Flea check and more food for you tonight, big guy." She kissed the top of his head. "If you can intimidate people with your ribs sticking out, you'll be a brute with more weight, right?"

His tail disturbed the leaves near his rump as it wagged.

A high-pitched scream brought Dani to her feet. She wasn't far from the old Standpipe and park. If the MP families hadn't left yet, she wasn't far from them either. Careful to remain quiet, she jogged toward the noise. Another scream made her feet move faster, with less regard for stealth. Dani reached the tree line and swore. The three Brigands she'd passed on the trail were attacking the women and children.

One woman was on the ground and not moving. One of the Brigand men was pinning the other woman to the ground, while the other two men were tying up three of the children.

Brody growled.

"Quiet," Dani hissed at him. She scanned the area for the fourth, the oldest, child but didn't see him. With the men occupied, she slipped around the park, moving closer to the woman on the ground. Still unnoticed, Dani shrugged out of her pack, left the trees, and knelt by the woman. She had a lump on her forehead. Dani shook her shoulder.

The woman's eyes fluttered open, and she gasped, recoiling from Dani's touch.

"I won't hurt you," Dani said softly. "Get in those trees"— she gestured behind her—"and circle that way. When you reach the road, go across it and stay in that direction until you reach the barracks."

"My son."

"I'll find him and send him to the trees to meet you. Okay?" The woman nodded.

"Hey!" one of the men shouted.

"Shit. Go, lady." Dani dragged the woman to her feet and shoved her in the direction of the forest. Dani approached the men with her hands up. The three younger children shrieked and cried, and Dani still didn't see the taller boy. The man— who, Dani now saw, had been preparing to rape the other woman—ended his efforts as Dani approached. He re-zipped his trousers, pulled the woman up by her hair, and kept her on her knees while he stood. The woman wept, but Dani kept her eyes on the men. Brody growled as he walked beside her.

"Gentlemen, not a good day to start a war with the MPs." Dani's eyes scanned the area, weighing options, looking for things she could use if the men decided to fight instead of leave the remaining woman and children alone. She proceeded through a mental list of options like Gavin had taught her.

"They're in our territory," the man holding the woman said. The children screamed, and the noise almost pulled Dani's attention from the men. Almost. "Yeah," she said, eyes on her opponents, "but you're fucking with MP families. There will be hell to pay for this, and I don't want to welcome an MP raiding party because of you three pricks."

"Shut up!" the man screamed at the two wailing girls he held, which only caused more crying.

"Why do you need the kids, anyway?" Dani asked.

"These three will trade for a lot of food and weapons to the right person," the third man said. "The reasons for their interest are their business." He yanked the young boy closer to him by the back of his shirt and grinned.

Sex slaves. Dani's stomach turned at the man's sneer. Movement behind him caught her attention, and she saw a young face peering down at her from a broken window embedded in the brickwork around the water tower. *You picked a terrible place to hide, kid.*

"Since you let the other woman escape, we'll take you instead," the man keeping the woman on her knees said. He struck her and she fell, unconscious.

Brody leapt forward with a vicious snarl and sank his teeth into the man's arm. His actions altered Dani's attack plan; she charged the man holding the two girls instead. She slammed her boot into his groin, and he released the children to hold his crotch as he crumpled.

Brody was keeping his Brigand busy, so Dani only needed to deal with the final man holding the young boy. He released the boy, and to her surprise, the child ran to her and clung to her leg. She struggled to dislodge him from her leg, and the man grinned. She didn't know someone so little could be so strong, and she didn't want to hurt him.

"Freakin' leech." Dani pried one of his arms free. When she looked up to locate the man, he'd closed the distance between them and was bringing his fist down toward her head. She twisted and almost avoided the blow, but his fist clipped her cheek. The boy wailed and remained attached to her leg. With her balance skewed and her ability to move freely compromised, Dani fell. She scrambled away from the approaching man and finally managed to peel the child off her body. She turned him toward the trees and was relieved to see his mother crossing the field to come back.

"There's your mom. Go." Dani gave the boy a shove. He recognized his mother and started running toward her.

The man's shoulder caught Dani in the side as she stood. They crashed to the ground in a tangle. She rolled and slammed her right fist into his unprotected left side, the same way Gavin had done to her so many times before. He grunted with the impact and swung for her head. She turned her body so the blow hit the back of her shoulder, then struck the same spot on his ribs several times before rolling back to her feet.

He cursed as he stood and held one hand against his aching side. "I'll kill you for that."

Brody's teeth found the back of the man's thigh, and he howled with pain. He spun to dislodge the dog, and Dani leapt onto his back. She wrapped her arms around his neck, hanging on as he whirled in a circle. She tightened her grip, and his steps faltered. Once he was on the ground and not moving, she unwound her arms.

Brody's first victim had fled, the man Dani had kicked remained whimpering on the ground, and the third man was now unconscious from her choking him. Dani wanted to take a moment to rest, but she instead went to the woman still on the ground. The two girls clung to their mother and flinched when Dani approached, though their fear lessened when Brody began licking their faces.

The woman stirred and sat up.

"Your friend is waiting for you," Dani said. "Go back to the barracks."

The woman nodded and winced at the movement.

"Yeah, bitch of headache, I know, but you have to leave. Wait just inside the trees, and I'll send the last kid. Okay?"

The woman nodded again, and Dani helped her stand. She watched them move across the field toward the trees for a moment, then headed for the Standpipe.

She stepped through the doorway that was missing a door and looked up the long, winding row of broken steps.

"Hey, kid. This place is a death trap."

A board creaked from somewhere on the stairs that Dani couldn't see. She poked her head outside. The two men still lay on the ground, though the one that had taken her kick to the crotch was moving more now. Dani checked the nearby forest. The two women and three children were leaving.

"Wait! Ugh. The idiots forgot the last kid," Dani said with a grumble. She returned her attention to the interior of the Standpipe. "Kid, c'mon. Your mother is leaving your ass."

"Neither of them is my mother," a voice said from above.

"I don't care. They're leaving without you. C'mon down."

"I can't."

"Look, I know you're scared—"

"I'm stuck."

Fuck! Dani closed her eyes and passed her hand through her hair. If she was going to get the kid back home with the two MP families, she needed to hurry. A missing MP child following a Brigand attack would create a shit storm she didn't want to be anywhere near. "Uh, okay. I'll come to you."

She stepped around the leaves and other debris that had blown into the entryway after years without a door. Garbage left by Brigands who had slept in the Standpipe crumpled beneath her boots as she moved along the inside portion of the brick wall. The first few steps of the spiral stairs leading around the tower to the uppermost level were gone. Brody leapt past the gap and started up the stairs before she could stop him.

"Brody!"

He continued his climb.

"Ugh! Hey, kid, my dog is coming up first, but he's harmless."

"My name is Oliver Jackman. My dad is an MP."

"Wonderful. Dad's an MP," Dani said, unable to keep the sarcasm out of her voice. "I'm Dani. The hound is Brody. I'm coming up."

CHAPTER
18

Most of the lower boards were gone—likely used for fires during the winter—so Dani had to climb along the rusted metal framing to reach the first real step. Brody's leap impressed her more following the difficulty she had getting her body off the ground. Without having seen Oliver close up yet, she assumed he was an agile little thing to have gotten up the stairs too.

The steps groaned beneath her weight, some buckling inward or sagging when she placed her boot on a damaged board. She was reduced to crawling on her hands and feet to try to distribute her weight better. Her body lurched forward when one hand fell through a rotted step, but she regained her balance.

"I like your dog," Oliver said.

Dani was too focused on not falling to her death to respond. She wound her way around the inside of the Standpipe and finally spotted the boy. Brody wagged his tail at her arrival and whimpered. Oliver sat on a step near the top of the structure; there was an almost five-foot gap between the last step on Dani's segment of the stairs and Oliver's rump.

"Once I got up this far, the steps broke apart behind me," Oliver said.

Dani peered down through the hole. A fall from her current height would cause severe injuries, if not kill her. If she died, she'd come back as an incapacitated ten-year-old girl with wannabe child sex slave traders in the field right outside. Retrieving this boy wasn't going to be a quick rescue. She needed rope, lots of rope, and at least one extra pair of hands. What she had was no rope and a dog that was entirely too happy with their predicament.

"Okay. B, I need you to move," Dani said.

Brody licked her cheek.

She grabbed a handful of fur at his neck to guide him down the first few steps. "Go."

The dog's tail lowered, and he started down the stairs. He paused to look back, and Dani pointed for him to continue his descent.

"Oliver, you have to jump."

The boy's eyes widened.

"I'm not kidding. You need to jump, and do it now. I'll catch you."

"The boards are rotten."

"You should have considered that before you climbed up here and got yourself stuck."

"Find my dad. Captain Miles Jackman. He'll come with other MPs to get me. Just tell Dad you're not with those men."

"You really think they're going to believe a Brigand after what just happened to those women and kids?"

"I'll tell Dad how you helped. I watched you through the window."

"Yeah, give Captain Dad my best when you see him. I'll stay away from the MPs all the same. Stop stalling, Oliver."

Oliver frowned, but he inched his rump closer to the last stair before the gap.

Dani looked out the broken window closest to her. The man

she'd kicked remained on his knees, hunched over. The man she'd choked into unconsciousness was stirring.

"Jump now, kid." She scooted as close as she dared to the edge of the gap and extended her arms. "Those men are getting up. We need to be out of here before they recover. We're both dead if they find us. Understand?"

Oliver nodded and took a deep breath. He shifted his feet a few times. Dani sighed audibly at the continued delay, and the boy's eyes met hers.

"I'm scared," he said.

"Jump anyway."

Tears formed in his eyes, and a deep frown crossed his face. He pinched his eyes closed and leapt. His jump was a little short. Dani lunged for him and caught him as he fell, but his weight pulled her more off balance. The uppermost step broke beneath her stomach, and her knee punched a hole through another board. The hole, though painfully pinching her knee, kept her from being dragged off the stairs. She wrestled with Oliver, who was struggling in terror at almost having fallen, and finally managed to pull him up and move them both away from the edge.

Breathing heavily, Dani leaned her back against the brick wall to rest. Oliver slid closer to her, trembling.

"You're fine," Dani said.

He nodded and continued to tremble.

The wood groaned beneath their combined weight. Dani ended her moment of rest and herded the boy down the stairs.

Brody's growl echoed up through the interior of the tower.

Dani groaned. "That can't be good."

Oliver turned to head back up the stairs, and Dani caught the back of his shirt.

"Don't panic. Stay behind me, but don't try to go back up the steps. They're falling apart, and we're still too high to survive a fall."

Oliver nodded, and he shifted to stand behind her. Dani picked her way down the stairs, the boy following her a few steps behind. Brody's loud snarl was matched by a man's shout as the two attacked each other. A sharp yelp followed, and Dani no longer heard Brody. She quickened her pace down the stairs, but her balance was shaken as the stairs shuddered beneath her feet. She clung to a piece of the rail and lowered her rump to the steps.

The stairs rocked when one of the men climbed on to the fragile staircase. He rounded the turn, ignoring any boards he broke in the process, and charged at Dani. It was the man she'd choked. He cursed and called her every foul name imaginable as he approached. Oliver cried out with fear, but Dani couldn't worry about the boy now.

She decided against waiting for the man's arrival and sprang toward him. The action startled the man, but he recovered quickly. They crashed into the brick wall and bounced down a few steps, breaking some on the way. He grabbed her by the shoulders and forced her away from the wall, pinning her against the stairs and pushing her upper body downward. The steps beneath her broke and the man shoved her more, bending her so her head was pointed at the ground. Pain gripped her back at the awkward forced position.

She drove her knee into the man's groin and he released her. She rolled to her side, her hip on a half a step, and used one of the handrail supports to pull herself up to a safer spot on the rickety stairs. The man growled at her as he straightened his body. He was standing right in front of a broken window now. Ignoring the pain in her back, Dani rushed him and pushed his upper body through the window. While he was off balance, she crouched, grabbed his legs, lifted up, and flipped him out the window. His body struck the ground with a *thump*.

She sagged to her knees and leaned her head against the bricks. Her ragged breaths and the thunderous heartbeat pounding inside her head deafened her to everything else. She jumped when something touched her arm.

Oliver knelt next to her. "Are you okay?"

"Look out the window to see where he went." Dani took the time to slow her breathing while Oliver stood on his toes. He hooked his fingers over the frame and looked down.

"He's on the ground, not moving. The other one is running off. I don't see Brody," Oliver said.

"Okay. Go to the bottom of the stairs. Brody may be there."

"What about you?"

"I'm coming."

Oliver nodded and picked his way down the steps, pausing when they shook or groaned too much for his comfort. Dani's back ached. She rubbed her side and winced when a muscle spasm tore through her back. She grunted at the pain but forced her feet to move as she half-crawled down the stairs.

"Brody's here," Oliver said from somewhere below. "He's limping, but he looks okay."

Dani couldn't see the boy or the dog yet, but the news made her feel better. She liked that dog. She reached the final bend in the stairs and spotted Oliver kneeling next to Brody. At the same time, the step beneath her boot snapped, and the board she grabbed to stop her fall crumbled in her hands. She crashed through the stairs and fell eight feet to the concrete below.

Her leg absorbed the initial impact, and she cried out as pain rocketed up from her foot to her thigh. She landed hard on her side and had just enough time to put her arms over her head before the lower part of the stairs that had followed her down crashed on top of her.

When she came to, Oliver was shaking her shoulder. Her entire body hurt, and she appreciated the boy's efforts in helping her sit up.

"I thought you were dead," he said.

Dani moaned, wondering if being dead hurt less. She wiped at something dripping from her cheek, and her fingers turned red.

"You're bleeding a lot," Oliver said.

"It usually looks worse than it is. Help me stand."

On the third try and relying on Oliver for support, Dani made it to her feet. Her ankle sent pulses of pain up her leg with each heartbeat. She didn't bother assessing the volume of new cuts and bruises.

"I can tell you how to get back to the barracks," Dani said.

"I'm not going without you."

"How old are you?"

"Twelve."

"You're old enough to make it back by yourself."

Oliver's eyes widened with fear.

She sighed. "I can't go with you, Oliver. I steal from the MPs. A lot. They'll add me to their ranks if they catch me. Odds are there will be a shitload of MPs coming here soon anyway. You can stay and wait for them."

"What if those men come back?"

Dani groaned and shifted more weight off her injured ankle and onto Oliver's shoulder. "Fine. You staying here is a bad idea."

"What if they come back for *you*? Can we hide at your house?"

Dani laughed at the absurdity of the idea, and a spasm in her back turned her laughter to a grunt.

She didn't have many choices. She couldn't fight off the men again, even if the one she threw out the window was dead. The other two could come back, possibly with more friends.

The MPs would come for the kid, and she'd be captured. She thought of places where she and Oliver could go to at least be safe, wait out the night, and give her time to rest.

"Dani?"

Dani groaned and wiped more blood from her cheek. "I already regret rescuing your ass."

He smiled. "Yeah, thanks."

Dani sighed and shook her head. She couldn't imagine the day getting any worse than now. "I need my pack."

"Where is it? I'll get it for you."

She realized having Oliver around might not be a terrible idea. She pointed him in the right direction and waited while he sprinted for the tree line. He put it on his back and darted back to her.

"If hell is real, I'm going there for sure," Dani said. "I know a place we can go for the night."

CHAPTER

19

Sweat dripped from Dani's face despite the cool night. The mile-and-a-half walk back to downtown Bangor was excruciating, and they stopped often.

During this stop, Dani made Oliver smear mud and dirt on his face and clothes.

After he was done, he wiped his hands across his trousers to remove some of the filth from his fingers. "Why do I need to be dirty?"

"Because I'm taking you to a place where a clean kid will stick out. I need you to look like a street urchin," Dani said. She rummaged in her pack, which Oliver still wore, and removed a notebook. She handed it and a pencil to the boy. "Write a note to your dad. Tell him you're okay and to come alone to Aunt Hattie's to retrieve you."

"Aunt Hattie? Who's that?"

"He'll know who and what it is."

"We just transferred here a week ago."

"He'll figure it out. Write the note, Oliver. Tear the page out, fold it, and write your dad's name on the outside."

When he finished, Dani took the notebook from him and

wrote two notes of her own. She stuffed the three slips into her pocket, then threw the book and pencil back in her bag.

She pointed forward. "That way."

She leaned on Oliver's shoulder as they approached a dimly lit room at the rear of a large house that was well lit from the front. Raucous laughter came from within. Dani knocked on the back door.

A woman in a neat, royal blue dress that exposed her cleavage opened the door. She held the door with one hand and an ax with the other.

Oliver flinched upon seeing the ax, but Dani remained still.

"Jesus, Dani, you look like shit," the woman said.

"Hi, Aunt Hattie," Dani said.

Hattie lowered the weapon, and her eyes shifted from Dani to Oliver to Brody. "What is this?"

"The kid got separated from his parents. . . ." Dani squeezed Oliver's shoulder when he took a breath to speak. He closed his mouth, and she continued. "I just need a place to stick him for the night, and I'll get him home tomorrow."

"You want a room for the kid?"

"The dog and I are staying too."

Hattie's eyebrows went up. "You expect me to let you, a kid, and a dog stay *here*? My rooms rent by the hour for entertaining. You're not getting one for the entire night. I know you don't have money, Dani."

"What do you want as a trade?"

Hattie flipped the ax to place the head against the floor. She leaned against the handle, using it like a cane. "I want one of your solar panels with a battery reservoir."

"What do you have to eat?"

"Brigand stew," Hattie said with a grin.

Sometimes it was best to not know what was in a Brigand stew.

"I want eight bowls, a loaf of bread, two—no, three pitchers of water, a basin of warm water for a bath, and a room for the three of us. Oh, and I need these delivered." Dani pulled the three folded notes from her pocket and passed them to Hattie.

"Jace, Gavin . . . Who is Miles?"

"An MP."

Hattie thrust the notes back at Dani. "Have you lost your damn mind?"

"Yes. On occasion. Give the one for Miles to an MP here for, um"—Dani glanced at Oliver—"entertainment. You have at least one MP in there, Aunt Hattie."

Hattie scowled at her.

"I'll bring you a lamp when I deliver your panel and battery."

The older woman's scowl slowly turned into a smile. "You would make a fine businesswoman, Dani. But don't get any ideas on opening your own brothel. I own this town in that respect."

"Yes, ma'am, you do."

Hattie waved them in and led them through the back of the lower level of the house. Dani was tempted to cover Oliver's ears with her hands. The sounds of moans, grunts, and screams of pleasure from behind the closed doors lessened as Hattie continued to the end of the hall.

"Business is good tonight," Hattie said, waving her hand as she walked.

Oliver's brow creased with confusion, and Dani was relieved he didn't ask any questions.

Hattie opened the door for them. "One of the girls will bring up the food and supplies."

Dani allowed Oliver and Brody to enter first. "Thanks, Aunt Hattie."

The older woman shook her head. "I don't ask questions of my customers, but Dani, you make me want to break that rule sometimes." The woman touched her chin and turned her head from side to side, inspecting her wounds. "It's a good thing I like you and Jace. I'll send up some medical supplies."

"Thank you." Dani limped into the room and closed the door behind her.

"Is she really your aunt?" Oliver asked.

"She's Aunt Hattie to all the Brigands and some MPs."

"Were the people behind the doors we passed in pain?"

Dani's face flushed. "Um, no. Not exactly." *What were you thinking, bringing a kid to a brothel?!*

"Why did you ask for so much food?"

"Most of it is for Brody." She limped to a chair near the wall, where she eased into it and sighed. The throb in her ankle lessened, but another spasm attacked her back. She tried unsuccessfully to get comfortable while Brody and Oliver curled up together on the bed.

Someone knocked on the door, and Dani's back refused to let her out of the chair. "Oliver, answer the door, please."

He went to the door and took the towels and other items from a young woman in a low-cut red dress.

"My, aren't you a handsome young man," she said. "My name is Mary."

"Oliver."

"How old are you?"

"Twelve."

"Well, Oliver, when you get a little older, you come back to Aunt Hattie's and ask to see me," Mary said. "I'll treat you right."

"How?" he asked.

"For starters, I'll—"

"Thank you, Mary!" Dani forced herself from the chair with a groan and hobbled to the door. "Food would be great."

Mary winced upon seeing Dani's battered face, but she still managed a smile. "I can take care of you too, Dani."

"I know. Thank you, Mary. Food and water will do for now."

"Are you sure?"

"Yes. Thank you."

Mary handed Dani a linen sack. "Medical stuff from Aunt Hattie. She said she put a bottle of medicine in there that will help with the pain. Don't drink too much of it though; it's potent."

"Thanks." Dani closed the door behind Mary and leaned her forehead against it.

"Dani, what's a brothel?"

"Ask your father when you see him tomorrow."

Oliver shrugged. "Okay." He placed the towels next to the basin on the top of the small table near the chair and returned to sit on the bed.

Dani rubbed her lower back with both hands and considered the chair. She instead stayed by the door to wait for Mary's return. Several minutes later, Mary arrived with the food and water, as well as two other young women Dani recognized as workers for Aunt Hattie. The three women brought the food, water, and bucket into the room.

"A lot of food for two people," Mary said.

"We're hungry," Dani said.

"We've been friends for a few years now, Dani. Don't bull-shit me."

She shrugged. "The food is mostly for the dog."

"What the hell kind of mess did you land yourself into today?"

"A big one." Dani waited while one woman filled the bucket with hot water, and the other woman placed the pot of stew on the top of another small table.

The two other women left, but Mary lingered. "Sure you don't need an extra hand?"

"I'm fine. Thank you, Mary."

Dani closed and locked the door after Mary left. She returned to the chair and slid into it with a groan.

Oliver scooped the stew into the bowls and put one on the floor for Brody, who finished his before they did. Oliver refilled Brody's bowl, and again the stew disappeared in seconds.

Dani set her half-eaten bowl of stew aside and rummaged in the sack for Aunt Hattie's medicine bottle. She unscrewed the lid and took a sniff. "Whoa!" The fumes made her eyes and nose burn. She closed her eyes and took a gulp—and her face pinched into a grimace at the bitter taste and insane burning as the liquid slid down her throat. She tried not to cough, but one erupted anyway, causing another spasm in her back.

The burning sensation moved from her stomach and out through her body. Her limbs relaxed, and the pain in her back eased. Her body felt warm, and her head dropped forward.

"Dani?"

Her head came up, and she opened her eyes, unsure when she'd closed them.

"Do you like the MPs? I know you don't want to be captured by them, but do you like them?" Oliver shoved another bite of stew into his mouth while Brody watched him in case he dropped the tiniest morsel of food.

With most of her pain gone, Dani stood and began the task of washing blood and filth from her face and hair. "The Wardens are the bigger enemy," she said. "But the CNA and their MPs are too busy maintaining the status quo instead of going after the Wardens."

"What's status quo?"

"It means keeping things the way they already are. The CNA isn't trying to change. The MPs waste their resources on capturing Brigands to increase their numbers and merely defend against the Wardens. It's not that I don't like the MPs, but they can be really fucking stupid sometimes. Sorry. Didn't mean to drop an f-bomb on you." Aunt Hattie's medicine had lowered Dani's vocabulary filter along with her pain.

Oliver giggled. "That's okay. The MPs I'm around swear all the time."

She placed the bloody towel aside and took a few more bites of her stew. She tore off a piece of bread and shoved that into her mouth. With the pain gone, she was ravenous.

"Dani?"

"Yeah?" she asked between chews.

"Is Mary a whore?"

Dani choked on the bread. When she managed to clear it from her throat, she said, "The men and women that work for Aunt Hattie are making money the best way they can. *Whore* is a terrible word, and don't ever call them that in person."

"Calling them that would be rude?"

"Very rude. They're people who work for a living, just like your father."

Oliver nodded and fed Brody the rest of his bread. "What do you do for work?"

"I scavenge for my food and supplies."

"You said before that you steal."

"Yes, but I never take from someone that needs something more than me. If you were starving, I wouldn't take that stew from you."

"Do you use weapons to rob people?"

"No."

"Are you sad?"

"About what?"

"You killed that man today."

Dani remembered the man almost snapping her spine. "Yeah, I did. I'm not sure how I feel. No more questions. Feed Brody another bowl of stew and go to bed."

"Where are you sleeping?"

"Floor. With Aunt Hattie's medicine, I think I could sleep upside down if I had to."

Oliver smiled. "Thank you for helping me today, Dani."

"Yeah." She picked up the cloth by the basin to finish cleaning the blood off her while Brody inhaled his third bowl of Brigand stew. His rounded belly swayed when he moved. He climbed back on the bed and settled in next to Oliver. The boy threw his arm over the dog, and both fell asleep.

Once clean, Dani applied some smelly ointment to the cuts on her scalp and cheek. She sat and removed her boots and socks. Her right ankle was swollen, purple, and tender to touch. She found a rolled length of cloth in her bag and used it to wrap her ankle before pulling her sock and boot back on. The extra padding made the boot tight, but her foot felt better.

Muscle tightness seized her back, and she took another drink of the medicine. *Aunt Hattie's magic bottle of goodness.* She smiled. The heat flowed through her body again, and she lowered herself to the floor. Her eyes closed and didn't open again until morning.

Dani rose slowly and stumbled out of the room and down the hall to the toilet. Once her bladder was empty, she took a moment to enjoy the cold water from the tap running over her hands. She splashed water on her face and woke up a bit more. Her blurred image in the mirror stared back at her, and Dani remembered the picture Jace had shown her yesterday—or was it the day before that? She wasn't sure. She and Jace didn't have a mirror at home, or indoor plumbing, so where was she? Her ankle hurt, and she didn't remember why.

She left the cramped bathroom and went back into the hall. She recognized Aunt Hattie's brothel then, but her memory didn't clear until her back tightened with a brutal spasm that threatened to drop her to her knees.

She used the wall for support to return to her room. Beads of sweat popped out on her forehead, the result of a mix of both pain and exertion.

The window was open and both Oliver and Brody were gone.

Shit.

She hobbled to the window and startled when Oliver's head appeared. He climbed through the window, and Brody leapt through after him.

"Where did you go?" Dani asked.

"We had to pee."

"Oh. Right."

"Your face is really pale."

"Yeah. Muscle spasms are back." She limped to the chair to sit but opted to stand and lean against it instead.

"Do you have any of that medicine left?"

Dani shook her head and closed her eyes, hoping the pain would leave soon. She did have more of Aunt Hattie's elixir, but she didn't want to drink it. Her mind was still fogged after two gulps of the liquid last night. The ongoing pain tempted her to drink the entire bottle, but she needed to keep her wits about her.

Oliver fixed three bowls of leftover stew and tore the remaining bread in thirds. Brody gobbled his bread and devoured his stew before Oliver sat on the edge of the bed to eat. Dani picked up her piece of bread and munched on it.

"How would you end the war?" Oliver asked.

"Huh?"

"Last night you said the MPs were only defending against the Wardens and not attacking. How would you end the war?"

God, this kid is a pest. So many questions. "Uh . . ." She picked up her bowl and ate a few bites of cold stew, stalling, and as she chewed her mind cleared a little more. "Brigands make up half of the total population on Earth. The Commonwealths are about 30 percent of the population with their troops, MPs, and such. The Wardens are around 20 percent, right? Wardens have the better tech, but if the Commonwealths and Brigands joined together, that would be 80 percent of the population—the war would have never lasted almost sixty years if that had happened. But the Wardens unleashed a shock attack, blasted the hell out of the major cities, and the governments folded. They panicked and unraveled. Panicking means death, Oliver. The CNA still unravels every time they have to fight the Wardens. Can't win like that."

"Why don't you get the Brigands and CNA to join forces?"

"Me? No."

"You said the MPs won't change."

Dani nodded.

"You're no different than they are. You scavenge, you hide, you do your own thing. You're angry that the MPs won't attack the Wardens, but you aren't willing to attack them either."

Dani opened her mouth to argue but realized she had no comeback, so she snapped it closed and turned her attention back to her cold stew. Someone knocked lightly on the door, saving her from the conversation. She placed her bowl on the table and hobbled to the door. Upon opening it, she smiled.

Jace and Gavin entered, and Dani closed the door behind them.

"Glad the dog is still alive," Jace said.

Dani sighed with disgust as her happiness to see her brother evaporated. She returned to the chair but didn't sit. Another spasm tore through her back and she moaned.

"Dani?" Gavin asked.

"Muscle spasm. It'll pass," she said through a tightened jaw.

Jace stood before the boy and stared down at him. "Who is this?"

"I'm Oliver," the boy said without hesitation. "I was with two families by the Standpipe when three Brigand men attacked. Dani got them away from us, but one of them beat the crap out of her when he came after her again."

"Again?" Gavin asked Dani, but she didn't answer.

"Jesus, Dani," Jace said. "Bangor is in an uproar about a Brigand woman with a dog seen earlier yesterday at the Standpipe. The body of a Brigand man was found there last night. You've never stooped to murder before."

Dani glared at her brother. "Check that accusatory tone, Jace. You weren't there. The convenient witness that saw me was probably one of the other two men trying to kidnap the women and children."

"He was going to kill her," Oliver said.

Her back pain wouldn't stop; she leaned her hands against the small table.

Gavin slipped his pack from his shoulder and began rummaging through it. He pulled a slender, clear slab, like a piece of glass, from his pack.

Dani gaped. "You have a MedPanel?"

Gavin nodded. "You're not the only one that steals from the CNA." He held the panel toward her back and tapped the side of the panel facing him. Dani couldn't see the view Gavin had, and he adjusted the display's sensitivity as he moved the panel parallel to her body.

"Spinal column is good," he said. "No breaks. Deep-tissue bruising in the lower back muscles. Some small tears, and I can see the source of the spasm." He turned the MedPanel off and put it back in his bag. He placed one hand on her shoulder and one at the base of her spine. "How did you hurt your back?"

"He almost folded me in half, except it was the wrong way to fold a body."

"Sounds painful." Gavin pressed his fingertips into her back, probing her muscles, until she flinched. He placed his palm over the most sensitive spot and pushed.

She groaned and shifted away from his touch, but he held her in place. "Be still, Dani. I can temporarily fix this."

"You're hurting me."

"I'm sorry. Give me a second, and stop squirming."

Dani tried to remain still, but her face was pinched into a grimace.

"Hattie said you sent a note to the MPs," Jace said.

"To Oliver's father, to retrieve him," Dani said between groans. Sweat formed on her face again as the pain continued to worsen.

Jace's voice boomed. "You *invited* the MPs to Hattie's? Are you crazy?"

"We only invited the one," Dani said. Her back still hurt, and her brother was annoying the shit out of her. Suddenly the knotted muscle in her back relaxed, and she sighed.

Gavin released her. "Better?"

"Yeah. Not as fast as Aunt Hattie's medicine, but your way has no side effects on the brain." Dani stretched her body, pleased to be able to stand straight again.

"What medicine?" he asked.

Dani found the bottle and handed it to him.

Gavin unscrewed the lid, took a sniff, and put the lid back on. "You drank this?"

Dani nodded.

He slipped the bottle into his pocket. "Killed a few brain cells with it, too."

Jace lingered in the corner of the room, his arms folded across his chest.

"Oliver, feed the rest of the stew to Brody, please," Dani said.

The boy's face brightened with something to do other than watch the bickering. Gavin's eyes remained fixed on her, and she tried to ignore the way he watched her. His face was softer than she'd seen it before.

"It's not murder when you're protecting yourself in self-defense," he said.

Dani nodded. Still, she *had* killed a man. *Is it still considered self-defense if I threw him out the window in anger?* She didn't know the answer to that question.

A knock on the door pulled her from her thoughts.

Gavin eased the door open a crack.

"I'm Miles Jackman," the man on the other side of the door said. "I'm here for my son."

"Daddy!" Oliver sprang toward the door.

"Fuck," Jace said. His face paled and his arms dropped to his sides.

Dani had never seen her brother startled before. He had been angry about Brody, but he looked almost terrified now.

Gavin opened the door, and Dani watched as a man in his mid forties, dressed like a Brigand, entered the room. Oliver threw his arms around his father, and the man returned his son's embrace.

Gavin leaned farther out into the hallway before coming back into the room and closing the door. "He's alone."

"Thank you so much for taking care of my son. He . . ." Miles's voice failed when his eyes landed on the other two people in the room. He stared at Dani in a way that made her more uncomfortable than Gavin had earlier. A mix of emotions crossed his face as he tried to speak. His brow creased, and he shook his head. "I don't . . . you were . . . um. *How?*" He looked at Jace and shook his head with disbelief before staring at her again.

A few more seconds ticked by in silence.

Miles took a step toward her. "*Dani?*"

CHAPTER

20

Rowan stood before an eight-foot-long glass window, one of three windows overlooking a medical lab below. He held his hands clasped behind his back and observed without emotion as a group of ten Echoes ranging in age from twelve to sixteen were marched into the room. A few wept and passively walked forward, but most fought back to try to escape the experiment. Warden soldiers wrestled them to the tables and strapped them down. The medical staff went to work next. They applied different-colored wires to various parts of the subjects' bodies and inserted needles, one into each of the restrained arms of the Echoes. The colored wires led to a screen that registered a myriad of squiggled lines of both brain and heart function.

Rowan glanced at the officer standing next to him for a moment before returning his attention to the medical lab. "Comm tower status?"

"Progressing, but it's a slow process," Curtis said. "We've had some delays getting the right equipment. Brigands are interrupting our supply lines."

"They're stealing tech?"

The lab workers rolled twenty metal poles, two for each

subject, into the lab. The five-foot lengths of tubing hanging from the clear bags of fluid swayed as the poles were moved into position.

"No. They're going after food, but they're finding new ways to harass the supply lines."

"Do more sweeps. Cover the whole fucking county if you must. Wipe the Brigands out and bring me more Echoes."

Curtis nodded. "I'll accompany the first sweep tonight."

"Try not to die, Curtis."

The man laughed. "I'll do my best. I know it irritates you when I look younger than you do."

Both men returned their full attention to the lab. Ten workers stood by their subjects and used a long syringe to deliver a dose of medication through one of the IVs. Four of the children suffered seizures immediately, and died seconds later. The remaining six breathed their last breath without any side effects. The erratically moving lines on each monitor screen stilled as their hearts stopped beating.

Minutes passed, then all ten bodies glowed. The blue hue filled the lab for several seconds before diminishing. The unmoving lines on the monitor screens ticked back to life, showing resumed cardiac and cerebral activity. The staff worked quickly to begin the larger infusions hanging from the poles. As soon as the first few drops flowed into the youngsters' bodies, they screamed and writhed while still strapped to their stretchers.

The infusions from the poles finished after a few minutes, and the screaming ended. The subjects, still tied down, were wheeled out of the lab. A crew entered a moment later to re-tidy the room and bring in empty stretchers. That done, soldiers marched the next group of ten youngsters into the lab.

"We'll know in a few hours if the dose of neurotransmitters successfully submits their minds," Curtis said. "If it doesn't work, they'll go back into the lab for reconditioning tomorrow. I wish it was a faster process, but our scientists are still adjusting the infusion cocktail to try to maximize conversion and stability. The ones that seize almost always need to be repeated."

Rowan moved away from the window and started down the bland white corridor. Curtis walked with him, and their booted feet sent echoes down the hall with each step.

"I can't do anything with a twelve-year-old in the army," Rowan said. "Eighteen to twenty is optimal. Any success on manipulating the regen age?"

"Some. We've had better luck getting a younger child who regens to ten to go up to twelve or thirteen. It's harder to get the ones who regen to their mid-twenties to go back to a younger age."

"I can work with mid-twenties. Have the labs focus on getting the younger ones to regen to an older age. Don't bother with manipulating the older ones."

"Yes, sir."

Rowan glanced at his friend and grinned. "You like taking orders, old friend?"

"Not as much as you like giving them," Curtis said with a smirk.

Rowan laughed.

The pitter-patter of rapid steps filled the hall. A child rounded the far corner and charged toward Rowan. "Daddy!"

Rowan increased his pace to meet his son and scooped the boy into his arms. A moment later, a pregnant woman turned the same corner, spotted them, and smiled. Rowan greeted her with a kiss.

"Beautiful as ever, Ana," Curtis said.

She smiled and kissed Curtis on the cheek, then passed her hand over her protuberant belly. "Devon is all yours, Rowan. I need to rest."

"Sure." Rowan kissed her again. "I'll see you later."

Ana left, and Rowan bounced his son in his arms as he and Curtis resumed their walk.

"Where are we going, Daddy?"

"To the training fields, where our newest Echoes are learning to become Wardens."

When they arrived on the grounds, training officers were barking orders at the recruits standing at attention while other groups practiced hand-to-hand combat or trained with weapons. A quake grenade disintegrated a wooden target six hundred yards away.

Curtis gave an approving nod. "That's the new grenade launcher. We've increased its range and submitted the new designs for mass production last week."

Rowan nodded. "Excellent. Devon, do you understand what's happening here?"

"They're learning to fight," the boy said.

"Yes. Do you know why they need to learn to fight?"

The boy nodded. "To take Earth for the Echoes."

"That's right. We lost our home planet to civil war, but Earth will become the new Ekkoh. We're united this time. The humans here are ignorant and weak. Ekkohrians would outlast the humans and own Earth in time, but the Wardens will take it. We don't need to wait for the humans to go extinct when we can speed that process up."

The boy smiled and hugged his father's neck. "Can I go play?"

"Sure." Rowan put Devon down, and the boy ran to climb on a cargo truck.

"He doesn't quite understand," Curtis said.

"Not yet, but he will." Rowan watched his son. "How much longer until we can field test the new tanks?"

"It may be a while. We still can't retrofit the plasma pistol tech into something that large. The prototypes either don't have enough power for the size of the tank, or it overloads and blows everything. We lose a tank driver every time that happens. Even an Echo can't come back from being blasted into a million pieces."

Rowan frowned and shook his head. "We can't lose our fighters to mistakes or substandard tech."

"Agreed."

"Keep me posted on progress."

Curtis nodded. "I will."

"Any news on my request to move north?"

Curtis shook his head. "HQ in Boston is content with our range as it stands."

Rowan's jaw tightened. "We need to crush the CNA and be done with this damn war. We have the weapons."

"We don't have the numbers, Rowan. We need both to destroy the CNA."

"I want the rest of Maine."

"Why? It's nothing but fucking trees north of Portland."

"There is a thriving Brigand community—well, thriving by Brigand standards—in Bangor. My resource there has been sending me intel on the MPs and Brigands. The Commonwealth ground troops are all but gone. I could take that entire region with a dozen Wardens."

"Who is the contact?"

Rowan smiled. "I can't tell you all my secrets, Curtis. He's already inside the MP base, and he's close to infiltrating the Brigands."

"Echo?"

Rowan laughed. "Of course not. Human. Expendable. He dies, no one cares, least of all, me."

Curtis shook his head. "You have always been a genius, Rowan, but sometimes you scare me."

"Good," Rowan said.

"Any other reason for your interest in Bangor? Still searching for her?"

Rowan's jaw tightened. His Brigand captures over the last several years had yielded him Danielles, Danielas, Dannikas, and the like, but none had been the woman he sought.

Curtis sighed. "Odds are she died a long time ago."

Rowan stepped away from Curtis to keep a better watch on his son once he abandoned climbing on the truck for a stack of crates that had the artillery insignia on them.

"Devon!" he barked. "Come here."

Devon ran to his father.

"Hungry?" Rowan asked him.

"Yes!"

Rowan extended his hand, and Devon's small hand slipped inside it. Rowan turned to his friend. "I'll meet you later."

"Of course." Curtis chucked the boy under the chin. "Bye, Devon."

"Bye, Uncle Curtis," Devon said with a wide smile.

CHAPTER
21

Dani didn't know what to do about Miles, so she remained silent. He recognized her, *knew* her, but she had never seen him before. His face kept shifting between joy and something much more distressing, like pain. He stepped toward her, and she took a step back.

"I'm sorry. I just can't believe it's really you. The last time I saw you . . ." Miles shook his head. "You were *dead*. But you're here, alive, and you look the exact same as I remember you. How can you stand there and not say anything to me?"

"I've never seen you before today," Dani said. "I'm sorry."

Miles pinched the bridge of his nose. "Making me believe you were dead for the last fifteen years hasn't been enough torture? Now you pretend you don't know me? How did you survive? You had a huge hole in your chest. I know! I put it there."

Oliver stared up at his father. "You *shot* her?"

"Well, I mean, I didn't shoot her on purpose," Miles said hastily. "I was on an MP raid and Wardens arrived. Everything went to hell. I lost most of my team in the firefight. Dani kept us from getting killed by a quake grenade, but I lost track of her after that. The Wardens attacked, and a few of us were pinned by sniper fire. The shooting stopped, and the sniper stood, so I fired, but . . ." He turned his gaze to Dani. "I'd already pulled the trigger when I realized I shot the wrong person. You fell, and when I found you, you were already dead—from my gun, the fall, or both, I don't know. Someone attacked me from behind, knocked me out. After that, two other MPs found me and dragged me out. They insisted there wasn't a woman's body, only blood, where they found me."

"She must be an Echo," Oliver said.

Miles shook his head. "She never turned blue. Dani, you remember that day, right?"

Dani shook her head.

"Christ! Do you at least remember *us?* You and me?" Miles took another step toward her.

Dani tensed at his approach, and he backed away.

"We were in a relationship, Dani. It was a bit tumultuous at times, but I loved you."

Dani remained silent.

Miles turned to Jace. "Have you lost your memories too, Jace?"

"No," he said.

"Please stop making us both suffer, Jace," Dani said. "Is what he says true?"

Jace sighed. "Yeah. He's telling the truth. Miles, Dani is an Echo. I struck you from behind before her body began to heal. I wrapped her in a blanket and took her away. I met your two MPs as I was leaving with her and traded information about your location for passage by them."

Miles's jaw dropped, and his gaze darted back to Dani. "You're an *Echo?*"

She nodded. She glanced at Gavin; he remained silent. He didn't seem at all surprised by the revelation. She returned her attention to Miles. "When my body heals, the injuries disappear, along with my memories. I come back as a ten-year-old kid and don't remember anything. I don't even remember the war or what started it. Jace is my brother. If I didn't keep dying, I'd be around seventy-one now."

Miles shook his head. "You lived as a human when we were together."

"At that time, she believed she was a human," Jace said. "I never told her she was an Echo in that life until the day she died."

"You let me believe that I killed the woman I loved." Miles trembled with anger. "For fifteen fucking years, I have carried that grief with me, Jace. Not only was she dead, *I* was the one who accidentally killed her. Do you have *any* idea the kind of torment I've lived with over that day?"

Jace scowled. "I don't give a shit about you. Dani is my sister, and I keep her safe. I've been with her for three regens, raising her from a child that forgets who I am each time. You think I'm worried about *your* feelings?"

Before the men could come to blows, Dani stepped between them. "Stop. Please, stop. I'm sorry I don't remember you, Miles. Whatever we had for a relationship is over. It died the day you shot me. I know it wasn't intentional, and I don't blame you. We can't change what happened. Please just agree to stop fighting for a few minutes. Oliver is here, he's safe, and I'm sure he wants to go home."

"I don't mind staying," Oliver said. "I like Brody."

"Brody? The dog?" Miles asked.

Oliver nodded.

The dog, still perched on the bed, wagged his tail upon having attention directed his way.

"Dani, you had a dog named Brody before," Miles said.

Jace groaned. "This is the fourth iteration."

"Did you nickname him B, too?" Miles asked.

Dani's brow creased. She had only nicknamed the dog

yesterday, but apparently this, too, was a behavior she repeated each regen. "Jace says I'm stuck in a cycle with my lives. I forget everything except survival skills. I also adopt a dog each time and name him Brody."

"Not this time," Jace said.

"Shut up, Jace. Miles, please take Oliver home. Make sure he takes a good, hot bath. Sorry to drag him into a brothel for the night, but Aunt Hattie's was my only option for no questions but plenty of privacy. Other Brigands would pounce on the chance to take him and hold him for ransom." *Or worse.*

"Thank you for looking after him." Miles looked shell-shocked. "Will I see you again?"

Dani shrugged. "I don't know."

"Do you still steal everything you can from the MPs?"

She shifted uncomfortably. "Maybe."

He smiled. "Then I imagine we'll cross paths again. I'll never arrest you, Dani. I know you hate the MPs."

"She doesn't hate them," Oliver interjected. "She hates that they 'maintain the status quo' and won't change their tactics. She thinks the Brigands and MPs should join forces to take out the Wardens."

Dani winced and cursed under her breath. "I said all that stuff after drinking Aunt Hattie's potion."

Gavin snorted a laugh. "An inebriated Dani. I'd pay money to see that."

Oliver gave Brody a parting kiss on his snout and hugged Dani. "Bye."

Dani patted him on the back, unsure what to do about the hugging. "Uh, bye."

He released her and returned to his father's side. Gavin opened the door for them, and closed it once they were out.

Jace stood with his arms crossed again. His persistent stubbornness annoyed her.

"*What*, Jace?"

"You took his side," he said.

"I didn't take anyone's side. That's what is pissing you off the most." Dani turned to Gavin. "Is there a place Brody and I can stay that's not a brothel? I think it's time I moved out of my brother's house."

"Sure," Gavin said.

Jace's face fell. "You can't move! If you die—"

"Yes, Jace, I go back to being a ten-year-old. I get it. You're still keeping secrets from me. I'm done. I'll pack my stuff today and leave."

"Gavin, if anything happens to her—"

"Jace! Give it a rest. He's an Echo too. He knows how this shit works."

Jace stared at Gavin. "Is this true?"

"Yeah." Gavin looked at Dani. "How long have you known?"

"Figured it out a while ago. It's not a big deal. C'mon, B."

The dog leapt from the bed. She scratched behind his ear, and he licked her hand. She shoved her things back into her bag. "Aunt Hattie will want her room back, I'm sure. Though she does enjoy seeing you, brother." Dani limped to the door and walked out with Brody. Gavin closed the door and quickly caught up to her with his long strides.

Mary stopped them before they could leave. "Quite the gathering in that room today. Fun?" She winked.

"Loads," Dani said with a flat tone.

Mary smoothed the nonexistent wrinkles from her dress. Her outfit was a stark contrast to Dani's faded and battered shirt and trousers. "Coming back tonight?"

"Not tonight, sorry. I like the yellow, Mary. It suits you better than the red."

Mary's face lit with a smile. "Thank you. I'll be sure to wear this dress when you decide to come back."

"Yeah, okay." Dani continued through the back of the house and out the rear door.

Brody trotted off into some tall grass to relieve himself.

Gavin gave Dani a searching look. "I know you're friends, but I think Mary genuinely likes you."

"Uh-huh. Stop grinning. I didn't mean to throw you in the middle of my issues with Jace, but I was desperate. I need to be away from him for a while."

"It's not a problem. I want to know how you figured out I was an Echo."

Since her limping gait created a horribly slow pace, Dani opted to walk while they talked. She wanted to reach her new home, wherever it was, sometime today. "You said you were a marine. It's a dated term. After the war started, all military personnel were reallocated to Commonwealth troops. They have ground, air, and sea troops. The formal troop branches for the army, navy, air force, coasties, and marines all dissolved with the United Nations."

"Yes, they did," Gavin said with a nod.

"You look like you're in your forties, and the war started fifty-nine years ago. You're too young, physically, to have been a marine without being an Echo with at least one or two regens." Dani's back began to cramp, and the throb in her ankle returned. "You had no reaction to the news that I'm one too. You already knew?"

"You were eighteen when Jace hired me to train you. There was too much knowledge locked away in your head for someone of that age. Your memories are in there somewhere."

She wasn't sure she wanted them to resurface. A war starting and her parents dying weren't memories she cared to recover.

Gavin squinted at her. "You really don't recall anything of your life with Miles?"

She shook her head. "I noticed you kept the medicine bottle. Can I have a sip?"

"No. That stuff will melt your brain."

"I never sleep well, and I slept great last night."

"Passing out is not the same as sleeping. We're not in a rush to be anywhere; we can stop as needed. Once you're settled for the night, I'll take a look at your ankle."

"Where are you taking me to stay?"

"Mount Hope."

Dani stopped. "The cemetery?"

"Yeah."

"Because that's not a creepy place to live."

Gavin laughed. Brody's heavy feet thundered by as he caught up from wandering in the grass outside Aunt Hattie's and raced ahead.

Dani resumed limping. "Brothel one night, cemetery the next. Lovely."

CHAPTER

22

After dropping off the final items owed Aunt Hattie for her solar panel, Dani walked to a large oak tree nearby and sat down at its base. She left her pack on her back, using it as a cushion to lean against. She extended her leg and rotated her sore ankle. It was healing well; the noxious-smelling green paste Gavin made her apply to it and her back every night must be working. She'd be back to fighting shape soon. In the meantime, she was using her time with Gavin to pester him about maps and military tactics.

A scuffling noise on the other side of the tree made her roll her eyes and chuckle. "You can stop hiding, Oliver. When Brody is done begging for food from Hattie's kitchen, he'll find you and lick you to death."

A sigh came from the other side of the tree, and Oliver emerged. He sat next to her and grinned. "You knew I was here the whole time?"

His clothes were rumpled, hems tattered. His shirt and the knees of his trousers were stained, and his face was smudged with dirt. He looked like he belonged in Brigand territory. Dani was impressed.

"Saw your big head poke out earlier. Nice clothes."

He smiled. "I met a Brigand kid my age the other day and traded him food for some clothes. I wanted to see you, and this was the only way to make it happen. You owed Aunt Hattie her solar panel, so you had to come back. I was afraid I had missed you, but Mary said you had to make more than one trip."

"Mary aiding your delinquency, no surprise there. You're a smart kid, Oliver. I'll give you that."

Brody galloped toward them and, seeing Oliver, barreled into the boy's lap, knocking him over. Dani laughed as Oliver struggled with Brody's weight and lashing tongue. When Oliver finally managed to sit up again, Brody sprawled in the grass on his belly.

Oliver wiped the dog saliva from his face. "I like his new collar. He seems happy, and he's put on some weight. Still a little bony, but not like before."

"His winning personality gets him lots of handouts."

Oliver studied her face. "You look tired though. Dad gets dark shadows under his eyes after working a night shift and staying up too long. That's how you look."

"I haven't been sleeping much."

"Is it because you killed that guy?"

"I normally don't sleep well, but that day does still bother me."

"Are you going to merge the Brigands with the MPs?"

She wasn't about to tell him that was the exact reason why she'd been sleeping so little lately. Oliver's words about her being the same as the MPs, unwilling to attack the Wardens, irritated her more than her lingering back and ankle pain. "Let's go."

Oliver scrambled to his feet faster than she did, and it annoyed her. She thought of Jace and his movement limitations due to his age. An injured Brigand scavenging alone was a dead Brigand. She decided she would find extra food today to bring to him later. A few days without seeing him had eased her anger.

Dani started up the hill, and Oliver and Brody walked with her.

"Where are we going?" Oliver asked.

"I'm taking you back to your father."

They talked as they hiked, and Dani took a different path to stay clear of the Standpipe. Though the uproar among the Brigands over the death of Dani's attacker had resolved once the witness had been identified as one of the would-be kidnappers, she wasn't ready to venture so close to the Standpipe again.

"Stay quiet," Dani told Oliver as they neared the Union Street boundary line. She heard distant voices. She gestured to Oliver to remain behind with Brody. "I'll whistle if it's safe for you to join me."

He knelt and took Brody's collar, and Dani crept toward the voices. She spotted two men and recognized them both. Xander stood with his arms folded across his chest. Miles waved one hand while leaning toward him. Both of their faces held scowls. She couldn't hear everything Miles said, but after a few more sharp words, Xan's arms fell to his side, and his body stiffened. Miles had used his rank, and Xan now stood at attention.

"Get the hell out of here!" Miles said.

"Yes, sir." Xan turned sharply and jogged back toward the barracks.

Miles passed his hand through his hair with a sigh. Dani continued to linger and observe. He turned to walk away, and she stepped into the open.

"Miles."

He jumped and turned to face her. "Christ, Dani. What are you doing here?"

"I'm not the one on the wrong side of the boundary."

"My son has wandered off, and I'm going to find him. Please tell me he's with you."

She whistled and seconds later, Brody reached her side.

Oliver took a little longer to catch up. Miles's face softened to see his son safe, but his look quickly turned to one of irritation.

"I wanted to make sure she was okay, Dad," Oliver said.

"Dani knows how to survive just fine without you checking in on her." Miles's lips pinched into a frown. "Where did you get those clothes?"

"Oliver," Dani said before he could answer, "can you go play with B for a few minutes?"

"Sure! C'mon, Brody."

Oliver led the dog to a more open area in the trees several yards away. He found a stick to throw—and quickly realized Brody didn't know how to fetch. While he took on the task of teaching him, Dani turned her attention to Miles. He was staring at her.

"He's a good kid. Don't be too mad at him."

"So I should only ground him for a few years instead of forever?"

Dani grinned. "Yeah, something like that."

"I'm glad to see you, Dani. You're moving around a lot better than before."

"Yeah. The first couple of days were miserable."

"I'm sure. You don't sleep much—well, I mean, you didn't before. You look tired."

Dani rolled her eyes. Miles knew her better than she had realized. "That hasn't changed. But I didn't send Oliver off to play with Brody so we could chat about my health."

Miles nodded.

She stalled for a moment and picked at some dirt on one of her palms before thrusting her hands into her pockets. "When is the next site visit by CNA higher-ups?"

"We only warrant mid-level CNA leadership coming to Bangor. Our barracks aren't big enough for a visit from the higher brass. They're due to arrive middle of next month. Why?"

"The less you know, the better for you if things go sideways."

"Shit. You're going to do something stupid."

Dani snorted. "You *do* know me."

"Yeah." Miles reached for her right hand.

She resisted the urge to back away from him. He was still a stranger to her, but he wasn't a threat. He pulled her hand from her pocket. His fingers curled around her hand, and his fingertips touched her palm.

Dani relaxed slightly. Miles was somewhat familiar to her, in the same way Jace had been when she was a child standing on the side of the road, watching him help push a truck out of a hole. She hadn't run away from Jace then, and she didn't flee from Miles now.

He passed his thumb over the back of her hand and sighed. "The day you died . . . we argued that morning. You burned the back of your hand, and it was my fault. But there's no trace of a burn now; it's gone, just like your memories of us when we were together. I am sorry for everything I did wrong that day." Miles released her hand and shook his head. "I'm so sorry."

Part of her wished she could remember her life with him. The other part of her was glad she couldn't. They stood in silence for a few minutes, pretending to watch Oliver play with the dog.

"Why are you interested in the CNA?" Miles eventually asked.

"What are the chances of a CNA–Brigand merger? I don't mean the Brigands becoming part of the CNA troops, but for the two to work together to end the Wardens and this war."

"You were *serious* when you told Oliver the two should join forces?"

"At the time, not really . . . except the little turd said something the next morning, before you arrived, that changed things."

"What?"

"He said I was a hypocrite for criticizing the MPs and CNA for not taking the offensive with Wardens and only defending when here I am doing my own thing and expecting someone else to deal with the war. He said it with fewer words, but the meaning was still there. It's been keeping me up at night and making me crazy. Oliver was right. I don't want to keep doing nothing."

Miles chuckled and passed a hand through his hair. "Sometimes the twelve-year-old insight is so plain and simple it's brilliant. Before you can think about the CNA, though, you'd have to get the Brigands to agree to that. There are decades of distrust between you guys and the CNA."

"The Bangor MPs don't conduct Brigand raids like Jace says they did in Portland. Why?"

Miles shook his head. "I haven't been here two weeks yet, but the CNA here is much more tolerant of Brigands. They certainly like visiting Aunt Hattie's and the other brothels. I'm told the pubs offer a range of food and drink that we don't have in the barracks. Both sides mostly respect the territories. Since the men who attacked the two women and children are being dealt with by Brigands, we haven't even needed to get involved."

Dani nodded. Of the remaining two men, one had been captured and jailed. The other one hadn't been caught yet, but the community was on the lookout. In fact, the whole town had come together to go after the attackers. Dani hadn't ever seen Brigands work together like that. She figured Miles had played a part in keeping the MPs out of the mess.

Aunt Hattie was one of Bangor's leaders—unofficial, but she had a tremendous amount of power in the town. Dani wanted to talk to her about formally uniting the Brigands, see if she thought it was possible. If so, next task was tackling the subject of partnering with the CNA.

"Thanks, Miles. Can you keep me posted about the CNA brass coming?"

He retrieved a small, flat device from his shirt pocket about one inch wide and three inches long. He slid the top of the device so it opened, doubling its size. He pushed a series of buttons on the lower half, and the screen went black for a moment before turning back on. "We use these on the base and during maneuvers for communication. It's the latest model. You can type or just talk into the thing. It holds a charge forever, but the screen also has a solar charging ability if the reserve is low." He continued to manipulate buttons on it as he talked. "I've rooted the device so it's no longer synced with the CNA comm system. You'll be able to use it and stay off their grid." Miles passed the comm unit to her. "It's easy to use. You'll figure it out. I'll request a new one when I am back on base and tell them I lost this one. I'll send you a message later today so we can stay in touch."

"Thank you."

"Since I took this one offline, and it was linked directly to me, I need to return to the base before anyone comes looking for me." He cleared his throat. "Oliver! Time to go!"

Oliver and Brody ran back to join them.

"He doesn't fetch, but he's starting to understand," the boy said.

Dani smiled. "Great! Thanks for trying to teach him."

"Take care, Dani," Miles said.

She watched them leave before turning to head back toward downtown. She almost slapped her forehead when she realized she'd forgotten to ask him about Xan. She was so curious to know what he'd done to piss Miles off. Still shaking her head, she slipped her new comm device into her pocket and decided to find Jace. He was the last person she needed for her plan to work.

CHAPTER

23

L
ate afternoon began to turn into evening as Dani walked north on the old road near the river. The water flowed out toward the bay, and a bald eagle soared above. She always enjoyed spotting eagles or ospreys patrolling the waterway. Her attention diverted to the sound of an approaching vehicle. Only the wealthiest Brigands owned cars or trucks, and with gasoline so limited, few were ever driven. There were solar cars too, of course, but powering them was an issue, as the charging equipment deteriorated over time. Repairs were ghastly expensive due to the scarcity of replacement parts, even used ones. The most successful business people in Bangor were brothel/pub owners, lumberjacks and jills, and mechanics.

Dani stepped off the road as the car crept over the battered asphalt toward her. She smiled when she recognized the driver.

"These roads are shit, but it sure beats walking," Hattie said, slowing to a stop beside her. "You're still a bit gimpy on that ankle. Want a ride back to Jace's?"

"Back? You were already there?"

Hattie gave Dani a wink and a grin. "Your brother is doing just fine for a man in his seventies."

Dani smiled politely, though the thought of her brother

having sex with Aunt Hattie made her cringe. Jace and Hattie shared a semblance of a relationship, but Dani could live without the mental image of them in bed together. "I'm fine to walk the rest of the way. Thank you for the offer."

"Suit yourself. I must be getting back. Work beckons as the sun goes down. Oh, and thanks for the solar panel, honey, but you will have to come by to put the damn thing together for me. I know that wasn't part of the deal; I'll feed you and the mutt well as payment."

"Yeah, I'll swing by."

"Good. I'll tell Mary you're coming," Hattie said with a wink. She removed her foot from the brake and rolled the car forward, maneuvering around the worst of the holes and buckles in the road.

Dani continued her walk to the small home she had shared with Jace until just a few days ago. When she arrived, she stood outside for a moment and watched him move around inside. He scooped food from a pot into a bowl and eased his arthritic body into a chair at the table. He poured a dollop of liquid from a bottle on the table into his bowl—a bottle the same size as the one Hattie had given her the night at the brothel. She was glad her brother had something to ease the pain. She considered leaving and coming back tomorrow, but she needed to end the battle between them. She made Brody wait a few feet from the house before she approached the door and knocked.

The chair scraped against the floor for a second, and Dani heard Jace's footsteps as he came to the door. He smiled as he opened it, but his smile faded upon seeing her.

"Sorry, I'm not Hattie," Dani said.

"Where's the dog?"

"Around back."

Jace grunted and, leaving the door open, returned to the table. Dani figured the fact that he hadn't slammed the door on her meant his temper had also cooled. She entered and closed the door.

"Hungry? There's a little stew left in the pot."

Dani recognized the smell as Hattie's recipe; she appreciated the older woman's efforts to take care of Jace. "I'll eat later." She removed her pack and pulled two smaller sacks from it. She placed the sacks next to the pot before sitting in the remaining chair at the table.

Jace ate in silence, and Dani glanced around the room. She'd tended to keep the house tidier when she was there. Now that he was living alone, Jace had a mix of clothing and tools in various places of his room. His bed linens were also in disarray; Dani turned her eyes from the sight. She didn't need the reminder of her brother's extra activities with Hattie.

"Ever think of moving closer to town?" she asked.

"Why would I do that? Too many people." Jace set his spoon aside and brought the bowl to his lips. He slurped the remaining stew until it was gone. He placed the bowl back on the table and leaned back in his chair. "Why are you here, Dani?"

"I wanted to apologize for being angry with you the other day. I never thanked you for coming to Aunt Hattie's to help me with Oliver."

"You thanked Gavin by moving in with him."

Dani's temper began to flare, and she pinched her lips closed so she wouldn't blurt anything back at him. She didn't need a fight; she needed his help, again.

"I'm not living with him, Jace. Near him, yes, but not with him," she said once she'd suppressed enough of her irritation to speak almost nicely.

"Food in those sacks?" he asked with a nod toward the sacks she'd left near the pot.

"Stuff foraged from the forest and fields, plus a little jerky and bread."

"So." Jace narrowed his eyes. "You come here bringing food and apologizing. You even remain polite when I jab you about Gavin. What do you want?"

He had intentionally tried to provoke her, *and* he knew she was up to something. "You can be a real prick, brother."

"Uh-huh. What do you want?"

She was tempted to stall. *This is what I came here for*, she reminded herself. She took a breath. "I want to end this war, Jace."

He leaned forward in his chair. "War? The one between us? You don't care—"

"No, Jace. No, no," she said, ending his rant before he could get going. "*The* war."

Jace flinched at her response. He shook his head. "*You* want to end the war? What exactly does that mean?"

"I'm not signing up with the CNA, so stop freaking out. But what if we—meaning the Brigands—joined forces with the CNA against the Wardens? Not as MPs, but as allies?"

Jace blinked several times without speaking. When he opened his mouth, Dani expected him to say something, but instead he erupted with laughter.

She rolled her eyes. Normally this would be when she'd become so annoyed with him that she'd leave, but she remained planted in her chair.

His laughter subsided when she stayed. "You're not serious."

Dani stared back at him.

"No, Dani, you *cannot* be serious."

"Brigands combined with the Commonwealth are 80 percent of the population. We have the numbers to crush the Wardens and their attempts to take over Earth."

"The Wardens have all the tech. They blow the CNA to bits every time they attack."

"*Yes!* That's my point. The Wardens are always the ones to start a fight. What if the CNA and Brigands did it instead?"

Jace shook his head. "The CNA never attacks first."

"And they get their asses kicked almost every time they only defend. They survive, but they get the shit kicked out of them for it. If we join and attack first, the Wardens will never see it coming, precisely because it's never been done before."

Jace remained silent. Dani took that to mean he was in some form of agreement with her.

"Jace, forget the war for a moment. Biologically speaking, we, Echoes, have the potential to be immortal. The human numbers are still higher than the Echoes', but we'll ultimately outlive them. Used to be uncommon to cross paths with an Echo, right? That's what you told me when I was little. That's not the case anymore. When the humans die, that's it. They're gone. In time, especially with this war killing everyone off, the Echoes will be the only ones left. And the Wardens are only interested in taking Echoes, which means we'll always be hunted until we're all caught or dead."

Jace folded his arms across his chest.

I fucking hate when he does that. She again pushed her irritation aside. "Oliver, Miles, and Hattie, along with every other human friend we have, will die. They'll *all* die, Jace. I can't live with myself if I do nothing and let that happen."

He unfolded his arms and scratched at his beard. "You've lost your mind."

"Be honest, Jace. I have never had a mind. Damn thing keeps resetting on me."

Jace's frown slowly transformed into a wry chuckle at her joke. "Okay, I'll bite. How do you plan on ending the war?"

"We need to bring the Brigands together. Stop operating independently of each other. If we can unite the Brigands, we can fight alongside the CNA."

"You mean join the CNA?"

"No. The Brigand army becomes its own entity. We *partner* with the Commonwealth."

"And you will lead this Brigand army?"

"Gavin will."

Jace erupted again with laughter. "So he's brainwashed you into thinking this is not only possible but is a good idea too?"

"*I* convinced *him*."

Her brother's laughter ended in a startled cough.

"We've always avoided the war, or tried to, but by avoiding it, we've made it worse, Jace."

"The Brigands partner with the CNA, and then what? Team scavenger hunts?"

"We retake Maine from the Wardens."

Jace's mouth dropped open, and his face paled. This was the second time in the span of days Dani had thought she might see her brother die of fright.

CHAPTER
24

When Dani had approached Aunt Hattie about her idea and the older woman hadn't come after her with her ax or thrown her out the door, Dani had assumed that was a good sign. Then Hattie had declared that she would call the council together for Dani to present her proposal. Dani had almost puked at this revelation.

She tended to skulk in the shadows; all of a sudden, she was expected to stand before Bangor's leadership? Dani had hoped Hattie would take the idea to them, but she should have known she wouldn't be that lucky.

The council's response had left Dani disheartened. Some had agreed that the Brigands should organize to help the CNA, but several council members had lashed her with flat refusals and insults, and the rest of the council had refused to commit either way.

Dani sat on the floor in a back room of the brothel surrounded by wiring, pieces of a solar panel, and a battery. Her frustration carried over into her work, and she yelped and dropped the pliers when she pinched her finger with them. Brody's head came up at the sudden noise but dropped back to the floor. His rounded belly, full of food from Mary, was making him lazier than ever. He resumed snoring seconds later. Dani envied the dog's ability to sleep so soundly.

"You okay?" Gavin asked as he entered.

Brody opened his eyes, thumped his tail against the floor a couple of times, and closed his eyes again.

"Yeah." Dani examined her sore finger and rubbed the bruised skin with her index finger.

"I've seen you put these things together in no time, but you've barely started and you've been in here for hours."

"Are you stalking me?"

"Nah. Mary told me you were having a bad day and hiding in here."

Dani frowned. She wanted to say she wasn't hiding, but that's exactly what she was doing.

"Still beating yourself up over the council presentation?"

"I thought it would go better than it did."

"You made a great case for partnering with the Commonwealth, and an even better argument for uniting the Brigands. No one could have done better, Dani."

"You should see the sneers I get when I walk down the street now. I feel like even more of an outcast than before."

"Just wait until they find out you're an Echo too."

"Shut up!" Dani hissed. She leaned around him to make sure no one was near the door. Reassured that it was empty, she punched him in the arm.

Gavin, unaffected by her assault, chuckled and stood. "You're not an outcast. Build your panel sometime today, will you? I'll see you tonight. I have something to show you."

Brody's tail thumped against the floor again when Gavin stopped to pet him for a moment before leaving.

Dani was used to scavenging alone; she enjoyed her independence. This was the first time she'd felt lonely. What was she thinking, trying to unite two enemies that had hated each other for decades? Her attempt to unite just one of the groups had already failed.

She brushed away the tear that escaped her eye, annoyed by her show of emotion.

"You really *are* having a bad day," Mary said as she entered the room carrying two mugs. She handed a mug to Dani before carefully kneeling in her simple blue linen dress. "Quite the shit storm during the council meeting the other night. Lots of stressed-out councilmen and women drowning themselves in alcohol and other activities when it was over. Also lots of talk of uniting the Brigands to form a partnership with the CNA."

Dani grunted and sniffed her mug. Ale. She loved ale. "I can't pay for this."

"It's on me. I think a partnership is a great idea. To the end of the war." Mary lifted her mug.

Dani tapped her mug against Mary's, desperate for the wish to come true. "To the end of the war." She took a sip of the ale and coughed. "What's in here?" she asked before taking another drink.

After swallowing her sip, Mary grinned. "Ale with a shot of courage."

Dani nodded. "I like it." The mixture burned her mouth and throat, left a soothing warmth behind that she enjoyed.

"Thought you might, but you'll want to slow down at bit before it catches up to you." Mary shifted from her knees to her rump and took another drink. "I heard your proposal caused quite the ruckus at the meeting."

"That's me, the stirrer of shit," Dani said with a giggle. She didn't know what was in the mug other than ale, but it had to be Hattie's elixir or something similar. She took another gulp, but a smaller one this time.

Mary smiled. "How is Oliver?"

"He's fine. I saw him and Miles, his father, the other day."

Dani's face was impossibly warm, but she wasn't sweating. Ale would help cool her off, right? She took another sip.

"Don't drink that so quickly, Dani."

"Uh-huh." Dani's eyes remained fixed on the liquid in her mug.

"Miles is handsome," Mary said.

"Uh-huh."

"Gavin is too."

"Yep."

"Planning to sleep with either, or both, of them?"

"Nah."

Mary's eyebrows went up. "I think you should reconsider that decision."

Dani laughed and shook her head. She felt like she was swimming though she was sitting on the floor, and her mug was almost empty now. Her eyes only left the bottom of her mug when Mary leaned in close and kissed her.

Dani was stunned by the act, but didn't pull away from Mary. Instead, she kissed her more deeply, until she tasted the lingering flavor of ale in Mary's mouth. Finally, she ended the kiss—just as a wave of dizziness arrived. She touched the side of her head and winced.

"I told you to drink it more slowly," Mary said.

"Did you drug me?"

Mary frowned. "Of course not."

Dani handed her mug off to Mary. "What's in mine is not in yours. Why not?"

"I'm on the clock, darling. I can't drink the heavier stuff."

"Christ. You're getting me drunk on purpose."

Mary shrugged. "You're stressed out of your mind. You were crying a moment ago."

Dani wanted to leave the room, but she didn't trust her legs to hold her up.

"Do you think I'm trying to take advantage of you?" Mary asked with a frown.

"What other motivation would you have?" Dani pulled her pack close and rummaged in it for a moment before removing her canteen of water. She drank the water fast, trying to dilute the mix of chemicals in her gut.

"Are you so dense that you still don't see how much I like you?"

"Yes—I mean, no. Fuck. I don't know what I mean. I can't think." Dani drained the rest of the water from the canteen. Beads of sweat formed on her face, and she wiped them away.

"I was only trying to help you relax, Dani." Mary stood. "I've never seen you so upset before. You're usually a bit on the gloomy side, all business. I gave you the drink, yeah, but I didn't expect you to gulp it. I warned you. Twice!"

Dani couldn't argue with her; Mary *had* told her to slow down.

"Granted, I probably shouldn't have kissed you, but I couldn't resist when you laughed. I love that sound . . . and don't hear it often enough. I'd never drug or take advantage of you."

Dani remained silent, unsure what to say. Her mind was still so fogged.

Mary shook her head and sighed. "I'll bring you more water."

She left before Dani could apologize. She'd hurt her friend's feelings, and the familiar sensation of feeling like crap returned as the effects of the mug's contents wore off a little. She stood, wobbled, and waited a moment for her legs to steady.

Aunt Hattie appeared in the doorway, glanced at the equipment on the floor, and scowled.

"Glad you don't get paid by the hour, honey."

"I know."

"Hell, I'm glad you don't get paid at all," Hattie said, and she burst into raucous laughter.

"I had a few delays," Dani said when Hattie was done. "I'll finish the build today, promise."

"Good. Your face is flushed."

"Hot flash."

"Ha! You're far too young to be having those. Enough bullshit. The council has decided that if you can convince the CNA to agree with your insane idea, they're willing to talk to them to work out an agreement."

Dani stared at Hattie, certain the chemicals in her system were causing a hallucination.

"That's great news!" Mary stepped past her employer to give Dani a mug of water and placed a second mug on the floor.

"She'll have to pull a magic rabbit out her ass to make the CNA agree first. Good luck—and finish my damn panel!" Hattie swept out of the room.

Mary picked up Dani's canteen. "I'll refill this for you. Just water." When she was done pouring, she turned to leave.

Dani caught her arm. "I'm sorry I accused you of those things, Mary."

"I may have been too forward. I didn't realize how much of a cheap date you are."

"My fault. Did Aunt Hattie really just say what I think she did? I didn't hallucinate that, did I?"

"You heard her right. Congratulations, Dani. There isn't a better person to create this partnership than you. I know you think you're in this alone, but there are a lot of people that will always be on your side. Other than Aunt Hattie, you may be the most-liked Brigand in Bangor."

"Me?"

"It's adorable how clueless you are sometimes. Now, finish that panel before Aunt Hattie skins you alive and makes you the most-dead Brigand in Bangor."

Dani stepped closer to Mary and embraced her. Hugging

wasn't something she'd done since she was much younger, so the action was awkward and stiff, but she felt compelled to do it. "Thank you for being my friend."

"Any time. Next time we have ale, it will be *just* ale, since you clearly can't handle the heavier stuff."

"Deal."

"You're good at kissing, but you suck at hugging." Mary winked at her. "Practice on Brody; he won't mind."

"No, he won't." Dani smiled.

Mary left, and Dani ran her hand through her hair. She was both elated and terrified at Hattie's news. She needed to tell Jace and Gavin—but she had a solar panel to build first. She chugged some more water, sat on the floor, and went to work.

CHAPTER
25

Jace lingered in the shadows between two dilapidated brick buildings that might have been nice apartments pre-war but now served as housing for the poorest Brigands. The stench from the alley—just as frequently used as a latrine as it was a walkway—kept most people away, but he didn't mind the smell. He considered taking the longer and slightly flatter way back to Hattie's after his meeting. Either way, his knees and hips would be killing him by the time he went to visit her.

Moonlight danced on the Penobscot River, and Jace half wished he was spending the night at his home farther upstream instead of with Hattie in the noisy brothel. But the walk home was too far for him to make at the end of a long day. His body was old, worn, and failing him. His worries about his sister had grown exponentially now that she wanted to become involved in the war. He hadn't told her about the pain he'd felt in his chest the night she revealed her idea to attack the Wardens. He knew he'd feel it again tonight after returning to Hattie's. But he would never admit this new symptom of old age to anyone.

The sound of approaching footsteps made him shift his hand to his knife at his belt. Miles's head swiveled as he moved past Jace in the direction of the river, but he didn't see Jace standing near the wall. Jace made a hissing sound, and Miles froze.

Jace removed his hand from his knife. "You move like a goddamn moose." The arthritis in his hands had stolen his strength years ago; he couldn't defend himself well against an attacker anymore. Luckily, his gruff manner tended to bluff most into thinking he was still a tough bastard.

Miles's shoulders relaxed as he turned.

Jace waited, allowing Miles to suffer a little longer before speaking again.

"I'm sorry I can't move with the shadows," Miles said, still unable to place exactly where Jace was standing.

"A skill Dani can't seem to learn," Jace said, stepping out of the shadows.

"You're the only Brigand who moves quieter than she does. You taught her well."

"Not well enough in regards to surviving. Entering the war will put her at risk in a way I never meant for her to experience."

"I don't like it either, Jace." Miles turned his attention to the glittering river. "This area might be called Hell, but the river is beautiful tonight."

"Used to be called Devil's Half-Acre. In the 1830s, Bangor was a booming town, and this was where the poorest of the poor lived. Shit literally flowed downhill from the rich bastards living in their mansions on the hill when their outhouses flooded during heavy rains. Dangerous place. Full of disease until the city finally cleaned things up. After the war started, it degraded back into that state, but they shortened the name to Hell." He snorted. "That's assuming everything Hattie told me about this place is true."

"It's still a dangerous place." Miles sighed. "The CNA meeting is just over three weeks from today. I still don't have a way to get Dani or Gavin in to meet them. The few officers I've talked to among the MPs have laughed me off."

"The MPs aren't interested in a partnership either?"

Miles shrugged. "Not the ones I've talked to—or maybe they're just in shock over the whole idea, like I was when Oliver first blurted it out. Of course, I was in shock over a few things that day."

The problem with meeting in dark places was being unable to read the other person's face. Jace was annoyed that he couldn't get any kind of read from Miles's body language, except when he shrugged or waved his hand. Without more physical clues, Jace had to rely on listening for pitch changes in the MP's voice. Thus far, he didn't believe the other man was lying.

"Any talk within the CNA, not just MPs, of them wanting to take the offensive to the Wardens?" he asked.

"Nothing that I've heard."

"Arrange for Gavin to meet them. Him only."

Miles turned to face Jace. "You want to leave Dani out of this; I get it. So do I, but she won't sit this one out."

"I don't want her anywhere near CNA brass or in the MP barracks. I don't trust any of them. Hell, I don't trust *you*. But I'm willing to help her do what she wants—as long as she's kept safe. She isn't safe inside the barracks."

Miles shook his head. "I know you hate me. I'm why you had to raise her again. Jace, I'm not asking for us to be friends, but I can't ask Dani to stay out of this meeting. The whole thing is *her* idea. She must be involved."

"The day you shot her—accidentally, yes, I know—Dani told me you warned her about the MP raid on C Block. You didn't want her to scavenge that day. I didn't either, but she didn't listen. She told me you would never arrest her. When I asked her why you wouldn't, she said she thought you loved her."

Miles slumped slightly. "I did. I do."

"She stopped listening to me years ago, but I think she remembers some of her history with you. As much as I hate it, I think she's still in love with you. I'm old and only half Echo. I may not regen. Someone needs to look after her in my absence. She's different this time, Miles. I think she'll listen to you."

"You just said you don't trust me."

"I did say that, but I'll do whatever needs to be done, including put my biases aside, if it's what is best for her. You would do the same for Oliver, right? Convince her to let other people do the fighting. Keep her away from the war." He wasn't lying about doing whatever he must, and that included playing on Miles's feelings for Dani.

Miles remained silent; he returned his attention to the river.

"Well?" Jace asked.

Miles sighed. "You said Dani has changed. So have you. Does Dani know you're trying to subvert her plan? No? I didn't think so. Smart to try to play on my emotions, but you're a real asshole for trying to manipulate me by dragging Dani and Ollie into your game. This partnership could work with the right people involved, and Dani is a requirement for the meeting. You, on the other hand, can go fuck yourself."

Jace tightened his jaw with disgust. "You and Gavin are so in love with her you can't see that this plan is ridiculous. You're encouraging her."

"Yeah, we are certainly guilty of loving her. You're her brother; you should be encouraging her too. You disappoint me, Jace."

"I don't need your approval."

"You apparently don't need Dani's, either."

Jace growled at Miles and took a step toward him. The insult cut him more deeply than the MP knew—or maybe he did know. Tightness gripped his chest, and Jace retreated a step.

Reflexively, his hand went to the center of his chest, where the pain was located.

"Jace?"

"Shut up. People are coming." Jace forced his hand off his chest and to his knife.

Miles shifted deeper into the shadows to stand next to him, but Jace kept his eyes turned toward the alley. Two men hurried past without speaking. Jace leaned his back against the building, hidden from sight, as they passed. The tightness in his chest eased a little, and he released the breath he held.

The men continued toward the river, and Miles touched Jace's arm. "The one with short hair is an MP," he whispered. "Name's Xander."

"The other is the Brigand everyone is still searching for," Jace said. "The one who attacked Dani." His pain forgotten for the moment, he pulled his knife from its sheath. "His name is Alan, I think, but he goes by Al."

"Before you go killing him, let's find out what they're doing here. I already knew Xander was trouble, but I want to know exactly what he's doing with that Brigand."

"Try not to be a damn moose." Without a sound, Jace started following the men, staying within the darkest shadows.

Xander and Al often turned to glance behind them, but they didn't see or hear Jace—or Miles, who was thankfully managing not to make as much noise as he had before.

Xander and Al stopped under a tree near the river next to a broken and buckled concrete walkway, once a scenic path through the park, which was now overgrown with brush and trees. Jace and Miles hovered a few feet away and kept their silence, waiting for the other two men to speak.

CHAPTER

26

Rowan studied the twenty-foot-by-twenty-foot wall displaying a digital representation of New England with his hands clasped behind his back. He tilted his head, eyeing the map for a moment, before approaching it. He released his hands and used his finger to shift the map's visual range. Hartford, Providence, and Boston were clustered close enough together that they could easily shift resources between them. He considered even Manchester, New Hampshire, close to Boston. Like Maine, Vermont and New Hampshire were more trees than anything else.

He touched the controls on the wall to focus more on Vermont. Burlington was close enough to Montreal for supply runs, and the Wardens holding the Canadian city were firmly entrenched, with plenty of resources. He shifted the map across to Maine.

Curtis was right.

"Nothing but fucking trees," Rowan said.

He turned to make sure he hadn't woken his son with his outburst. Devon slept in a ball on a small couch in the corner of the briefing room. The top left of the screen showed the time: 2249. Rowan should have taken him home already, but the boy was a handful. He wanted Ana to have time for herself. She loved to read and couldn't do that if Devon was awake and getting into everything. The boy always woke at least once during the night, so Rowan planned to wait until that happened and then take him home late. In another month his daughter would be born; the thought made Rowan smile.

He returned his attention to the map and moved it beyond Maine's borders. Quebec City's river access was perfectly located for shipments up from Montreal, or even coming from London. He could do a lot for the Wardens and control the entire northeastern corner of North America if he was in charge of a place like Quebec City. He'd have plenty of room to expand the Wardens' reach as Vice Regent of the Northeast.

Brigands continued to occupy the more rural locations of the continent, and that irritated him. The Brigands often made attempts to unify themselves but never succeeded; only a dozen or so people ever figured out how to work together before everything fell apart.

Except Bangor.

Rowan shifted the map back to Maine and stared at the town tucked almost in the center of the state. The town was a shithole, but it had river access and was centrally located. HQ didn't care about anything but Portland and the southern portion of Maine, but Rowan did. Bangor's Brigands were more organized than they had any right to be. They didn't pose a threat to the Wardens, but Rowan wanted to obliterate the town, along with the Brigands and small CNA base there, just for the sake of wiping the vermin off *his* planet.

Xander had his orders to disrupt the Brigand community in Bangor, but the Brigands he'd hired to start a fight with the MPs had suffered a spectacular failure. Rowan was still furious about it. Xander's new orders were to finish cleaning up the mess he'd created.

A soft beep at the door drew his attention away from his hatred for Earth's civilian human population. He opened the door and found one of his aides waiting.

She snapped to attention. "Sir, sorry to bother you so late, but we have our latest captures from western Maine."

"Good. Follow the usual protocol with them tonight. Don't wait until morning. No need to waste resources on humans overnight when we can terminate them now."

"Yes, sir." She turned to leave.

"Where's Curtis?"

"R and D, sir."

"Thank you." Rowan closed the door and wondered what the research department had come up with that required Curtis's attention so late. Devon stirred, and he decided answering that question could wait. He picked him up. *Time to go home.*

He got the boy settled in his own bed, then checked in on Ana. She was sitting up in bed, her thumb holding her place in a book at her side. Her eyes were closed, and she appeared to be sleeping.

He kissed her forehead, and she smiled. "You're finally home."

"Not yet. I need to head back out, but I'll be back soon. Promise."

She pulled him closer and kissed him.

"No more than an hour," he said.

"Better make it less than that if you want me still awake."

"Deal."

He arrived at the door marked Research and Development and entered. R&D crews worked around the clock under his orders, and the team was responsible for a significant portion of new technology used by Wardens across the globe. The war had stunted space travel, so he always kept a portion of the team working on that project. The Ekkoh ships that had brought his people to Earth had been destroyed—foolishly—by that generation of Ekkohrians. They cited humanitarian reasons for destroying the space tech, altering their DNA to blend in with the humans, and integrating themselves into society. They had periodically made significant scientific "discoveries" to benefit the humans and help them along in their quest for whatever they were trying to accomplish with their existence. Rowan just wanted an aerial pesticide to wipe them out.

If the Wardens could recreate their old ships, the war would be over in a day. Rowan wanted his R&D team to be the ones to accomplish the feat. Then he'd be free of Brigands, the CNA, and Maine's fucking trees. That kind of victory would get him promoted to regent and running the entire continent.

Tonight, though, Curtis was busy playing with a new combat helmet.

"Rowan! You must see this." Curtis grinned as he pulled the helmet off.

"I want weapons, Curtis, not toys." Rowan took the helmet from his second-in-command and frowned.

"You'll like this one. Put it on." Curtis turned to one of the technicians. "Cut the lights once he has it on."

Rowan pulled the helmet on. The soft padding auto-conformed to create a custom fit to his head, but left openings around his ears. He shifted his jaw; he liked not having a strap confining his movement. "The fit is nice. Snug but not too tight."

"It has enhanced audio so we don't sound muffled," Curtis said. "How do you like the night vision?"

Curtis's voice was indeed clear. Their current helmets

slightly obscured voices from those not also wearing a helmet with a linked comm. As for the night vision . . . "Turn off the lights, and I'll let you know."

Curtis grinned. "They are off."

Rowan didn't believe him. He removed the helmet, swore in the darkness, and put the helmet back on.

"Great, isn't it?" Curtis said, sounding gleeful.

"I can see everything."

"Yeah, and watch this." Curtis put another helmet on.

Rowan saw his face as though no visor existed. The helmet's shell wrapped around Curtis's head and his face appeared exposed, though it wasn't.

"Well done!" Rowan slapped his friend on the back.

Curtis removed his helmet. "We're shipping a prototype and plans to Boston tomorrow, but we have everything we need to mass produce them here. Our Wardens will be the first group to use them. It will take us some months before all our troops are equipped, since we are still getting new arrivals, but—"

"Perfect!" Rowan took his helmet off. He congratulated each of the technicians in the room on their success before leaving with Curtis.

"There are a few other things in the works to show you," Curtis said as they walked.

Rowan nodded. "I'll come by tomorrow. Ana has ordered me home tonight. I want to talk to you about Bangor."

"Again?"

"We need that town."

"The VR isn't giving her blessing to move in."

"I know. And my contact botched his assignment. He hired Brigands to attack the MPs to stir up tensions there, but the Brigands went after MP families instead."

"Even better. Attacking family members would really piss off the police."

Rowan shook his head. "No. Another Brigand interfered, stopped the whole thing, killed one of the attackers, and the MPs let it all go. The police still should have retaliated, but they didn't."

"Okay, so the Brigands are fighting each other now. This is still a good thing."

"Again, no. The Brigands caught the attacker that escaped and are still hunting for the other one. They're more organized in Bangor than we realized. They have their own justice system in place for crimes against each other. I've given my contact orders to kill the two idiots he hired to sever that link back to us."

"What does it matter if they find out Wardens were involved?" Curtis shook his head. "They can't come after us."

Rowan shook his head. "I want them to think their own kind are the biggest immediate threat. They can't be allowed to organize like this, Curtis. We need to put them down forever. File another request to Boston in the morning. Send a request every goddamn day if you must. I want the green light."

"Will do."

Rowan nodded and left his friend to return home. If he hurried, Ana would still be up and waiting for him when he got there.

CHAPTER

27

Dani straightened and stretched her back, stiff from leaning over the table of maps. She walked to the wall—covered with more maps—and rubbed her eyes before stepping closer to inspect the updated sketch of the Warden compound in Portland. Parts of the base were detailed with numerous small notes. Other parts were swaths of blank paper, waiting to be filled in.

The lanterns in Gavin's one-room home provided enough light for them to continue planning after dark, but after a few hours of studying the lines and notations, the low light was beginning to cause some strain.

Gavin caught her rubbing her tired eyes. "Why don't you take a break?" he asked. "Ale?"

She recalled her latest experience drinking ale. "Water, please."

"Really?" He knew she loved ale.

"It didn't sit well with me the last time I had it." She tapped her finger against the largest blank spots on the compound sketch. "We need to bring in Miles and Jace on this. Miles has knowledge of what's in the barracks, and Jace knows Portland like the back of his hand. I, meanwhile, can't remember a damn thing."

"Their information is fifteen years old, Dani. This is the best current intel we can get, short of going down there ourselves." Gavin handed her a mug of water.

She took the mug and stared at him.

He shook his head. "No. No!"

"I like that idea."

"That's what terrifies me. No, Dani. Jace will kill me, literally *kill* me, permanently, if I take you to Portland to snoop around."

"Take me? I don't need your permission."

"But you do need my help."

Dani sipped her water; he had her there. She returned her attention to the wall maps. "Your contacts are confident the terrain maps are accurate?"

"Yeah. Topos are good. There's been some additional construction; they're still researching what it's for. They've been trying to keep track of weapons shipments, but stuff is constantly moving in and out, as are transport trucks and helos. The guy who runs the place makes rounds every day. He's always making changes to schedules, troop rotations, everything."

"The inconsistencies could be a problem."

Gavin nodded. "Yeah, which is why we need *this* map." He stared at the mostly blank piece of paper, three feet long and two feet wide, lying on the table. "The sewers will likely be our best way in and out."

"Mmm, can't wait to be crawling around in shit."

Gavin chuckled.

Dani frowned. "If trucks are going in and out, could it be a manufacturing site?"

"It's possible. My people found the demo area where they're firing off new weapons, but they can't get close enough to see what the weapons actually are."

"Damn. It would be nice to know what they're up to. Other birds?"

Gavin moved to stand next to her and took a drink from his mug. He pointed to the runways, indicated by long lines on the compound diagram. "They have at least three fighter planes that stay armed with bombs, but my contacts have never seen the jets leave. The Wardens are holding them in reserve—or, if we're lucky, they simply lack the fuel to put them in the air much."

"What kind of firepower do they carry?"

"Long- and short-range missiles. Dual high-caliber-round guns on the front and four incendiary bombs strapped to the belly."

"Fuck."

"Yeah."

"We need to assume they're operational."

"Yep."

"Guards?"

Gavin shrugged. "They have regular patrols, but overall the base isn't swarming with people on the outside. Hell, they don't even bother trying to encrypt on-base communication anymore."

"What about guards around the planes?"

"Light. Why?"

"Just thinking. Security is light, and they don't care who intercepts messages. They don't fear an attack from anyone, which means they'll never see us coming." Dani had an idea about how to immobilize the planes without destroying them. Warden fighter planes in CNA hands would be a nice win.

Gavin disagreed. "We'll show up as bright little dots on their radar miles before we arrive."

"Not if we're wearing CNA skins."

"CNA tech lags behind the Wardens', always. The suits may not work if the Wardens upgrade their radar." He stopped and looked at her. "Wait. How do you know about skin tech?"

"You're not the only one who steals from the CNA," she

said, echoing his words to her the day he revealed he owned a MedPanel.

"You're assuming the CNA will agree to meet with us."

"We don't need them to agree."

Gavin placed his mug aside and turned his full attention to her. "What are you talking about?"

"The CNA meeting will happen whether they want it or not, Gavin. I've been inside the MP barracks, many times. You and I both can slip in without being caught."

"So if they don't agree to us joining their meeting, you plan to crash it. Great." Gavin sighed and shook his head. "Now I understand why Jace looks much older than he is—and he probably doesn't know half the shit you do on a daily basis."

"No." Dani laughed. "Hey, why have we stopped hand-to-hand training for so long?"

"You needed time to heal."

"I've been healed."

"There isn't much more I can teach you."

She realized he was avoiding the topic. "Can I beat you?"

"No."

Dani took a long drink from her mug before setting it on the table. "Then there is more to teach me. Let's go." She headed for the door.

Brody trotted out behind her, and headed off toward the trees. Dani stretched her arms and shoulders, waiting for Gavin to emerge. They had decent light from the moon, and tonight would still be a good warm-up after time off from training.

Gavin started by throwing light attacks at her, each of which she easily defended, though he effortlessly swatted aside her more aggressive counters. His punches to her side when she failed to protect her ribs landed with enough force to make her stumble, but he didn't work her as hard as he had the last time they trained.

Dani dropped her hands after he landed another soft hit. "What the hell is wrong with you? You're pulling your punches."

He shrugged. "Your movements are still stiff. How's your back?"

"Cut the shit, man. I'm fine."

"I don't want to hurt you."

"When did that change? You kicked my ass at the Standpipe. You had no issues leaving me in pain that day."

"And because of that, you had a difficult time when those men attacked you later."

Dani shook her head. "That wasn't your fault. I was fine by the time I ran into them. Granted, you never taught me how to fight with a child attached to my leg, but we can call that one a fluke. The stairs falling apart in the Standpipe wasn't your fault either."

He stepped closer and touched her cheek. "When Jace and I arrived and saw you like that, it killed me. You were in so much pain. I never trained you to deal with that kind of fighting. It *is* my fault you were injured that day, and I'm sorry."

He leaned toward her, and she put her hand on his chest and lowered her head. He was going to kiss her, and she wanted him to—God, she wanted him to—but she couldn't let him. The feel of his chest beneath her palm weakened her resistance; all she wanted was to kiss him and drag him back into his house, all the way to his bed. She let her hand fall and took a step back.

"What's wrong?" he asked.

"Miles."

Gavin tightened his jaw. "You remembered your life with him."

"No. I don't remember a damn thing. That's the problem. You were there; you saw his reaction when I told him I didn't know him. It ripped his fucking heart out. If anything happens to me, I'll forget you. Do you really want that heartache too?"

"I'm already in that boat, Dani."

Her brow creased. "What does that mean?"

"I love you."

Dani stared at him for a moment before blinking. It took her another moment before she could speak. "I care about you, Gavin. I do."

"But?"

"I want to wait."

"Why?"

"Can we revisit this after we retake Maine?"

"After retaking Maine?! Jesus, Dani, we don't even know when we're going to Portland."

"This winter," she said without hesitation, "six months or so. We need to attack around January, worst part of the season. It'll be stupid cold and a perfect time to hit them—when they're freezing their balls off. Plus, I need the extra time to focus on becoming as good a fighter as you, or at least as close as I can get."

Gavin shook his head and frowned.

Dani took his hand. "You're not understanding me. I need you to teach me everything you can in that time so we're *both* still around after Portland. Let's get past that part first."

Gavin squeezed her hand. "It won't be easy for me to wait."

"Please trust me when I say it won't be easy for me either."

"Okay." He released her hand. "So we're back to just business for a while."

"Yeah, but you have to work me harder than before."

"You don't understand what you're getting yourself into, Dani."

"I never do, but I intend to be neck deep in the fight."

"I'll make sure you're ready."

Dani smiled. "Thanks. I'll come by in the morning to start."

She went inside his house to grab her pack. When she came

back outside, she whistled; she heard Brody's heavy feet thundering through the brush long before she saw his form emerge from the trees. He arrived panting and wagging his tail.

"He's got some basic commands down, but he needs more," she told Gavin. "Can you work with him too?" she asked.

"No, but I know the MP who runs the Bangor K-9 unit. We were in the marines together."

"Echo?"

"Human. He's in his seventies, but don't let his age fool you."

"Noted. Handy contact on the inside. See you in the morning."

CHAPTER

28

iles inched closer to hear the conversation between Xander and Al. The moonlight helped him identify each man by their silhouette, but the overall darkness of the night made it difficult for him to clearly see their faces.

"Where's my money?" Al asked.

"Money?" Xander spat back. "You're as stupid as the rest of the Brigands. You weren't supposed to leave any witnesses, and you left plenty. How's life in Hell? It must be as shitty as it smells down here. Fucking Brigands."

"You hired us to provoke the MPs, and we did."

"Hardly. Dani took one of you out, and your other partner was caught. The Brigand council promised to handle the issue on their own, and they will once they find you."

Miles tilted his head. It seemed odd to him that Xander would know Dani by name. Sure, Brigands knew her, but he was an MP.

"You can't do anything to me, Xan. You'll be shot for treason when the MPs find out you're working for the Wardens."

Xander's arm arced out in a blur of motion. Al stumbled back, clutching his throat. Blood sprayed out from between his fingers. He made a few gurgling sounds before collapsing under the tree.

"Not if they don't know," Xander said with a shrug.

Xander had attacked the Brigand so quickly, Miles hadn't had a chance to stop him from killing the other man. Miles reached for his service weapon and realized it wasn't there. He'd dressed as a Brigand to meet Jace, so he didn't have his pistol. They were impossible to conceal when wearing threadbare and tattered civilian garments. He gripped the hilt of his knife and emerged from the darker shadows, Jace beside him.

"Drop your weapon, Xander," Miles said.

Xander's eyes widened with momentary surprise that turned to a sneer. He turned the knife in his hand and wiped Al's blood from his face with his other hand. "Always the pain in my ass, Miles."

Miles stalked closer. Jace held his own blade ready as he knelt to check the fallen man.

"Dead?" Miles asked without taking his eyes from Xander.

"No, but he will be in a few more seconds," Jace said. "An MP killing Brigands is bad news for MPs in Brigand territory. Good luck getting out of this one alive."

"Drop the knife, Xander," Miles said. "You're under arrest."

Xander laughed. "For killing a Brigand?"

"Murder and treason." Miles really wished he had his plasma pistol instead of a knife. He'd killed the last MP he'd caught murdering Brigands, and he wanted to avoid having to kill another one.

"Treason? You're taking the word of this piece of shit?" Xander pointed his blade at Al.

"I am."

"You're pathetic, stupid—and alone."

Miles flicked his eyes to the side. Al's corpse remained at the base of the tree, and Jace had vanished. *Shit.*

Xander lunged forward, and Miles darted aside. The blade still sliced through Miles's shirt and caught the skin on his ribs. He winced at the injury, hating Xander more for his youth and speed. He wanted him arrested, not dead, but if forced to kill him, he would.

"Add slow to that list," Xander said.

When Xander attacked again, Miles moved in to close the distance faster. He caught Xander's wrist and twisted it to lock the joint, immobilizing his arm. Then he drove the grip end of his knife into the side of the younger man's head. Miles kept his hold as Xander stumbled from the blow.

Despite being off balance, Xander managed to swing one leg out and clip Miles's knee. Both men toppled into each other. Xander righted himself first, and Miles cried out in pain when Xander's blade cut across his left jaw, leaving a deep gash. Miles rolled away from the follow-up attack, and Xander's knife stabbed into the ground, all the way up to the hilt.

Miles rolled back toward Xander and drove his blade into his thigh.

Xander howled with pain. He growled and yanked his knife from the dirt. The pair tumbled on the ground, kicking and punching each other when able, and both men lost their weapons in the struggle.

Xander slammed his fist into Miles's already wounded jaw, and Miles was stunned by the fresh wave of pain. He blinked a few times, and his vision cleared enough to see the stone Xander was holding in his hand. As he swung the stone downward, Miles got one arm up, just in time to keep the blow from connecting with his skull.

Pain filled his arm at the impact. He swung his uninjured arm up and grabbed Xander's throat. He squeezed as hard as possible before realizing Xander had stopped fighting. The young man's staring eyes turned toward the blade lodged in his chest.

Jace grabbed Xander from behind and pulled him away from Miles. He let the dying MP fall.

Miles sat up and tried to catch his breath and process everything.

"Think you'll live?" Jace asked him.

"Uh, yeah." Miles's jaw and arm throbbed, but he was still alive.

Jace picked up Miles's knife and stooped to pick up Xander's as well.

"Stop!" Miles snapped. "Don't touch his blade."

Jace's hand hung in the air a moment before he righted himself. "You and me, we're deep in the shit now. MP kills a Brigand, Brigand kills the MP. Folks are coming after all that noise."

Miles held his injured arm close to his body as he stood. People were indeed approaching. Three people came out of one of the buildings and joined two others heading toward the river. Xander's eyes stared lifelessly at the sky. Miles placed his hand on the knife still lodged in Xander's chest. He moved his palm and fingers over the grip, replacing Jace's fingerprints with his own and transferring Xander's blood to his hand.

"Do you have any of his blood on you?" Miles asked.

"No."

"Good. Remove my sheath from my belt and put it on yours. Put your sheath on my belt. Hurry. Stop thinking so much, and do it!"

Once Jace's sheath was attached to his belt, Miles used the lower part of his shirt to wipe it clean of any of Jace's fingerprints. He then smudged the sheath with his own fingers. "Now wipe my knife and take it as yours."

Jace nodded. "What about you?"

"The MPs would execute you for killing an MP, but I think I can get myself cleared as acting in self-defense."

"So, you want me as your witness?"

"I want you to send someone to Hattie's to contact the MPs and keep the Brigands from hanging me until the police arrive."

Jace squinted at him.

"What? We don't have much time left before the civilians get here."

"You're really taking the blame?"

"Yes."

"Why?"

"Because you need to be around for Dani, not executed and in a grave."

"Huh," Jace said.

Miles wiped at the blood dripping from his jaw and winced at the tenderness around the laceration. "What?"

The footsteps neared, now only twenty or so paces away, and Miles raised his hands, palms out, to show he held no weapon. His arm throbbed worse with the movement, but he still held it up.

"Maybe you're not as stupid as I thought," Jace said.

Miles would have smiled at the sideways compliment, but his face hurt and the Brigands had arrived. Jace intervened while Miles remained silent, his hands raised. One of the men left for Hattie's immediately; he increased his pace from a walk to a sprint when Jace yelled at him.

It seemed liked forever before the MPs arrived in their trucks. Miles was exhausted and sore from his fight with Xander. Two officers interviewed him and Jace while others examined the bodies and gathered evidence. They scanned the weapons, and the blood and fingerprints matched the story Miles had given them of Xander's collaboration with the Brigands that attacked the MP families. They also bought the slightly concocted version of the fight he told them. Jace, deemed merely a witness to two MPs fighting, was allowed to leave, and Miles rode back to the barracks with the officers and corpses.

To keep Jace out of an MP jail and away from the executioner, Miles needed to take this secret to his grave. It would torture him to lie to Oliver and Dani, but Miles mostly wanted Dani to continue to believe her brother was just an overprotective curmudgeon—not a killer who would stab another man when he wasn't looking. Jace had saved Miles's life, but Miles didn't think for one second that Jace had done it out of goodness. Jace had wanted Al dead; Xander had just beaten him to it. He'd been after blood, and he'd gotten it.

CHAPTER
29

nstead of the twice-a-day training Dani assumed she'd be getting, Gavin insisted on working with her all day. He began teaching her how to shoot, beyond what Jace had taught her as a teenager, and showing her how to set traps to take down people, not rabbits. She enjoyed the first day. The second day she hated him. He made her run with him to establish the route and pace he wanted her to complete every other day. Following the run, she found a place to sit and rest. He barked at her to get on her feet. When she did, he charged and tackled her. Fighting while standing was a different matter than fighting on the ground, and he pummeled her.

He didn't coach her as before, by showing her a technique and then letting her try it; instead, he flattened her, told her everything she was doing wrong, made her get up, and then clobbered her again.

Brody wasn't concerned with the punishment Gavin was giving her—though a couple of times, when she was on her back, out of breath, and in pain, he did come over and lick her face. She appreciated his support but secretly wished he would bite Gavin at least once when he pulled some crazy Judo shit and sent her crashing to the ground.

"You'll learn to protect your exposed sides, or I'll break every one of your fucking ribs," Gavin told her that morning.

She did finally protect her left side, and when she did, he drilled her left thigh with a vicious punch instead. She cursed him while lying crumpled on the ground. She was pretty sure getting kicked by a mule would hurt less than taking his punches.

"There are no rules when you're fighting for your life, Dani," he said. "You need to play dirty and expect the same from your opponent."

She grumbled in response.

"You have four hours to scavenge or lie on the ground," he said. "Be at Hayford Park by 1300. We're meeting Javi to start work with Brody." With that, he walked away.

After two full days of training with Gavin, plus this morning, lying on the ground sounded like a great idea. Dani couldn't imagine what kind of permanent damage one of his punches to the head could cause. Or what a kick from him would feel like. Thus far he'd only tripped her or swept a leg out from under her. Dani figured a kick to her middle would forever transplant her spleen into her neck. But she'd asked for this torment, and Gavin was just delivering.

She forced herself to her feet and limped to her pack, cursing him with each step. She took a long drink of water and decided to use the next four hours, time she now regarded as a break between beatings, to find food and her brother. Brody had eaten more than she had in the last two days. As for Jace, he was probably in town. She shouldered her pack and started the three-and-a-half-mile walk to Aunt Hattie's. It was on the way to Hayford Park, so she could take a break and rest before venturing into MP territory.

The knot in her thigh eased the longer she walked; by the time she started up the gentle hill that would take her through the middle of the town, her limp was almost gone.

Brody had quickly learned the way to Aunt Hattie's, and he raced ahead. By the time Dani arrived, Mary was standing at the back of the brothel. She rushed to meet Dani in the street.

Dani frowned. "What's wrong?"

"Where have you been?" Mary demanded. "Shit hits the fan and you vanish?"

"I didn't vanish. I've been training"—*getting tortured*—"by, I mean, *with* Gavin. What happened? Where's Jace?"

"He's not here. He said he had business in Waterville and borrowed Aunt Hattie's car. He left the morning after Miles killed that MP."

Dani shook her head. "*What?*"

"God, you're clueless . . . as usual." Mary took Dani by the elbow and ushered her toward the house. Brody bounced around them as they walked, expecting food, but they ignored the dog.

Without a word, Mary led Dani to the same room she had borrowed before. "Sit."

Dani was alarmed by Mary's urgency, but she gladly dropped her pack on the floor and put her rump in the offered chair.

Mary closed the door and sat on the other side of the small, round table in the room.

"When did you last see Jace?"

"Uh, what's today?"

"Tuesday."

Dani stared at the ceiling for a moment, thinking back over the last few days. *Today is Tuesday, so Monday was the ass kicking from Gavin. Sunday was weapons training. Saturday, Gavin tried to kiss me.* "Saturday morning, or midday, something like that."

"Saturday night there was a fight in Hell. This MP named Xander murdered Al after Al said something about how he was working for the Wardens."

Dani blanched. *Xan, a murderer?*

"Miles was there and tried to arrest Xander, but everything went wrong. He killed Xander. Jace saw it happen, told the MPs his side of things, and they let him go. Miles is back at the barracks, confined to quarters, until the investigation is complete, but he should get off with acting in self-defense."

"How do you know all this?"

"Jace came here that night, and I brought him something to drink while he told Aunt Hattie what happened. He said Miles should be cleared of any charges. He was sweaty and pale, Dani. When he thought no one was looking, I saw him put his hand on his chest like this. . . ." Mary placed the palm of her hand on the center of her chest with her fingers splayed. "He took several deep breaths every time he did it."

"Heart attack?"

"I don't know. Aunt Hattie wanted to call the town doc to come see him, but Jace refused. He went to Aunt Hattie's room for the night and left early the next morning for Waterville."

"Anyone with him?"

Mary shook her head.

Dani ran her hand through her hair. She and her brother fought often, but she didn't want him dropping dead from a heart attack. Until he died, there was no way of knowing if he would heal like an Echo. He was having chest pain and leaving town alone. She didn't have a way to track or catch up to him.

"There's more," Mary said. "It didn't matter to the council that Al was a piece of shit; they were pissed that an MP killed him. Even if you could get the CNA to meet with them, the council would still reject the merger now, based on the Commonwealth's interference in Brigand matters."

Dani leaned her elbows on the table and dropped her head in her hands. Everything had unraveled in a matter of hours—and she hadn't found out until days later.

Mary stood and placed her hand on Dani's shoulder. "I'm sorry to hit you with all this at once. Can I bring you anything?"

"No, thanks. I need time to think."

"Stay as long as you like. Aunt Hattie's blocked this room for non-brothel-related business."

"Thank you."

Mary left, and Dani leaned back in the chair. Her mind raced and her thoughts collided with each other, creating a jumbled mess. She reached into her pack and removed an item wrapped in cloth. Dani unwound the fabric, revealing an antique revolver. Despite his prior, repeated refusals to let her carry a weapon other than a knife, after the Standpipe incident, Jace had brought her the weapon and told her to keep it with her.

She didn't like the weapon: it was old and heavy, and if she needed more than six rounds, she was out of luck. She wanted a plasma pistol, but Jace said he didn't have one. The weapon now lived in her pack, since she never planned to use it.

She removed another cloth from her pack and began the task of dismantling the weapon. The pistol was clean, but she didn't care. The tedium of cleaning or tinkering with things engaged a different part of her brain, which helped her think. Her racing mind kept her up many nights, so when she couldn't sleep, she tinkered.

Brody settled on a rug on the floor and napped while Dani removed the shells from the weapon. She set them aside and turned her attention to the other parts of the gun. As she manipulated the parts, she ran through the list of things Mary had told her, sorting through them one at a time.

Miles killed Xan. Why? Xan was a prick, sure, but killing him seemed extreme, even if he had been working for the Wardens. She'd have to talk to Miles about that, assuming Miles was cleared and released. *Shit. What is Oliver doing during all this?*

Jace might have heart issues and was too stubborn to see a doctor. *Shocker.* Brigands lived a hard life, but they could still obtain medical care with the right connections. And no one was better connected than Aunt Hattie. *What the hell is in Waterville?*

She had no ideas on how to salvage the CNA–Brigand partnership that hadn't even had a chance to begin.

Dani placed the cleaned gun on the table with the cylinder open. She wiped one of the shells with the cloth and rolled the shiny, brass-covered bullet in her fingers. *The ultimate sleeping pill*, she thought. *For a human, not an Echo.*

A soft knock on the door diverted her attention from the shell.

Brody leapt from the rug to the door and yipped.

"Go away, Oliver," Dani said.

He opened the door and stepped in, welcomed by the dog.

Dani wiped the shell to make sure it was free of any oil from her fingers before inserting it into the pistol's chamber. She picked up the next bullet and held it between her thumb and fingertip.

"Mary told me you were here," Oliver said.

He moved to stand next to the table but kept his hands away from the weapon and ammunition. Dani figured the boy had watched his father clean his service weapon many times, and knew better than to touch anything. She shook her head. "I need to talk to Mary about what 'time to think' means. Why are you here? Shouldn't you be at the barracks?"

"Dad's not arrested, but he can't leave. I waited every day for you at Union Street, but you never showed."

"I didn't know any of that stuff happened until today."

"I sent you a message."

Dani inserted the second round into the gun and wiped her hands with the cloth. "What message?"

"The comm Dad gave you."

"Oh." Dani dug through her pack. She removed the unit and a light on it blinked. "Sorry. I haven't been in my bag at all the last couple of days."

She tossed the comm on the table and set to work cleaning the remaining four shells. Once they were loaded back into the gun, she snapped the chamber closed. "What does your mother think of you bailing on school so often? Neither you nor Miles ever mention her."

"Her name is . . . was . . . Emily. She died three years ago trying to save Brigands from Warden capture."

Dani softened. "That must have been difficult."

"She always told me it was her job as an MP to help the Brigands, because one saved her life a long time ago."

"Hmm, MPs and Brigands helping each other. Too bad that idea has been shot to hell."

"I wish she was here to help you, Dani," Oliver said quietly. "You would've liked her."

Dani winced. "Shit. I'm sorry, Oliver. I'm sure she was a great person. I didn't mean to make a bad day worse by dragging your mom into it."

"It's okay to have bad days, but I don't think you should be messing with a gun when you're neck deep in a pity party."

Her temper flared at this remark, but Oliver didn't say anything else to her. He had turned his attention to Brody. He rubbed his head, and the dog's tail wagged in a blur.

Dani wrapped the weapon back in its cloth and slipped it into her pack. "Ready?" she asked.

"For what?"

"I'm taking you home." She stood. "Shit!" She leaned against the table for a moment, crippled by a thigh cramp.

"What's wrong?" Oliver asked.

"My leg is sore. It's fine." She straightened.

When Oliver scooped up her pack, she didn't argue. Her limp had returned, and she hobbled her way out of the room. Brody trotted ahead, followed by Oliver.

They passed through the back of the building, and Mary met them before they left. She tossed a palm-sized piece of bread to Brody, and he snatched it from the air. He trotted outside to lie in the grass and chew on his treat.

Mary handed a sack to Oliver. "There is another piece in there for him so the two of you can eat without him drooling at you."

"Mary, you shouldn't—"

"Don't bother, Dani. I like fixing a little extra food for you, Oliver, and even Brody."

"You don't need to spend your money on us," Dani said.

"I'll spend it where I like, thank you."

"Thanks, Mary." Oliver hugged her and left to join Brody.

"I put an extra flask of water in the sack for you," Mary told Dani. "I'll need it and the sack back."

"I'll come by after I'm done returning the street urchin and meeting Gavin. Thank you for the food." Dani stepped forward and hugged Mary for a moment before releasing her.

Mary smiled. "Better. Still some work to do, but you've been practicing."

Dani's face flushed.

"Gavin? You spend a lot of time with him."

"Brody."

"You're a piece of work," Mary said with a laugh. "I'll get you moved up to practicing on people. I'll see you later and let you know if I hear any word on Jace."

"Thanks. I'm worried about him."

"Me too."

Dani's pace remained slow until the knot in her leg relaxed. Mary had given them a pair of baseball-sized tomatoes that Dani and Oliver ate like apples. Dani couldn't remember the last time she'd eaten a tomato. Oliver dug in the bottom of the sack and passed her a piece of bread and a cucumber, keeping one of each for himself. He bit into his cucumber, chewed a few times to force the lump in his mouth into smaller pieces, then spoke. "This is great!"

Dani nodded as she chewed on her own cucumber.

"Most of our food is freeze-dried or dehydrated. It all tastes like plastic." Oliver took another bite and shoved the rest of the cucumber into his pocket. "Dad might not kill me if I bring him the rest. Will you thank Mary again for me when you go back?"

Dani finished her cucumber. "Yeah, will—"

"Dani!" a woman's voice shouted.

Oliver turned. "Who's that?"

Brody wagged his tail at the approaching stranger.

Dani shrugged. The woman's face wasn't familiar.

The woman arrived mildly out of breath and managed to both smile and shake her head with disbelief at the same time. "I can't believe it's you. I never thought I'd see you again after you helped us. I knew you were lying that day when you tried to make us think you were human. You must have died since then, because you haven't aged a bit."

Dani glanced at Oliver before returning her gaze to the stranger, who only paused to take a breath when she dug through her bag.

"Your son?" the woman asked.

"Friend," Dani said.

"I've been carrying this for years just in case I ran into you again." The woman pulled an old, rumpled, black jacket from the bottom of her bag and thrust it at Dani.

"Do I know you?"

"I'm Rebecca." The woman shook the jacket in front of Dani. "This is yours. You gave it to us after you clocked a Warden in the head with a stick the size of a bat. Hit him twice in the head and once in the wrist." She directed this last statement at Oliver.

"When did this happen?" Dani asked.

"You don't remember? God, I remember everything that happened that day. You were out roaming in Portland, lost as a goose and walking in the sunlight. You had a bandage on your hand. The MPs were raiding C Block, and then the Wardens showed up. One of the Wardens shot my brother. He was about to shoot me when you attacked him. You gave your jacket to my brother after he regenned. I've kept your jacket so I could give it back to you if I ever saw you again. You really don't remember any of that?"

Dani took the jacket with her free hand and stared at it. "Where's your brother?"

"He died a few years ago cutting lumber in the north. He was hit by a falling limb and went into the river. He drowned during regen, before his friends could pull him out."

"I'm sorry."

Rebecca smiled. "He didn't die a captive of the Wardens or MPs, and that's all we wanted. What happened to you that day after you left us?"

Dani shrugged. "I died."

"How?" Rebecca asked.

"Uh, freak accident."

"Sorry to hear that. Still saving lives?"

"She saved me!" Oliver said.

"Wonderful!" Rebecca clapped her hands. "Some things never change."

"Yeah," Dani said, "and I need to take his butt home before his father finds out and ends him this time. Thanks for the jacket."

They parted ways, and Dani wanted the remaining walk to the park to be in silence. Oliver had other plans.

"You may still be having a crappy day, but you made that lady's decade," he said.

"Apparently." Dani only heard a snippet of what had happened to the woman and her brother, and it sounded terrible—yet the woman had to be the happiest person Dani had ever seen. Oliver was another person that didn't seem to have too many bad days. "Hmm."

"What?" Oliver asked.

"Nothing. Just thinking."

When Dani and Oliver arrived at the park, Gavin was already there, talking to another man she assumed was Javi. Brody trotted up to the pair of men, tail wagging.

"Hi Javi," Oliver said. "Hi, Gavin."

"Ah, skipping school again," Gavin said.

Oliver smiled. "Just for a little while." He pulled Dani's pack off and placed it by her feet. "Ask Dani about the jacket," he said, then skipped away toward the barracks.

Gavin glanced at the jacket in her hand. When his eyes met hers, she avoided his gaze by leaning down to drape the garment over her pack. She looked at the other man. "You're Javi?"

He wore seventy years better than Jace. His face was wrinkled, but his body wasn't damaged by arthritis.

"Yep." His hand engulfed hers in a solid grip. "That's an old, MP-issue jacket. From before we got upgraded gear."

"Yeah. You'll have to ask Miles how I got it, because I don't know."

Javi grinned. "I will. Gavin has told me a lot about you, Dani. Pleasure to meet you, and I see you found our runaway, Acer."

Dani's heart sank. "His name is Acer?"

Javi grinned. "Not anymore, I guess. Brody is a good name for him. He bolted from his trainer months ago, so he's not MP material. Congratulations, Dani. You have yourself a military K-9 dropout, and you can keep him."

"Of course I'm keeping him." She scowled. "You didn't think I'd actually let you take him from me, did you?"

Javi laughed. "Not at all. Sometimes the dog and handler aren't a good match. You and Brody seem happy to be stuck with each other, so I'm sure he'll make progress in training now. Ready to go to work?"

"One sec," Dani said. "Gavin, can we talk for a minute?"

"About Miles and Jace and the scuffle by the river? Javi told me."

Dani threw up her hands. "Okay, so I'm the last to know everything. Fine."

"Javi will help us with insider intel, since Miles is unavailable now. Miles's former commanding officer, Lieutenant Colonel Houston, is coming. The CNA visit just got moved up, so she'll be here in a week."

Dani frowned. "That's not much time."

"The CNA is tense over an MP killing another MP. We'll never get invited to speak to the brass when they're here. I'm sorry."

"I told you we don't need an invitation, Gavin."

"You're not serious."

Dani nodded.

"Crash the meeting because the CNA brass won't mind that little invasion and will never arrest us? No, Dani."

"Yes, Gavin. We can easily do this."

"*Easily?* On what planet will this be easy? You won't be able to get that close to the brass, even if you're wearing a skin."

"No tech. We go in as we are. Brigands. Breaching the barracks and getting into the meeting without any tech will show them we know what we're doing."

"And we just hope they don't arrest us?"

"Yeah, that's a potential complication." Dani shrugged. "We'll need Jace. Butterflies make more noise than him. No one can penetrate an MP base like he can."

"You think he'll agree to this?"

"We'll know when we ask him. Minor problem there, though."

"What?"

"He's in Waterville."

Gavin groaned. "Perfect."

"We can talk about this later. Javi has already ditched us to work with Brody."

"Fine. You're limping."

"Got punched in the thigh by an asshole," Dani said, already moving to join Javi and Brody.

Javi worked with Dani and Brody for hours that day, giving Dani time to practice the lessons under his instruction. Before leaving, he told her to practice with Brody until they met with him again in two days.

She and Gavin walked back to Aunt Hattie's after the session, with Brody leading the way. She shared her leftover bread and water with Gavin, but they didn't talk much.

As they neared the brothel, Dani felt a surge of relief to see Hattie's car tucked behind the building. She passed her pack, Mary's bag, and her jacket to Gavin and strode into the building. She found her brother in the back, having dinner with Aunt Hattie.

"Though this is *my* house and *my* dining area, I guess I'll give you two a minute," Hattie said with a frown.

Once she was gone, Dani dragged a chair to sit closer to Jace. He continued to eat as though she weren't there.

"Jace, stop being a dick and look at me. Were you having chest pain the other night?"

He didn't look up. "No."

Dani slid his plate out of his reach before he could continue eating. They glared at each other for a moment.

She tried a softer tone. "Jace, please, don't lie to me."

"My heart is fine."

"Why were you in Waterville?"

"Business."

"Bullshit."

"Hattie's birthday is coming up. I went there to buy her something."

"Stop lying!" she shouted, then forced her voice down again. "We're Brigands, Jace. We'll never be robbed because we never have money. You go to Waterville the day after you're a witness to Miles killing Xan to go *shopping*? You're hiding something from me again."

"Because you never hide anything from me, do you? Care to explain why you called that MP *Xan* instead of by his full first name?"

Dani hesitated and fidgeted for a moment. He had a point. If she didn't want him hiding things from her, she couldn't do the same to him. "I met up with Xan a few times. Semi-dating, if it can be called that, before we stopped seeing each other."

"*God* you're a pain in my ass, Dani. You always have this thing for MPs, though I'll never understand why." Jace shifted in his seat and pulled a small box from his pocket. He placed the box on the table. "I'm giving that to Hattie tonight. You moved out to live your own life, and I am moving on with mine. You killed the mood when you barged in, though. Thanks for that, by the way."

Dani stared at the box for a full minute before opening it. The small, silver ring rested on a piece of red silk. "Holy shit."

"Yeah, something like that."

"I am so sorry."

Jace grunted in response.

"Congratulations, brother."

"She hasn't seen the ring or said 'yes' yet, so hold on the celebrations."

"Okay."

"So what do you want?"

"Huh?" Dani asked.

"Miles is stuck at the barracks, the council killed the concept of meeting the CNA, and you're up to something."

"Oh. Yeah. Gavin and I need your help to interrupt the CNA meeting. The brass are visiting early due to the crap with Miles."

Jace took a deep breath and let out a long sigh. "How early?"

"Next week."

Jace nodded. "That shouldn't be a problem; their security is full of holes. What do you need from me?"

Dani's mouth dropped open. She hadn't expected Jace to agree; she certainly hadn't expected him to agree *and* freely offer his services. She recovered before he could change his mind. "Here's what I'm thinking. . . ."

CHAPTER

30

Miles stood on the floor of the small auditorium. He'd led officer briefings in the same room, but now, he was thankful the room was mostly empty. He stood before a long desk with five senior Commonwealth officers seated behind it. Two additional MPs, armed, stood near the wall, one to his left and one to his right. He was in his dress uniform with his back straight, his feet slightly parted, and his hands clasped behind his back. He'd been before a review like this before, after killing an MP on one of his fireteams for murdering Brigand Echoes in Portland. That investigation had been easily closed because he'd had witnesses who'd corroborated what he said about the murders. This time, he hoped his story held again—but the fabricated evidence around Xan's death made him nervous.

The major he'd served under in Portland was now a lieutenant colonel. Houston was a fine leader, and Miles wished he was seeing her again on better terms. She'd arrived in time to testify on his behalf, but one of the other panel officers, Major Moore, had made sure everyone else knew it had been a seven-year gap since Miles had served under her. "A lot can change in that time," Moore had said.

Miles couldn't argue with Moore's assessment. Seven years ago, Miles had been happily married. Emily had died only three years ago, and within two weeks of transferring to Bangor, Miles had discovered that Dani was alive.

Moore wasn't finished with his complaint. "You shouldn't be on this panel, given your preexisting bias," he told Houston.

"I don't see any other senior staff offering to preside over this review, Major," Houston responded. "My vote won't matter if the rest of the panel sees fault in his actions."

Moore had his own bias: he hated Brigands. Xan killing a civilian was a non-issue for him. Self-defense be damned; Miles knew Moore wanted him to pay for causing the death of the MP.

They argued a bit longer, and Miles didn't move. He thought of Oliver. He'd need someone to look after his son if he had to serve time in the brig before his dismissal from service. He considered Dani for the briefest of seconds before tossing her as an option. She was an impulsive wild card. While it was something he loved about her, it didn't mean he thought she'd be a great guardian for Oliver. The first day Oliver met her, she'd sheltered him in a brothel. *No, not her.*

Houston didn't waver. "The captain's record is exemplary. I don't know why we are rehashing this again. The only thing he's guilty of is saving lives, including those of CNA troops and civilians."

Three of the officers agreed with her assessment; only Moore did not. When Houston called for the final verdict, four cleared him of any wrongdoing, agreeing that he'd acted in self-defense. Moore refused to concede and find him innocent, but he was outvoted.

"Based on the vote results, Captain Miles Jackman, you're free of all restrictions previously placed on you," Houston concluded. "Please return to duty."

"Thank you, ma'am." Miles snapped to attention and saluted—and the room sank into darkness. The power was out.

He heard the two guards moving toward the center of the room. He lowered his saluting hand and turned, but he couldn't see anything.

"Secondary power should come on any second," one of the guards said.

The room remained dark, and the officers at the table began to stand.

"Sit," a familiar man's voice said. "Make yourself comfortable."

Miles spun around, unable to see Gavin or detect where his voice had originated from. One of the MPs was fumbling to release his flashlight from his belt when he yelped with pain. The light clattered to the floor.

Seconds later, the overhead lights finally came back on. Gavin was standing next to Miles now, Jace next to the MP he'd relieved of his flashlight and weapon before kicking both out of reach.

The other MP held his weapon up and shifted his aim from Jace to Gavin, unsure what to do.

"Christ," Miles muttered.

"Shoot them!" Moore said.

"Sergeant, lower your weapon," Houston ordered. "They're unarmed."

When Miles turned to face the officers now standing behind the table, his body tensed. Dani was leaning against the wall behind them. The MP spotted her too, and swung his weapon in her direction. The officers spun, and several swore upon seeing her. Miles tried to keep his eyes on Houston. Her jaw tightened for a moment before relaxing.

"Sergeant, I gave you an order," she said with a calm but firm voice.

The MP lowered his pistol, and Miles felt a slight release in the tightness that gripped his body. He desperately wanted to ask Gavin, Jace, and Dani what the fuck they thought they were doing, but he remained silent.

Houston returned her attention to Gavin. "Who are you? What is this?"

"I'm Gavin, this is Jace, and the one behind you is Dani. As you've figured out already, we're Brigands. Don't bother calling for backup to arrest us, because your comms are down."

"How exactly did you manage to penetrate the barracks, let alone this secure room, and take down our power and comms?" Houston asked.

"The same way we'll infiltrate the Wardens in Portland if you'll help us," Gavin said.

Fuck! Miles thought. Dani wasn't kidding about the merger.

Houston narrowed her eyes at Gavin. "Help you?"

"Brigands have united to take the fight to the Wardens. The Commonwealth should partner with us to expedite their defeat."

"You're volunteering to join the CNA?"

Gavin laughed. "Never. We're Brigand forces and will remain as such. I'm proposing a *partnership.*"

Houston remained silent for a moment. Another bit of tightness in Miles's body eased when the senior officer reseated herself at the table. "Go on."

"Ma'am!" Moore said.

Houston raised her hand and waved him off. Moore fell silent, and he and the other officers sat again.

"Brigands are experts at surviving," Gavin said. "Our lives depend on hiding, stealth, and living off the land."

"And stealing from CNA supplies," Houston said.

Gavin nodded. "Guilty. And the CNA never steals from Warden supplies, does it?"

"Of course we do," Houston said. "It's all part of surviving."

"Agreed. Think of what your resources would look like if we stole from you because we wanted to hurt you, take you down. We steal food and clothing almost exclusively. If we focused on taking your weapons, you'd have another war on your hands."

"Is that a threat?" Houston asked.

"Not at all. We've shown you what we can do here in your own barracks—and we did this without enhanced tech or weapons. This war with the Wardens has gone on too long. Imagine what we, CNA and Brigands joined, could do with a bit of cooperation."

Houston nodded slowly. "I'm listening."

"It's time to end the war. Miles here has a son. Ma'am, you have two daughters, right?"

Miles shot Gavin a glare that he ignored. Instead, he approached the table. The officers tensed, but none tried to stop him. "My point is, Brigand or CNA, we've been living under the Warden threat too long. You're in our town. Brigands run Bangor, and we know your troops here. I've seen Major Moore on Harlow Street more than once, in fact. We do have some fine brothels and pubs in that area, don't we, Major?" Gavin grinned.

Moore's face flushed with rage, but he held his tongue.

"Ma'am," Gavin said, returning his attention to Houston, "the CNA only defends against Warden attacks. You've been slowly losing for decades. It's time to change tactics if we're going to change the outcome of this war."

"What do you propose?"

"We have ways of gathering intel. With your tech, we can help you do more than just defend. We can attack the Wardens for a change, do some real damage."

"You gather the intel, and the CNA does the fighting?"

"No. The Brigands will be your recon and sabotage forces. We'll fight together."

Houston tapped a finger on the table in front of her. "While

I'm intrigued by the idea of hurting the Wardens' cause, I need a better reason to loan out our tech to a civilian force that's effectively holding us hostage."

"Dani," Gavin said.

Miles hated the smirk on her face as she strode around the table and dropped a palm-sized black box with several wires coming out of it in front of Houston. She pulled Miles's old comm device from her pocket, and he tightened his jaw. She flipped it open and manipulated the touch pad. "Your engineers will need that to restore power back to the primary." She nodded toward the black box on the table and entered more commands on the comm. "Your secondary power is back under your control, and comms are now up again." She tossed the unit on the table and walked past Miles to stand behind and to his right.

Miles glanced at her as she passed and tightened his fists, ready to throttle her for invading the barracks. Her smirk disappeared when her eyes fell on the new scar on his face, courtesy of Xander. He hadn't seen her in over a week, and he wanted to talk to her about more than just this foolish intrusion.

Houston picked up the comm unit and examined it. "You wiped the device. We have ways of retrieving the data to find out what you did to commandeer our equipment."

"Good luck," Dani said.

Gavin stepped forward. "Three Brigands took control of your barracks, and all we needed to do it was that little black box. Ready to take us seriously now?"

As Gavin spoke, Jace left the MP he'd been standing beside and eased himself into one of the seats in the front row of the auditorium. He moved, as usual, without a sound. The squeak from his chair was the only noise when he sat. Dani watched to see if he touched his chest, and was relieved when he didn't.

Her eyes moved to Miles. From her angle, she couldn't see his face, or the scar she'd spotted when she walked by him before. She'd known Xan had attacked him; no one had told her that he'd slashed his jawline open. She wanted to talk to Miles, ask him about the incident with Xan, but she'd have to wait. She still needed Houston to meet with the Bangor Brigands and not throw her, Jace, and Gavin in jail.

"Three Brigands." Houston stared at the box on the table. "What you've accomplished today is impressive; I'll give you that. Though you've broken at least two dozen CNA laws as a result."

"We know," Gavin said.

"Yet you still came?"

"We believe this partnership is more important than worrying about the risks we took to come."

"More important than our laws, you mean," Houston said.

Gavin shrugged.

"Other than the three of you, how many people do you have on this Brigand force?"

Gavin hesitated, and Houston leaned forward. She placed her arms on the table and laced her fingers together.

Shit, Dani thought. *Gavin flat lied about the Brigands agreeing to join together, and Houston just flushed out the truth.* The woman was smart.

"Ah, a bit of an exaggeration you made earlier," Houston said.

"This is ridiculous," one of the other officers said.

"Arrest them!" Moore growled, seeing his chance.

Houston silenced them again with a flick of her hand. Dani admired this woman. One dismissive wave and the others fell silent. Sure, she outranked them all, but they—Moore excluded—clearly respected her for more than the shiny pins on her collar. The officer reminded her of Aunt Hattie.

"We have a high concentration of Brigands in Bangor, and we have a strong community," Gavin said. "Bangor has leadership and laws where other Brigands can't even claim a community larger than a handful of people able to work together."

"Our council had agreed to meet with the CNA," Jace said. "Then one of your MPs killed a Brigand. They didn't much like that."

Houston turned her attention to Jace. "So you speak for your council?"

"Nope," Jace said. "We speak for ourselves. If you agree to meet with our people and we can reach a partnership, more Brigands will join."

"I see," Houston said. "And what's your role in this, sir?"

"Locksmith," Jace said with a grin.

Dani's eyebrows went up, and she stifled a laugh. Her brother was genuinely enjoying himself.

"Captain Jackman," Houston said.

Dani suppressed her smile when Miles flinched to hear his name called.

"Yes, ma'am?"

"Your son was protected by a Brigand woman when three men attacked MP wives and their children, correct?" Houston asked.

"Yes, ma'am."

"Is the Brigand woman in this room?"

Miles's voice failed, and he coughed. "Yes, ma'am."

"Speak up!" Houston said.

"Yes, ma'am!"

"So you know each other?"

"We've crossed paths, yes, ma'am. She kept Oliver safe that night and sent word to me through an MP who was visiting a brothel in town. I met her the following morning when I picked up my son."

Dani shifted her feet. Miles was leaving out *a lot* of details about their former history, that visit, and their subsequent path-crossing. Houston was clearly good at sniffing out the truth; Dani hoped she wouldn't press for more information here.

"And you've seen her since then?" Houston asked, dashing Dani's hopes.

Miles nodded. "Yes, ma'am. My son likes to skip school to visit her."

"Is Oliver a good judge of character?" Houston asked.

"He is."

Houston leaned back in her chair. "Has Oliver met these other two?"

"Yes, ma'am."

"And?"

"He thinks Gavin is the friendlier one of the two," Miles said.

"He's right," Jace said and laughed.

Dani disliked this interrogation, but Miles withstood the barrage of questions without complaint.

"How many other Brigands has Oliver met?"

"Several," Miles said.

"And?"

"Other than the one incident at the Standpipe, he's made friends among them."

"Have you made friends too, Captain?"

Dani stepped forward. "He has. Why does it matter?"

Houston grinned at Dani and leaned across the table again.

Fuck.

"I wondered how long I'd have to press him before you interrupted. Now I know. Your poker face sucks as badly as his," Houston said with a nod toward Miles. "Ready to end the bullshit?"

"Yeah." Dani's temper flared, though the logical part of her brain knew it was her own fault she'd fallen into Houston's trap.

"What do you know about our tech that makes you think you can penetrate the Warden base in Portland?"

"If you have it stored at these barracks, we know it exists and may have one of our own. We've been gathering intel on Portland for months and know when we need to attack. We can fine-tune how the attack will play out once we partner."

"When are you planning this event?"

Dani shook her head. "Partnership first."

Houston turned to Gavin. "You're former military, yes?"

Gavin nodded.

"Branch?"

Dani pinched her lips into a thin line, willing him to stay quiet. If he told the truth, Houston would figure out he was an Echo.

"Marines, ma'am," he said.

Goddammit, Gavin.

"You know what Wardens do when they catch Echoes—what they will do to *you*—yes?" Houston asked.

Houston had figured out he was non-human far more quickly than Dani had. Dani wondered if the woman exceeded smart and leaned into genius territory.

"Yes, ma'am."

"Still worth the risk?"

Gavin nodded.

"Her life too?"

Gavin's jaw muscle flexed before he answered. "Dani knows what's at stake."

"Does she?" Houston stood, and the other officers did the same. "I'll meet with the Brigand council and hear what they say on the matter."

Moore trembled with rage, but he did not speak out against

his superior officer. Dani grinned at the man's discomfort and at Houston's answer.

Houston turned and addressed the other officers. "Thank you for the time you took today to review Captain Jackman's case." They accepted their dismissal, saluted, and left. "You're excused as well, gentlemen," she said to the guards. "Not you, Captain."

Dani waited next to Miles and Gavin while the room emptied. Jace pried his body from his chair and joined them as Houston walked around the table to face them.

"If there's any chance you want to join the CNA, I can find jobs for you," Houston said.

"Pass," Gavin said. Dani and Jace nodded their agreement.

"I figured as much." Houston turned to Jace. "You're too old and banged up to be taking on this kind of mission, so I'm guessing you came along for the ride today because they asked you to."

Jace smiled. "I just helped get them through the front door."

"Uh-huh." She turned her attention to Miles. "Captain Jackman, you lied about Dani. You know her far better than you implied a few minutes ago, and I expect you to fill in the gaps for me later. Never lie to me again."

"Yes, ma'am," Miles said.

"Gavin, you're the face of this movement, or whatever the hell it is, but"—Houston focused her eyes on Dani—"*you* are the force behind it."

Dani tensed.

"Thank you for confirming my suspicions." Houston smiled. "If the Brigand council rejects the partnership, I'm still open to using your help to attack the Wardens. I can't tell you how tired I am of getting my ass handed to me or being forced to flee every time those fuckers show up looking for a fight. I'm still pissed I had to leave Portland to them. I want it back."

Dani nodded. "So do we."

"Good. Next question: where's the best place to eat in town?"

"Hattie's," Jace said. "Ask any MP based here for directions. They can get you there, no trouble."

"Excellent!" Houston picked up the comm unit from the table and took a moment to reprogram it. She tossed the unit to Dani and picked up the box from the table. "Contact me when the council is ready to meet. That comm will link directly to mine." Houston headed for the door. "You showed yourselves in, you can show yourselves out."

Dani continued to stare at the door after it closed behind the woman. Her attention diverted away from it when Miles grabbed her arm and spun her around.

"Christ, Dani, have you lost your mind? Houston is a fucking master at reading body language. She presides over most investigations because she can sniff out lies like no one else can, and *you*—my god, Dani, *you* interrupt the panel's meeting just to show you can break into the barracks while *she's* here?"

"How was I supposed to know she's a genius?"

"I would have told you, but you didn't bother to speak with me before you dropped in."

"You were confined to quarters!" Dani roared back at him.

"You had the comm. All you had to do was use it to contact me—but no, instead you use it to fuck with the power."

"We got the meeting. That's what we wanted, Miles."

"It's what *you* wanted."

"Not just me. They did too—uh, where did they go?" Dani looked about the room; only she and Miles were left in it. She abandoned their argument and jogged to the door. She found Jace and Gavin waiting for her on the other side.

"Took you long enough," Jace said as Miles followed her out.

Dani scowled at him. "Shut up."

"Miles, congratulations on the results of the investigation," Gavin said.

"Time to go," Jace said, glancing down the hall both ways. A few MPs were hovering and watching them. "Think we've worn out our welcome."

Dani left with her brother and Gavin. She glanced back at Miles, who said nothing as they walked away. She had wanted to talk to him about his altercation with Xan. Instead, they'd shouted at each other and parted on bitter terms. That wasn't at all what she'd wanted.

CHAPTER
31

Oliver knelt on the floor by one of the tables at Aunt Hattie's, occupying himself with finding Brody's favorite places to be scratched. Three days earlier, the Bangor barracks had been turned upside down by a trio of Brigands, and Oliver wished he could've seen it. Instead, he'd been in school when the power went out for a few minutes before coming back on. At the time, it had seemed like a non-event, but his mouth had gaped open when his father had told him what really happened. Oliver was far more excited about the mini invasion than his father.

A group of Commonwealth MPs, ground troops, and a few senior officers had visited the town that night and spent a lot of money on food and drink in the pubs. Oliver, of course, had been in bed when this happened. He hated missing out on big events. The CNA officers had started an all-day meeting with the Brigand council yesterday, and it had resumed again today. Oliver had insisted that his father bring him to town so he could hear the results for himself.

"It's all the political bullshit now, Ollie," his father had told him. "This could go on for days."

"So?" he'd demanded. "We're out for school break now. Let me go to town, or I'll go anyway."

Oliver had gotten his wish, but he had to admit the waiting around *was* boring. Gavin, Jace, and Aunt Hattie were involved in the meeting, though they weren't formally part of the council. His father was on duty and would join him later in the day. Dani sat at the table tinkering with an electronic something-or-other Aunt Hattie had asked her to fix before leaving for the meeting. *At least it's not a gun*, he thought. He didn't like guns.

Dani's food remained untouched, and her mood worsened the more she fought with the tiny wires. She released a burst of curses at the device, and Oliver decided to interrupt her small project.

"Hey," he said.

Dani sighed and tossed her screwdriver on the table. She leaned back in her chair. "What?"

"Let's go to the river so Brody can have a swim."

She stood without argument. "Sure."

Oliver tried to have a conversation with Dani as they headed down the street, but she was distracted and only gave him one-word responses.

At least the meeting hadn't ended with the two sides storming out after the first few hours. Oliver saw that as progress. He had enough classmates, himself included, with a deceased parent as a result of the war. A few of his friends had been orphaned by the war and adopted by other military families. Children from barracks all ended up in the CNA ranks once they turned seventeen. Oliver didn't want to be part of the ground, sea, or air troops. He didn't want to fight and kill. He needed this war to end as much as everyone else did.

They arrived at the river, and Brody wasted no time

clambering down the slope to reach the water. Dani stood a few feet up the embankment, staring at the water, her arms crossed. Oliver followed Brody's path and stopped at the waterline. He picked up a few small, flat rocks, and threw them across the water, counting the number of skips they made. Brody swam after them until they disappeared, then paddled off in another direction until Oliver threw another rock.

"Six!" he cried out, raising his arms. It was a new personal best record.

"How do you do that?"

Oliver hadn't heard Dani come down to the sandy area where he stood. "Do what? Skip rocks?"

"Yeah."

"You've never skipped rocks before?"

Dani shook her head.

Oliver held up one of his stones. "You need a nice flat one with rounded edges, like this. Sharp edges will make them catch and dive into the water instead of skimming the top." He took her hand and placed her thumb and first two fingers around the stone the way he wanted them positioned. "Hold it like that and throw side-arm. Before you release it, give your wrist an extra flick. Got it?"

Dani nodded. "I think so."

Oliver stepped aside. He'd never taught her something before; in fact, he'd grown to believe she knew everything.

Dani threw the first stone, and it plunked into the water a few feet from shore.

Oliver handed her another rock. "More side-arm. Watch me." He made another throw—slower than he normally would, to show her the motion—and his stone skipped three times before sinking. "You're not trying to hit the water with the rock; you want it to glide just above the surface so when it hits it'll skim the top."

Dani nodded and made another toss. This time it skipped twice.

"Great! Go again." He gave her his last rock, then began searching for more stones along the water's edge.

Oliver rubbed his shoulder. "I think I need to stop. My arm is sore."

"Mine too." Dani laughed. "That was fun."

Oliver had no idea what time it was; he'd lost track during all the fun. Dani had celebrated with him when he'd made another personal best—nine skips!—and when she'd clocked her own best, seven. Brody, tired from the swim, was sprawled in the sun on the bank, napping.

They headed back up the slope. Brody roused himself and walked beside them instead of racing ahead.

"I think he'll will sleep a long time tonight," Oliver said.

"I'm sure he will."

"Dani," Jace said.

Oliver and Dani turned. Jace stood under a tree, and Oliver was surprised to see him smiling. Granted, it was the tiniest of smiles, but it was still a smile.

"Why are you here?" Dani demanded. "Is the meeting over? What's the decision?"

"Relax, Dani. We ended it early today. Things are going well, and we should wrap up tomorrow. Though it might drag on, since Houston likes the food in town way better than what is served at the barracks."

"We have terrible food," Oliver said.

"Part of the agreement we sign will be that Brigands aren't forced to eat CNA rations," Jace said and laughed.

Oliver grinned. He thought the old man was joking, but maybe he wasn't.

"Dani, Hattie wants to speak with you. She said 'yes,' if you can believe it." Jace shook his head.

A smile spread across Dani's face. "Congratulations, brother."

"Thank you. Now go on, we'll catch you later. I need to speak with Oliver."

Dani paused at this unexpected dismissal. Oliver shrugged when she looked at him. He wasn't sure why Jace needed to speak with him either.

"Okay," Dani said slowly. "See you later, Oliver. Let's go, Brody." She strode off with a slightly confused look on her face.

Jace and Oliver started the walk back at a meandering pace.

"Thank you for teaching her to skip rocks, Oliver." Jace rubbed the back of his neck. "I was always too busy teaching her how to survive. Thank you for showing her how to live."

"She knows how to live."

"No, not really. Surviving and living aren't the same. Dani doesn't laugh much, and I've never seen her as happy as she was throwing those silly rocks. *That's* living, and that's something I regret not doing myself. Though I will say, I'm learning how to do it now." Jace smiled. "Hattie and I are getting married."

Oliver's eyebrows went up. "That's great!"

"You don't think of me as the friendliest of people, and I can't blame you."

Oliver felt his face flush with embarrassment.

"This bag," Jace said, patting the messenger bag resting just behind his hip. "I have a journal in here that I want you to have if anything happens to me. I think you know Dani better than anyone else does, and you'll know when she's ready to read it."

"Why don't you give it to her now?"

"The last time I let her read it, she died a few hours later. When that happens, Dani resets to a child of about ten years."

Oliver nodded. "At Aunt Hattie's, when Dad came for me,

Dani said she forgets everything after a regen. Why does she forget?"

"I don't know."

Oliver remained silent for a few minutes. "That must be terrible when she forgets you too," he said and looked up at the man. Jace's eyes flicked down at him. Oliver wasn't sure what emotion Jace was feeling, but his eyes were shining.

Jace nodded. "You're a good kid, Oliver. Your father did a fine job raising you, even if he and I aren't always on the best of terms."

"Mom raised me too, up until three years ago."

"She left?"

Oliver shook his head. "Died."

"What was her name?"

"Emily," Oliver said. "Emily Coulson. She didn't take Dad's name when they got married."

Jace glanced down at him again. The man's eyes were dry this time, but they scanned Oliver's face before returning his attention to the road. "She an MP like Miles?"

"Uh-huh."

"Interesting."

"What is?"

"That two MPs could raise a good young man like you."

Oliver didn't reply, but he knew Jace wasn't being honest with him. They arrived back at Aunt Hattie's, and Jace left him before he could ask more questions. He spotted Dani and Aunt Hattie talking alone at the side of the room while other people moved around them. Mary delivered several mugs to tables occupied by a mix of council members and Commonwealth officers. Lieutenant Colonel Houston said something that created raucous laughter just before the group bumped their mugs together and drank.

Jace wasn't kidding. The meeting seemed to be going well—

so well that it was continuing after the formalities ended. Oliver had never seen CNA troops and Brigands sitting, much less *celebrating*, together. This was a miracle.

His eyes wandered back to Dani. She and Hattie smiled as they talked, and Oliver remembered Jace's words. Oliver had made a promise to Dani that she'd never know existed. As long as he was alive, he would do anything to make his best friend happy.

CHAPTER

32

Following his usual routine, Rowan traversed the base, getting updates and performing small inspections when needed. Curtis remained at his side, as always, feeding him any additional necessary updates as they went: supplies, munitions, troop numbers, and anything else relating to base operations.

Rowan stepped aside and observed a platoon as they jogged past. Their uniforms were crisp, their movements in sync. He nodded with approval before turning to his friend. "Have you sent requests to Boston, as I asked?"

"Every day, sir," Curtis said.

Rowan sighed and shook his head. "They're too passive."

"My aide has word to find me immediately if anything comes through about Bangor. We'll hear something eventually. I must be pissing them off by now."

"Good. They need to remember how to be angry."

Once the base and barracks were covered, they got into a truck and drove through the region. Rowan continuously scanned the landscape while Curtis drove and talked. They reached the eastern end of Portland's peninsula, the Eastern Promenade, and Rowan had Curtis stop near the monument displaying the four names the city had been dubbed with during its history. The obelisk was broken and smeared with decades of dirt.

They stepped out of the vehicle, and Rowan walked the length of the overlook before returning to the monument. He paused and turned to look back at the city. He pointed toward Congress Street, which stretched out before him and ran from the Eastern Promenade to the center of the city. "We need to make some changes here."

Curtis's comm beeped an urgent notification alert, and he turned it on. "What is it?"

"Sir, we received word from Boston on your inquiries," his aide said.

Rowan grinned.

"And?" Curtis asked.

"We have permission to raid Bangor in the spring," the aide said.

Rowan's grin disappeared, replaced by a scowl.

"Anything else?" Curtis asked.

"No, sir. That's all the message said."

"Thank you." Curtis closed the comm link.

"Spring? Fucking *spring?*" Rowan shook with anger. The incompetence of his superiors never ceased to amaze him, or to make him livid. "Why so long? What the fuck are they doing in Boston that means I have to wait *months* before obtaining more resources for the Wardens? Do they not realize this raid is for all loyal Echoes?"

He continued his rant for several minutes before calming. Curtis remained silent during his tirade. He'd said things and issued threats that would get him tried, convicted, and executed for treason if anyone above him heard any of it, but he knew Curtis would never betray him. He took a deep breath to calm himself a bit more before speaking again. "I've lost contact with my insider in Bangor."

"Captured?"

"Not sure. He made such a mess of things, I imagine he failed at the cleanup and got himself killed."

Curtis shrugged. "You said he was a human."

"Yeah. Nothing lost there, other than word on what the Brigands and CNA there are up to. The Commonwealth can't be doing much, since their leaders are somehow bigger idiots than ours. The Brigands, though—I want to know more about their unification attempts. I'll need another resource."

"I have an aide that is dying to move into another role. She would do well blending in with the Brigands. She's smart."

Rowan shook his head. "She's an Echo, so she's not expendable. What about one of your Brigand insiders in the Portland area? I want a human."

"I have a couple in mind that should do well. I also maintain people in Augusta and Waterville, but there really isn't anything happening in those towns—not with the Commonwealth or the Brigands."

Rowan turned to Curtis. "Both towns?"

Curtis nodded.

"And you're only just now telling me this?"

"Any news they've been able to send me has already been passed straight to you, Rowan."

"Hmm, so the Brigands there are doing absolutely nothing?"

"Correct."

Rowan grumbled with frustration. "We won't be doing anything for a while either. *Spring.* Fuck. The only consolation is that we can hit Augusta and then Waterville on our way north to Bangor. What's the term for three goals in hockey?"

"Hat trick."

"Yes! We shall plan for a hat trick in the spring, then, if HQ doesn't modify our orders." Rowan smiled. "Back to business. I can barely see the observatory from here; all the trees and old homes and buildings still on this end of the peninsula are in the way. Knock it down, burn it, I don't care. I want a clear line of sight from the observatory out to sea from any angle. Start at Washington Avenue and level everything from there to the Eastern Promenade. Once the area is cleared, start building a newer, taller tower with better optics. We have forty miles of visibility with the current optics. I want more." He looked at his friend. "You're smiling. What?"

"When we returned to the base, I planned to take you out to the fields to show you a new weapon. I think you may have more fun watching it in action on something other than dirt targets." Curtis turned on his comm. "I'll let the R&D team know we're waiting for them out here."

Thirty minutes later, two trucks arrived. Six Wardens leapt out of the back of each one while the R&D scientists, designated by the green stripe on their uniforms, climbed out of the cabs of the vehicles and gathered near the rear of the trucks. They instructed the troops on how to unload and where to place the crates inside.

One of the scientists brought a grenade launcher to Rowan. He held it out with both hands, like an offering.

Rowan took the weapon and examined it. "Grenade launcher. We have plenty of these."

"It's what's on the inside that counts," Curtis said with a grin. "Pick your target."

Rowan lifted the launcher to his shoulder, and his eyes landed on a house on the corner.

"Uh, not that one, sir," Curtis said. "It's a bit close."

"Fine." Rowan started up the street to find a target far

enough away to meet Curtis's approval. Two blocks up Congress Street, he spotted a square, three-story, red brick building with another two levels of roofing. "That one?"

Curtis nodded. "Perfect."

Rowan flipped the optics open and aimed the launcher at the center windows of the second level of the structure. He'd launched many quake grenades as a Warden; one could collapse a wooden building, but it took a few hits to bring a brick or stonework building down. He expected to blow out all the windows and maybe part of a side wall with this first grenade.

He squeezed the trigger, and the grenade left the launcher. It shattered the glass window as it entered the building.

For a second, nothing happened.

Then a blast ruptured the brick building from the inside, followed by a secondary blast that brought the structure and the buildings on either side of it down too.

Rowan wobbled from a momentary loss of balance as the ground shook. He stared at the ordinary-looking launcher in his hands. "What the hell was in this thing?" he asked with a wide smile.

"They call it a cluster grenade," Curtis said. "Two blasts within each of the individual ones you witnessed, so four total. First a sonic pulse, then the typical expansion blast. It'll easily rupture brick, but it can also take down heavier stone or granite structures. It's about five times more powerful than a standard quake grenade."

"It's perfect!" Rowan strode back down the street and returned the launcher to the scientist who'd given it to him before addressing the R&D team. "Ladies, gentlemen, the cluster grenade is a thing of beauty. Well done! Reload it for me and bring a map. I'll show you what we're leveling today."

When the troops were gathered around him, Rowan traced his finger over the digital map along the streets he'd called out to Curtis earlier. "This is a roughly one-and-half-square-mile area. I want it leveled so nothing obstructs the views of water or land from the observatory."

"Yes, sir," they said in unison.

Rowan disliked how much time he'd been spending in his office and in meetings lately. He reveled in this chance to use the new tech. Over the next couple of hours, he destroyed several buildings, and whooped with glee when his troops fired their own weapons. Soon, every structure that stood in the targeted radius had been leveled. He congratulated the research team again before returning to the base with Curtis.

Back at the base, Rowan returned to his office and pulled up his familiar map of Bangor. "I'll introduce you to our new cluster grenades in the spring," he said to the map, smiling.

CHAPTER 33

"The town's celebrating, and you look like hell," Mary said. She placed a mug in front of Dani and sat in the chair across from her.

Dani rubbed her hands over her face and groaned. She leaned back in her chair, careful not to bump her sore ribs. "I'm thrilled we have a treaty with the Commonwealth, but Gavin's training hasn't let up. He's a fucking machine. He never stops. I took my beating this morning and have one more to go this evening. I don't know how he does it. I swear he's not human."

"Because he's not human," Mary said.

"I mean, I know, but I'm an Echo too, and I still can't go like him. He never gets tired. I'm exhausted." Dani sipped at her ale, glad her mug lacked any other surprise ingredients.

"We are still talking about your combat training, right?" Mary asked with a sly grin.

Dani laughed, but her face flushed red.

Mary leaned forward. "What are you hiding?"

Dani kept her eyes on her ale. "Nothing."

"You suck at lying. Are you sleeping with him?"

"No. We . . . like each other. But we agreed to put things on hold until after we sort out Portland."

"That's the stupidest decision ever."

"I thought you were in favor of us taking Portland back."

"*God*, you're so dense. I mean, you're ridiculously intelligent, but there are some things you just don't have a goddamn clue about, Dani. Why put your life with him on hold for anything other than, I don't know, the world exploding and taking everyone with it? As a human, I understand how finite my life is; I only get one shot. And you're not much different, since your mind reboots back to zero." Mary's attention diverted for a moment to another area of the crowded room. She stood to leave. "Aunt Hattie wants me for something. Rethink your plans with Gavin. Better yet, forget him altogether and spend an evening with me." She squeezed Dani's shoulder as she walked out.

Dani smiled and resumed drinking her ale. She sat alone for a while, wondering where her friends were. The room was packed with Brigands and CNA troops eating and drinking together, but she didn't see Miles, Gavin, or Jace among them. Oliver had taken Brody for a walk, and they hadn't returned yet.

She stood, her side still aching from Gavin's punch that morning. It didn't matter how many times she *did* guard her ribs, he still exploited the one time she didn't.

"Hey," Jace said.

Dani flinched at his unexpected arrival at her side; as usual, she hadn't heard him coming. Before she could greet him, he picked up her mug and pressed it into her hand. He then took her arm and led her from the crowded room. He didn't say anything until he brought her to the private dining area where she'd barged in on his evening with Hattie.

He closed the door behind them. "I need to talk to you."

"I figured as much," Dani said.

"I noticed you're avoiding Miles."

"That must thrill you."

"Normally, yes, it would make me quite happy, but things have changed. Stop avoiding him."

"He shoved a knife into a Brigand's heart, Jace. He was cleared by the military brass, but the other day I asked him what really happened with Xan, and his answers were evasive. I don't think I want to be around him."

"You may want to sit, Dani."

She refused.

"Miles didn't kill Xander; I did."

Dani stared at her brother.

"I killed Xander," he repeated.

She placed her mug on the table so she wouldn't drop it, then leaned her palms against the wooden tabletop. "Why?" she asked without looking at Jace.

"I went after Al to kill him for attacking you, and Miles stopped me when Xander showed up. We overheard their conversation, and when Al threatened to expose Xander for working with the Wardens, Xander killed him. Miles tried to arrest Xander, and that went horribly wrong. He was about to beat Miles to death with a stone; I stabbed him in the heart."

"If you kill to protect yourself or someone else, it's not murder."

"I killed him because I wanted him dead. Saving Miles was just a side effect."

Dani remained silent.

"Miles insisted on taking the blame to keep me out of jail. The MPs would've executed me for killing one of their own."

Dani turned to face her brother. She suddenly doubted everything about his character. He was nothing like the person she'd believed him to be. "He offered to take the blame, and you let him?"

"He put his prints on my knife and gave me his blade."

"Why did he put himself at risk to keep you safe?" Dani asked.

"He should probably explain that part to you."

"Who else knows?"

"Outside of Hattie, Miles, and me, you're it."

"Oliver?"

Jace shook his head.

"Shit, Jace, you and Miles cannot have that kid believing his father killed a man when he didn't."

"That's for Miles to decide. I wanted you to know the truth because, well, things are changing. I didn't kill Xander out of any love for Miles, but now I'm glad I didn't let him bash in his skull. Miles is a decent fellow."

Dani's eyes widened. "Wait, what? You're saying you like Miles now?"

Jace snorted. "I wouldn't go that far, but I don't hate him." He rose and put her mug back in her hand. "Keep this information to yourself, and process it all later." He ushered her out a different door than the one they'd come in through. They emerged into an unfamiliar hallway.

Dani pulled her arm from his grasp and stopped. "What the fuck is going on?"

"There's something I need to show you."

"Why?"

"I realize you've just learned your brother is a killer, and I understand if you hate me. But I need you to come with me. Please."

Dani sighed and relented.

They made a turn, passed through a small door, and went down a set of narrow, poorly lit stairs. They walked through another room, lined with barrels of ale, and came to a stop before a wall. Jace passed his hand along the flat surface, and the wall slid aside.

Dani's mouth opened but no sound emerged. He took her arm and guided her into the next room, where Miles, Gavin,

Hattie, and Mary waited. The size of the underground vault would have impressed her on its own, but it was the stash of neatly organized weapons, tech, and radio equipment filling the room that left her speechless. She recognized the battery unit hooked to the radio as the one she'd traded to Hattie following the Standpipe incident.

Dani stared at the racks of several dozen older-model plasma rifles, with a few more modern quake rifles mixed in. Plasma pistols had their own racks. Antique rifles and pistols with boxes of ammunition took up another space in the room. She walked past a row of several tables laid end to end. They held boxes and piles of various pieces and parts of Warden and Commonwealth tech. She picked up one device that had a corner of its housing broken off.

"Took that off a downed Warden helo near Montreal," Mary said.

Dani tried to speak, but her mouth had gone dry. She took several sips from her mug and tried again. "It's part of the rear rotor."

Mary nodded. "The motor still works, but I haven't had a chance to fool around with it to see what I can build."

"You and Hattie never needed me to assemble the solar panel. You could've done it."

"Yeah. We needed to give you a few test runs to see if you could build as well as Jace said you could."

Dani tossed the part back into the heap and set her mug aside. She used her fingertips to rub her forehead. The radio crackled with static, and she lowered her hands.

"How long has this been going on?" Dani asked.

"Since the start of the war," Hattie said. "Bangor is sitting on the largest stash of weapons in the northeast. We have six more bunkers, all larger than this one. They're also all connected by the tunnels under the city used during Prohibition in the 1920s and '30s. We don't have the newest gadgets, but these will still put holes in the Wardens. The only thing we've lacked for the last five, almost six decades is a reason to pull them out and use them. We always knew we'd have an easy time uniting the Brigands in this area, but we also knew we could never take on the Wardens alone. Seems we just needed someone insane enough to put a Brigand–Commonwealth partnership in motion."

"Holy shit," Dani muttered.

Hattie shrugged. "I'm not sure how holy it is, but the shit has certainly gotten way more interesting the last few days. I brought Houston down here today but didn't tell her about our other sites. Still feeling her out for how much we can trust her, you know? Anyway, that panel you built for me wasn't for a silly lamp. My old panel broke, so our communication with other locations had been cut off for a while."

"What other locations?" Dani asked.

"We have people in Saco, Gorham, and Freeport keeping an eye on Portland. We have other sites, but those three have been the most important lately."

Dani turned to Gavin. "This is how you've been getting your information fed back to you so quickly?"

He nodded.

"The beauty is the radio tech is so old, the Wardens don't pick up the transmissions," Hattie said. "They could if they wanted, but they're too busy monitoring the CNA traffic to worry about us. The CNA has the ability to intercept Warden signals between Portland and Boston, but they can't always unscramble them."

"Do the Wardens oscillate their frequencies?" Dani asked Gavin.

He nodded. "Can you build something to handle the variance?"

"Maybe. Their comms are always so far ahead of the Commonwealth's tech."

"Which is how the Wardens planned and coordinated their attack fifty-nine years ago without anyone knowing until it was too late," Hattie said. "We must have a way to know what they're up to, Dani."

"I'll need one of their devices to figure it out," she said.

"We have one, but it's damaged. See what you can do with it once Miles gets it from Houston."

Dani shook her head. "I still can't believe this."

"We were going to tell you sooner, but other things kept coming up," Jace said.

Dani's frustration released in a wave of fury. "I've lived here for fifteen years, and Houston still found out before me!"

"Pout, punch something, cry, I don't give a shit, Dani," Hattie snapped. "Get over yourself real quick, honey, because we have a hell of a lot of work to do now. The treaty is signed. The attack on Portland *will* happen. Gavin, I need Dani to help fix the tech my people couldn't. Stop beating the crap out of her every day."

"She can tinker in your dungeon between sessions," Gavin said. "I still have a lot to teach her. I have a personal interest in her being able to protect herself."

Miles scowled at Gavin. "That personal interest includes inflicting pain on her for fun."

"Jace didn't come to you to teach her how to fight," Gavin said.

"Exactly where is your line between abuse and training?" Miles asked.

"Both of you, shut up," Hattie said.

"I don't get a say in any of this?" Dani asked.

"Nope. Mary, let's go. There's a business to run upstairs." Hattie and Mary left, and Dani followed Jace, Miles, and Gavin out. She stopped and leaned her hand against one of the barrels while Jace closed the fake wall.

"Careful with that," Gavin said. "It's not full of ale."

Dani jerked her hand back as if burned. She eyed the barrel with suspicion. "What *is* it full of?"

"Explosives."

With that, he walked away. Jace went with him, leaving Dani in the dank cellar with Miles.

"How long have you been in on this?" Dani asked him.

"About twenty minutes before you arrived. I think. Like you, I couldn't breathe or speak for a while upon first coming down here. It may have been only five minutes, for all I know."

Dani half laughed at his remark. She drained her mug and found a barrel with a spout. "This one doesn't have explosives in it, I assume."

Miles chuckled. "Let's hope."

Dani refilled the mug and passed it to him. She wondered how many of the barrels contained ale versus something that could blow a crater in Bangor.

Miles drank deeply from the mug before filling it again and passing it back to her. She drank half of the contents in one go.

"Jace told me what really happened in Hell."

Miles nodded.

"Tell Oliver. Nothing sucks more than family keeping the truth from you," she said. She handed the mug back to him and left.

CHAPTER 34

Gavin barked at her. "Again!"

Dani rolled to her side and pushed herself up from the ground. Gavin remained standing, and she hated him for it—as usual. Another morning filled with pummeling, and she was angry.

She shifted her feet and raised her fists. She swung at him a few times, then sprang away from his attempt to sweep her feet.

"Good," he said. "You're finally learning."

She replied with a right hook at his head. As she swung, she shifted her left elbow up and away from her side. Gavin ducked below her punch, sidestepped, and prepared to strike her in her exposed ribs—but she rotated away from his incoming punch and brought her right fist down on his jaw.

The unexpected blow caused him to stumble. He stopped a few steps away from her and touched his jaw. A slow grin formed on his face. "You baited me. Well done. Solid hit, too." He worked his jaw side to side a few times.

He'd baited her enough times, only to launch counters that either put her on her back or in a crumpled heap on the ground. She felt somewhat pleased she'd been able to return the favor, though she still hadn't managed to flatten him.

Gavin pulled a knife from his belt and stalked toward her.

"What the hell? I'm unarmed." Dani backed away from him.

"Oops. Did I forget to tell you to wear your knife?"

He charged, and Dani had no choice but deal with him and the weapon. She left her feet planted and leaned her upper body aside when he made his initial stab at her. She grabbed his wrist, twisted it, and wrapped her other arm around his neck, folding his upper body back as his momentum continued to carry his lower half forward. She drove her knee into his lower back then slammed him to the ground. They scrambled for a moment in a flurry of motion and strikes. It ended with Dani lying on top of him with his knife in her hand. She held the blade against his neck, unsure how she'd even ended up with his weapon.

Gavin smiled. "Good. Except . . ."

Dani flinched when the tip of a knife poked her in her side. "You would've been dead before you could cheat," she said.

"Not if you hesitate like that."

"So you want me to cut your throat to prove I beat you?" She was still holding the knife to his neck, and he was keeping his second blade's tip against her skin.

"Seems more like a draw to me."

Dani got off him and threw his knife on the ground beside him. "Asshole."

Gavin laughed as he stood. "You win. Is that what you want to hear?"

"Yes! You've beaten the shit out of me long enough. I won that round."

"One round out of how many?"

"Fuck you." Dani left him to find her canteen. She took a drink of water, trying to ignore him and calm her anger, while he brushed dirt and leaves from his clothes.

Brody trotted over. She knelt and poured water into her palm. His soft tongue lapped it into his mouth.

Gavin dropped his knife so it lay next to the first one he'd pulled on her. "I can't use you during the assault on Portland, Dani."

"What?" Dani stood and faced him.

He approached her. She took a step back.

"I'm going."

"Never said you weren't. I just can't use you as infantry when the firefight starts. I didn't think I could, but I needed to be certain. I—"

"You agreed to train me so you could weed me *out?*"

He moved closer to her and slipped one hand around her side to her back. "Let me finish," he said in a softer voice. "You're not a killer. You hesitate, and you don't go into full survival mode unless you think your life is in imminent danger. When you do react, your reflexes are quick and your instincts are spot-on. But you don't play dirty, Dani, and that will get you killed."

"Teach me."

"I can't. You either have it, or you don't. You're among the latter group."

She flinched again when the sharp tip of another knife poked her back. She glanced behind her and saw the knife he was holding against her skin. She pushed his arm aside and moved several steps away from him. "You're a real dick, Gavin."

"Always carry three blades on you. Most people carry two, as you typically do. Hide a third on you somewhere," he said. He flicked his wrist, and the blade stabbed into the ground between her feet. "You can have that one."

"Keep it." She turned to leave.

"Dani, you're still misunderstanding me."

She paused but didn't turn to look at him. Her eyes burned with tears of frustration, and she'd die before she let him see her cry over this shit.

"I can't use you in an assault fireteam, but you're perfect for sabotage. The first day I showed you how to make a few traps, you excelled. You shoot well enough, but not enough to be part of a sniper squad. The second day, I made things harder. Hell, I thought I was going to die after that run. The fucking pace I set almost killed me. I was trying to make you give up, but you didn't. Everything I've thrown at you has been to see how far I could push you before you'd lash back with an attack meant to kill. Not once have you done that. Not even today, when I came at you with a knife. Sure, you fought back, and *won*, but there's a part of you that keeps you from taking a life."

She turned to face him. "I killed the Brigand at the Standpipe."

"You reacted to his attack and threw him out a window, but you didn't know how high up you were, did you? You didn't know the fall would kill him. That wasn't your intention. You got pissed off, like you did with me, and just needed to get him off you. The window was the quickest way. Right?"

Dani shrugged.

"You were threatened, and you reacted. Do you even know how you ended up with me on my back and you holding a knife to my throat?"

"No."

He nodded. "I'm changing your regimen. We'll continue hand-to-hand drills to keep you fresh, but they won't be as physical as before. I'm moving you into the recon and sabotage platoon—assuming we have more than just you in it." He exhaled. "Let's head into town early to eat. I'm starving, and I could use some rest."

"*Rest?*" Dani gaped at him. "*You* need *rest?* I've never heard you admit any kind of fatigue before."

"I just got my ass handed to me by a woman."

She smiled.

"C'mon. Care to wager on how many volunteers show up?"

"I'm hoping we get a hundred total," she said with a shrug.

"A hundred? Hell, I'll be thrilled with half that. I just don't know how many people, CNA or Brigand, are willing to be the first line of attack against a Warden base."

Dani had no issues letting Gavin pay for their lunch, especially since he'd just admitted to purposely abusing her under the guise of training.

After eating, they walked to Hayford Park and waited.

Gavin turned in a full circle. "This doesn't look good."

"We're a little early," Dani said.

Brody walked through the tall grass with his head down. His tailed bobbed above the grass as he walked, and Dani smiled as she watched him. His head popped up, and Dani turned to follow his gaze. A few Brigands emerged from the trees to cross the field. A moment later, several more people appeared. Gavin bumped her arm, and she turned around. A dozen CNA troops approached from the direction of the barracks, with Miles, Oliver, and Javi at the front of the group.

Oliver ran ahead, and Brody greeted him. He gave the dog a treat from his pocket.

"Why are you here?" Dani asked sharply. "Please tell me Miles isn't stupid enough to let you volunteer."

"I'm just here to watch and keep Brody company," Oliver said with a broad smile.

"Ah," Dani said, deciding she'd better keep an extra eye on Oliver to make sure he didn't try to steal her dog.

Within an hour, around 200 Brigands and 150 CNA ground troops had joined Dani and Gavin. She recognized Mary and a few others among the civilian group as Aunt Hattie's employees. They were no longer in the nicer clothes they wore when working for Hattie; instead, they'd donned faded and tattered pants and shirts, same as Dani.

"What do you think of the new clothes?" Mary asked, sidling up to her.

Dani laughed. "I've never seen you dressed like a street urchin."

"I prefer guttersnipe." Mary smiled.

Jace appeared and walked between them. "We'll have to keep you two separated or the Wardens will hear you giggling miles before we reach Portland."

Dani's retort was interrupted by Gavin's booming voice.

"Commonwealth troops, you're now responsible for helping teach the Brigands how to line up and use military terminology. Brigands, you're responsible for teaching your CNA associates stealth and survival skills. Each group has a skill set so ingrained it might as well be in your DNA. Help your fellow volunteers survive another day, and he or she will do the same for you. Line up!"

Dani joined in the shuffle of people to create a block-shaped arrangement of just under four hundred people. She followed the direction of an MP in the group on how and where to stand. When the shuffling settled, Gavin spoke again.

"We have a mix in this group of Echoes and humans. Get over it now. We're all on the same side here. Also, understand that this is a *partnership*. Brigands are not becoming formal CNA troops, and the CNA isn't converting to civilian life. Today we're together as people of Earth who are sick of the Wardens' genocide. Yes, the Wardens are Echoes, but the Echoes among this group aren't the same as the Wardens. Wardens hunt Echoes too, and it all must stop. That's what we're here to do." Gavin scanned the crowd. Seemingly satisfied that everyone was still with him, he continued. "Everyone will count off one to four. Jace, take group one to assess stealth. Miles, you have group two and will assess endurance and agility. Javi, take group three to the rifle range. I'll take the fourth group and start hand-to-hand combat drills. Count off and reform your lines with the others matching your number."

Dani and Mary landed in the third group together; Dani was pleased to have her friend with her. She recognized some of the other Brigands around her, but she didn't know any of the Commonwealth troops.

"This is the first of four days of initial training," Gavin bellowed. "We'll rotate each of you through the four rounds of assessments to understand strengths and weaknesses. We'll resort you again on day five. A partnership like this has never been formed before. Today we start a new history—for the people of Maine, and for everyone on Earth."

CHAPTER

35

As the weeks of training continued, some people quit and others were released for medical reasons. Their initial number of volunteers fell to 364—still far more than anyone had expected. The walk to and from Mount Hope Cemetery to Bangor after training quickly grew old; it was also an extra energy expenditure Dani couldn't afford. She was eating more food than before and still dropping weight. The last thing she wanted was to get booted from the ranks, so she moved into Aunt Hattie's shed with Brody. Gavin didn't like her relocation, but she didn't care.

She spent any spare time she had in Hattie's cellar, fixing items and digging through the plethora of parts. It was the only way she could pay for all the extra food she was consuming. Many nights she was asleep seconds after collapsing on the thin, lumpy mattress on the shed's floor. She'd sleep a few hours, then wake early and start the routine again. Eliminating the extra walking time gave her time each day to spend with Brody— time she often spent with his broad head resting on her thigh, gently scratching behind his ears while she sorted through her thoughts. It was more relaxing for her than cleaning the gun or building something, and sometimes she fell asleep.

The summer had waned. Dani stood in the shed staring at the gear spread out on the small table before her. Brody slept on her bed, and she watched him as he snored. She was going to miss him.

Gavin had turned the training sessions over to Houston and picked three others to go with him to Portland for reconnaissance. Dani was one of the people chosen. Patel and Lee, the other two members, would gather surface intel while Dani and Gavin scouted the sewers. They would be gone for at least a month, possibly two.

She checked the time and sighed. She needed to stop screwing around. She was meeting Miles and Oliver to hand over Brody to them. She was already regretting leaving the dog for so long. "I'm more distraught over leaving the damn dog than I am my brother." She shook her head, annoyed by the mix of emotions she was feeling, and began packing. She clipped two knives to her belt and slipped the third into a concealed sheath she'd created on the inside of her belt. The third blade was small, sharp, and likely to go undetected even if she was frisked.

She began placing the gear on the table in her pack, a CNA-issue rig that held more than her usual daypack could ever carry. With more space and more gear came more weight. Gavin had given her explicit instructions on what to pack, so she needed to make sure she didn't forget anything.

A light knock on the door pulled her from the task. She opened the door and found Jace.

"Nice guard dog," he said. "Didn't even bother to bark."

She laughed. "Yeah, he's fairly useless most days. Come in. I need to finish packing." She left the door open and returned to the table. A vague image flashed in her mind. "Jace, have I ever lived in a shed before?"

"No. Why?"

She shrugged and resumed filling her pack. "Something

about this place seems familiar. It's like seeing an out-of-focus picture of a room similar to this. Crappy bed to the left of me, table in front, the totes stacked on the right."

"A memory?"

Dani shrugged again. "Doesn't matter. I'm so damn tired after training, I can barely see straight. This trip will be a good break, I think."

"Dani."

She refused to turn around. "I know you don't want me to go, Jace. We've already had this conversation."

"Be careful, please."

She'd expected another argument, not this semi-blessing. She turned to face him. "I will. I promise."

"I'm too old to raise you again. I mean it this time, Dani. Well, you don't remember those prior conversations, but I really am too old. I lied when I told you I wasn't having chest pain. I stopped in to see a doctor when I got Hattie's ring. He couldn't do anything for me, but since then I've been to see some CNA doctors, and they've been able to help some."

"What are you saying? Are you dying?"

"No, not yet. They can't keep me from aging, but they were able to help my heart with some treatment." Jace held up his gnarled, arthritic hands and flexed his fingers into tight fists. He smiled. "I haven't been able to do this in years."

"What about regen?"

"They don't know if I will or not. I don't want you to make this trip to Portland, but I know you'll go no matter what I say. Gavin's smart, and a fine soldier even if he pretends he's a civilian now. Do what he says, and be careful."

Dani approached Jace and took his hand. "I remember standing on the side of the road while you helped push a truck out of a hole. My hand was a lot smaller then. You didn't raise me as a brother, though that's what I called you . . . you've raised me like a father. I know we fight, a lot and often, but I do appreciate everything you've done, including the sacrifices you've made. I'm so excited for you and Hattie. I promise I'll be careful, and I will be back." She hugged him. "I love you, Jace."

He gasped when she said the words, and she was a bit surprised herself. She couldn't remember ever having told him she loved him. They had their ways of showing it, in between their arguments, but neither of them was great at verbally expressing themselves.

When she released him, he fidgeted and stared at the floor while she cleared her throat and fiddled with the zipper on her jacket.

"Um, yeah, love you too, and I, uh, should probably let you finish packing," Jace said.

"Yeah." Dani scuffed a foot against the floor. "This is new territory for both of us. Guessing it'll take some time to get used to it."

Jace nodded and turned to leave. "Oh, uh, I'll help Oliver with the mutt if either of them needs anything. I know you love that damn dog more than you like breathing, so he'll be here when you return."

"Thanks, Jace."

After he left, Dani dropped into the chair next to her. Had they ever had this kind of conversation before? Given his reaction, probably not. *Well, I'll have plenty of hiking time to think it over on the way to Portland.* She rose, finished packing her things and straightened the shed. When everything was in its place, she slipped her arms through the heavy pack's straps. She grunted under the weight as it settled on her back. She picked up her daypack from the floor and headed out the door, Brody beside her. Before shutting the door behind them, she stopped to look at her room once more. It still seemed familiar to her. She pulled the door closed. *Time to go.*

Oliver and Miles were waiting for her at the Standpipe, as promised. She handed her daypack to Oliver. "There's some food and a couple of toys in there for him."

"I'll take good care of him," Oliver said.

"I know. Jace said he's willing to help you if you need it."

"He did?" Miles lifted an eyebrow.

"Yeah. He surprised me with that too." Dani chuckled.

"Hmm. He's different somehow. He's still grumpy most of the time, but now I think it's just part of the act." He looked at Oliver. "Hey bud . . ."

"Want me to take a hike so you two can chat? Yeah, you always do. Bye, Dani. Have fun." Oliver hugged her and took Brody's collar. "Do you need to tell him 'good-bye' again?"

"No. Thanks though." She absolutely wanted to hug the dog once more, but she feared she'd unravel if she did.

Dani tried to not watch Brody as he left with the boy.

"I know you adore that dog, Dani," Miles said. "Leaving him must be tough on you."

She nodded.

"He'll be here when you get back."

"Thanks."

"I won't tell you to be careful because you likely won't, but I do hope you stay safe and get the information you need."

"Me too. I'm meeting Gavin at the barracks. You heading back that way?"

"Yeah. Care for some company?"

Dani smiled. "Always."

When Gavin spotted them approaching, he checked his watch.

"Relax," Dani said. "I'm early."

< 241 >

He grunted in response.

"See you soon," Miles said.

Dani didn't miss Gavin's scowl as she hugged Miles good-bye, but she didn't care about it, either. Miles was a good friend. She would miss him.

"You're smiling. Why?" Gavin asked. He checked his watch again while they waited for Patel and Lee.

"I'm happy."

"Happy? We're about to spend several weeks sleeping on the ground, being eaten by mosquitoes, and crawling around sewers hoping we don't set off any traps the Wardens may have left in there for us. We'll be pissing in bottles and shitting in cellophane to pack it out of the area. And you're happy?"

"It's not my problem you're in a foul mood," Dani said, and her smile widened. She was leaving on peaceful terms with her brother. When had that ever happened before? She was *very* happy.

CHAPTER
36

ani pulled the towel from around her body, and her bare skin prickled in the cool air. She passed the towel over her head before tossing it aside and running her fingers through her hair. The oil lamp in the room cast a sickly yellow glow, but she didn't mind. It was lighter than what she and Gavin had encountered in the sewers.

After weeks of eating and sleeping in Portland's sewers, she was enjoying being clean for a change. She and Gavin had met up with Patel four days earlier and spent two nights at a camp in Freeport. She'd washed last night, but she'd only managed to get so much dirt off her in the freezing nighttime temperatures with the bucket of icy creek water she'd used.

The Wardens had waste recycling systems in place, so she and Gavin hadn't had to deal with urine and feces in the sewers, but the pipes had still reeked of other filth. She hoped to never eat or sleep near rats again.

At least they'd gathered great intel. Gavin was thrilled with their findings. The Wardens had only set a few traps for intruders, and had apparently forgot about them since; they'd proven to be old and in disrepair, and she and Gavin had had no trouble disarming them. They'd found access to the base at the airport, and Dani had spent hours listening to Warden comm traffic from directly beneath the base using the device she'd repaired for Houston while Gavin updated his map, marking areas on it where structural supports for the former MP barracks resided underground.

The Warden's comm tower had remained lit and guarded, but Dani had noticed heavier security in place at a second, newer structure one day. It had similar equipment but was not lit. Once they returned underground, Dani drew a circle on Gavin's map.

"This is the real tower," she said. "The men guarding it rotate and are far more alert than the guards on the lit one. I think the one with lights is just a decoy."

"Smart bastards." Gavin shook his head. "The spies said the man running this place kept things on a tight schedule. The troops here are bored, though. They spend a lot of time yapping and laughing when on duty."

"Complacency is good."

Gavin grinned. "Good for us."

They heard a voice over the manhole lid they'd climbed through and scrambled to extinguish their lights. They waited without breathing as the Wardens above chatted.

"Rowan will beat you himself if he catches you smoking that shit," one said.

"I know, but I don't care," the other said. He paused, and Dani heard him expel a long breath, probably of smoke. "The man's sharp, but he really is a little crazy. He works those fucking R&D teams around the clock cranking out new gear and tech. The cluster grenade is a beast." He chuckled. "Have you fired one yet?"

Dani's heart thundered in her chest. Her breaths quickened. The Wardens weren't the only ones that had become complacent. She wished they had been more cautious; they'd grown overconfident in the safety of the sewers. Rumors always swirled about the Wardens and their reconditioning process. The only thing consistent between the rumors was that the process was horrific. She and Gavin couldn't get caught. *Don't panic. Don't panic.*

Gavin's hand touched her forearm, and she realized she was trembling. He squeezed her arm and motioned for them to move. She nodded and followed him deeper into the pipe. They moved almost soundlessly and didn't speak until they were well away from the men and any manholes where someone else might overhear them.

"Shit, that was close," Dani said. She passed her hand though her hair and immediately wished she hadn't. The foul goop from the sewer walls transferred from her hand to her hair. *Ugh.*

"Yeah." Gavin's face was grim. "We've been here too long, got cocky. It won't happen again."

Dani nodded.

"I wanted to hear more about that cluster grenade, but when I saw you shaking. . . ."

"I'm sorry." She flushed. "Hearing them so close freaked me out."

"You have to be able to get much closer to them and remain calm. I know this is the first time you've done anything like this, but you must be able to stay in control."

She nodded again. Everything always sounded so easy coming from him.

Four weeks had passed since that day. They'd had other close calls more often as they moved beneath and around the base and rest of the city, but Dani had managed to remain somewhat calm during subsequent encounters. Her heart still raced each time, but she didn't turn into a trembling mess.

Lee wouldn't be returning to Bangor. He and Patel had been

on the western side of the peninsula when the Wardens started blasting old homes and buildings to create better sight lines. The pair had just finished surveying the area and were on their way out when the blasting started. Lee wasn't quite clear when the building they were exiting was leveled.

Later that night, Patel had returned and retrieved Lee's body. He'd tied bricks and debris to the corpse and dropped it in the bay to remove any sign that non-Wardens were lurking in Portland. Dani felt horrible for Patel, having to do something like that. She didn't think she could ever dump a friend's body in a bay and continue on.

They were out of Portland now, farther north and closer to home, and Gavin had arranged for them to stay in a home south of Augusta—hence the shower. Dani pulled on a pair of denim trousers, clean by Brigand standards, and a T-shirt. Both were too tight compared to her usual clothes; the stuff she scavenged was always too big for her. She wiggled her toes and realized she'd forgotten to ask the man for a pair of socks.

Dani knocked on Gavin's door. "Hey, you have any clean socks I can borrow?"

"Yeah," he said from within his room. "I'll bring them by when I'm done cleaning up."

"Thanks."

She returned to her room and considered asking the owner for a different set of clothes. She decided not to bother. He'd fed them and given each of them a room as a way of supporting their efforts. She didn't want to appear ungrateful for his help. A chilly breeze drifted through the room, and she realized the window was partly open. She tried to close it, but the window was stuck.

There was a light rap on her door, and it cracked open. "You decent?" Gavin asked.

"No, I was walking the hall naked looking for socks," Dani said, still fighting with the window.

"Sounds good to me," Gavin said with a laugh as he entered the room. He closed the door. "Damn."

She glanced over her shoulder at his remark. He'd shaved, and his hair was still wet. He wore faded jeans, a dark T-shirt, and a red plaid shirt that was open down the front. He was barefoot and stood with socks in his hand. His eyes were cast slightly downward, and he wasn't blinking.

"Stop staring at my ass," she said and resumed her fight with the window.

"Hard not to. Are you sure we have to wait until we retake Maine?"

Dani grunted in response as she tugged up on the window. It slid up easily enough, but when she tried to push it back down, it lodged in place, now more open than before. She swore under her breath and leaned on the window as the room grew colder.

"Need a hand?" he asked.

"No, I think I've got it." She wiggled the lower part of the window, and the frame slid down—too quickly for her to get all her fingers out of the way. She released a string of curses as she pulled her mashed finger from beneath the window, cradling it with her other hand and groaning.

Gavin placed the socks on the sill and took her hands. "Let me see."

"It'll be fine."

"Is it broken?"

Dani shook her head but kept her other hand wrapped around the injured finger.

Gavin peeled her hand away and inspected the bluish lumps forming along the top and bottom of her index finger. He moved his thumb and forefinger around the joints, pressing as he went. Dani flinched, and he stopped. "It's just a bruise."

"I don't care. Shit hurts."

"We spent seven weeks crawling around sewers and sleeping with rats, and you're whining about a bruised finger?"

"Yes, I am." She tried not to smile. Her finger *did* hurt, but when he put it that way, worrying about a dinky bruise on a finger did seem silly.

He continued to hold her hand. "I like those jeans."

"They're a little snug."

"Not at all. I'll ask Mr. Ashe if you can keep them." He placed his other hand on her hip and shifted closer to her. She didn't stop him this time.

"Can I have my hand back?" she asked.

He released it, and she pulled his head down. She opened her mouth and kissed him deeply as his arms pulled her close. But as they shifted toward the bed, she froze.

"Wait. Is this a good idea?" she asked.

His mouth traveled down the side of her neck, sending a tingle along her spine. "Yes, of course," he said, his voice muffled. "This whole waiting thing has sucked from the beginning."

She struggled to ignore his wandering lips while his hands found their way under her shirt. He pulled her closer; she liked the sensation of his body against hers.

"I agree, but what about the military structure? I'm one of your underlings. There must be rules about superiors sleeping with their subordinates or whatever, right?"

He sighed and lifted his head to look at her. "We aren't military, Dani. Those rules only apply to the CNA. We're still civilians."

"So this won't change anything, and you will still send me into the fight like any of the other volunteers?"

"You'd just disobey if I tried to hold you back."

Dani smiled and leaned in for another kiss as she reached for his belt. Their clothes landed on the floor as they moved toward the bed.

Dani stared at the ceiling as Gavin slept beside her. The oil lamp still burned, and a mouse scratched at something in one of the walls. Her feet were still cold, but it didn't matter when all other pieces of clothing had come off too, she supposed.

She'd almost called Gavin "Miles" at one point, but had managed to cover up her near mistake with a moan. She hadn't thought much about Miles over the last several weeks, so she wasn't sure why his name had popped into her head at such an inopportune time. She was far more excited about going home and seeing Brody than she was about seeing Miles. He was right; she adored that damn dog. *Shit.* Now she couldn't get Miles out of her head.

She sat up and closed her eyes for a moment. She'd forgotten all about the familiarity of her space in the shed until tonight. She had the same feeling now, with Gavin in her bed, but Miles was the name lodged in her brain. Her memories seemed to be fighting to resurface. Dani didn't want them back.

Unsure what else to do, she retrieved her clothes from the floor and dressed. That act, too, seemed familiar. She dressed without a sound, then took the socks from the windowsill, where Gavin had left them, and pulled them on. They were too big for her feet; she didn't care. She slipped her boots on and laced them.

She glanced at the bed and saw Miles in it.

He slept on a small mattress on the floor in a room lit by a candle instead of an oil lamp. He had a jagged scar on his right shoulder that extended to the right side of his chest, over his pectoral muscle.

Dani gasped. She blinked, and once again recognized Gavin in the bed.

I'm losing my fucking mind!

This time the memory had been clear, and it frightened her. She shivered, but not from the cold.

She pulled her jacket on and slipped out of the room. She needed to think about something else—anything but her past and the tangle of memories interfering with her current life.

CHAPTER
37

They'd been back in Bangor for three days now. Since their return, Dani had been busy catching up on her training, and Gavin, Houston, and other CNA brass had been spending hours each day discussing tactics based on the new information they'd brought back from Portland.

She'd slept with Gavin once more since the night near Augusta. He wanted her to move back to Mount Hope, but she'd said no. He hadn't hid his irritation at her refusal, and she didn't blame him. But she couldn't lose herself with him like she wanted to, for fear of calling him the wrong name. Her face flushed impossibly hot any time she saw Miles, so she was trying to avoid him too.

She and her brother walked toward the waterfront clad in CNA-issue fatigues, Brody leading the way.

"We're running squads of fifteen volunteers," Jace said. "We have three four-man teams, plus two sabs and one squad leader. One sab for two fireteams. Patel is with teams Alpha and Bravo; you're with Charlie and Delta."

"Sabs?"

"Saboteurs. You handle the tech. Disarm shit you find. Once the building is cleared, you blow it."

"Okay."

"You're armed, but only with a pistol, since you need to be mobile and quiet. The rest of us will have rifles, and our job is to keep you alive so you can do your damage. We happen to have a hound with us, too." He pointed at Brody.

"He's not trained for that," Dani said.

"While you were gone, Javi and Oliver worked with him to teach him to alert us when a person is in a room before we enter to clear it. I have to say, the damn dog is impressive."

Dani frowned. "Us?"

Jace smiled. "I bummed some medical care off the Commonwealth. The arthritis is gone. I'm like a pup again. Ask Hattie."

"Ugh. No. I can't handle you talking about sex."

Jace's boisterous laugh surprised her. "Marcic, Elmore, Miles, and I are fireteam Charlie. You'll be Brody's handler; Javi will brush you up on that today before we start. You and the mutt will check for and disable traps and bombs, and we'll be right with you. If someone is detected in a room, you back off, and we'll clear it. We continue through the structure, room by room. Delta team follows a few minutes behind to clean up any Wardens when they regen."

"Ah. Good idea."

"We're using sim, simulated, rounds in our weapons today. They won't kill you, but they do still sting like a bitch when you get shot with one. I recommend not getting hit. But if you do take a hit, if it's non-fatal, you keep going with a limp or one-armed or whatever until we drag you out of the building. If it's a fatal shot, play dead. Got it?"

"Yeah, I think so."

"It's the closest to the real thing as we can get." Jace retrieved a tiny, clear device with a round piece of metal inside from his bag and handed it to her. "Here. Comm unit. Stick it in your ear. You speak normally to talk to someone else through it."

She rolled the device around on her palm. "It's so small. Won't it fall out?"

"No. Somehow the techies rigged them to stay in and be practically invisible. They're not hard to remove, either. Takes some practice, but you'll figure it out."

Dani's mind reeled with all the new information. Jace acted like this was just another day—and it was for him, she supposed. While she was in Portland, everyone else had been training. She hoped she didn't screw up the team too much while she adjusted. Miles being on the team she'd be working with most closely didn't help the other issues going on inside her head. She inserted the comm in her ear and tried to think of other things.

"Javi has cameras rigged everywhere, so he'll be watching us," Jace said. "On the uppermost level of the buildings we're training in today, people will be firing grenades into empty buildings to create real combat noise, dust, and smoke. Some of our volunteers are young and have only lived in Bangor, so this is their first time hearing these kinds of explosions. It's good practice so they don't freeze when the real shit hits the fan in Portland."

Dani nodded. She and Gavin had almost been deafened inside the sewers when the Wardens started blasting the Western Promenade. They'd survived with only minor injuries and a persistent ringing in their ears that had lasted a couple of days. She hoped the noise from today's training didn't have the same effect on her.

Dani got a quick lesson from Javi on how to work with Brody before training began: he did a practice run with her and the dog with first an empty room, and then one with someone hidden inside. After that, he pronounced her ready.

Once everyone had their gear ready, Javi, who was serving as their platoon leader, spoke into his comm, giving the four fireteams, those that would be firing grenades, and the people serving as hidden civilians or hostiles inside the buildings their orders. The fireteams moved into position, and they began.

Dani drew her weapon and crept through the door of the first building. Brody stayed beside her, and when she stopped, he did too. She was impressed; the ninety-pound goof had a serious switch she hadn't known existed until now.

She inched forward and spotted a trip wire. She gestured for Brody to back up, then holstered her weapon. She repeated the list of steps Gavin had taught her and quickly disabled the wire.

She signaled to her team that it was safe to proceed. Miles was the first of the four-man fireteam to follow her into the building. She and Brody moved toward the first room off the entryway. She wouldn't be killed by the sim rounds, but her heart still raced. The tension of creeping through rooms without knowing who or what was waiting for them frazzled her nerves worse than the sewers had.

At the second room, she missed Brody's alert that someone was inside. As she stepped through the doorway a sharp pain struck her neck, and she stumbled. She fell on her back, clutching the side of her neck.

"Fuck!" she said with a grimace.

"Charlie and Delta, reset," Javi said through the comm. "You just died, Dani."

She wiped at the wetness on her neck, expecting blood, but her hand was spattered with yellow paint. Still, her neck burned with pain, and she felt a welt begin to form.

"I told you it hurt to get hit," Jace said.

Miles, Jace, Marcic, and Elmore stood over her, grinning. Brody wagged his tail and licked her cheek.

"Charlie, stop screwing around and reset!" Javi said.

Miles extended his hand and helped Dani up while the others returned to the outside of the building. Her face flushed. Thankfully, he mistook it for embarrassment over taking a sim round in the neck within her first five minutes of urban warfare training.

"Don't feel bad," he said. "Our entire fireteam was wiped out in the first fifteen minutes of training our first day. I know it's easy to get rattled, but keep a close eye on Brody. He alerted that someone was in the room—you just missed it. Also, after you cut the trip line, you didn't re-draw your weapon."

"Well, I guess I just fucked that up every possible way." Dani continued to rub the burning lump on her neck.

"You'll get the hang of it. Javi resets us if we really screw up, and we'll keep going until we have the building clear. Sometimes it's easier to get popped with a sim round early on. It's like learning to ice skate."

Dani nodded. "Once you bust your ass, falling is no longer a big deal."

"Exactly."

"Why didn't you just tell me when I was screwing up?"

Miles smiled. "Do you think you'll ever miss Brody's alert or forget to redraw your weapon again?"

"I get it. Learn from your mistakes." Dani rubbed her neck again. "When does the stinging stop?"

"In a few hours, so it's a constant, but good, reminder."

They spent the next several hours working their way through the building, resetting, and doing it again all while grenades tore apart nearby buildings and shook the one they were in. By half-way through the day, every member of Dani's fireteam had at least one or two spatters of yellow paint on them. Dani had six.

They approached what felt like their hundredth room of the day. Brody signaled a person's presence, so Dani backed away and waved her team into the room to clear it. Jace winked at her as he went by.

Seconds later, a young man ran out of the room. He stopped and turned after passing Dani. She spotted his weapon and fired her pistol first. Paint spattered on his chest and he fell. He tried to play dead, but he reflexively clutched the sore spot on his chest.

Dani gaped at the gun in her hand. She'd reacted without thinking, which was the whole point of her years of training with Gavin, but still, the ease with which she'd shot the young man startled her.

"Nicely done," Miles said and patted her on the back as he came out of the room. Marcic and Elmore congratulated her as well.

"Good job," Jace said. "Those fake civilians are the ones that usually shoot one of us. Quick little bastard slipped out before we could stop him."

Before Dani could respond, shouts rang out from above, and Javi's voice blasted into their comms. "Take cover! Take cover!"

Dani thought it was part of the training—until she noticed that Jace's eyes were wide with fear. The young man who was "dead" sprang to his feet and sprinted for the stairs. Jace threw his arms around Dani and took her to the floor as the blast erupted from two floors above.

Pain tore through Dani's body, and all air was forced from her lungs with a second impact to her back. She groaned and tried to breathe, but everything hurt. She couldn't think. She tried to sit up, and everything went dark.

The next time she woke, she was in a bed in a room she didn't recognize. She tried to move and winced. Mary appeared from nowhere and sat on the bed beside her.

"Hey." Mary smiled, though tears spilled from her eyes.

Dani resisted the urge to go back to sleep. "What happened?"

"How do you feel?"

"Don't change the subject. What happened?"

"The launcher malfunctioned, and the armed grenade dropped on the top floor of the building you were in. It caused a partial collapse of the two floors above you, and you were injured."

"What happened to everyone else?"

"The men using the launcher were killed. Miles was injured, but he still got you out. He'll be fine."

"Jace? Elmore and Marcic had him, I think. I'm not sure. Where's Brody?"

"They're still looking for Brody."

Dani tried to sit up, but sudden pain in her left shoulder and back made her stop. She wore a sling on her arm and had some sort of bandage stuck to her skin running from her elbow to her shoulder, where the bandage split and ran to her back and along her neck. Tiny lights on the dressing blinked. She'd never seen anything like it before.

"Your shoulder blade and collar bone are broken, and your shoulder was dislocated by falling debris. You bruised your lung, and you have a concussion. Some of the debris cut your neck, but it wasn't bad enough to make you bleed out."

That explains why I feel like shit.

"You're in the hospital at the barracks," Mary said. "The stuff on your skin helps speed healing."

"Jace was on top of me when the explosion hit. How is he?"

Mary stared at her hands for a moment before answering. "He died last night."

"What age did he regen to? Is he younger than me now?"

Mary shook her head. "He . . . died, Dani. He didn't regen."

"But . . . he's half Echo," Dani said. She felt a sudden tightness inside her chest; she could barely breathe.

"I'm so sorry, Dani."

"Brody is missing, and Jace is . . ." Dani closed her eyes and groaned. "This wasn't supposed to happen." She shook her head, and tears began to fall.

Mary stayed with her until she quieted and fell asleep again.

CHAPTER

38

Dani sat at the table in her shed. The hospital had released her that morning. Brody remained missing, and her brother was still dead. She'd eaten enough food in the hospital to make them happy, though she had no appetite and wasn't sleeping. She wanted to help search for her dog, but her body wasn't healed enough for that much activity. She continued to wear the sling, and healing patches still covered her shoulder and part of her back.

Mary was the only person she had allowed in the shed since returning to it. The food Mary had left for her remained untouched on the table before her. She'd turned both Gavin and Miles away today. She wanted to thank Miles for getting her out of the building, but she wasn't ready for company. Oliver and Houston had sent her messages on the comm unit, but she hadn't yet bothered to see what they said.

The tiny light on the unit blinked, begging for her attention. Dani flipped the unit over to make the blinking light go away.

Jace wasn't coming back. How could that be true?

"Dani, I'm coming in, honey," Hattie said from the other side of the door.

Dani didn't have time to protest before the woman was

through the door and had it closed again. She shifted her stiff body to glare at her visitor.

"Life fucking sucks for you and me," Hattie said. "No need to sugarcoat the bullshit; it'll still stink. I'm not here to try to cheer you up, because that's just bullshit too. Neither of us is in a mood to be cheery, right?"

Dani's face softened, and she nodded. She appreciated Hattie's blunt, honest approach.

"I asked Jace to wait for you to get back from Portland, but he insisted we get married."

"I'm glad you didn't wait. He loved you, and he was genuinely happy." Dani's last memory of Jace was his terrified face, but she didn't mention that part. She was just glad that they had talked before she left for Portland, and that her brother had seemed happy in his relationship with Hattie.

The older woman spoke, but Dani's mind was on her brother. "Huh?" she asked, realizing she'd missed something.

"He said the two of you spoke before you left," Hattie said. "He didn't say what you discussed, but he was at peace. I'm not sure how else to explain it. He had a calm I hadn't seen before. He kept saying, 'This time is different,' but I don't know what he meant."

Dani stared at the table. "This is my fourth life. In the prior three, I've died the same way—friendly fire, at the age of twenty-five. I've been stuck in a loop of making the same choices and mistakes. Jace told me parts of the pattern were broken this time, and that some events had changed. Others, like me getting a dog, remained the same. When he said things were different, I didn't know that meant he would die to keep me alive." Fresh tears slid down her cheeks, and she wiped them away. "I'm sorry. I never would have gone on that training run if I'd known it meant he wouldn't come back."

"He knew he might not regen," Hattie said. "It's clear he

loved you more than his own life, even if he never said the words. And no one could have predicted an accident like this. No one is to blame, Dani. We both loved that crotchety bastard, and it sucks to be the ones living without him."

Dani nodded. Right now, she didn't want to live, period.

"Folks are still searching for Brody; we haven't given up on him."

"I want to help look for him."

"Not today. Get some rest, honey." Hattie laid a gentle hand on top of Dani's head for a moment, then left.

Dani stared at the closed door blankly and traced her fingertips over the closed wounds on her neck. Without Commonwealth tech, the deep cuts would have taken at least a week to close. Bones that would normally take six to eight weeks to heal on their own healed in under two weeks with the patches they'd put on her.

Her shoulder ached, and she wished she'd asked Hattie for some of her medicine. She used her foot to scoot her pack closer to her. Instead of picking it up from the floor, she used her free hand to unzip the pack and pawed around inside it, hoping to find the packet of a few pills the hospital had given her when she was discharged. Her fingers landed on the pistol in the bottom of the bag. She pulled it out, placed it on the table, peeled back the cloth wrapping, and let her eyes travel the length of the weapon.

Put it away.

No, pick it up.

Instead, she lowered her head as new tears came. She wanted the ache in her chest to go away more than she needed the physical pain to disappear.

She moved the pistol from the table to her lap.

What if she died in this life by her own hand? Regen would make her current wounds and scars disappear—plus she could forget everything with one squeeze of the trigger. It tempted her more than she would ever admit. She didn't want to forget Jace and all he'd done for her, but. . . .

Grief consumed her thoughts, and she pulled the hammer back with her thumb. She slipped her hand over the grip, and her index finger touched the edge of the trigger.

She sat with the weapon cocked and lying in her lap for several minutes.

No. Jace would be so disappointed if she took the easy way out now. He'd raised her four times, and she couldn't, wouldn't, undo everything he'd done for her over several decades with one bullet. She placed her thumb on the hammer, squeezed the trigger, and eased the hammer down. She put the weapon back on the table and dropped her hand back to her lap.

She closed her eyes for a moment and sighed. When she opened her eyes again, the room had changed. She assumed she was dreaming. The sling was gone, and she shivered when cool air drifted across her bare arms. The gun was gone, and she had a mix of wiring before her. A dog slept on an old blanket on the floor near her feet. She recognized him, but he was not her current Brody. Dani turned in her chair, no longer stiff and sore from her injuries, and spotted Miles. He rolled to his side to sit up. He passed his hands through his hair and yawned. The dog lifted his head for a moment before going back to sleep.

"What are you working on?" he asked.

Dani blinked a few times before answering. "Nothing, really."

"Did you sleep well?"

"Um, yes?"

Miles chuckled. "You don't sound too sure."

"Weird dreams."

"Yeah, I hate those kinds of nights. Hard to know when

you're awake or asleep sometimes."

"Uh-huh," Dani said.

Miles retrieved his clothes from the floor and dressed. He pulled his boots on last and paused when lacing them. "You waxed my boots."

"Yeah." *He hates wet socks*, she thought, and wondered how she knew this detail.

"Thanks! Nothing is worse than wet socks."

Dani shivered again. She'd had this part of the conversation with him before, of that she was certain.

He finished lacing his boots and approached her. He leaned down, gave her a long kiss, and she didn't resist or try to avoid him. "See you tonight, yeah?"

Dani nodded, though she wasn't sure if that was the right answer.

He smiled and left. The door latched behind him with a loud click. She jumped at the noise—and found herself back in the shed. Brody's blanket on the floor was empty.

More images filled her mind, and she pieced together a few more memories—against her will. She wasn't ready to cope with the mix of emotions these memories of her prior life with Miles stirred up inside her. *Where is that damn medication?* She stood with a groan and used the table for support until some of the pain lessened. She intended to make the pain, physical and emotional, disappear with some of Hattie's elixir. She was sure the older woman would give her some if she asked.

She pulled the door open to leave and instead found Oliver, poised to knock on the door.

She scowled. "What do you want?"

Oliver lowered his hand. "To talk to you."

"Go away."

He ducked under her arm and slipped between her and the door to enter.

"You're such a little shit." She sighed, turned, and glared at him.

Oliver ignored her as he placed the book he was carrying on the table, covered the pistol with the cloth it sat on, and eased the weapon off the table.

"Leave that alone."

He darted past her again. She turned too quickly to try to catch his arm, and drew in a sharp breath when her body reminded her of her injuries.

Oliver ran across the yard and vanished through the back door of Hattie's brothel. Seconds later, he reappeared without the weapon.

"What did you do?" Dani shouted from the doorway of her shed. "Bring it back."

"No." Oliver moved past her and entered the shed again.

"I'm not in the mood for this crap. Bring the gun back and go away, Oliver."

He slid the book off the table. "Have you seen this before?"

Dani's eyes landed on the object, and she nodded. "It's Jace's."

"It's his journal, and he asked me to take it and read it if anything happened to him."

"And?"

"You need to read it too."

Dani shook her head. "I can't read his journal, Oliver. My shoulder is fucking killing me, and I need medicine to make it go away. Make yourself useful instead of being a pain in my ass, and get a bottle of Hattie's medicine for me."

"No. Gavin took it away from you before. The hospital didn't give you medicine?"

"It's somewhere in the bottom of my pack," she said with a wave of her hand at the pack on the floor.

Oliver knelt by the pack and dug through the zippered

pouches until he found a small pouch with four orange pills inside it. "This it?"

Dani nodded.

"How many are you supposed to take?"

"All of them."

"Liar." He placed one tablet in her hand.

She put the pill in her mouth, and he passed her the mug of water sitting on her table. She took a drink and swallowed the tablet.

He took the mug back and pointed to the mattress on the floor. "Sit."

The command reminded her of something he would say to Brody. Her temper flared, but he wasn't listening to anything she said, and he was too fast for her to catch him and throw him out, so she relented. She eased her rump onto the mattress and leaned her back against the wall.

Oliver shoved the packet of remaining pills in his pocket before sitting next to her with the book.

"I'll find out when it's time for you to have another pill and come back to give it to you. Aunt Hattie has the revolver, but don't ask her for it. I told her not to give it back to you. I know you're sad, Dani. You weren't cleaning the gun. What were you going to do with it?"

Dani tightened her jaw.

"I'm glad you didn't. We're all sad about Jace." His face fell. "And I miss Brody. I don't want to lose you too. Promise me you won't hurt yourself."

Dani nodded.

"Say it."

"I promise I won't do anything to hurt myself," Dani said.

"Good. Thank you. You're an important person, Dani."

She shook her head. "You're wrong."

"I'm sitting here next to you because of things you did

fifteen years ago. Maybe you don't remember them, but it was you. When the Wardens attacked Portland, you saved my mom. And my dad. I know you died, but everything is in here." Oliver held the book out for her to take. "My mom and dad lived that day because of you, and that's the only reason I am on this planet. You fought for my future, though you didn't know it at the time."

Dani took the journal from him and placed it in her lap.

"Jace wrote a letter to you. It's in the book, and it's sealed, so I didn't read it."

She flipped open the book and used her good hand to turn the pages to the front. She stared at the words, written in Jace's hand and dated the year the war began. She closed her eyes for a moment and took a deep breath. "I don't think I can do this."

"You can. I'll stay with you."

She took another deep breath and opened her eyes. She gazed down at the book in her lap and started reading.

Dani turned the pages as she read entries about her parents, and the family trip to Boston that coincided with the Wardens' attack on the planet.

"My last name is Ireland?"

Oliver furrowed his brow. "You didn't know that?"

She shrugged. "That was a detail that wasn't ever important to surviving, so I never thought to ask Jace."

"Dani Ireland." Oliver smiled. "I like it."

"I think I'll stick with just Dani."

Trying to read a book with one arm in a sling was awkward. Oliver helped by holding the left side of the pages down for her as she turned pages. She resumed reading for a while, and stopped to look at the few pictures between the pages. She didn't bother wiping away tears as she read Jace's accounts of her deaths and the things he'd done to care for and protect her when she regenerated back to a child.

"Why didn't he give me this before? I didn't know what he went through, and he never told me."

"Keep reading," Oliver said.

She continued turning the pages and paused after the account of her last death. Oliver had told the truth. She'd saved Coulson from being shot in the back by Wardens, then killed the Warden trying to kill Miles. She looked at Oliver. "Does your father know about this book?"

"Yeah. He hasn't read it since Jace didn't give me permission to let anyone but me and you read it, but I did tell him that Jace wrote an entry about him seeing you save Mom and another MP with her. You saved her and Dad, then Mom let Jace pass when you were back to being a kid again."

Dani nodded. "Jace told me a lot about my history, but he left some big pieces out."

"I wouldn't be here if it wasn't for you, Dani."

She wasn't sure how to respond, so she resumed reading until she reached the folded paper sealed with a blob of wax. Her name was written across the paper. Oliver helped her break the seal, and she read the note from Jace. It made her cry, but she forced herself to finish it.

Afterward, she and Oliver sat in silence for a while.

"Bring me my pack, please," Dani said.

Oliver sprang up from his place on the mattress, and she envied his agility. He returned with the pack, and she reached into it, removed a pencil, and flipped to the back of Jace's book, where she wrote her own entry—two full pages. When done, she folded the pages so the edges tucked into the center of the book and wrote her name on the outside.

"What's that?" Oliver asked.

Dani returned her pencil to her pack. She closed Jace's book and handed the journal back to Oliver.

"It's a letter from me, to me. You're the keeper of this book,

Oliver. If anything happens to me, you're in charge of getting this book and that letter back to me. Understand?"

He nodded.

She leaned the back of her head against the wall. "I'm so tired."

"Get some sleep. I can stay in case you wake and need anything."

"You don't have to stay. I'll be fine."

His face grew serious. "Remember your promise."

Dani gave him a small smile. "I remember it." She hugged the boy. "Thank you for everything, Oliver."

After sleeping soundly for a few hours, Dani got up and left the shed for the brothel. There, Mary helped her wash and change clothes, a task not easily done alone and with one arm.

The first thing Dani did upon returning to her shed was empty her pack on the table. Fifteen minutes later, a knock on the door interrupted her gear organization. She opened the door and gasped to see Brody in Miles's arms. She lunged for them both—threw her arm around Miles and buried her head in Brody's fur, despite his wiggles to try to lick her face.

"Ollie is bringing food and water for him," Miles said. "I guess you didn't see his message."

Dani pulled her face from Brody's fur and kissed his head. "I was asleep for a while."

"He'd fallen through a hole in the floor and was trapped. We were searching for him on the upper levels, which is why we couldn't find him. Javi called the MP's vet, so he's already been checked. Other than being hungry, a little dehydrated, and banged up from the fall, he's fine."

Dani touched the bandage on Brody's right front foot.

"He has a nasty cut on one of his pads, so the vet wrapped his paw. He can limp along on his other three legs, but I opted to carry him since that was the fastest way to get him to you." Miles lowered the dog to the floor, and when Dani knelt down to pet him, Brody wagged his tail so hard his body shook.

"Food!" Oliver announced as he arrived with two bowls. Brody thrust his head into the bowl of stew as soon as it touched the floor.

Dani stood and hugged Miles again. "Thank you for finding him."

Miles smiled. "He's a good dog."

"He is," Dani said, unable to stop smiling. She realized she still had her arm around Miles. She moved her hand to her pocket, her face burning with embarrassment.

Oliver darted back to the house to get more stew for Brody, and the dog moved to his bowl of water, sloshing liquid across the floor as he lapped it up.

"What's this?" Miles asked with a nod toward the table.

"I was just starting to resort my gear for Portland when you knocked."

Miles scratched at the stubble on his jaw. "Dani, they're meeting today to discuss Portland. The training accident has people rethinking the attack. Many are calling for it to be canceled, and a lot of people think the Brigand council will agree."

"Canceled?"

Miles nodded.

"When is the meeting?"

"It's about to start."

Oliver arrived with fresh bowls of stew and water.

"Can you keep Brody company for a bit?" Dani asked.

Oliver nodded and knelt by the dog while Brody started on his second bowl of stew.

Dani grabbed her jacket from the back of the chair. She slipped her arm through the right sleeve and pulled the other side over her left shoulder.

"What are you doing?" Miles asked.

"Crashing another meeting."

CHAPTER

39

fter reaching the top of the stairs to the old courthouse, Dani stopped. Her breath fogged in the cold night air. She wanted another moment to rest, but she instead forced her feet to keep moving.

"Dani, the doctors worked their asses off to save you," Miles said. "Don't undo everything and drop dead over this stupid meeting."

"You think we should give up on Portland?"

"No."

"Neither do I." Dani pushed the heavy door open and stumbled. Miles caught her before she fell to the floor.

"Thanks," she said. "That would've hurt. Maybe I should go a little slower."

"Think so?" Miles kept his arm around her as they walked.

Dani appreciated his assistance, and she didn't stumble again.

They continued down the hall. "Why must they meet way the hell in the back? Plenty of rooms closer to the entrance."

"Stop whining."

She chuckled, but her fatigue remained. He held the final door open for her; when she entered the room, the people seated around the large table inside quieted. Gavin shot up from his chair as she walked through the center row between the empty chairs on both sides of the room and met her halfway. She leaned on one of the empty chairs to rest a moment.

"You look like shit," he said.

"Thanks. Sorry I'm late." *Not that I was invited.*

When she finally reached the front of the room, she lowered herself into a chair in the row closest to the table and wiped at the sweat running down her face. The night air was far too cold for her to be sweating like this. Her shoulder pain had returned with a vengeance; she wished she had one of those pills with her.

Gavin and Miles sat on either side of her.

"Why did you bring her here?" Gavin asked Miles with a frown.

"She wanted to come, so she did." Miles shrugged. "You know you don't have a choice in anything when she insists on doing something, regardless of how stupid it seems."

Dani scowled at Miles.

"What? It's true."

"It's good to see you, Dani, though this meeting doesn't require your presence," Houston said.

"Well, ya have it anyway," Dani said. "Let's make this quick, since I could pass out any second. We had a cluster fuck of a training accident and people were injured, some killed. Now folks are skittish about attacking Portland. That's the short version, yes?"

Houston nodded.

"Show of hands," Dani said, raising her own. "Who wants to stay on course for Portland and boot the Wardens out of Maine?"

Miles, Gavin, Houston, and another CNA officer Dani didn't recognize raised their hands.

Dani looked at the four remaining people at the table who

were keeping their hands either in their laps or on the table. "Okay, if you didn't raise your hand, you're either undecided or want to quit. If you want to quit, the door is back there," she said with a wave of her hand in the general direction of the rear of the room. "If you're undecided, you're not anymore, unless you make a last-second sprint for the door."

No one moved.

"Good. Everyone is for attacking Portland. Now, it's time to stop pissing yourselves and get on with it. We have an invasion to plan."

"It's not that simple," Houston said.

"It is." Dani looked at Gavin. "Did you already explain the plan to them?"

"We didn't get that far yet. We were trying to come to a consensus about the attack when you came in."

"Consensus?" Dani said with a laugh. "Arguing and not getting anywhere is what it sounded like to me."

Gavin shrugged.

"No one ran for the door. Consensus reached. The only piece left to figure out is when. Lieutenant Colonel Houston, would you please use your panel to search long-range forecasts for major storms due to hit Portland this winter?"

Houston paused. "This winter?"

"Yes."

Houston lifted the device in front of her from the table, and Dani slumped a little in her chair while waiting.

"You're really pale," Miles whispered.

Gavin nodded. "You look terrible, Dani." He looked at Miles. "Take her back to Hattie's."

Dani lifted her chin. "I'm staying."

"Okay, in a few weeks, early November, four inches of snow projected, followed by a six-inch storm a week later," Houston said.

"Nothing less than a foot," Dani said.

"A ten- to twelve-inch one is forecast for early December, and an eighteen-inch one mid-December."

"Temps?"

"Upper twenties, Fahrenheit, for the first one, and upper teens for the second one."

"January?"

"January sucks. Single-digit highs most of the month. Zero and lower on several nights. Well into sub-zero for wind chills, and a projected two to three feet of snow, with strong winds on the twelfth going into the thirteenth."

"When is low tide on those dates?"

Houston tapped a few times on her screen. "Uh, right around midnight on the twelfth."

"Perfect!" Dani sat up straighter. She instantly regretted the quick movement but tried to hide the wave of nausea that accompanied the shock of pain in her shoulder.

"You want to attack before the storm or after?" Houston asked.

"During."

"*During?*"

Scattered murmurs came from others seated at the table.

"Saltwater freezes at seventeen degrees Fahrenheit. Even if the Wardens are able to break up the ice in the bays and harbors, they won't be able to keep their bigger boats close to the port without risking them getting stuck in the ice. We attack before midnight, so the tide will be low and still going out. If they have broken the ice, they still won't be able to get anything near Fore River at that time, and then for several hours after that, until the tide comes back in. You have pilots for helos and fixed-wings, yes?"

Houston nodded.

"If we can't commandeer the aircraft onsite for your pilots, we can at least ground them so they can't be used against us during the attack. Planes don't like ice, so again, we can use the colder temps to our advantage."

"The Warden crews in the observatories on the Promenades will be too concerned with freezing their balls off to stay out in that weather," Gavin said.

"What about our own troops freezing their balls off?" Houston asked.

"Please," Dani said. "If our Mainers can't handle the cold after growing up in this shit, they shouldn't be volunteers."

"How well do you think we'll be able to move in that much snow?" Houston asked.

"Visibility will suck, but we'll be fine using the sewers—no snow down there."

"What about the snow covering the drains and manholes?"

"We'll only need a few of them cleared—enough for us to surface when setting charges prior to the full assault. Once the initial charges go off, there will be no more hiding."

Houston tapped more commands on her screen and placed the panel in the center of the table. A 3-D, topographic map of the Portland area that spanned most of the length of the table sprang up. "Show me."

"This is all you," Dani said to Gavin. "I can't stand for that long."

He nodded and left her side to approach the table. "We'll maintain radio silence beginning now, and only the people in this room will know the details of the attack," he said. "Understood?"

The group nodded.

"If we have an info leak," he said, "I'll find the source and kill you myself. It won't be quick or painless."

"I will need to report our plans to my superiors," Houston said.

"Lie," Gavin said. "Tell them whatever you want except what we're actually doing."

"I'm using CNA resources for this, Gavin. I can't lie."

He rapped his fist on the table. "Not everyone in the CNA is loyal to the Commonwealth. Lie. Tell them we're going anywhere but Portland."

Houston looked uncomfortable, but she nodded slowly.

"Okay," Gavin said. "The first parts of the attack will have to be done according to time, since we will keep long-range communications quiet until the larger attack begins. We won't have audio and visual signaling initially. We have maps of most of the sewer system beneath Portland, including the airport and Warden base. We have three hundred sixty volunteers that we'll split into two companies. The volunteers will leave for Portland, six weeks prior to January twelfth."

Houston checked her tablet. "That would be December first."

"Good. Three weeks later, ma'am, your battalion will head south. Put two hundred troops in Yarmouth with our Brigand contacts already there. That group will be four hundred strong with the Brigands added, and you'll take the power plant on Cousins Island at the appointed time. The rest of your battalion will continue inland to circle around Portland and approach from the south. You'll pick up more Brigands along the way who will help guide you through the terrain."

Miles leaned close to Dani's ear. "You planned all this with him?"

She nodded and smiled. "It gets better."

"Send two hundred troops with another two hundred Brigands to take Portland Head Light and Fort Williams area at your scheduled time. Secure the bunkers, here, here, and here." Gavin pointed to specific areas along the coast by the lighthouse. "Once secure, you'll leave those posts manned and move on to take the petrol port in South Portland on the other side of the river from Portland. It won't be as iced in as the shallower parts of the river, but you shouldn't have any boats. The Brigands report that tankers rarely make port in the winter."

"What about the other forts on the islands in the bay?" Houston asked.

"Bomb the shit out of them later, when the storm moves out. The ice will prevent the Wardens there from being able to send reinforcements to the city."

"Where is the rest of my battalion, since you're only leaving me with six hundred ground troops?" Houston asked.

"Your numbers will be closer to a thousand with the Brigands added. You'll place those troops at the Warden base along the airstrips. All these areas are accessible through the sewers, so you'll be moving underground most of the time. The airport has two runways: this one, which runs east-west, and this one, which runs northwest-southeast." Gavin indicated the areas on the map.

"You're having me put a thousand people in the sewers?"

"Yes. We will use the weeks before you arrive to clear any hazards underground and set up markers that will allow you to navigate without getting lost. There are deep drainage ditches on the far sides of those strips with sewer lines just below the surface. We'll rig the pipes to create a fake top. You'll be underground, out of sight, and able to come out of the ground when it's time to attack."

Houston nodded. "L-shaped ambush."

"Exactly, but that doesn't happen until we, the volunteers, signal. When I split the volunteers, Alpha Company will be further broken down into smaller platoons. They will move in waves, concealed by the snow, and come in from the north over the Back Cove bridge to the Eastern Promenade. They'll take out the Wardens in the observatory and move across the peninsula to other strategic points such as City Hall, the Custom House, and the old armory, all of which have high vantage points that overlook the city. This first wave will continue on to their next targets without stopping. The second, larger wave will move in a few minutes behind them to kill the Wardens as they regen and place people in the towers. Visibility will be low for them too, but when the weather clears we'll have those areas secured."

Dani looked around the table. So far, everyone seemed to be on board with the plan.

"Bravo Company will be responsible for getting their assigned saboteurs and pilots to designated locations around and *within* the base," Gavin continued. "Bravo will also be responsible for taking out the real comm tower. These attack points in Yarmouth, South Portland, and the Portland peninsula will be done with as much stealth as possible. Noise-suppressed weapons, knives, choke wires, and the like will be used. We won't blow anything unless it's too well defended for us to take. These attacks will occur simultaneously, and we'll have people inside the base, accessible via the sewers, to blow secondary power sources once the comm and air traffic towers are down."

Dani was part of Bravo Company, which Gavin would lead. Javi was her platoon leader, and Miles was still part of the fireteam she was assigned to. The other members needed to be shuffled a little, since they'd suffered losses with the training accident. At this thought, Dani's vision blurred, and she pinched her eyes closed for a moment.

Miles's voice was in her ear again. "You okay?"

"A little dizzy is all. I'm fine." She felt terrible; she'd started sweating again. She fidgeted with the strap of her sling where it lay across her neck.

Gavin paused to take a breath. "Ma'am, you'll send a team of fifty to a hundred troops through the sewers beneath the airstrips to the base. They will wait there until the tower explosions, which will be your audio and visual signal to begin the ambush. Once that starts you can open radio comms to whomever you want, because the Wardens will know we're on their doorstep. As your ambushing troops close in from two sides, signal your final sewer troops to come up. They should emerge from behind or within the defending Wardens. Your ambush troops will switch to take out periphery targets so they don't shoot their own people, while your close combat troops wreak havoc from within the Warden defensive lines."

"What about the artillery mounts on top of the base?" Houston asked.

"Best-case scenario, we remotely detonate the towers and take the cannons before the Wardens can fully man them. Since that part of the plan has a lot of unknowns, you'll still prep for an airstrike follow-up with birds from Bangor."

Houston shook her head. "I don't have the resources for that kind of aerial assault."

"We just need to use them for the cannons. Once we start the major assault on the city, I expect the CNA will happily send in more troops and aircraft to finish cleaning up. They'll be dying to capture the island forts and greater Portland region once we have the base back."

Houston nodded. "The CNA needs a win. We all do."

"Agreed."

"You planned all this by yourself?" Houston asked, looking impressed.

"I had help," Gavin said with a glance back toward Dani. "We'll use the areas around the Bangor barracks to lay everything out as close to scale as we can to start drills tomorrow. We'll rehearse until we can navigate the Portland base with our eyes closed. Any other questions?"

"Nice work planning the assault, Dani. How about I give you a ride back to Hattie's?" Houston asked as they left the meeting.

"Thank you," Dani said.

Gavin and Miles helped her into the truck and sat with her for the short ride to Harlow Street. Dani's knees wobbled when she stepped out of the vehicle.

"When was the last time you ate?" Gavin asked.

She couldn't remember and closed her eyes. When she opened them again, she was sitting in her room on the mattress with her back against the wall, and Gavin was kneeling on the floor in front of her with a bowl in his hand.

"What happened?" she asked.

"You passed out," he said.

"I did?"

"Here," he said, and held the bowl of cold stew up to her mouth.

She took a sip of the broth and winced.

"Drink it."

"It's cold," she said.

"Drink it anyway."

She took a few more sips. "I don't want any more."

"Too bad." Gavin put the edge of the bowl back to her mouth and tipped the bottom upward.

She swallowed several gulps of the liquid to keep it from spilling down her face and shirt as Gavin tilted the bowl. When it was half gone, she pushed the bowl away and wiped her mouth with her hand. "Christ, you trying to drown me with it?"

Gavin smiled. "Welcome back. Feel better?"

She nodded.

"Still dizzy?"

"Not anymore."

"Have you eaten anything since leaving the hospital?"

Dani shrugged with her uninjured shoulder.

"That's a 'no,' then." He placed an orange pill in her hand. "Take that and drink more of the broth."

She put the pill in her mouth and took the bowl from him. She drank the cold broth and swallowed it and the pill.

"Want me to bring more stew?" a boy's voice asked.

Dani looked over Gavin's shoulder and realized Oliver and Miles were also in the room. Brody sat next to Oliver. The dog had a droplet of drool at the corner of his mouth and was staring at her bowl. The injury to his foot clearly hadn't impacted his appetite.

"Sure," Gavin said to Oliver.

Miles squatted near Dani. "Your color is better."

Oliver darted out and returned with another bowl in record time. As he moved to give it to his father, Gavin extended his hand for it. "I've got this if you want to head home," he said to Miles.

"Dani, is there anything else you need?" Miles asked.

"No," she said. "I'll be fine. Thank you for your help today." She ignored Gavin's subsequent frown.

Miles nodded and stood.

"Bye, Dani," Oliver said with a small wave before leaving with his father.

"Bye," she said, waving with her good hand. When they were gone, she looked at Gavin. "I'm sorry I passed out."

He traded bowls with her. "You pushed yourself too hard today."

"I didn't mean to; it all hit me at once when I got to the courthouse." She drank the broth—warm this time. She enjoyed it much more than the cold version. She picked a few pieces of the vegetables from the stew with her fingers and ate those before placing the bowl on the floor.

Gavin moved the bowls to the table to keep them out of Brody's reach. He returned and sat next to her on the mattress.

Dani slipped her right arm between his arm and body. She laced her fingers through his and squeezed his hand. "You were amazing tonight explaining the plans for Portland."

"I had a lot of help working out the details." He leaned toward her and kissed her forehead. "You really need to rest."

He shifted to rise, and she kept a grip on his hand. "Stay here tonight."

"Are you sure? Seems like you've been avoiding me."

"I know. I'm sorry. Mentally and emotionally, I haven't been in the best places lately. I've had these little snippets of memories coming back. I never know when they will return, and they freak me out."

"Memories of what?"

Fatigue clouded Dani's mind, and she leaned her head against Gavin's shoulder. "Uh, Boston, I think. Buildings collapsed and Jace carried me away from them. I, uh, also remembered the dog I had when I lived in Portland, and I saw Miles."

"What else?"

"The one of Miles . . . he and I talked a little. I don't know if it was a memory or a dream. It's almost like that one was a mix of the two; I'm not sure what was real and what was my imagination."

"You had a life with him before."

"One I don't remember," she said. Her eyes closed, and Gavin repositioned her to lie on the mattress. He draped a blanket over her, and she stirred. "Will you stay?"

"Yeah." He settled next to her, and Dani shifted closer to him as he put his arm around her.

CHAPTER

40

Dani lost track of the next few days. She was out of the sling, but her shoulder remained stiff and sore. The Commonwealth doctor she had a follow-up appointment with assured her it was normal and would improve with more time. She spent her days training with her new fireteam. Jace had been replaced by a woman named Rosen, a CNA troop member and transfer from another fireteam. What the woman lacked in friendliness, she compensated for with lethality. She was an assassin—one with skills that made Dani both respect and fear her. Even Brody didn't bother to try to make friends with her.

In the evenings, Dani spent the bulk of her time with Mary in Hattie's cellar, catching up on how to use the CNA's newer explosive devices. She crossed paths with Gavin a few times, but since he spent his days and evenings finalizing plans with Houston, Dani wasn't seeing him much.

She yawned as she and Mary walked the last hundred yards to the MP barracks, where they were to meet the CNA supply officer and receive their new fatigues, winter camo, and the last of their gear before leaving for Portland.

"Late night with Gavin?" Mary asked.

"Nah. I didn't sleep well is all. Besides, I never know when I'll run into him anymore. Sometimes we're around each other constantly, and he spends the night . . . then I don't see him for days and we don't speak. I don't know what that means for whatever the hell it is we have going on."

"Don't overthink it. You care about each other. Go with that."

Dani shrugged. She was too tired to think much about anything this morning.

They walked into the supply depot—and, unexpectedly, found Gavin there waiting for them. Several tables were set out in a row with identical sets of packs, gear, and uniforms grouped neatly together. Gavin, clad in a crisp set of fatigues, waved them over. As they approached, Dani noticed that the left, upper part of his uniform had a name on it: Marcus. Last names had been so unimportant to her, she'd never thought to ask his. She'd known him for years and had never known his surname until now. Of course, she hadn't known her own until recently, either. She glanced at Mary and wondered about her last name too.

"These are the saboteur packs," Gavin said. "Go through them before you leave and memorize the contents and the order in which they're packed. These are your skins: winter camo and regular." He placed his palm on a stack of two, folded sets of clothes. "They will automatically adapt to your surrounding environments' lighting conditions to help conceal you, but your stealth is what will keep you alive. Remember that." He took one side step and placed his hand on a folded, thin, black set of clothing that included a pair of socks. "This is the CNA's newest armor. Body size and type doesn't matter too much with this gear. It'll conform to the wearer. Thin, lightweight, and it will thermoregulate for you. The socks will also keep your feet warm, even if wet. Put these on first, then put on your fatigues."

Gavin tossed the armor to Mary, then handed her a set of fatigues. "Change behind the doors over there to make sure everything fits well, though I expect it will," he said with a wave of his hand toward the side of the room. Mary headed for the line of bi-fold doors with her items. "This is your set." Gavin picked up a set of fatigues with two sets of armor on top and handed them to her.

"Why the extra armor?" Dani asked.

"Just put it on and wear it under your uniform at all times."

"Only one set of socks?"

"There's another pair in your pack."

"We're only issued two pairs?"

"Yes."

"Can I get a spare?"

Gavin sighed and left the table to dig in a tote on the floor. He returned with another pair of socks and put them inside her pack. "Happy?"

Dani rolled her eyes. "So today is all business again?"

"Dani." Gavin lowered his voice. "There's a lot going on, and a shitload of work left before we leave tomorrow."

"I get that; I do. But you confuse me when you spend the night and then disappear."

"That's not my intent. I specifically relieved the supply master this morning so I could see you."

"To give me my new uniform in person? Great." She sighed and followed Mary to the changing area.

Once behind the bifold doors, she stripped and pulled on the first set of armor. The second set slid over the first layer with ease. She dressed in her new fatigues and passed her fingers over the patch embroidered with her name on the left side of her chest.

She and Mary emerged from the changing area to return to the tables. Dani read the name on Mary's uniform.

"Smith?" she asked. "Really? Mary Smith?"

Mary chuckled. "No, but it's easier to pronounce than my real one. Mary Smith or Marella Sigursveinnsdottir?"

"That's a mouthful."

"Yeah. Icelandic. Not sure they could even make a name patch that long, so I just told them it was Smith." She glanced at Dani's patch. "I see you didn't bother with a last name."

"I wouldn't answer to anything other than Dani anyway," she said.

"You ladies done chatting?" Gavin asked. He didn't wait for an answer before he began giving them their helmets and the rest of their gear, including exterior armor.

By the time they left with their seventy-pound packs, Dani was also laden with a second, smaller pack of things for Brody. The dog had his own body armor, winter equipment, and food. She loved the gear, but left the supply depot far more irritated with Gavin than she'd been when she arrived.

Oliver and Miles were waiting for Dani and Mary back at Hattie's. Oliver took Brody for a walk while Dani, Mary, and Miles sat in the dining area to eat and relax.

"I think he's going to miss Brody more than he'll miss me," Miles said.

"Yeah." Dani smiled. "The damn dog has a way of making you fall in love with him."

Miles nodded and stared at her. Dani's face felt hot, and she smiled at the sight of one of Hattie's young men carrying three mugs of ale in for them.

"Aunt Hattie says this round is on her because you're leaving tomorrow, but you're buying your own after this," the man said.

"Fair enough," Dani said and took a sip from her mug. "Wow." She placed the mug back on the table. "This has that extra stuff in it. What did you call it?" She tilted her chin at Mary.

"Courage," Mary said with a smile. "Drink it slowly, Dani. Remember what happened last time."

Dani grinned and took another sip.

"What happened before?" Miles asked.

"She's a cheap date," Mary said. "Less than one mug in, and she doesn't mind making out with you."

"That's not true . . . well, the first part is."

Mary's eyebrows went up.

Dani took another sip, then set the mug aside. "Okay, fine, it's all true."

Miles leaned forward. "You and Dani?" he asked.

Mary grinned and nodded. "It was unfortunately cut short when she panicked."

"I didn't panic . . . much. This shit just makes my brain fuzzy. Oh!" Dani pulled the pair of socks from her pocket and handed them to Miles. "I mooched these for you as a spare set in case your other two pairs get wet. I know you hate wet socks."

"Thanks," Miles said, looking puzzled. "How did you know?"

"Oh, uh . . ." Dani made a grunting sound, shrugged, and reached for her mug.

Mary caught her hand. "Not so fast. Answer his question."

"I've been able to remember a few things here and there," Dani said. She frowned at her friend when she still wouldn't let her pick up the mug.

"Like what?" Miles asked.

"Well . . ." Dani reddened. "Do you have a nasty scar on your right shoulder that extends down to the right side of your chest?"

"Yeah," he said.

"From a fight with the Wardens soon after you joined the MPs, right?" That part of the memory had just resurfaced in the last few seconds, and it startled her. She pushed Mary's hand away, snatched her mug from the table, and took a long drink. She clutched the mug with both hands to keep them from shaking.

Miles nodded. "So your memories are back?"

"A few," Dani said.

"That's good, right?" Mary asked.

"No. They kinda show up unexpectedly—like seeing Miles in my bed when it's actually Gavin. Well, I mean, not always when we're having sex. Sometimes it's after. Christ, what's wrong with me? It's like I can't shut up." Dani placed the mug on the table and pushed it away from her. "This shit messes with my head. I'm sorry," she said to Miles. She pushed her chair back from the table, and Miles caught her chair to prevent her escape.

"Dani, relax," he said.

"Please don't tell Gavin what I said."

"We won't say anything to him," Mary said. "You really need to calm down."

"It's understandable that these memories would startle you," Miles said. "Hell, they would freak out anyone who was in your place."

Dani shook her head. "I don't know what to do. What if they pop up when I'm trying to set explosives?"

"First, stop panicking," Mary said. "You have three prior lifetimes of memories stuck somewhere in your head. When they come back, don't freak out. Just let them come, and sort through them later. You don't always have to figure everything out right away."

Miles nodded. "We're here if you want to talk about them. If you're uncomfortable talking to me, go to Mary. Neither of us will mind, and we won't ever tell anyone else about them."

Dani nodded and stared at the table.

"I'm glad you've had a few memories return," Miles said.

Mary excused herself for a moment and returned with two mugs that she set before Dani. "Water—to dilute the other stuff—and plain ale. Food is coming." She took Dani's first mug and finished it. "I've never seen someone get shitfaced as easily as you."

"It's embarrassing," Dani said and drank her water.

"It is." Mary smiled. "Can't take you out drinking, you freakin' lightweight."

Dani snorted a laugh. She took a deep breath, relieved that Miles didn't seem to mind her awkward confession about mixing up him and Gavin. She doubted Gavin would be as forgiving. Maybe it was a good thing he was too busy to spend time with her now.

CHAPTER

41

D ani's form almost disappeared in the mounting snow drift at the base of the air traffic tower. Wind gusts whipped snow around her body, and the driving snow stung her face. As expected, the Wardens had opted for shelter instead of standing out in the weather at their posts. This was making it much easier for Bravo to move around the base. She checked her watch: 2150. Alpha Company would start its assault on the Promenades and other targets in ten minutes. Houston's troops at the power plant and Alpha had an hour to secure their positions before Dani and Mary started the fireworks.

At 2210, Dani needed to be underground with her fireteam to meet with Javi and the rest of her platoon to take the fixed-wing jets on the river side of the north-south runway 740 yards away. At the same time, another platoon on the far north end of the same runway was assigned to secure the fixed-wing transport planes and helos in their hangars.

That left Javi's platoon with thirty minutes to take the birds, leaving enough time for Dani and Mary to get in position to detonate their bombs. Dani was due to blow the air traffic tower and the cannon on it at 2300; Mary was to destroy the real comm tower, tucked tightly in the corner of the Warden base's main building between the west and north wings, at the same time.

Following the start of the war, the Commonwealth had taken the former airport's main building, terminals, and parking garage and converted the three structures into one sprawling, five-story base, including barracks. When they'd abandoned the base to the invading Wardens fifteen years ago, the Wardens had expanded the base's buildings and operations. The new comm tower was flanked by the two wings of the base, each of which had a cannon. Mary and her fireteam had the more difficult task: accessing the real tower. Dani hoped her friend was successful.

The foul weather hindered their progress, but it also shielded her and the rest of the volunteers from the Wardens' view. Dani wiped snow from her eyelashes and turned her body to better protect her face from the blizzard's wrath and bitter wind chill.

Her helmet would have shielded her face from the wind and snow, but she could see better without it. She placed the last of the explosive charges at the base of the air traffic tower and pushed a mound of snow over the devices. A thumping noise from within the tower caused her eyes to widen. She was near the tower's external stairwell door, and someone on the inside was jogging down the stairs.

She flattened her back against the tower and sank into the drift. She pulled her knife from her belt and waited. The door opened, and a gust of wind jerked the door so it clanged noisily against the hinges. The Warden cursed and wrestled with the door. When he finally slammed it shut, he sprinted toward the barracks. Dani sent a mental "thank you" to Houston for the winter camouflage. The Warden never saw her, though she was inches from the door.

A harsh shiver shook her body, and she wasn't sure if it was from the cold or nerves. She rushed back to the open manhole five yards away and dropped through it. Miles helped her down, then slid the cover over the hole to seal it.

"What was that banging noise?" Rosen asked.

"A Warden coming out of the tower. Gave me a good scare, but he didn't see me." Dani pulled her gloves on and yanked her knit hat down so it covered her ears.

"Charges set?" Miles asked.

"Yeah. We're good. Where's Mary?"

"Her team hasn't finished yet."

"Should we assist?" Dani asked.

"No. Javi's been in my ear for us to get our asses back to the river. Mary will be fine. Go."

Dani checked her watch: 2202. The first wave of coordinated attacks on the Promenade had started.

The half-mile sprint through the sewers warmed Dani's chilled face and fingers. Her group passed through the CNA ground troops' line along the north-south runway before exiting the large drainpipe protruding from the side of the river bank and scrambling along the ice and up the embankment to join the three other fireteams that were gathered behind the hangar closest to the river.

"Where the hell is Tamu's fireteam?" Javi asked Miles. "They stop for a picnic?"

"They'll be here," Miles said. "If they'd been detected, this place would be going bonkers."

"We can't wait. We're already running behind. We have two fixed-wings in this hangar behind us that can launch vertically. The four fixed-wings in the open area need the runway, so they should be iced in, but we need to make sure they're disabled.

Miles, take your team and Tamu's team, if Mary ever finishes setting her charges, and take the east armory opposite the fixed-wings on the tarmac."

"Got it," Miles said.

"Patel, your team will set charges on the four jets if they're not iced in. I don't want to lose those birds, but we'll blow them if we need to." Patel nodded, and Javi continued. "At 2255, we'll use a plow to clear snow and hopefully get the two birds from this hangar in the air just after the air traffic and comm towers blow. This weather is worse than we expected."

"Welcome to Maine," Dani said, and Javi chuckled. She hadn't intended for her comment to be heard, but she was glad some of the tension around the attack had eased a little.

Movement close by made her and Rosen raise their weapons. Dani squinted; five people were coming toward them through the snow. She smiled and touched Rosen's arm. "They're ours."

"How do you know?" Rosen asked.

"The smallest one is Mary. Weaver is the tallest, Tamu is next tallest, Jens is built like a truck, and Zykov walks like he's been riding a horse for a hundred years."

Rosen grinned and lowered her rifle. "Zykov does walk like that."

"Glad you finally made it," Javi said to the arriving fireteam. "Miles, fill them in as you head out. We don't have time to re-review."

Dani walked with Mary as the two fireteams left the rear of the hangar to move toward the east armory, just over three hundred yards away. "Any problems?" she asked her.

"Nothing Jens couldn't handle," Mary said. "We left a dead Warden in the sewers below the base. You?"

Dani shook her head.

They continued in silence, Dani and Mary at the rear of

their teams. As they neared the armory, Miles and Tamu signaled the teams with hand gestures, and Rosen and Jens left the group. Dani soon lost sight of them in the blowing snow.

She hated waiting. Miles, Marcic, and Elmore always looked calm, but she felt like she had a hamster on a wheel inside her chest. She took a few deep breaths to calm herself, and a moment later Rosen and Jens returned carrying a body. The dead Warden was clothed in heavy, black body armor and wore a helmet.

Miles glanced over the body. "Dani," he said to them.

They dropped the body on the ground in front of Dani. She couldn't tell if the small-framed Warden was a man or woman. The body glowed blue under the heavy body armor, and Rosen jerked the Warden's head to the side. The sickening crunch of cervical bones snapping turned Dani's stomach. The glow stopped.

"That never gets old," Rosen said with a grin.

Christ, Rosen's a genuine fucking psychopath.

"Strip the body and put the gear on, Dani," Miles said. "I need someone on the inside, and you're closest to this Warden's size."

Dani shrugged out of her pack, unfastened her belt and pistol holster, and peeled off her winter camo layer as Mary and Elmore stripped the corpse. She tried not to look at the dead Echo. She stuffed her hat into a pocket in her fatigues before pulling them off too. The dual layers of CNA armor she was wearing helped keep her warm, but not warm enough. As she put the Warden armor on, her ears and face grew numb from the cold.

When she reached for her pistol and belt, Miles took them. "You're a Warden now, and you need to look just like this one. Use his."

Dani did as she was told and also traded gloves with the

dead man. Miles didn't argue when she moved her knives from her old belt to the Warden's. As she slipped the Warden's weapon, a far newer plasma pistol than her own, into the holster at her upper thigh, she made a mental note that she'd have to remember to reach lower to pull the weapon, since she typically wore her gun on her hip.

She slipped the helmet on, gasped, and pulled it off. "Wow." She put the helmet back on. "I can see everything out here like it's in the daytime. You guys have to get one of these."

"Marvel over it later," Miles said. "Get inside."

She checked her watch. 2223. *Shit.*

Mary picked up Dani's pack. "I'll keep this safe for you. Be careful."

Dani took a deep breath and circled to the rear of the building. The blowing snow had started filling in the prints made by Jens and Rosen. Dani followed them until she found the larger imprint in the snow where the Warden's body had fallen. She spotted the rear door and walked to it. The flat security panel near the door's handle blinked green. Her new suit contained some kind of proximity access somewhere on it. She had no idea what she was walking into or how many Wardens might be on the inside. Dani lowered her hand to the former Warden's pistol, took another deep breath, and pulled the door open.

CHAPTER
42

Dani was wishing she had Brody with her as she stepped through the door. The canines were being held well away from the worst of the firefight tonight, however. They would be brought in later, once they had the base, to help clear the remaining structures. It was a good plan—except Dani wanted him there with her now.

She scanned the immediate area; it was free of Wardens. The armory's interior was all metal beams and walls. It wasn't much warmer in there than it had been outside, except there wasn't any wind. Crates were stacked in groups and covered much of the floor. Several forklifts were parked in the far left corner.

She signaled, and the waiting fireteams entered without a sound. One of them eased the door closed, and Dani moved forward alone after it clicked shut.

Two Wardens sat in an open area at a table, playing cards next to a portable heater. Their helmets rested on the floor by their feet. A coffee pot and a couple of mugs sat on a table next to them. A path through the crates would lead Rosen to their rear, but she would need some time to get in position. Dani needed to create a distraction to give her that time.

She communicated her intentions to the others with hand signals, and Miles shook his head. Dani ignored his silent protest. Keeping her helmet on to conceal her face, she strode away from the door and crates toward the table.

"Longest smoke break ever, Walker," one of the Wardens said. "Thought we'd have to come look for you, but it's cold as shit. Easier to just let you freeze to death." Both men at the table laughed.

She couldn't risk speaking, so she extended her middle finger at them. They laughed again and continued their game.

Forcing herself to take slower breaths, Dani headed for the pot of coffee. She fumbled with one of the mugs and dropped it on purpose. The glassware shattered—and almost simultaneously, the lights went out. Dani's helmet allowed her to see everything. The two Wardens were blinded in the darkness, but didn't panic.

"Damn storm took the power out," one said, reaching for his helmet.

Rosen stepped out from behind the crates and jerked the Warden's head to the side while Jens looped a wire over the other Warden's head. A tiny gurgle escaped the second man's mouth, but Jens extinguished any other sounds as he pulled the wire tight around his neck.

The remainder of the fireteams emerged from the maze of crates. Dani identified each member except Mary. She must be the one who'd taken out the lighting.

A third Warden appeared behind Miles with his pistol out, and Dani drew her weapon. The lights came back on as Dani fired. Her shot clipped the Warden in the arm. He stumbled, and Marcic was on him and thrusting his knife into his neck in an instant.

Miles signaled for the two teams to perform a sweep of the facility. Dani rejoined her group as they searched the rest of the armory for more Wardens. None surfaced, and the rest of the base remained quiet. Dani feared the third Warden had alerted the base to their presence, but it seemed Marcic had stabbed him before he could.

They gathered at the center of the structure, and Dani removed her helmet. Elmore, Marcic, and Zykov opened some of the crates and celebrated their new stash of weapons. Dani busied herself by checking her watch while Rosen and Jens dispatched the regenerating Wardens. 2234. They were running out of time.

Gavin's voice boomed into Dani's ear comm, startling her. "Javi, Wardens are moving helos out of the hangar, and the fire-teams there can't take them on their own. Move three of your teams in to support and keep them on the ground. Take the west armory next to the hangar while you're there."

"On it," Javi said.

"Javi, wait," Dani said. "Gavin, are they moving the birds to leave or to attack? Any signs that we've been discovered?"

"Their movements aren't rushed and no other Wardens have been dispatched to defensive positions. Nothing on their comms shows that they know we're here."

"Then let 'em leave," Dani said. "We can't take the helos without making a ruckus. Blow the fake comm tower first, and the birds will be recalled, then we can blow the place as planned."

"Miles?" Javi asked.

"We have a shit ton of toys we just took in the east armory," Miles said. "We can blow the helos out of sky from the ground when they return."

"Javi, send one of your sabs to meet me at the decoy tower," Gavin said.

Dani slipped her helmet back on. "Gavin, I'm coming."

"Javi, I want Patel," Gavin said.

"He's still working on the fixed-wings," Javi said.

Dani grumbled with annoyance. Gavin was trying to keep her back, and she refused to let him. "Gavin, I'm dressed as a Warden, so don't shoot me. Javi, tell Patel and his crew not to kill me when I go by." Dani took her pack from Mary and removed the detonator for the explosives she'd placed on the air traffic tower.

"I'm still in the winter skin," Mary said. "I'll go."

"I can walk out in the open as a Warden and cover the half mile above ground quicker than you can make the three-quarter-mile hike underground in the sewers. Just blow my tower for me, will you?" Dani handed the detonator to Mary and headed for the door.

Miles walked beside her as she went. "Don't do anything crazy. Set the charges and leave. The comm and air traffic towers come down at 2300."

Dani resisted the urge to check her watch. "Understood."

The wind battered her as she waded through the snow covering the roadway between the base and the east armory and fixed-wing hangars. She gave a thumbs-up when she spotted Patel's fireteam working below the four fixed-wings, hoping that Javi had relayed the message to them about her disguise. One of the volunteers returned the gesture, and a slight amount of the tension in Dani's shoulders eased. Now she just needed to cross the rest of the airfield without dying.

She pushed her feet and lower legs through the knee-deep and sometimes thigh-deep drifts. The wind had swept some of the north-south runway free of snow, and Dani realized she was walking directly over the CNA troops at that moment. She hurried across the runway, then slowed again as she encountered more drifts.

Some lights near the helo hangar across the airfield flickered as the waves of snow swirled over the area. Dani wondered what the hell would possess the Wardens to make a flight in these conditions. The air traffic tower she'd crept beneath before, she now walked right past.

She crossed a few other paved and wind-swept areas before arriving at the decoy tower. She tried to steal another view of the helos, and her head snapped back around when she almost walked into another Warden standing at the base of the fake comm tower.

"This weather is shit," the woman said. "Doesn't matter where you stand, the snow finds you. I'm really missing Florida tonight."

Dani chuckled and hoped it didn't sound as nervous as she felt. Her body was tense, and her heartbeat felt out of control. The Warden wore the same type of helmet as Dani, and Dani had a full view of the woman's face through the shield. She assumed the woman could see her too.

"I bet. What's all the fuss with the helos?"

"Boss wants to strike Bangor tonight is what I heard from one of the pilots. He was asleep and got called out to fly in this storm."

"Ah." Dani struggled to keep her face neutral. "Glad it's him and not me."

"Me too. I'd puke my guts up on a flight that rough."

"Hey, head in to warm up a bit if you want," Dani said. "I just transferred in from Boston, so the cold doesn't bother me as much."

"You're a lifesaver. I owe you a beer. What's your name?"

Dani said the first name that popped into her head. "Jackman."

The woman tilted her head, confused, and Dani realized she was asking for her first name.

"I meant—"

Hands grabbed the woman from behind and snapped her head in an unnatural direction. Dani started to bolt, and then she recognized Gavin. He pulled the woman to the ground.

"You're going to give me a fucking heart attack," she said.

"You suck at lying, Dani. You're going to get yourself killed. You say your name is Jackman when your uniform says Walker. Brilliant."

Dani looked down at the name label on her stolen body armor. *Fuck.*

"We're not here to make friends," Gavin said.

"I wasn't. I—"

"Stop arguing. We have work to do."

Dani knelt and dug through her pack. "They're hitting Bangor tonight."

"I heard. Hurry."

"Don't rush me."

"We're right between the real comm tower and the air traffic tower. When those blow, we don't want to be between them. Hurry."

Dani removed the charges from her pack and used her teeth to remove her gloves. She spit the gloves out and adjusted the wires on the units.

The fallen Warden's body began to glow, and Dani's eyes fell on her body as it writhed inside her armor. Based on her now much smaller body size, Dani guessed the woman returned to a child's age after regen.

"Pay attention to what you're doing, Dani." Gavin shifted closer to the Warden and wrapped a wire around her neck until the glow faded.

Dani stared at the little body inside the oversize Warden armor. She flinched when Gavin touched her hand.

"I know all you see is that I killed a child, but you must

remember she is still a Warden, a target, regardless of age. Focus on your work. That's your only job."

Dani nodded and blinked several times to try to clear her mind.

Gavin removed charges from his pack, and Dani continued to prep her own explosives. Once finished, she scooped her devices into her hands. "I'll cover the interior. Let's go."

CHAPTER
43

"This weather is horrible." Curtis stood at the windows in Rowan's office that faced the south, but all he saw was the blowing snow swirling past the glass. "Can't see a damn thing."

"What are the odds my troops are keeping watch like they should?" Rowan organized and straightened various items on his desk again.

"There's a minus twenty-five wind chill, Rowan."

"I don't care. Ready one of the trucks. I'll make rounds to remind them not to slack off."

"We have almost two feet of snow on the ground now, not including the drifts and the remaining foot yet to fall. The plows stopped because they couldn't keep up with the snowfall."

Rowan left his desk to stand at the window too. The snow blocked his views of everything, and he frowned. "Trees and snow. I hate this state."

Curtis chuckled. "And you're interested in a post in Canada? It's more trees and more snow there."

"Quebec City and Montreal are still bigger cities than this one."

"Agreed. Bangor is smaller than Portland, though."

"Bangor is a pain in my ass."

"You *make* Bangor a pain in your ass. It's a nothing town that you're only slightly less obsessed with than you are with finding the girl."

Rowan turned and stared at his friend.

Curtis shrugged. "Just being honest."

Rowan grunted in response and left the window. He retrieved his coat and pulled it on.

"Where are you going?"

"To make rounds where I can. We still have snow machines that can handle the deeper snow."

Curtis groaned but followed his superior. As they walked down the corridor, one of Curtis's aides rushed up to him and handed him a palm-sized panel.

"What is this?" Curtis asked.

"Intel reports from across the state, sir," the young man replied. "It mentions Bangor."

"Thank you," Curtis said. He dismissed the aide and scrolled through the report while Rowan waited.

Rowan shifted with impatience. "Anything of interest?"

"Not really. The usual stuff. Wait." He passed the panel to Rowan and pointed to a particular paragraph. "Read this part."

"Commonwealth troops have been observed actively training with resident Brigands in the town and completing military maneuvers," Rowan said, reading from the report. "They have a cache of weapons but exact numbers are undetermined. Their intent of training is unknown but is likely for the defense of Bangor." He shook the panel at Curtis angrily. "Fuck. The groups united anyway. I specifically didn't want this to happen. Why is this information only coming in now? How old is it?"

"Keep reading."

Rowan sighed and returned his attention to the report. "Blah, blah, blah. Lieutenant Colonel Catherine Houston of the CNA leads the Commonwealth division and a former military member turned Brigand, Gavin Marcus, leads the civilian troops." Rowan lifted his eyes from the report. "Houston's the one that was in charge of the MPs here when we took over. The CNA rolled right over and let us in without much of a fight that day. I'm not worried about her."

Curtis gestured toward the panel.

Rowan glanced back down at the report. "Both are assisted by various leaders in the Commonwealth and Brigand communities. Marcus is closely assisted by fellow Brigands Jace Ireland and a woman named Dani, last name unknown. . . ." He reread the last sentence again before turning to Curtis. "Dani."

"It might not be the girl you're looking for, Rowan."

He grinned and gave the panel back to Curtis. "It's her. It has to be."

"We'll find out when we hit them in the spring."

"Fuck the spring." Rowan spun and headed down the corridor in the direction they'd come from with long, determined strides.

Curtis jogged to catch up. "Where are you going?"

"Change of plans. I don't need to inspect the soldiers on watch. I want troops to load the helos. We're going to Bangor tonight."

"You don't have orders to attack."

"I've received intel indicating a significant threat to the Warden initiatives regarding Earth. I have the authority to act on that threat."

"You're stretching the boundaries of that authority. Let me contact Boston, sir. If you attack without clearance, you can be stripped of your post here."

"No one, not even the CNA, wants Portland. The vice regent sits in Boston and has never bothered to make the short flight here to see everything that we do. Without me, the Wardens don't get new tech. They can't strip me of anything. I'm attacking Bangor *now*."

"We're in the middle of a blizzard!"

"We can fly in the snow."

"This is more than a passing squall or snow."

"Get the birds ready, Curtis. We leave as soon as we stow our gear and troops are on board."

"If we wait a couple of hours, the worst of the storm will be over."

"Within an hour. That time is non-negotiable."

"Sir—"

"Do it, or I'll find someone who can."

Curtis nodded. "Yes, sir. Within an hour."

"Good. You're in charge of the base until I return," Rowan said. He'd never slowed his pace during the conversation, and they were already close to the barracks where his elite Wardens were housed. Like him, they were always ready and willing to attack the CNA and Brigands. A little snow and cold wouldn't bother them. They could leave, capture Dani, burn Bangor, and be back in Portland before this storm was done. Boston wouldn't know until it was over. He might receive a reprimand for disobeying the order to wait until the spring, but he didn't care. He'd gotten enough commendations over the course of his career to cancel out a negative mark for attacking a town he technically had permission to attack. He could also fudge some numbers regarding the weapons stores they had in Bangor to further justify the trip.

As expected, his elite troops were eager to gear up for an easy trouncing of Bangor. They stood at attention while he walked among them.

"The weather could be better, but none of us are worried about a few snowflakes, are we?"

"No, sir!" they shouted in unison.

"Bangor Brigands and Commonwealth troops have been training together, and our sources say they're making significant progress," Rowan said. His troops would never know that he was lying a bit—and even if they did find out, they wouldn't care. "Our task is to destroy that progress; burn it to the ground."

"Yes, sir!" they said as a collective.

"There is a woman there helping them, a Brigand. Her name is Dani, no recorded last name. Find and capture her alive. She has important intel on the inner circles of the Brigands, so no harm is to come to her. Once we have her, we incinerate Bangor. Capture what Echoes you can, but that is not our main objective. The woman is the one I need captured at any cost."

"Sir, do you have an image or description of her?" one of the Wardens asked.

"No. The only description we have is over a decade old. But Bangor isn't that big. Round up the locals and interrogate them to find out where she is."

"Yes, sir!"

"Gear up, and get on the helos ASAP. I'm going with you."

Though the prep time took longer than he wanted, by Warden standards, his team was ready in record time. Rowan strode toward the running helicopter wearing his body armor, a quake rifle slung across his back. He carried his helmet and used his hand to keep the swirling, wind-whipped snow out of his eyes as he neared the bird. The storm had intensified, but he had four helos loaded with troops and weapons.

He stepped up into the helicopter and placed ear protectors over his head.

"How are we looking?" he asked the pilot.

"I've flown in worse," the pilot said.

Rowan grinned. "Good. Take us up."

"Yes, sir."

Once the doors on the helicopter closed, the spinning blades picked up speed. A blast of wind rocked the helo as it left the ground, but the pilot didn't flinch. The other helicopters lifted from the tarmac successfully despite the thrashing wind.

Rowan lost sight of the ground and base within seconds as the helo gained altitude and turned in a northerly direction. His heart rate quickened with anticipation when he thought of what would happen when they reached Bangor. Even with the poor weather, the flight would be quick.

Finally.

CHAPTER

ᴸⅠᴸⅠ

After placing one of the charges near the base of a support beam on the fake comm tower, Dani scrambled under the stairwell to place another device. That done, she climbed back down and moved through the lower level, where she planted two more before stepping back outside to meet Gavin.

"I'll place this last one beneath the tower once we're in the sewers," she said.

"Go. We have company coming." Gavin carried her pack with one hand and dragged the dead Warden with the other.

Dani spotted the two Wardens leaving the air traffic tower. They were busy fighting with the door and didn't notice her and Gavin. She rushed to the nearest manhole, placed the explosive device she was holding on the ground, wrestled the lid up, and slid it aside. Her hands ached with the cold, and she blew warm air across her fingers. *Shit.* She'd left her gloves at the base of the fake tower.

The Wardens had the door closed and were now heading toward them.

Gavin dropped the corpse through the manhole, and it landed with a thud inside the pipe. He shoved Dani's pack into her hands, and she slipped her arms through the straps before picking up the device from the snow and climbing down into the pipe.

Halfway down, she dropped from the ladder to the tunnel floor. Her boots squelched in the filth that the Warden's body lay in. Dani forced her eyes away from the small corpse.

Gavin slipped into the pipe opening and pulled the lid back over the hole just in time. He froze in his position, and the Wardens walked through the snow and over the manhole lid. Their boots knocked some snow through the tiny openings in the sewer cover, but Gavin didn't move.

The Wardens continued past, and Dani released the breath she held.

Gavin jabbed his finger in her direction before jabbing it in the direction of the decoy tower. She understood his intended command: *Get your ass moving.*

She raced back toward the tower and placed her final charge as high up on the sewer wall as she could reach. She pressed a few buttons, and once the light started blinking, she splashed through the muck to rejoin Gavin. Her fingers were numb, and she was out of breath.

"I left my gloves up there," she said between gasps.

Gavin took the Warden's pistol and checked her for other weapons. "I have them."

"Time?"

Gavin stood, grabbed Dani's shoulder, and shoved her ahead of him in the pipe. "Not enough."

She had never seen Gavin look stressed before, so she knew they were in trouble. She darted ahead, and he sprinted behind her.

They wove their way through the maze of pipes for a few minutes, until they reached a manhole 150 yards away from the air traffic tower. The pipe walls were too thick for them to detonate from within the sewers; they would have to do it from the surface.

Dani held the detonator in one hand and used her other hand to climb up the ladder.

"Time?" she asked.

"2246."

Dani groaned. They wouldn't have enough time to blow the decoy tower and clear the comm and air traffic towers before they were detonated at 2300.

The heavy thumping of helicopter blades increased in frequency. "They're leaving," she said. She looked at her watch and her insides tightened more.

"Javi," Gavin said.

No response came through the comm.

"Javi, if you can hear me, delay detonation until 2305. Copy?"

Again, no response.

Dani interrupted him before he tried to raise Javi again. "He planned to clear snow at 2255 to get the two fixed-wings in the air for 2300. When the helos get word of the blast, they'll be fourteen minutes out. If any of the Wardens still here spot the plow and head that way, I need to detonate the decoy at 2256 so they'll abandon investigating the plow and come back this way."

"It's not enough time, Dani."

"It'll be slim; that's for sure. But we can't push the 2300 time back. The CNA has been on radio silence this entire time. They're waiting for our signal."

"They won't come out of the ground until we start blasting."

"If they hear the decoy tower blow at 2256 they'll emerge then, not at 2300."

"Can't have that happen."

"Having them out a little early is a good thing. It'll give

them a few more minutes to assault the base before the helos return."

"Give me your detonator and head back across the airfield."

"Not a chance. We'll have four minutes to clear the air traffic tower."

Static crackled in their ears before Javi's voice. "Gavin, are you in position?"

"Affirmative," Gavin said. "We can blow the decoy at 2256 to pull back any troops that try to intercept your plow and fixed-wings."

"That will give you enough time to clear the 2300 blasts too?" Javi asked.

Gavin looked at Dani, and she nodded.

"Affirmative," Gavin said.

"Copy. Go at 2256."

"You sure about this?" Gavin asked.

"No," Dani said. "I'm terrified, but we don't have a choice. Give me your detonator."

He fished the device from his pocket and handed it to her.

She checked her watch again.

"Ready?" he asked.

She nodded.

He slid the cover partway open, just enough for her to poke her upper body out. Her hands trembled from a mix of cold and fear. She glanced at her watch one more time, then pressed the buttons on both detonators. The red light on the switches in her hands began blinking, and she slipped back through the opening. Gavin lowered the manhole lid, and they dropped into the pipe. The ground shuddered as the blast ripped the decoy tower apart.

Without a word, they darted through the network of pipes, trying to put as much distance between themselves and the air traffic tower as possible. Gavin stumbled in the muck behind her once, but he recovered and caught back up to her. Her lungs burned and her legs fatigued as they struggled to maintain their frantic pace.

She didn't bother to check her watch. The time didn't matter anymore. They just needed to get as far away from the coming destruction as they could.

As they made yet another sharp turn through the pipework, a powerful blast shook them both off their feet. Gavin was up first; he helped her up. They sprinted a few more yards before the piping behind them began collapsing. Dani refused to look back.

The farther they got away from the destroyed air traffic tower, the safer they would be, but they were too close and the aged sewer system was more fragile than Dani had expected. They needed to navigate to stronger pipes that wouldn't crush them as they fell apart.

"This way," Dani said, shifting to make a left.

"Nope," Gavin said, and her body jerked to the right as he grabbed her pack and shoved her in the opposite direction.

She stumbled as her feet dropped into the lower, flooded pipe. Gavin stayed behind her, and as debris fell on them from above, Dani began to fear that they'd made a terrible mistake.

The knee-deep water slowed their progress, and the destruction caught up to them. Just as the sewer's structures collapsed around and on top of them, Gavin shoved her into another side pipe, and she fell.

She pinched her eyes closed and curled into a ball. Falling debris pelted her body, and she had nowhere to go.

When the destruction finally stopped, Dani was too dizzied to move at first. Static and voices filled her ear comm, but she couldn't understand anything that was being said.

Water seeped into her helmet, and she realized she was underwater. She watched the bubbles leaving her helmet to figure out which way was up, then turned her body to place her feet beneath her and rolled her upper body to shift debris off her. As she righted herself, she stumbled back into a portion of the sewer wall.

She got her bearings while water drained from her helmet. She was standing in thigh-deep water. She wanted to take the helmet off, but she could see better with it on. She tried not to panic. "Gavin!" she cried, and began searching through the rubble.

A hand reached out of the water. Dani gasped. Gavin was pinned beneath a collapsed portion of the pipe, and was trying to push the object upward. She sloshed toward him, flinging smaller debris aside, and submerged most of her body so she was positioned beneath the debris trapping him. She pressed her right shoulder against a piece of pipe and pushed up with her legs to lift it. With her left hand, she groped the water until her fingers met Gavin's. He gripped her hand, and she pulled. His head and upper body emerged from the water, and he gasped for air.

Dani made sure he was clear of the pipe, then lowered it back down before dragging him farther out of the water. He groaned with the movement. Blood spurted from his mouth when he coughed.

Dani slid her pack off her back and pulled a headlamp from it. She turned the light on, removed her helmet, and slipped the strap around her head. "Gavin, you're the medic. What do I do?"

"My pack, left side pouch," he said between labored, raspy breaths. "Bottle."

Dani turned him as little as possible and pawed through the side pouch. She removed the bottle and recognized it.

"This is the one that you took from me at Hattie's."

"Enough chemicals in one bottle to take out an elephant."

Dani unscrewed the lid with her cold fingers and held the

bottle to his lips. He took several sips before resting his head back with a sigh. She opened the front of his outer armor, expecting to find his CNA armor underneath, but instead she touched skin. With each difficult breath he took, his ribs ground against each other and moved in ways they weren't supposed to move.

"Crush injury," he said. "Multiple fractures, probable flail chest, and a pneumothorax if I had to guess."

"I don't know what the fuck any of that means. Where's your armor?"

He smiled. "You're wearing it."

Dani shook her head. "The extra set you gave me . . . It's the one the CNA issued you?"

Gavin nodded. "It went to a better cause. When I regen, I don't forget everything."

"I wish you hadn't done that."

"You're not the one with internal bleeding, and that was the whole point." He coughed several times, and more blood sprayed from his mouth.

"Gavin, what do I do?"

"Nothing. I'm dying."

CHAPTER
45

Rowan was determined to find Dani in Bangor. Fifteen years had passed, but he'd never forgotten her face. She'd attacked and beaten him twice during the Portland invasion. The first assault, she blindsided him with a stick. The second attack, she'd been the much weaker opponent, yet had somehow managed to kill him before he killed her. *Bitch will die this time.*

A wind gust hit the helicopter, making it bounce roughly, but Rowan didn't care.

He'd find her tonight.

The pilot interrupted his thoughts. "Sir, we have a message coming in from the base."

"Goddammit, we've been gone what, ten minutes? Is it Curtis?"

"Yes, sir."

Rowan sighed and considered ignoring the man. "Put him through."

The pilot pushed something on the console. "You're linked now, sir."

"Curtis, go," Rowan said, not bothering to hide his disgust.

"We're under attack."

"Under attack?" he snarled. "What kind of stupid game is this?"

"Sir, our decoy comm tower has just been destroyed. CNA troops are attacking from the ground, and I'm unable to raise our observatories on the East and West Promenades. I'm located on the southeast corner of the base."

"Why there?"

"The blast took out part of our command center. I'm setting up our secondary now."

God. Dammit.

Bangor and Dani would have to wait.

Rowan held up his finger and moved his hand and fore-arm in a circular motion. The pilot nodded at the gesture and banked the helicopter to the left to turn around.

"Where is the concentration of fire coming from?" Rowan asked.

"I'm not sure. We have enemy fire coming from across the airfield, but the storm is hindering visibility. It could be coming from more than one location."

"We're coming back now and will fly over the base to locate them. Get this shit under control, Curtis."

"Yes—"

"Curtis, do you copy?" Rowan asked. He leaned toward the pilot. "I lost him. Get him back."

"Communication to base is disrupted," the pilot said.

Rowan leaned forward in his seat, willing his eyes to see through the blinding snow. "The CNA is attacking. Make a pass over the area so I can see where they're located. Come in over the peninsula, east to west, then circle toward the base. Radio the other helos to follow us and to look for CNA troop movements."

"Yes, sir."

Rowan wanted to be part of the ground forces—somewhere

where he'd be in a position to return fire—but he needed to get back to base command and take over coordinating the defense and counterattacks. The CNA had never brought the fight to him before; he was eager to burn every man and woman, human or Echo, who was daring to attack his Warden base.

The storm battered the helo as the pilot flew low over the city from the Eastern Promenade to the western portion of the peninsula. Rowan didn't see any fires or signs of destruction below, so he wasn't sure why Curtis couldn't raise the east and west observatories. As they neared the base, however, he saw the glow of multiple fires. The air traffic, decoy comm tower, and actual comm towers were collapsed piles of flaming rubble. The normally well-lit base was otherwise barely visible.

Rowan grumbled. "Goddammit. Primary power is out too."

Thousands of tiny lights flickered below as weapons fired.

"Bring me lower," Rowan said.

"Sir, we'll be at risk of taking ground fire."

Rowan glared at the pilot.

"Yes, sir," he said.

The helicopter banked to come back around, and Rowan gazed at the scene below. The Wardens were holding their positions at the base but taking fire from both sides of the air strips. The CNA's ambush-style attack was effectively pinning the Wardens in their positions.

The remaining two cannons on the base's roof were firing nonstop, but the CNA lines were long and relatively unaffected by the cannon fire. A sudden flash of light erupted from the ground near the east armory, and a rocket flew past the front of the helo, just missing the nose.

"Turn around and shoot the hell out of the bastards that fired that shot," Rowan commanded.

The pilot turned the helo and launched a pair of missiles at the ground. A fireball sprang into the air when the fuel depot exploded as a result. Rowan turned in his seat and smiled at the expanding flames spreading along the ground. CNA troops scattered to escape the inferno, many of their bodies alight with fire. Who cared that he'd lost his primary fuel reserves, as long as the CNA burned.

One of the helicopters behind them was ripped apart by an explosion, and Rowan spotted the fixed-wing that had fired the shot. The attack was far worse than he expected. The CNA had captured at least one of his newest jets.

"Radio the other two helos to drop their forces behind the CNA lines along the airstrips. Put me as close to the air traffic tower as you can. I'll take the Wardens on board inside with me to secure the base. After that, get this bird back in the air, and don't bother returning to the hangar until you are out of munitions."

"Yes, sir."

Rowan unfastened the straps holding him in his seat and he fought to reach the middle of the helo as the wind and storm slammed it from all sides. When he reached the area where his elite forces were riding, he barked out his orders for which Wardens would accompany him to the southeast corner of the main barracks. With the air traffic tower gone, that corner of the barracks was the only place left where he could view both the north-south and east-west airstrips. He assigned the remaining troops on the helicopter areas of the base to secure.

Like him, they were ready to fight.

"Kill them all," he said.

"Yes, sir!"

"If they surrender, kill them anyway. I want them all slaughtered. Every last one."

The Wardens vocalized approval of their orders.

"If you die, regen and put your ass back in the fight. We die *permanently* before they take what's ours."

The helo landed hard on the ground, but Rowan kept his feet. He took his quake rifle from the weapons rack while one of the Wardens opened the helicopter's side door. Rowan hopped out first and started jogging toward the base, ignoring the sounds of gunfire coming from all around him.

One of Curtis's aides met him as he entered the barracks and handed him a new earpiece. "This one is linked to our secondary comms, sir," she said. "They're somewhat limited, but it's the best we can do right now."

Rowan removed his old comm and inserted the new one. "Curtis, you copy?"

"Yes, sir."

"I'm coming to you." Rowan passed his rifle off to one of the Wardens with him. His strides covered the distance to the lift in seconds. As he rode to the uppermost level of the barracks, Curtis updated him on the status of the battle.

When Rowan arrived at the ops center, he strode to the corner of the room without a word. He gazed out the windows to the south, then moved to the east-facing windows. All he could see was snow, a few flickers of light, and the periodic burst of more light each time an explosion went off. He turned to Curtis and glared. "How the fuck did this happen?"

CHAPTER

46

"Don't look so terrified," Gavin said. "I'll regen and be back."

Dani frowned. "Fine. Hurry up and die, then. I'll stay until you recover."

Gavin shook his head and moved his hand to his pocket. He removed her gloves and handed them to her.

She trembled from the cold as she put them on. CNA and Warden armor weren't meant for swimming.

"Javi," Gavin said.

"Jesus, Gavin, where the hell have you been?" Javi said over the comm.

Gavin coughed, and Dani wiped the spattered blood from his lips. "Delayed. Your location?"

"At the fixed-wings on the tarmac trying to de-ice the damn things."

"Sending Dani to you. She's still dressed as a Warden. Don't shoot her. Javi, you have Bravo Company until you hear back from me."

"Understood," Javi said.

Gavin leaned his head back against the sewer wall and groaned. Dani helped him take another drink from the bottle.

"You have your orders, Dani."

"They suck."

He tried to laugh, but it turned into a grimace. "My regen will put me close to your age now. I want to spend my life with you."

A lump formed in her throat. She didn't want him to die, even if he would come back. "Picked a nice romantic spot to spring this on me."

Gavin smiled and touched her face.

Dani leaned forward and kissed him. She tasted the blood in his mouth but didn't care. She didn't want to watch him die, so she ended the kiss and prepared to leave.

"You really do suck at this cloak and dagger shit," Gavin said. "You can't even lie well."

"I know."

"Remember, your name is Walker now."

"Got it."

"Be careful," he said.

"Yeah," she said, unsure what else to say. She handed him the headlamp so he wouldn't die in the dark, then put her helmet on.

He placed his palm on the shield concealing her face. "You're in there. I can't see you, but I know you're in there."

"Hattie's special medicine is addling your brain. You're starting to babble."

"No pain," he said with a broad smile.

"Good. Glad you'll die with a drunken grin on your face. Find me when you're back."

"I will."

Dani found her pack and put it on. Gavin was still watching her; she gave him a small smile, though he couldn't see it. She turned and started picking her way through the sewers. She had a fight to get to.

After leaving Gavin, Dani had a difficult time keeping her mind focused. She was lost. She finally found a manhole and began to climb. When she eased the lid up, she spotted the flaming wreckage of the air traffic tower twenty yards southwest of her location. She and Gavin hadn't gotten very far from it when it blew, and her disorientation in the sewers had put her back closer to the base instead of farther from it.

The CNA troops were bombarding the base with plasma rifles shots. She heard and felt aftershocks as quake grenades exploded.

A rapid *boom-boom-boom* came from above. Dani couldn't see the cannons due to the snow, but she saw the blasts of flame each time one was fired from the roof of the barracks. She was caught right in the middle of the fight; she cursed her terrible luck.

A helicopter passed overhead and lashed snow into the air as it neared the tower's wreckage. Not that she knew how to fly one, but a helo would be an effective weapon against a cannon. Dani lowered the manhole cover and removed her pack. She didn't want to be blasted into oblivion if a plasma rifle shot hit her pack while she wore it. She lashed one of the straps to the ladder to keep it near the opening and then crawled out of the manhole, leaving the lid partially off in case she needed a quick retreat. She stayed low and crept toward the helo as it landed.

As soon as the bird touched down, Wardens leapt out and went in different directions. Dani jumped up and sprinted for the helo. The whirring of the blades increased as it prepared to leave again. She slipped through the door before it closed and slammed her shoulder into the Warden attempting to close it, sending him flying. Without a thought, she moved to the front and pressed her pistol against the exposed skin between the pilot's armor and helmet.

Shit. Now what? She hadn't thought this plan through. She couldn't fly the damn helo herself, and if it stayed on the ground, the CNA would blow it up.

"Javi, I—"

Dani's body flew sideways as the Warden she'd struck to get on the helo now returned the blow. Her pistol flew from her hand, and she fell between the two front seats. Javi's voice sounded in her ear, but she didn't have time to bother with whatever he was saying. The Warden was on top of her, and the pilot was scrambling for her dropped weapon.

She wedged her knee up and pushed the Warden off. As he reeled backward, she pulled her knife and slashed the pilot's arm. Her pistol fell from his hand just as three Brigand volunteers boarded the helicopter. They killed the first Warden then came after her and the pilot.

Dani dropped the knife and jerked her helmet off. One of the volunteers struck her cheek, and her body collided with the empty front seat before bouncing off and landing on the deck. She couldn't see straight, but she still put one hand out to protect herself from additional blows while she used the other to scramble away from the blurred, approaching man.

"I'm in Bravo Two-Three under Gavin Marcus," Dani said.

"Aw, shit," the man said. "Dani?"

She looked up and blinked at him. She recognized his face but didn't recall his name. "Yeah."

He took her outstretched hand, meant to stop his attack, and pulled her to her feet. "I'm Dresden. Attacking a Warden helo alone? It's true. You really are insane."

The two other volunteers dragged the dead pilot to the rear of the helicopter before hopping into the front seats to prep to leave.

Dani shook her head to clear the fuzziness.

Dresden passed her knife and pistol to her. "We've got it from here, unless you want to fly in this shit too."

"No, I'm good." Dani holstered the pistol and sheathed her knife. She touched her sore cheekbone.

"Sorry about that," Dresden said. "I thought you were one of them."

"No harm done," she lied. She put her helmet back on. "Best of luck, guys."

"You too. Try not to die," Dresden said with a chuckle.

Dani slipped out the helicopter door and darted for the nearest structure, seeking shelter from the snow and blasts of wind from the helicopter as it left the ground. She circled around behind the building to get out of the wind. She knelt and tried to think, but an explosion overhead sent her running for cover. A Warden helo, shot down by the volunteers in the stolen one, blew apart, and the tail section fell toward her. She dove behind a row of transport trucks. Three of them were toppled by the helicopter's falling parts.

She scrambled to one of the trucks that was still standing upright and tucked her body in tightly behind the rear dual tires just before a blast of hot air flooded the area. It seemed the flaming tail section had caused something in one of the toppled trucks to explode too.

She was alive still, somehow, but she couldn't focus on anything else. Her battle to control her breathing was a fight she was starting to lose. Her heart raced, and her chest began to tighten.

"Dani!"

The sound of Miles's voice brought her back from the brink of panic. She slowed her breaths enough to be able to speak. "Yeah?"

"Where are you?"

"Did you see where the ass end of that helo broke off and fell?"

"Yeah."

"I'm here, there, whatever."

"Okay. We're coming to you. Sit tight."

Provided nothing else fell from the sky and tried to land on her, she was happy to stay out of the fight for a few minutes.

"Gavin?" she said into her comm. She waited and was answered with silence.

Dani's pack was in the sewer drain, and she didn't dare try to retrieve it now. She checked the gear she had on her: she still had her three knives and plasma pistol. She pulled the pistol from the holster, and her hand trembled. She reholstered it, then removed her helmet and wiped at the sweat on her face. She had been freezing before; now she was sweating. Her body still felt cold, though, or she thought it did. Maybe she was going into shock; she wasn't sure.

Before she hyperventilated and passed out, she drew in deep breaths of the icy night air. She scooped a handful of snow and wiped it over her face. The cold shock of the snow against her skin made her gasp, but it also made her thoughts clearer. She put the helmet back on. After a few more deep breaths, her heart rate slowed to something less than a thousand beats per minute.

Ten yards away, people began emerging from a hole in a snowdrift. She grabbed for her pistol, just in case, but lowered it when she recognized Zykov's telltale swagger.

"Miles, I'm at your nine o'clock."

The group turned, crouched, and headed toward her. She counted only six people. Elmore, Lee, and Tamu were missing. Miles reached her first, and she saw that he had a mix of blood and soot on his face.

Dani was glad her face was hidden by the helmet. She almost cried with relief upon seeing Miles and Mary.

Miles grasped her upper arm. "You hurt?"

"No," she said. Her body would have answered differently.

Miles gave her arm a squeeze before releasing it.

"Where's Gavin?" Mary asked.

"He should be regenned by now, but I haven't heard from him. What are our orders?"

"Get inside the base and take out their secondary power," Miles said.

"What about the cannons?"

"Other platoons are in charge of disabling them. Let's go."

"Hang on." Rosen slid a crate from the back of the truck Dani had been hiding behind. "Quake grenades."

Rosen passed the grenades to the others in between filling every possible pocket in her clothing. Dani took the two grenades handed to her and put them inside the waist pocket of her Warden armor.

"That's enough, Rosen," Miles said. "Leave the rest."

Rosen looked like she might weep over leaving the massive stash of grenades behind.

They slipped around the remaining trucks, Miles in the lead. The cannons continued to fire from the roof of the barracks. He led them to the top portion of the air traffic tower, which now lay on the ground, smoldering. It offered them a cramped area to crouch in while the fight raged on.

One of the jets they'd stolen was hit, and the wing burned as the pilot guided it to a rough landing on the north-south runway. A few Wardens fired their quake rifles at the jet to destroy it, but the CNA returned such heavy fire that the Wardens retreated.

Dani reached to wipe the sweat from her face, and her hand bumped into her helmet.

"Sure you're okay?" Mary asked.

Dani nodded.

Mary squeezed her hand, and Dani tensed.

"I can't see your face inside that thing, but I know you. What's wrong?"

CHERYL CAMPBELL

"I'm trying not to panic," Dani said through a tightened jaw.

"Good luck with that," Mary said. "I've almost wet myself three times now."

The remaining jet fired missiles at the cannon closest to their position and obliterated the target. The debris sprayed in all directions before falling. Not even an Echo came back from that kind of destruction. Smoke and dust flooded the area.

"Make that four times," Mary said and coughed.

Dani laughed. She didn't think she should be laughing, but she couldn't help it. Her nerves were fried.

Miles ordered them to move, and Dani followed until he made them stop again.

"This entrance is blocked," he said. "We have to go underground or move around the building to find another way in."

Four Wardens huddled behind the carcass of a fallen helo and fired across the airfield at the CNA troops.

"Hit 'em with a grenade," Rosen said.

"We don't want to announce that we're breaching the interior of the compound," Miles said.

"I can get in close," Dani said.

Miles shook his head. "And get your ass shot? No."

"I can lure them away from the entrance."

"How?"

"Since I suck at lying, I'll tell them the truth," Dani said.

"No," Miles said.

"Let her do it," Mary said. "She's right; she sucks at lying. She has the sewer stench all over her, so she can pull it off."

"See?" Before she could lose her nerve or Miles could refuse, Dani stood. She pulled her pistol and placed her other hand against her side. She faked a limp and stumbled away from their cover toward the huddled Wardens. The enemy turned their weapons toward her, but she waved and continued her limping approach, and they lowered their weapons.

Dani reached their location and dropped to her knees among them.

"If you die, you're on your own," one said to her.

"I'm not dying yet, asshole," Dani said. "The CNA is using sewers to move around the base. I fell through one of the pipes when they started blowing shit up. I found a pack of explosives at one of the manholes a hundred yards that way." She nodded her head in its direction. "But I couldn't retrieve it."

"Why not?" the Warden asked while the other three continued firing at the CNA.

"Damn thing is tied to the ladder. I couldn't free the pack. Too much heavy fire." Dani pointed. "Put a quake rifle shot on the ground a hundred yards over there."

The Warden eyed her for a moment before instructing another of the Wardens to shoot where Dani had pointed. On the second shot, the ground erupted in an explosion.

"Huh," the Warden said.

"I found where the fuckers are using a pipe to come in close," Dani said.

"Good. The boss wants everyone dead. Show us their access point."

Dani fake grunted and struggled to her feet while still holding her uninjured side. The Warden in charge left one person at the door, then followed Dani away with the other two Wardens. She did not have to fake dodging the incoming CNA fire. She led them to a manhole a good distance away, firing her pistol in the general direction of the CNA as she went. She sent her shots high and hoped she didn't hit any volunteers or CNA troops beyond the front line.

The manhole cover was askew. The Warden dragged it the rest of the way off, and he and the other two Wardens dropped into the sewers. Dani released her side and pulled a grenade from her pocket. She was about to kill three Wardens; her fingers tightened over the grenade. She jumped when Mary appeared at her side. Without a word, she peeled Dani's fingers off the weapon, armed it, and dropped it on top of the Wardens.

Dani and Mary sprinted away from the pipe. The quake grenade shook the ground when it exploded, and both women tumbled forward. They righted themselves quickly and raced back toward the rear entrance.

"Why did you do that?" Dani asked.

"Gavin told me a long time ago that you'd hesitate to kill. In case he was right, I followed you out. Call it a Plan B."

"I—"

"Relax, Dani. It's okay to not be like Rosen."

They rejoined the group as Jens finished killing the Warden left to guard the entrance. He stripped the corpse of its upper layer of body armor. Dani approached the door, and the access panel's light switched from red to green.

"Miles, report," Gavin said through the comm.

Dani smiled to hear his voice again.

"We've accessed an exterior entrance to the base," Miles said. "We're going for the secondary power."

"Dani with you?"

"She's here."

"Have her fall back and proceed underground to the fixed-wings," Gavin said.

"Why?" Dani asked, her smile fading.

"Do as you're ordered," Gavin said.

He was trying to pull her out of the fight to keep her safe. "Fuck off. My team needs me to use the Warden armor to gain access through locked doors." She didn't bother waiting for his reply before entering the base. Miles and the rest of the team followed her in.

Jens held up the stolen Warden jacket. "I have this."

"Shut up," Dani growled at him.

"Miles, send her to Javi at the fixed-wings," Gavin said.

"We're already inside," Miles said.

Dani started moving through the corridors. She led, since her stolen uniform gave her access to otherwise locked doors.

They arrived at a set of lifts. The lights indicated that one of them was descending from an upper level. Dani hurried toward the stairwell and opened the door, and the team rushed through. She hadn't quite gotten the door closed when the lift stopped and the doors opened. She held her breath as six Wardens poured out of the lift. Their boots echoed in the corridor as they jogged toward the far end of the hall where Dani and the others had entered.

Once the Wardens were out of sight, Dani eased the stairwell door closed so it clicked shut. "Shit, that was close."

"Five times," Mary said.

Dani snorted a laugh.

"Five what?" Miles asked.

Still chuckling, Dani started down the stairs. They continued down until they reached the lowest level. There, they exited the stairwell.

"Secondary power should be down here somewhere," Dani said. "Possibly guarded. There are sewer access points, but they're a bit scattered. As soon as the secondary is out, we should go underground. The hornets are angry."

"Angry is an understatement," Miles said. "Mary, stay with Jens and Zykov and search the southern third of this level. Marcic and Rosen, take the center portion. Dani and I will take the northern third. If you can't quietly disable their secondary power, blow it."

"How does this work?" Jens asked, holding his stolen jacket up.

"It's a proximity thing," Dani said. "Hold it close to an access panel, and it should let you through."

"We'll steal one to use," Rosen said with the same grin Dani had seen her flash when breaking Warden necks.

The group split up, and Dani left with Miles.

"One of the Wardens I led out to the manhole said they had orders to kill everyone," Dani said.

"I'm not surprised. I know better than to tell you why you need to stop taking so many risks."

"Good. I don't want the lecture."

"You're going to catch hell from Gavin later."

"What else is new?"

A blast shook the lower level of the building. The dim lights flickered but remained on. Two more explosions erupted, and Dani winced as shouting voices filled her earpiece.

"Taking heavy fire! Rosen is wounded," Marcic said.

Mary's voice was next. "They know we're inside!"

Dani's eyes traveled the length of the ceiling. She spotted an irregularity in one of the corners of the corridor. She fired her pistol, and the upper corner exploded in sparks. "Cameras. Shit."

"Abort," Miles said into his comm. "They have surveillance on the lower levels. Everyone, fall back and get out or go underground."

Blasts shook the compound, and parts of the structure collapsed around Dani and Miles.

"Gavin, stop firing on the fucking base," Dani barked into her comm. "We're still inside!"

"It's not us. The Wardens are blowing all the entrances to keep us out," Gavin said. "We got the jets out of the ice and in the air, but the Wardens are firing cluster grenades from the ground. We can only provide limited air support. Leave *now!*"

Miles spoke up. "Our team is split up and pinned. We need internal support. You can come in through the sewers. The Warden body armor jackets will get you through any interior doors."

Dani tuned out of the chatter between Gavin and Miles and tried to think. Their well-planned battle had gone to shit. Marcic's comm chatter had stopped altogether; Dani assumed he was dead.

"Mary, where are you?" she asked.

"Uh, trying to return to the stairs we came down," she said. "We're close, but the stairs are blown to hell. Can't go out that way. Zykov is wounded. Jens is dead."

"Miles and I aren't far from you. Find a place to sit tight. We'll find you."

Miles touched Dani's arm. "Houston has CNA pilots in the jets. She wants to bomb the shit out of the base. We have to leave."

"After we find Mary, I'll gladly leave."

"Where is she?"

"Near the stairwell we came through, but it's blocked."

"Okay. We'll figure out what to do about the stairwell when we get there."

An explosion struck the upper portion of the base directly above them, and Dani dove away from the falling debris. More parts of the building came down, and she scrambled farther away from the wreckage. Something struck the side of her helmet with enough force to knock her down. When she stood, she realized that her helmet's visual field now had multiple cracks, rendering it useless. She had to remove it and retreat farther from the smoke.

Miles's voice sounded in her ear. "Dani!"

His voice sounded strong, so she assumed he wasn't beneath the debris. "Yeah. Where are you?" The smoke burned her eyes and made them water. She wiped at the tears with her filthy gloves, smearing dirt on her cheeks.

"Other side of this heap. The ceiling is still crumbling, so I have to find another way to reach you. Any injuries?"

She coughed. "No."

"I'm coming to you. Stay put."

"I can't with this smoke. I'll meet you at the stairwell."

"Dani . . ."

She stopped listening to him and started creeping through the corridors, shooting cameras out when she could. She ducked through a door when she heard the sound of approaching Warden boots. She didn't dare take a shot at any of them; she wouldn't stand a chance against multiple Wardens within a storage room with only one exit.

After they passed, she emerged from the room and followed them at a distance, hoping they didn't turn and double back.

A blast hit the building, shaking it, and she heard a mix of screams and shouts. Wardens wouldn't be screaming in fear. She left the main corridor to move toward the new sounds. She neared a set of double doors, and they swung open before her.

Stretchers, medical equipment, and shelves with a myriad of devices and stuff she didn't recognize lined the sides of the medical bay. She continued toward the shouts, though they'd lessened between explosions. Dani passed through another set of doors and down a short hall lined with more doors on both sides. The building rocked, and the cries rose again. "We're down here! Help!" They banged on the insides of the doors.

They sounded young. What, exactly, was she was walking into?

The proximity lock blinked green as she neared one of the doors. She readied her pistol and released the manual lock on the door. She pulled it open to find eight children on the other side. They backed away when they saw her pistol and huddled together in the dim room.

"What the hell are the Wardens doing with kids?" Dani asked.

A teenage girl stepped forward. "Who are you?"

"Not a Warden."

"Clearly, or you would've shot us already. Who's attacking the base?"

"The CNA and Brigands."

"Bullshit."

Dani blinked at the girl. "I know it sounds absurd, but it's true. Christ, are you Echoes?"

Some of the kids flinched, and she realized she was waving her pistol at them when she addressed the group. She lowered the weapon.

"Yeah," the girl said. "Don't let our physical appearance make you think we're helpless children."

"Right. I'll do my best. Why are the Wardens holding you down here?"

"They force us in the med room with the stretchers, kill us, and inject stuff into our veins to recondition us into Wardens. If it doesn't work, they stick us down here to try again a few days later."

"Fuck." Dani had heard the rumors of reconditioning, but now she knew it was real. "How many of you are here?"

The girl shrugged.

She didn't know any underground access points in this portion of the lower level. She'd gone to the wrong part of the floor for a quick escape. "Any chance you know a way out of here or know somewhere close where we can access the sewers?"

"The original holding area for us has a big drain in the floor that we used before they moved us here and installed toilets."

"Perfect."

"The Wardens sealed it when one of the smaller boys almost escaped that way," the girl said.

"I have a grenade that can unseal it," Dani said, hoping that was true. "I'll open the rest of the doors, and you lead the way to this other holding area. Okay?"

The girl nodded.

Dani moved down the hall and opened the remaining doors, releasing more children. Some were younger than Oliver; others were approaching their late teens. There was an even mix of boys and girls, and they appeared more angry than terrified. Dani jogged behind the last group and reminded herself that their childlike appearance was external only. Most of the Echoes she'd just released were likely older than she was—and unlike her, they remembered their past lives.

The girl made two turns through the halls and pointed to a closed door. Dani approached, and the door unlocked. She peeked into the room of concrete walls and floor. She spotted the indented area of the floor where the drain had been sealed. "Sure hope this works." She activated the grenade, rolled the device along the floor toward the center of the room, and closed the door.

The building trembled with the force of the blast. Dani waited a second, then cracked the door open. The floor was damaged but intact, part of the ceiling had fallen in, and one wall was half gone. The scent of sewer mixed with the smoke.

As the smoke cleared, Dani spotted the sewer pipe that had ruptured open when the wall collapsed. It wasn't the floor drain as planned, but this would do.

Dani held the door while the Echo children rushed into the room. She caught their de facto leader by the arm. "Move through the pipes and head in *that* direction." Dani pointed. "You'll need to make a few turns, because the pipes don't go in straight lines, but keep trying to go that way."

The girl nodded. "Can I have your pistol?"

"No. I'm not leaving yet."

The children stayed close together, and the bigger ones helped the smaller ones into the pipe.

"Miles? Miles! Shit. Gavin, can you hear me?"

Static filled her comm.

Dani held the door open with one hand. She still held the pistol in her other hand, so she shifted her foot to prop open the door to free her hand. She used the body armor's sleeve to wipe grime from her face. The last child moved past her and into the room.

"Gavin!"

"Dani, the Wardens are abandoning the base," Gavin said. "There isn't a need to go after their secondary power, but you still need to leave."

"Can't leave yet."

"It's over."

"No, it's not. Children are coming out through the sewers."

"Children?"

"Yeah. The Wardens are—"

Her response was cut short when she was struck from behind, so hard that she was sent sprawling, face down, on the corridor floor. The door swung closed, and her pistol skidded away from her hand when she landed. For a moment she couldn't breathe or move due to the pain in her back. She managed short, shallow breaths, and tried to move. A blurred image of black boots appeared near her head, and she winced when the Warden pressed his pistol's muzzle against the side of her skull, pinning her to the floor.

"Echo or not, you can't survive without your head. You're *here?* Impossible."

He lifted his pistol, grabbed her by the back of her collar, and rolled her over. As her blurred vision cleared, she was able read the name on the Warden's uniform as he loomed over her. *Rowan.* Two other figures that Dani assumed were also Wardens stood with him in the hallway.

Rowan laughed. "I've searched for you for fifteen years, Dani, and today you walk through the goddamn front door."

She didn't know how he knew her name, since she'd traded her uniform for the Warden disguise. She reached for her knife, and he ripped it from her hand and tossed it aside. While he was leaning over her, she partially sat up, swung her fist, and clipped his chin. Unfortunately, her punch wasn't hard enough to stagger him, and he responded by striking her in the side of the head with his pistol.

The blow rocked her; she collapsed back to the floor in a world of dizziness and pain.

"Still full of fight," he said. "I like it."

Voices filled her ear—Miles, Javi, and Gavin, all calling to her through the comm. Her mind was too fogged to respond to any of them.

Rowan dragged her through the hall by her collar, and the other two Wardens followed. They passed through double doors, and Dani realized she was back in the medical bay.

"Put her on a table and strap her down," Rowan said.

The two Wardens picked her up and roughly deposited her on one of the stretchers. She tried to resist, but they restrained her. Her left arm was pulled straight and tied to a part of the stretcher to immobilize her arm. Her right arm was pinned against the side of her body by strapping.

A banging noise caught everyone's attention. Dani looked up—and saw Miles. He fired shots at the long, glass-like window overlooking the medical bay, but the shots barely cracked the pane.

"Looks like someone wants to save you," Rowan said to Dani. He turned his attention to the other Wardens. "Bring him alive if you can."

Dani struggled against the straps. "Miles, run!"

He disappeared from the window, and Dani believed he'd listened to her—except he returned a moment later with a metal bar. He slammed it into the glass with wild, repeated swings.

Rowan grinned. "He'll break his arms before he gets through that glass. Curtis," he said into his comm, "meet me in Med Bay Three. I have the woman; she's here."

Rowan pulled his knife and cut through the uniform fabric and the layers of armor covering Dani's left arm until her skin was exposed. He replaced the blade in its sheath, then rolled a cart closer to the stretcher. He pulled drawers open and removed a length of tubing, a bag containing a clear liquid, and an object that resembled a needle inside some packaging.

Miles's attack on the window stopped, and he sprinted away from the glass. The two Wardens fired their weapons as they pursued him. Within seconds, they were all out of sight. Dani hoped he could find a way to escape them. She needed to find a means of doing that herself. She moved her right hand and discovered that the strap over her wrist wasn't too tight. Her head pounded with pain, but she forced her mind into some sort of working order.

"Do I know you?" she asked.

Rowan abandoned the cart for a moment and stared at her. She froze her right hand.

"You haven't aged since the day you killed me, so you must be an Echo. You don't remember me?"

"No."

"Oh well," he said and returned his attention to the cart. "I remember you. The sneaky bitch that had the balls to come after me, *twice*. I thought it was impressive until you stabbed me with a knife and watched me bleed out. You didn't finish the job, though, which was stupid for you; if you had, I wouldn't be here to torture you now."

Rowan turned around with a three-inch-long, catheter-covered needle in his hand. Dani tried to squirm away as he approached, but the straps held her. She winced when he pierced the skin in the bend of her arm and threaded the catheter into her vein. He left the catheter in her arm and tossed the needle to the floor. Rowan attached one end of the tubing, now full of the clear liquid, to the catheter. He applied tape over the contraption to hold everything in place. He picked up the bag of liquid and squeezed it.

"Normally we kill the kids before we start this part of the process. Killing them helps prime their brains for conditioning. This step is exceptionally painful, so I'm sure I'll enjoy it more than you." He smiled.

She thrashed against the straps as the cool fluid entered her bloodstream and quickly turned to a fiery sensation, like she was being burned from the inside. Pain flashed up her arm, and she screamed.

CHAPTER
47

Dani pushed with her feet and arched her back as far as she could move within the straps. The blinding pain that was steadily moving up her arm toward her shoulder threatened to make her pass out. She reached for the knife at the back of her belt. Upon removing it she slashed at the tubing first—and missed. But Rowan lunged away from the blade, and as he did he dropped the bag of liquid. As it fell, the weight of the bag tore the tape and intravenous catheter from Dani's arm.

She cut the straps around her body and rolled off the stretcher. Her legs refused to hold her weight, so she scrambled across the floor and used one of the other carts to pull herself to her feet. Blood dripped down her arm from where the IV had been, and she held the knife out with a quivering hand.

Rowan, standing on the other side of the stretcher she'd abandoned, looked at her and smiled.

"Dani and whoever else is left, get the fuck out of there," Gavin said into her earpiece. "We have the children, and Houston wants to pummel the base. The jets are inbound."

She couldn't respond; she needed what wits she had left for dealing with the Warden focused on killing her. Blood matted her hair where he'd hit her with his pistol, and her entire left arm still burned from whatever it was he'd just given her.

Rowan lazily clapped his hands a few times. "Well done, Dani."

She flinched when a loud bang echoed through the medical bay. Miles was back at the window with his pipe. He and Mary alternated turns striking the glass with their weapons. Part of her was glad to see her friends; the other part screamed that they were all in terrible danger. Even if she survived her encounter with Rowan, none of them would survive the CNA's bombing of the base.

Dani kept her knife pointed at Rowan. Her hand continued to shake. Rowan placed his hands on the stretcher and grinned wider. He pushed it forward and charged toward her, clearly planning to pin her between the stretcher and cart she leaned against. Dani, too, grinned as he neared. His eyes widened when she leapt from the floor to land with her left hip on the stretcher. Before he could recoil, she kicked her right boot and struck his head. As he stumbled, she slid off the stretcher, swung her knife, and sliced his face with its tip.

He dropped, arced one leg out, and swept her off her feet. She landed on her already sore back with a grunt and automatically rolled into a crouched position. He pulled his pistol, and she charged before he could aim the weapon at her. They collided and tumbled to the floor. Rowan managed to knock the blade from her hand, but she pinned his pistol hand to the floor and drove her knee into his wrist.

As she pulled the pistol from his hand, his fist caught her in the ribs and unbalanced her. The weapon spun across the floor to the other side of the room.

"Shit," she said. She separated from him and rolled to put a few feet between them before she stopped and crouched again. Her breaths were deep and ragged; her chest heaved to bring in more air. Miles's and Mary's voices filled her ear, and she removed her comm and tossed it aside to eliminate the distraction.

"You're a much better fighter than you were before." Rowan stood and rubbed his sore wrist for a moment, then wiped at the blood on his face.

Dani stood and tried to slow her panicked heart rate and breathing. She'd tricked Rowan into thinking she was a trembling mess after leaving the stretcher. Though it hadn't been far from the truth, the deception had worked to land some good strikes against him. Still, this wasn't a training session with Gavin. Rowan planned to end her life today—and, possibly, let her regen and do it again. He was a twisted fuck; he wouldn't be satisfied with killing her just once.

She placed her right hand on her hip, near her one remaining small blade, and kept focusing on slowing her breaths. Rowan's eyes flicked around the room. They both ignored the continued banging against the window. Bits of glass broke away and rained down inside the room. Dani hoped she could stall Rowan long enough for the glass to fully break, but she wasn't resting all her hopes on that plan.

They moved in arcs, circling away from each other. Rowan pulled the knife that he'd used to cut open her sleeve from his belt and shifted as if preparing to charge her, but Dani wasn't tricked by the feint.

He shifted a second time, and this time he committed to the charge. Dani removed her own blade from its hiding place as she spun away, and she sliced his arm open as he moved past her. He didn't flinch at the injury; he immediately attacked again.

They slammed into medical equipment as they wrestled to free their wrists from one another's grip. Dani used her small blade to cut into Rowan's forearm. He loosened his grip, and she pulled her wrist free. He shoved her back into a wall and pushed his body against hers. As he did, she drove her blade into his neck—and he stabbed her in her right side with his knife.

She shuddered when the blade penetrated her body. Severe pain registered in her mind, and she cried out and shoved him back.

Rowan dropped his blade to use both of his hands to slow the blood pouring out of his neck. Dani leaned forward, clutching her side. Blood covered her hand, seeped through her fingers, and spattered onto the floor.

"Bitch!" Rowan growled.

More glass fell from the window, and both Mary and Miles shouted at her from above. Dani still couldn't give them her attention. She remained focused on Rowan. The high-pitched whine of a quake rifle turned her attention to the Warden entering through the double doors. There was no time to duck before the blast struck her in the chest.

"Curtis!" Rowan scowled. "Why did you do that? I had her."

"She's not the one bleeding out of her neck." Curtis fired his rifle at the man and woman screaming and banging on the glass above them. They dove aside as the glass exploded into the corridor around them. Curtis used one hand to yank med cart drawers open and remove contents. He used his teeth to tear open a few packages of bandages.

Rowan watched to see if the man and woman returned to the window. No sign of them so far.

"Grab the tape," Curtis said.

Rowan found the roll he'd used on Dani's IV, and Curtis pressed the bandages against the wound on his superior's neck. Rowan held the dressing in place with one blood-covered hand

and unwound a length of tape with the other. Curtis took the tape and placed several wraps around the bandage and Rowan's neck to secure it.

"It's tight," Rowan said with a grunt.

"Not nearly as tight as I want to wrap it, I promise. Besides, it's just to keep you alive for a few minutes longer." Curtis pulled Rowan toward the exit.

Rowan resisted. "She's an Echo. We have to take her."

"She's a human corpse, Rowan. Look! I hit her in the chest with a goddamn quake rifle. No human survives that." Curtis resumed herding Rowan out of the medical bay.

"But—"

"If she was an Echo, she'd be regenerating by now. Move!" Curtis gave him a violent shove.

"Wait. She hasn't aged a day since we first took Portland."

"You're mistaken, Rowan."

"I'm not."

"We've lost the base, no thanks to you fucking around with your girlfriend down here instead of leading the counterattack. You've got about five minutes before you bleed out anyway. I already evacuated your family. You're welcome." Curtis shook his head.

Rowan stared back at the med bay though the doors had closed. He felt dizzy; he stumbled. "I might pass out."

Curtis sighed. "If you do, I'll carry you."

As soon as the Wardens were gone, Miles took Mary's hands, helped her over the window's edge, and lowered her into the room. She still had an eight-foot drop.

She hit the floor boots first, rolled along her hip and side, then hopped back up to her feet. She pushed a stretcher over to shorten Miles's longer drop. Once he landed, denting the stretcher with the impact, they went to Dani's side. Mary rolled her to her back and pressed her fingertips against her neck.

"She's alive. I don't know how, but she is."

Miles felt a mix of relief and terror. "Gavin, I need a medic for Dani, *now!*"

"Air strike is inbound," Gavin said.

"Delay it. We're in some sort of medical part of the base, and I don't know how to get out of here." Miles turned to Mary. "Do you have any idea how to treat her with anything in this room?"

She shook her head.

Miles scooped Dani into his arms. "Then we'll just have to find our way out of here."

CHAPTER 48

Within a few hours of the Wardens abandoning the base, those that did not escape into the tunnels were captured or permanently killed. Some Wardens chose to terminate their own lives with grenades instead of surrendering. CNA ground troops had now arrived to relieve the troops who had mounted the initial attack, but Gavin refused to rest.

He stood inside a field tent, staring at the map of the base on the table before him. He rubbed his eyes when his vision blurred. The attack plan had been solid until everything went wrong.

Houston entered. When she looked up from her panel and saw Gavin standing there, she frowned. "I told you an hour ago to leave. I don't care if you're in your twenties again, you're relieved."

"Where's my replacement?" Gavin asked, bitterness in his voice. He waved his arms, highlighting the fact that no one else was inside the tent with them.

"For a man that used to respect my position, you're mighty defiant now."

Gavin looked away. "What's the casualty count?"

"High." Houston tossed the panel to the table between them. Gavin stared at the device but didn't pick it up.

"Why the bullshit game, Gavin? You ask for the casualty count, but you don't really want to know the answer, do you? Have anything to do with Dani needing surgery to put her back together?"

"She's tough; she'll be fine."

"Will she? Will you?"

Gavin tightened his jaw and lifted the panel from the table. He scanned the numbers, which kept ticking upward as the constant feed of data was relayed to Houston's device. He dropped the panel back to the table with a clatter and passed his hand over his face. "Fuck."

"Yeah. We took a damn beating, that's for sure."

"What percentage were killed after the Wardens started fleeing the base?"

"That's the wrong question."

Gavin glared at Houston. "Don't try your mind games on me."

She shrugged. "No games, just stating a fact. You're asking the wrong question."

"How many died because I made you delay the air strike?"

"*Now* we have the question you wanted to ask the first time."

"What's the answer?"

"It doesn't matter. As field commander, all combat-related decisions, the right ones and the wrong ones, are mine. You begged for an air strike delay, and I agreed. You didn't 'make' me do anything. We had key people inside the base who we needed out before tearing the place to shreds."

Gavin shook his head and returned his attention to the map.

"Go ahead and hang on to that guilt as long as you want. Take it to bed with you, let it eat at you, Gavin. It's not yours to keep, but you'll do what you want anyway. Right?"

He didn't answer her, and they both gazed at the map in silence for a few minutes.

"What are you working on for new assignments?" Gavin asked.

"In Maine?"

"Outside of Maine."

"Before or after Dani is out of the hospital?"

Gavin tensed, but said nothing.

"So, you want to leave before she's out. Your decision." Houston shrugged. "You want a small team, or to work solo?"

"Either is fine."

"I need recon to the north, west, and south, all along Maine's borders, to identify any Warden outposts in the state. I'm planning to use the local fisherman along the coast to keep an eye on anything coming in from the east. I also want to start probing New Hampshire. Portsmouth is of interest, but we have some CNA presence already in the White Mountains—in Lincoln. I need someone to help organize the Brigands there."

"I'll handle the Brigands. Send me to Lincoln. Enlist me as a CNA soldier so I can formally represent you."

"Enlist? You refused my offer before."

"I'm not refusing now."

"As a volunteer, I can put you where I want. If you enlist and become CNA, the brass above me can deploy you where they want. I may not be able to keep you on my assignments."

Gavin shrugged. "You'll find a way to keep me if you want me, ma'am."

"Ah, back to the formalities now? God, you're fickle."

"Just handle the goddamn paperwork, Catherine."

Houston chuckled at his outburst, which infuriated him more.

"Gavin, you're a mess. You're exhausted and need to rest before making this kind of decision. Right now, you can't even decide if we're on a first-name basis or if you're still acknowledging military protocol. I bet if I give you a few more flippant answers I can make you homicidal."

He took a deep breath. "I admit that I am tired, but I know what I'm doing. Put me in the CNA as a soldier, not a volunteer. Do it soon and give me my orders."

"You are certain?"

He nodded.

"If you change your mind—"

"I won't."

"Okay. I'll give you want you want, now get the hell out of my tent."

Gavin saluted and left. He wanted to find a tent to rest in, but his feet carried him to the field hospital. CNA troops escorted Warden prisoners in I-cuffs away from the hospital toward a temporary brig. He hoped the prisoners would provide the CNA with some decent intel. He was desperate to know that the cost of this battle was worth something other than so many dead and wounded.

He knew he must look terrible, because several of the staff he questioned regarding Dani's location tried to triage him. He found Miles and Mary pacing outside one of the field hospital's surgical tents and cradling mugs of coffee in their hands.

"Where is she?" he asked.

"Out of surgery and in a recovery area," Mary said. "They only let us see her for a minute."

"She's awake?"

Mary shook her head. "It's bad, Gavin. That fucking Warden got her good with the knife and the other one shot her right in the chest with a quake rifle. She shouldn't be alive."

Gavin sighed.

"Are you okay?" Miles asked him.

"Yeah. I look like shit, but regen fixes the internal damage."
Most of it.

"Knocked a decade or two off you, too," Miles said.

"When did you die?" Mary asked.

"After the towers blew. Sewers collapsed right on top of us."

"You and Dani lied when you said you would be clear of the air traffic tower?" Mary asked.

"Yeah."

"And had me detonate on time."

Gavin nodded.

Mary sighed and shook her head with disgust. "Great. So I almost killed Dani and did manage to kill you. You're an asshole, Gavin."

He shrugged. "Not the first time I've been told that. Do they know when she'll wake up?"

"No," Mary said.

"We can't continue to hover around here while she sleeps. In a few hours, we go back on duty to start clearing the areas around the base for any Wardens in hiding." Gavin took Miles's coffee from him. "You're on the first rotation, so take your rack time now. Thanks for getting Dani out of the base alive."

Miles nodded and left.

Gavin lingered. "Mary, I'll be on patrols most of the time over the next few days, but send word on how she is when you have a break to check on her, will you?"

Mary stared at him a moment. "Why wouldn't you visit her yourself?"

"I'm taking a new assignment from Houston, so I'll be leaving soon."

"How soon?"

"I'm not sure."

"You'd leave before Dani woke up?"

"If I'm ordered to go, yes."

"That's bullshit."

"I will visit her, Mary. I want to be the one to talk to her before I go, okay?"

"Absolutely. No way in hell would I want to deliver the news to her that you're heading out of town right after she wakes up. I don't know what's up your ass or why you'd agree to an assignment like this, but that's your problem. Don't expect her to be happy."

Gavin nodded, his shoulders hunched.

Mary finished her coffee and left.

He considered drinking Miles's leftover coffee but instead tossed the brown liquid into a snow bank, found a tent with an empty bunk, and collapsed into it. His body was so fatigued that even his guilt-stricken mind couldn't resist the pull of sleep.

CHAPTER

49

Dani stirred and reached for Brody. She opened her eyes when her hand instead touched something hard. Eight-inch-tall, white walls surrounded her upper body like a capsule; above her she saw only ceiling.

Her first thought was that she was lying in a coffin. She twisted and reached for the side to climb out and gasped as pain shot through her side and chest. The coffin's walls now blinked with tiny lights and beeped, but she kept her grip on the opening near her head, undeterred. Then Mary's face appeared, and Gavin's, and she relaxed a little.

Mary touched her shoulder. "You're fine."

"Where am I?" Dani asked. "What is this?"

"You're in a field hospital, and this is a healing pod," Mary said.

"Not a coffin?"

"No, not a coffin. A Warden stabbed you in your side. You had major internal damage, and it took the surgeons hours to put you back together."

"I don't like this pod thing."

"Tell me when to stop," Mary said. She pressed a button somewhere, and the top part of the pod angled upward.

Dani could now see more of the room, which decreased her feeling of claustrophobia.

"That's good," she said. She winced as she released the pod's wall to lie on her back again. She remembered getting stabbed in the ribs. She touched the center of her chest. "The last thing I remember is the whine of a quake rifle."

"Another Warden showed up and shot you in the chest with one."

Dani shook her head. "If that happened, I'd be dead—well, I'd be a ten-year-old kid, at least."

"You did your best to die, but Gavin threatened the medics with their lives if they lost you."

Gavin nodded. "Apparently wearing Warden body armor over two layers of Commonwealth armor helps you survive an almost point-blank quake rifle blast. We also learned that the newer Warden body armor can stop a plasma pistol. You had a hole in the back of your jacket."

"I didn't know what he hit me in the back with, other than it hurt like hell and I couldn't move. Did those two Wardens escape?"

"Yeah." Gavin sighed. "After the airstrike, we went back in. We followed a shitload of blood before it stopped. I'm guessing the one you cut died, but his buddy with the rifle still got him out. By the time we unlocked the tunnels they'd used to escape, they were long gone."

Dani blinked a few times and realized how young Gavin appeared now. The wisps of gray in his hair were gone, and he smiled without any wrinkles. "I'm still mad you made you made me leave you dying in the sewers."

He shrugged. "It would've been a waste of time for you to stay with me until regen. You completely failed your mission to take out their secondary power source, of course . . . but you rescued a couple dozen kids from those psychopaths. All in all, not a bad day's work."

"Rowan," Dani said.

Mary and Gavin glanced at each other.

"What?" Mary asked.

"Rowan was the name of the guy who stabbed me. He said we'd run into each other before, but I didn't remember him. God, he wanted me dead—well, tortured first, then dead. He called for someone named Curtis to come to the med bay. I'm guessing he was the one with the rifle."

"Rowan was the one in charge of the base." Gavin shook his head in disbelief. "Curtis was second-in-command. Jesus, Dani, what did you do to make the head Warden come after you like that?"

"No idea."

"I'll notify Houston," Gavin said. "Some of the Wardens we captured may have more information on them."

"Where's Miles?" Dani asked.

"He's in a different wing of the field hospital. The day after we took the base, we started clearing the area around Portland. He took a plasma pistol shot in the leg; the med teams are still putting his femur back together."

"He'll be okay?"

Mary nodded. "You're both on the same transport back to Bangor to finish healing there. You leave tomorrow. We're still digging through the base, but crews found Rosen, somehow still alive. She needs more surgery. Marcic, Jens, and Zykov didn't make it."

"Rosen's made of tough stuff." Dani grimaced. "Man, we took a beating."

"Yeah," Mary said.

"When do you two go home?"

"I should be back there in another week. The CNA was so impressed we retook Portland, they've flooded the area with troops to help us keep it. We don't need to keep all the volunteers down here."

"And you?" Dani looked at Gavin. "You're also back in a week?"

He shook his head.

"I'm glad you're awake," Mary said, backing away. "I'll tell Miles."

Dani frowned at Gavin when Mary darted out the door. "Why did she leave like that? What's going on?"

"I'm not going back to Bangor, Dani."

"Why not?"

"I'm taking a post with Houston to help advise the Commonwealth."

"Why?"

"They need the help."

"Bullshit." Dani gripped the sides of the pod to pull herself up. More blinking lights and beeps protested her movement; she ignored them, but couldn't ignore the pain in her side. She grunted with the effort of sitting up. She batted Gavin's hand away, though, when he tried to help. "You're lying. Why?"

He stalled for a moment before answering. "You. I'm not returning to Bangor because of you."

"What?"

"The first night we were together, do you remember the questions you asked me?"

Dani shook her head.

"You asked if we were allowed to sleep together since I was a superior officer of sorts."

"Oh. Yeah, I remember some of that. You said it was okay."

"I lied, but I couldn't wait anymore. I love you, more than I want to admit, and it compromised my ability to lead my team.

I bent the rules and put people at risk to keep you alive. We were taking heavy fire from the Warden cluster grenades, and I delayed the air strike to give Mary and Miles more time to help you. Those troop deaths are on me."

Dani shook her head. "You can't—"

"When you're healed, will you rejoin the volunteers?" he asked.

"Yes."

"I figured you would. That's why I'm taking the post with Houston. I can't lead troops when you're among them. I can't make the right decisions when your life is at stake."

Dani leaned back in the bed, wishing the complaining pod would stop freaking out every time she moved. "You've already made your decision?"

Gavin nodded.

"So the shit you said in the sewer before you died was a lie too."

"No. I wanted to spend my life with you as a physically younger man. But once the battle really started, my decisions were compromised because I *needed* you to survive. I gave you orders so you'd back off, but you kept pressing the attack."

She wiped the tears away as her heartache shifted to anger. "You were wrong to think that you could order me to stop."

"I know. You're the best fighter I've ever seen—better than me, because you fight for the right reasons. We would've bombed the place and killed those kids without knowing we were killing them until it was too late. You saved *generations* by saving those Echoes."

Gavin reached for her hand, and she pulled it away. She didn't want to be placated with niceties. Not when he was ripping her heart out. "You say the fault is yours for the lives lost because you altered orders to keep me alive, but ultimately, you're blaming me for everything you did wrong. It's *my* fault you made poor decisions that got others killed. Do you have any idea how fucked up that is?"

"Dani—"

"Get out."

"I've hurt you, and I'm sorry."

"Get. Out."

"When you go home, move into my place if you want," he said. "It's yours."

She turned her head away. Seconds later, she heard him leave the room.

Once he was gone, she tried to hold back the pain and anger, but the tears still slid down her face. She took a deep breath to calm herself and grimaced at the sharp pain the movement created in her chest. The coffin-pod beeped at her again, and she slammed her fist into the blinking lights—which only made it alarm more.

Hospital staff came into the room to check her.

"Turn this damn thing off," she snapped at them.

Mary rushed into the room just then and shooed the staff away. "I wasn't gone that long," she said. "Yet in those fifteen minutes you lose your shit and make your side start bleeding again. What the hell happened?"

Dani filled her in on her exchange with Gavin.

"He told me he was taking an assignment with Houston, but he didn't say why. He's blaming *you*? That asshole. I'll fucking kill him. Permanently!" Mary turned to leave the room, as if to go find him.

Dani caught her friend's arm. "He isn't changing his mind. He wants to run away; let him."

"He's still a dick."

"I agree." Dani sighed. Her body felt heavy and tired.

"Are you sure I can't kill him?"

Dani offered her friend a tired smile. "How is Miles?"

"Thrilled you're awake. I left to come back here when they took him for more treatment. I'll make sure they put you near each other on the transport."

"Thank you. What happened after the Warden shot me in the chest?"

Mary told her of the subsequent events, and Dani peppered her with more questions. Everything Mary said confirmed Gavin's side of the story. He had held the air strike, as he said. While Dani was glad to be alive and not ten years old, it was true: Gavin had risked and sacrificed many lives by putting hers first.

"Where's Brody?"

"Javi is keeping him here for clearing all the buildings around the base. The field hospital wouldn't let him in, but I'm serving as his new handler. He'll come home with me."

"You're not keeping my dog."

Mary laughed. "I'll give him back—temporarily, at least."

"You and Oliver are trying to steal my dog. I know you are." Dani smiled, but her eyelids seemed impossibly heavy.

"You need to rest. I have to run out, but I'll be back before you leave. Next time you wake up, take a look around before you lose your mind. It's not a coffin."

"Got it. Thanks, Mary."

When Dani was loaded onto the transport plane the next day, Miles sat up on his stretcher and smiled. His entire left leg was wrapped in a swath of healing patches that constantly blinked beneath the blanket over his lower half. The medical crew secured Dani's pod to the plane's deck before leaving her to load the rest of the wounded.

"You looked like shit the last time I saw you," Miles said.

"So I've heard. My coffin does a decent job bringing people back from near death."

They talked for the duration of the short flight from Portland to Bangor. Whenever Gavin's name came up, Dani steered the conversation away from him. She wasn't ready to feel all the emotions that threatened to spill out every time she thought of him.

CHAPTER

50

Miles helped Dani into the passenger side of the MP Jeep. After a week in the hospital back in Bangor, she'd finally been released.

"Oliver made me promise to tell you that he'll visit this afternoon when he's out of school," Miles said.

She nodded.

February's weather was continuing on from January's bitter cold trend, and Dani was glad to get out of the biting wind and into the warm Jeep. A light snow fell outside; she watched the falling flakes land on the windshield and melt.

"It's okay to tell him to go away if you need to rest," Miles said.

Dani smiled. "He hasn't listened when I've told him that before."

"Wish I could blame that on his mother." Miles closed her door and limped around the vehicle to climb into the driver's seat. He used his hands to adjust the position of his left leg, still partially immobilized by CNA medical tech.

"There. That's better," he said once he had his leg in a comfortable position. "I only have a few more days in this thing, and the limp should be gone by the end of next week."

"Are you sure you can drive with that thing on?"

"Sure. I can still move my knee. Warm enough?"

"You don't have to coddle me, Miles. I won't break."

"I know." He started driving. "I planned to roll past Hattie's and let you jump out so I didn't need to stop. Bloody cold out today, and I want to stay warm." He glanced at her with a grin.

Dani laughed.

"Hattie had your things moved into a back room in the brothel, away from the noise of evening business activities. She said she refuses to let you hang out in the shed while you heal."

Dani didn't protest. The shed gave her flashbacks of life with Miles, and she had memories of Gavin there too. She was fine with the move.

Miles slowed the Jeep. "You're not arguing about the change. Are you feeling okay?"

"If you take me back to the hospital, I'll give you a permanent limp."

He chuckled and sped up again. "I figured you'd want your own space instead of a room at Hattie's. Will you move back into the place you shared with Jace once Gavin is back?"

"He's not coming back." She gazed out the window at the snow.

"Sure he is. Mary and Brody come home tomorrow. Gavin won't stay gone too much longer."

"He left, Miles. He's not coming back."

Miles remained silent until they arrived at Hattie's. He pulled up to the house and brought the Jeep to a halt, then turned in his seat to face Dani. "He ended things with you?"

Dani finally met his eyes and nodded.

"When?"

"The day before we flew back here."

"You didn't say anything."

"What was I supposed to say? 'Glad to see you're still alive,

Miles. Oh, by the way, Gavin blames me for his poor decision making and getting people killed, so he bailed. Have a nice flight.'"

"Wait. Is that true about him blaming you?"

Dani nodded.

Miles took a deep breath and shifted in his seat. He stared ahead for a few minutes while they sat in silence.

"I've never wanted to murder anyone before now," he said.

"You sound like Mary." Dani chuckled. "I stopped her from going after him. I think she would've killed him."

"I'm sorry he hurt you. Look, I know you're going to say you're fine, but you cared for him. He's wrong to blame you for his issues. Don't believe whatever bullshit he told you is your fault. He's wrong."

"I know, and thank you." She truly appreciated Miles's support.

"What if he does come back?"

"He can kiss my ass."

"Good!" He smiled. "Let's get you inside."

Dani's new room had a heater, three lamps, a desk and chair, and another comfy chair by one of the lamps next to a wall that had been turned into a bookshelf. She also had her own small bathroom, attached to the bedroom.

Hattie came in as she was surveying the space.

"I can't afford this," Dani said.

Hattie waved her hand, dismissing the remark. "Family doesn't pay. How are you feeling? I didn't want to go to the hospital to hover over you—plus, I don't have warm, fuzzy feelings for the place where Jace died."

"I'm much better, thank you. Still working out some stiffness. What do you mean family doesn't pay?"

"Exactly what it means, Dani. Sit."

Dani moved to the soft chair near the books. She patted the soft armrests and slid her palms over the fabric, tracing the patterns on it.

Hattie pulled the wooden chair away from the desk, turned it, and sat facing Dani. "That's a great chair," she said. "Thought you would like it."

"I've never felt anything so soft."

"There are plenty of books to keep you occupied until you're back up and running again."

Dani turned her head upward and followed the neatly lined up rows of books on the shelves, which ran from the floor to the ceiling. She wasn't sure what to say.

"Are we done with the chitchat?" Hattie asked.

Dani's eyes left the books. "Yeah."

"Good. Chitchat is a pain in the ass." She folded her hands in her lap. "I sit on the council now. No more behind-the-scenes and pulling-strings bullshit."

"That's great news!"

Hattie shrugged. "Took a few folks a while to get over themselves and what type of business I run. Turns out when you own enough weapons and explosives to protect the city from a Warden invasion, they suddenly don't give a shit what you do for work." She cackled. "Anyway, Houston said Gavin is now part of the CNA, and she's using him for 'sensitive' assignments. That tells me the two of you are over."

"Never could keep secrets from you," Dani said.

Hattie nodded. "Miles."

"What about him?"

"He's a good man."

"Hattie, are you really giving me dating advice?"

"Jace approved of him. Well, actually, Jace hated his fucking guts for a long time, but after Miles took the blame for killing that idiot Xander, he changed his mind."

"Yeah. Jace told me he thought Miles was decent not long after that—which, coming from him, was high praise."

"He admitted to me that he'd misjudged Miles and wished he hadn't given you such a hard time about dating him in your prior life. Jace said if you and Miles got back together, he wouldn't interfere."

"Oh." Dani wasn't expecting that for an answer.

"Miles still loves you. Any moron can see that."

"I know."

"It's your life. Do what you want, but don't wait around too long. Jace and I could have had more time together, but we waited. It's the only decision I've ever regretted." Hattie stood and walked to the door. Before she walked out, she paused. "A few hundred years ago, Maine used to hold their elections earlier than the rest of the states. The politicians used to say that the way Maine voted would determine how the other states would vote. 'As Maine goes, so goes the nation' was the saying. It wasn't always accurate, but I think the saying has new meaning now."

Dani shook her head. "I don't understand."

"For decades, we—Brigands and Commonwealths—have cowered under the Wardens' might. With this attack, we proved that not only do the Wardens bleed, they can be beaten. Maine is now out of the Wardens' hands, and other states and nations have seen and heard what a few hundred volunteers started with the help of only one CNA battalion. Less than two thousand people joined together to push the Wardens out of our state. The Brigand council believes in a new saying: 'As Maine goes, so goes the world.'"

"I don't know, Hattie. The world? That's a big leap."

"You'll see."

"How do you know so much about history? Are you the one who knew about this saying from centuries ago?"

"We all have our secrets, don't we?" Hattie winked. "You created a shit storm in Portland, Dani. Jace would be proud. Well done, honey."

Dani stared at the closed door for a while after Hattie left. She hoped she was right.

CHAPTER
51

Rowan tried to contain his disdain for the vice regent as he stood before her. She held a tremendous amount of power over the eastern portion of North America, but she wielded it with too much caution. She could order the immediate destruction of Maine and turn the state into a pile of ash, but here, sitting in her comfortable office in Boston, she sipped her tea and finished reading the report on Portland's loss to the CNA with zero visible reaction. Rowan resisted the urge to glance at Curtis, who stood beside him.

"This is a thorough accounting of the events of and leading up to eleven January," the vice regent said. "You believed Bangor to be such a severe threat that you left Portland in a snow storm to attack it earlier than your orders stated."

"That is correct," Rowan said.

"We had no such detail of massive weapon stores in our intel from that region. Some weapons, yes, but not massive by any means."

Rowan's lies came easy to him. "We had spies in Bangor giving us different information."

"Who were these spies?"

"We did not maintain records regarding those informants out of a desire to protect their identities," Rowan said.

"Where are your informants now?"

"One was killed months before the January attack. The remaining two have since gone missing." More lies. But the vice regent was incompetent, and he was confident that the report he and Curtis had compiled would clear them of any charges of mishandling Portland resources. Curtis had included some falsified documentation—what he called "creative elaboration"—in the report that only the most detailed individual would detect, and even then only if they cared to perform hours of research. The Boston VR was lazy, so they were safe.

I hope you choke on that tea, Rowan thought.

"But Brigands and CNA troops were already in position at *your* base when you decided to leave, correct?"

"They used the sewers to move without detection," Rowan said. "You have the reports for the last six months from my troops. We conducted sweeps throughout the city multiple times a day, Vice Regent. Nothing regarding spy movements in the sewers was recorded."

"Did your troops lie?"

"I fear their sweeps were not as thorough as their reports indicated. Also in the records are accounts of my personal rounds; I assure you they were thorough in every respect, but I could not inspect every manhole and sewer pipe in the city."

The vice regent set the report aside.

"Ma'am, Bangor is still a threat. Please give me troops to take into Maine so we can retake Portland and eliminate Bangor."

"No. You've lost enough of our troops, Rowan. The CNA and Brigands have a solid hold on Portland now. Seems the clever Lieutenant Colonel Houston got her own revenge for you taking Portland from her years ago. Despite this embarrassment, you won't be formally charged for failing to hold the city.

However, you will not be reassigned to another overseer position. Consider it an unofficial demotion. You are reassigned to Boston as part of R&D."

The vice regent stood. Rowan's eyes never left her.

"Please, ma'am. Let me retake Maine for the Wardens."

"Request denied."

Rowan tightened his jaw. "We cannot claim Earth for the Ekkohs if we do not control it in its entirety."

"Maine is not important strategically—thus, it is not a threat. Until our internal intel reports declare otherwise, Maine is a non-issue. The CNA can have their spit of land."

"Vice Regent, it's a mistake to underestimate this Brigand–CNA partnership. We have more than enough resources in Boston to attack Portland."

"Rowan, not another word."

"But—"

"Enough! There will be no retaliation on Maine. You are dismissed."

Rowan trembled with rage, but he turned and left the vice regent's office without further protest. Once he and Curtis were well away from Warden officials and anyone else who might overhear him, he exploded. "She's wrong!"

"Control your anger," Curtis said in a low voice. "We no longer have the freedom to speak as we wish. That report we put together has kept us within the Warden ranks despite our obvious fuckup in Portland. For that, we must be grateful. You get to stay with your family, Rowan. This could have meant a formal demotion, even jail time. We got off easy."

Rowan took a deep breath and nodded. "Do you agree with me?"

"Yes, but we're in Boston now. We have to play by different rules—by their silly, political rules. The only way she'll change her mind is if she gets pressured by other vice regents."

"I need to present them our case for attack."

"No! You can't go at them head-on, Rowan. The political games don't work that way."

"I don't have patience for games."

"I know you don't. Let me work our case discreetly. It needs to be done more subtly than calling our VR nothing short of a fucking moron."

"Well, she *is* a fucking moron." Rowan clenched his fists and then released them. "You will manage the politics of this?"

"On one condition. You must give up this obsession with Dani. She's dead, Rowan. She is a dead human."

She's not dead, and I want her to suffer.

"You can't have your revenge on a corpse."

Though he still didn't believe his friend, Rowan nodded.

"Say it. I need to hear you say it."

"She is a dead human. You shot her with a quake rifle in the chest, and she did not regen."

"Good. I'll work on Portland. Manage your R&D teams and keep your head down with work. Don't speak to anyone else but me about Maine. You must appear as though you agree with the VR."

"That won't be easy, but I'll do my best. Thank you, Curtis. Things would have gone differently had I listened to you in Portland. Still, you kept me from capture and stayed by my side during the inquiry. Thank you."

"I'm sure it's not the last time I'll save your ass."

Rowan offered his friend a small smile. "You're probably right."

"Go home to your family."

"Come by for dinner soon. Devon always likes to see you."

"I will. He's a good kid."

Rowan turned to head to his quarters, his mind racing. Dani was an Echo; he had no doubt about that. She hadn't regenned, so that meant Curtis hadn't killed her. How she'd survived a quake rifle shot to the chest, he couldn't explain, but he wanted to know. Rowan would let Curtis play his games while he figured out how to track Dani down and capture her. He would find a way to go back to Maine.

CHAPTER

52

"Yes!" Dani raised her arms in celebration, then lowered them to high-five Oliver.

"That's your longest one so far today," he said.

"You're still beating me. Easily."

"Stop throwing the heavier rocks. I'll find the ones you should use."

Oliver scavenged the beach area for more stones. He picked up several and handed Dani half of his collection. The river was still iced over, so instead of skipping stones, they were throwing them across the ice to see how far they could make them slide.

Dani threw a few more, and Brody whimpered and paced the shoreline. He wanted to chase the stones across the ice, but she wouldn't let him. This rock didn't go far; Dani frowned and touched her side where Rowan had stabbed her. The wound and internal injuries were healed, but sometimes her side still ached.

The CNA had chased several leads to find Rowan, but the Warden had reached the safety of Boston before they could catch him. The CNA didn't bother with further pursuits. Boston was too dangerous for any non-Warden to go near.

"Do you want to stop?"

Dani blinked and turned to the Oliver. "Huh?"

"You're holding your side. Does it hurt?"

Dani smiled and lowered her hand. "It just aches a little sometimes, like a sore muscle. I'm fine."

Oliver nodded and left to search for more rocks. Many were stuck to the ice on the ground, so he wrestled with some to break them free. Dani pulled her hat farther down to cover her ears and watched him.

The cloudless sky bathed them in sunlight; it reminded Dani of a time in Portland when she'd stood among the buildings and enjoyed the sun. Her memories continued to come to her in disorganized snippets, but they didn't startle her like they used to—except the ones with Miles. Those still tended to catch her off guard.

She thought back over her current life. Jace had made a smart decision when he'd taken her to Bangor after fleeing Portland. They'd never lived a life of luxury; meals, shelter, and clothing had only ever come with a lot of work, whether by scavenging, trading, or stealing. But they'd been happy in Bangor.

Dani thought back to the last time she'd stolen something. *The day before I met Oliver,* she thought.

She'd almost been killed a few times rescuing him. And he'd been a colossal pain in her ass afterward, until she'd accepted his stubbornness. He, of course, had accepted her on sight; he'd even trusted her to get him out of the mess with the Standpipe falling apart around them when he didn't even know her.

Good kid.

Her thoughts shifted. He was the one who'd annoyed her into taking action and creating the Brigand–Commonwealth merger. He was also the only person that had known the truth of her sometimes suicidal thoughts after Jace's death. She'd made him a promise to not hurt herself, and she was determined not to break it. That revolver needed to stay with Hattie, permanently. She didn't want the reminder of how close she'd come to killing herself.

Tears burned her eyes as she remembered the very dark places she'd gone to after losing Jace. Oliver bringing her Jace's journal was the only thing that could have brought her back from those depths.

She watched him throw a few more rocks across the ice and smiled. He'd shown her how to skip rocks. The happiness she'd experienced that day was something she'd never felt before.

He caught her watching him, and he walked over. "Are you sure you're okay?"

"Yeah. Just thinking. Oliver, people have been giving me credit for the partnership forming and for us taking Portland, but I'm not at the root of this thing. I never was."

"What do you mean?"

"You started it all. Meeting you at the Standpipe changed everything. You called me out for my bullshit when I blamed the CNA for not merging with Brigands and taking the fight to the Wardens. I was so mad at you that day, but I always knew you were right. Everything that's happened to retake Maine started because of you."

Oliver shook his head. "You're forgetting the part where you saved Mom and Dad."

Dani frowned. "You're missing my point."

"No, I'm not." Oliver smiled. "We're out here freezing and throwing rocks because you don't want to be at the meeting in town. Right?"

Dani narrowed her eyes. "Maybe."

"The day I taught you to skip rocks, Jace thanked me for teaching you how to live. He said you'd spent your entire life surviving, and that wasn't the same as living. I wasn't exactly sure what he meant at the time, but I think I get it now."

"Good. Enlighten me."

"You laugh more now than you did the day I met you."

Dani nodded. "Yeah, that's probably true."

"It *is* true. You have friends who love you as family, and you love them. You've even learned how to hug. You used to suck at it."

She adjusted her winter hat and turned her eyes to the river. "You're right. I guess I'm just saying that . . . you're important to me, and you're a factor in other, bigger things happening around us."

"You're important too." Oliver took her hand. "You're my best friend."

Dani turned to him and tried to swallow. "I am?"

Oliver nodded. "I never had a best friend until I met you."

She took a deep breath and let it out slowly.

Oliver giggled. "This is the part where you relax and live, Dani. Stop stressing so much over everything."

"Okay. Don't stress. I'm trying."

"Here." Oliver turned her gloved hand palm up and placed a stone in her hand. "You like to think when you're occupied doing something else. Like when you tinker with cleaning or building stuff. So start throwing."

Dani threw the stone, and Oliver passed her another one.

She threw that one and nodded. "Yes, this helps. You're right. How did you get so smart?"

Oliver continued to pass her a steady supply of stones. "My parents, I guess."

"I wish I could've met your mom. I mean, I did, but I don't remember. I'd like to have that memory back."

Dani tossed the stones Oliver gave her, and her mind and body relaxed. She wondered if that was what living was like: just being somewhere and not worrying about other things or about being someplace else.

Peace, she thought.

Hattie had used that word to describe Jace before he died. Her brother had been so happy on his final day of life.

Dani had lost count of how many stones she'd thrown, but Oliver didn't break her supply line. Since he seemed to have a lot of answers she didn't, she asked him the most pressing question on her mind: "If someone is at peace—not like rest-in-peace dead, but alive and *at* peace—what does that mean?"

Oliver thought for a moment. "Are you happy right now?"

"Uh, yeah. I am."

He put another stone in her hand. "Throw. Do you want to be here at the river chucking rocks?"

"Yes." Dani threw her rock.

Oliver gave her another. "Mom said it was important to be content—happy with what you have, not worried about what you think you might lack, and happy to be where you are. I think that's the same as peace."

"Your mom was really smart."

"She didn't want me to always be afraid of the war and all the things that were happening. She said she couldn't shelter me from the horrible things that happened, and she was right. Almost every kid in school has lost at least one parent. Some have lost both."

"Too many people have died in this war."

"Can I tell you something?"

"Of course." Dani halted her rock throwing and faced him.

"When I turn seventeen, I'm required to join the CNA." Tears formed in his eyes. "I don't want to."

Dani discarded her stone and pulled him close. "You won't have to become part of the army, Oliver. I won't let that happen."

"The law—"

"Screw the law. Damn thing won't matter anyway if the war is over, right?"

"When will it end?"

Dani knelt so she wasn't looking down at him. "I don't know, but sometimes having a deadline helps speed the process."

Oliver frowned with confusion.

"We'll find a way to end this shit before you're seventeen. I don't know how, but we'll figure something out. Okay?"

Oliver nodded.

"Best friends don't let each other get stressed out of their minds, right?"

He smiled, nodded, and wiped at his tears with the back of his mitten.

She hugged him again before standing. "Now, we have a competition to continue. You're beating me, and that's not allowed either."

Oliver gathered more stones, and they continued to talk as they bounced rocks across the iced-over river.

CHAPTER 53

"Dani!" Miles scrambled down the rocks toward the frozen, sandy area where Dani and Oliver were still skipping stones. "The CNA is meeting with the council. *Now.* You're supposed to be there."

"This is more fun." Dani winked at Oliver, and he grinned.

"Hattie has threatened me with bodily harm if I don't bring you back."

"She was probably joking," Dani tossed another rock on the ice. It bounced several times before sliding to a stop—well short of Oliver's record-breaking stone. She frowned.

"I assure you, she was not," Miles said.

Dani rolled her eyes.

"You should go," Oliver said.

"Fine," Dani said. "You hold the record for distance, but don't plan on keeping it for long."

Oliver grinned again.

Dani gave him her rocks and started up the slope with Miles.

"Can I come to the meeting?" Oliver called after them.

Miles shook his head. "I don't think—"

"Sure!" Dani said.

Oliver discarded the rocks. "C'mon, B."

Whatever injuries Hattie had threatened him with, Miles seemed to believe the woman would follow through, because he kept urging them to walk faster. Dani obliged so he would calm down.

They made the final turn up the last hill and walked up the steps to the old courthouse. Their footsteps echoed in the halls as they moved through the building. Miles opened the door and allowed Dani, Oliver, and Brody through before he followed and closed the door.

Every set of eyes in the room turned to see who'd come to the meeting so late.

Hattie sat with the rest of the Brigand council at one half of a long table; Commonwealth leaders were seated along the other half.

"It's about fucking time," Hattie said.

"Happy to see you too," Dani said.

The room was full of many of the volunteers who had fought for Portland and the remainder of Maine. All seats were taken, so Dani took a place along the wall among several others who were also standing. She leaned against the wall, wondered why she *had* to be here.

Dani spotted Mary seated among the group in attendance. She was wearing the yellow dress Dani liked. When Dani smiled at her, she pointed at her wrist and mouthed, "You're late." That only made Dani smile wider. She was with her friends, and she was happy. She could do without the meeting, but she remembered Oliver's words and tried to be content.

"We wanted all the Bangor Brigands that took Portland here so we could formally offer our thanks and congratulations to you," Houston said.

"Is that it? Can we go now?" Dani whispered to Miles. She

gave him a mischievous grin, and he tightened his jaw and glared at her in reply. Dani sighed and realized she wasn't going to get out of this meeting. Oliver covered his snickering laugh with his hand.

Brody sat patiently next to Dani's leg. She scratched his head while the people seated at the table made various announcements she ignored.

Dani noticed an insignia change on Houston's uniform. She leaned close to Miles. "Promotion?"

He nodded. "Full colonel now."

"Huh. Good for her."

Several commendations were presented to CNA troops and Brigand volunteers. Dani's mind wandered while everyone clapped. Then Gavin's name was mentioned as a recipient, and her attention snapped to the present. She glanced around the room but didn't see him.

"Good thing he's not here for me to pummel him," Miles said.

Between herself, Miles, and Mary, Gavin would receive more bruises than awards if he returned to Bangor. That thought made her smile again.

"Still can't believe that asshole left you," Miles said. "I just shoot my girlfriends when I'm done with them."

Dani snorted a laugh that her hand was too slow to conceal.

"Shh!" Oliver hissed at her.

She glanced at Miles. "You're going to get me in trouble."

He shook his head. "You don't need anyone's help to do that."

"Captain Marcus is on an assignment in New Hampshire and couldn't be here today, but I know he was a long-term member of the Bangor community and has friends here," Houston said.

Fewer friends than before. Dani leaned closer to Miles so it was easier to talk to him and not be too disruptive to the proceedings. "Captain? That was a quick promotion."

"He's an Echo; he has more years of military experience than I have of being alive."

"What's in New Hampshire?"

"You'd know if you'd been here when this thing started."

She opened her mouth to respond, but he shushed her.

Houston continued talking, and Dani resumed rubbing Brody's ears. Her middle grumbled with hunger, and she shifted her stance when one of her legs started to cramp from standing still for so long. Oliver, also bored with the announcements, dropped to his knees to pet Brody. With all the extra attention, the dog's tail didn't stop moving.

"In retaking Portland, we have acquired major quantities of food, munitions, tech, and other equipment and supplies," Houston said. "The shipments designated for delivery to Bangor will start arriving tomorrow, and Brigands and the CNA will receive equal portions of the spoils."

Several in the crowd cheered.

"The CNA fully understands that we could not have taken Portland without support from residents of Bangor and other towns across the state," Houston continued. "We also understand that the Brigand partnership with the CNA would not have happened if certain rogue Brigands had not interrupted a CNA meeting and forced us to hear them out."

People in the room shifted in their seats, and all eyes turned to Dani.

She lifted her eyes from Brody to see everyone staring at her.

"We all suffered a huge loss when Jace died," Houston said.

Dani wasn't sure what to say, assuming her voice would actually work even if she came up with something, so she just nodded.

"We're converting one of the old airport hangars here into

a center specifically for training CNA troops on the stealth techniques he taught us early on. Dani, we'd like you to help oversee the training regimens in his place."

"Yeah, sure," Dani said, though her voice sounded a pitch higher than normal.

"Great. Thank you." Houston returned her attention to the greater crowd again. "The CNA has reinforced the Maine borders now that we've retaken the entire state. We'll continue to hold Portland while we rebuild our supplies and weapons. The Wardens' Research and Development division in Portland was working on groundbreaking tech that we've never seen before. We have that research now, and will continue to build upon it with our own engineers and scientists. We will also remain in Portland and reinforce her defenses."

"When is the next attack on the Wardens?" Dani asked. *Shit. Didn't mean to say that out loud.* She swallowed hard, wishing she hadn't blurted out the question.

Houston shifted in her chair. "Next attack? We suffered heavy losses retaking Maine, Dani. We must conserve our troops and resources to defend—"

"No!" Dani burst out. "God. When will you people learn? We can't just sit on our asses. The Wardens still control Canada. They also still have New Hampshire to our west and south. You think they're going to conserve their troops?"

"No, but—"

"You think they won't come at us from the east?"

"We're planning for that event."

"We have secured one fucking port, Colonel. One. How do you plan to get naval reserves in when we have *one* port? All the lobster boats in the world won't be able to take on a Warden carrier." Dani realized she was now standing directly in front of the table. She wasn't sure when she'd left her spot against the wall to confront the colonel, but she was committed now.

"We can still defend—"

"Can you defend Portland and not lose *one* person? No. Defending only works if you never take *any* damage, which you can't do. This is not the time to sit and regroup."

Houston leaned forward in her seat. "What do you propose?"

"Rally more Brigands and bring in more CNA troops. Take the ports in New Brunswick and Quebec."

"Canada?"

"Canada is still part of the Commonwealth of *North America*, right?" Dani asked.

Houston tightened her jaw.

"Start taking parts of Canada. Only then can we attempt to establish supply routes with other parts of the East Coast and the UK. Troops are spread out so thin across North America they can't hold anything for long if the Wardens want to take it from them. Abandon non-strategic areas to take the important ones."

"Bangor Brigands will be part of this offensive?" Houston asked.

"No."

"So the CNA can do the rest of the fighting on our own?"

"Bangor—both CNA and Brigands—will have a different target."

Houston laced her fingers together and stared at Dani. "Which target?"

"The largest city in New England."

Several at the table with Houston gasped; some swore. But most of the Brigands seated and standing behind Dani murmured their support.

"You're not serious."

Dani didn't answer. They had a deadline to end the war; everyone else just didn't know it yet.

"Jesus, you're insane," Houston said, leaning back in her chair.

Hattie grinned and winked at Dani. "As Maine goes, so goes the world."

Dani turned to face the room. "Portland was the first target, and we have many others to take before we're done. We have a long fight ahead of us, but Boston will be ours again. It's time for the Wardens to get the fuck off our planet."

"Boston! Boston!" the crowd chanted.

"Won't exactly be a sneak attack this time, with everyone knowing the target—not to mention how we took Portland," Houston shouted to Dani over the noise.

Maybe she really *was* crazy. But her flicker of doubt disappeared when Miles appeared at her side and gave her left shoulder a reassuring squeeze. She felt a tug on her right hand, and found Oliver looking up at her from her other side with a smile on his face.

Dani squared her shoulders. "We'll find another way in."

"Boston?" Houston said. "Are you sure? What about Portsmouth instead?"

Dani grinned. "We're retaking Boston."

ACKNOWLEDGMENTS

I am forever grateful to my friends and family for their support during my writing adventures.

A special thank-you goes to my friend and adviser on military tactics for this novel, Major Mike Henderson, USMC, retired. He tackled the task to make sure I kept things as realistic as possible within the looser realms of futuristic science fiction.

Other test readers who provided invaluable feedback on the early draft of this book were James Lardie, Jennifer Thompson, Rebecca Hardman, and Chris Clements. I cannot thank you enough for your patience, time, and feedback.

Mainers, thank you for sharing your beautiful state with me. I'm proud to call myself a resident.

Thank you, the reader, for taking this adventure with me.

ABOUT THE AUTHOR

Irvin Serrano of Irvin Serrano Commercial Photography

Cheryl Campbell was born in Louisiana and lived there and in Mississippi prior to moving to Maine. Her varied background includes art, herpetology, emergency department and critical care nursing, and computer systems. When not traveling as a nomadic wanderer, she lives in Maine, the place she calls home. Cheryl has won five awards through the New England Book Festival for her Burnt Mountain fantasy series.

Echoes of War is the first book of her new science fiction trilogy, Echoes.

To follow her blog, visit www.cherylscreativesoup.com or www.facebook.com/cherylscreativesoup.

SELECTED TITLES FROM SPARKPRESS

SparkPress is an independent boutique publisher
delivering high-quality, entertaining, and engaging
content that enhances readers' lives, with a special focus on
female-driven work. www.gosparkpress.com

Firewall: A Novel, Eugenia Lovett West. $16.95, 978-1-68463-010-3. When Emma Streat's rich, socialite godmother is threatened with blackmail, Emma becomes immersed in the dark world of cyber-crime—and mounting dangers take her to exclusive places in Europe and contacts with the elite in financial and art collecting circles. Through passion and heartbreak, Emma must fight to save herself and bring a vicious criminal to justice.

Resistant: A Novel, Rachael Sparks. $16.95, 978-1-943006-73-1. Bacteria won the war against our medicines. She might be evolution's answer. But can she survive long enough to find out?

Ocean's Fire: Book One in the Equal Night Trilogy, Stacey L. Tucker. $16.95, 978-1-943006-28-1. Once the Greeks forced their male gods upon the world, the belief in the power of women was severed. For centuries it has been thought that the wisdom of the high priestesses perished at the hand of the patriarchs—but now the ancient Book of Sophia has surfaced. Its pages contain the truths hidden by history, and the sacred knowledge for the coming age. And it is looking for Skylar Southmartin.

Alchemy's Air: Book Two of the Equal Night Trilogy, Stacey L. Tucker. $16.95, 978-1-943006-84-7.Now that she's passed her trial by fire, Skylar Southmartin has been entrusted with the ancient secrets of the Book of Sophia. Ahead is her greatest mission to date: a journey to the Underworld to restore a vital memory to the Akashic Library that will bring her face to face with the darkness within.

Deepest Blue: A Novel, Mindy Tarquini. $16.95, 978-1-943006-69-4. In Panduri, everyone's path is mapped, everyone's destiny determined, their lives charted at birth and steered by an unwavering star. Everything there has its place—until Matteo's older brother, Panduri's Heir, crosses out of their world without explanation, leaving Panduri's orbit in a spiral and Matteo's course on a skid. Forced to follow an unexpected path, Matteo is determined to rise, and he pursues the one future Panduri's star can never chart: a life of his own.

ABOUT SPARKPRESS

SparkPress is an independent, hybrid imprint focused on merging the best of the traditional publishing model with new and innovative strategies. We deliver high-quality, entertaining, and engaging content that enhances readers' lives. We are proud to bring to market a list of *New York Times* best-selling, award-winning, and debut authors who represent a wide array of genres, as well as our established, industry-wide reputation for creative, results-driven success in working with authors. SparkPress, a BookSparks imprint, is a division of SparkPoint Studio LLC.

Learn more at GoSparkPress.com

CPSIA information can be obtained
at www.ICGtesting.com
Printed in the USA
BVHW030254241019
561922BV00002B/4/P

9 781684 630066